Second to None

Alexander Kent

arrow books

Reissued in the United Kingdom by Arrow Books in 2007

1 3 5 7 9 10 8 6 4 2

First published in the United Kingdom in 2000 by William Heinemann
First published in paperback in 2000 by Arrow Books

Arrow Books
The Random House Group Limited
20 Vauxhall Bridge Road, London SW1V 2SA

Addresses for companies within The Random House Group Limited
can be found at:
www.randomhouse.co.uk/offices.htm

The Random House Group Limited Reg. No. 954009

A CIP catalogue record for this book
is available from the British Library

ISBN 9780099497752

The Random House Group Limited makes every effort to ensure
that the papers used in its books are made from trees that
have been legally sourced from well-managed and credibly
certified forests. Our paper procurement policy can be found at:
www.randomhouse.co.uk/paper.htm

Printed and bound in Great Britain by
Cox & Wyman Ltd, Reading, Berkshire

Especially for you, Kim,
With all my love.

CONTENTS

The wave cry, the wind cry, the vast waters
Of the petrel and the porpoise. In my end is my beginning.

The midshipman stood beneath the cabin skylight, his body accepting the heavy motion of the ship around him. After the cramped quarters of the midshipmen's berth of the frigate in which he had taken passage from Plymouth, this powerful man-of-war seemed like a rock, and the great stern cabin a palace by comparison.

It was the anticipation which had sustained him when everything else seemed lost. Hope, despair, even fear had been ready companions until this moment.

The shipboard sounds were muffled, distant, voices far off and without meaning or purpose. Someone had warned him that joining a ship already in commission was always hard; there would be no friends or familiar faces to ease the jolts and scrapes. And this was to be his first ship.

It was still impossible to accept that he was here. He moved his head slightly and watched the cabin's other occupant, who was sitting behind a desk, the document the midshipman had carried so carefully inside his coat to avoid spray from the boat's oars turned towards the light of the sloping stern windows, and their glittering panorama of sea and sky.

The captain. The one man upon whom he had placed so much hope; a man he had never met before. His whole body was as taut as a signal halliard, his mouth like dust. It might be nothing. A cruel disappointment, the end of everything.

He realised with a start that the captain was looking at him, had asked him something. His age?

'Fourteen, sir.' It did not even sound like his own voice. He

1

saw the captain's eyes for the first time, more grey than blue, not unlike the sea beyond the spray-dappled windows.

There were other voices, nearer now. There was no more time.

Almost desperately he thrust his hand into his coat again, and held out the letter which he had guarded and nursed all the way from Falmouth.

'This is for you, sir. I was told to give it to no one else.'

He watched the captain slit open the envelope, his expression suddenly guarded. What was he thinking? He wished he had torn it up without even reading it himself.

He saw the captain's sun-browned hand tighten suddenly on the letter, so that it shivered in the reflected light. Anger, disapproval, emotion? He no longer knew what to expect. He thought of his mother, only minutes before she had died, thrusting a crumpled paper into his hands. How long ago? Weeks, months? It was like yesterday. An address in Falmouth, some twenty miles from Penzance where they had lived. He had walked all the way, his mother's note his only strength, his guide.

He heard the captain fold the letter and put it in his pocket. Again, the searching look, but there was no hostility. If anything, there was sadness.

'Your father, boy. What do you know of him?'

The midshipman faltered, off guard, but when he answered he sensed the change. 'He was a King's officer, sir. He was killed by a runaway horse in America.' He could see his mother in those final moments, holding out her arms to embrace him and then to push him away, before either of them broke down. He continued in the same quiet tone, 'My mother often described him to me. When she was dying she told me to make my way to Falmouth and seek your family, sir. I – I know my mother never married him, sir. I have always known, but . . .'

He broke off, unable to continue but very aware that the captain was on his feet, one hand on his arm, his face suddenly close, the face of the man, perhaps as few others ever saw him.

Captain Richard Bolitho said gently, 'As you must know, your father was my brother.'

It was becoming blurred. The tap at the door. Someone with a message for the captain.

Adam Bolitho awoke, his body tensed like a spring as he felt the uncertain grip on his arm. It came to him with the stark clarity of a pistol shot. The ship's motion was more unsteady, the sea noises intruding while his practised ear assessed each in turn.

In the dim glow of a shaded lantern he could see the swaying figure beside his cot, the white patches of a midshipman. He groaned and tried to thrust the dream from his mind.

He swung his legs to the deck, his feet searching for his hessian boots in this still unfamiliar cabin.

'What is it, Mr Fielding?' He had even managed to remember the young midshipman's name. He almost smiled. Fielding was fourteen. The same age as the midshipman in the dream which refused to leave him.

'Mr Wynter's respects, sir, but the wind is freshening and he thought . . .'

Adam Bolitho touched his arm and groped for his faded sea-going coat.

'He did right to call me. I'd rather lose an hour's sleep than lose my ship. I shall come up directly!' The boy fled.

He stood up and adjusted to the motion of His Britannic Majesty's frigate *Unrivalled*. *My ship*. What his beloved uncle had described as 'the most coveted gift'.

And it should have been his greatest prize. A ship so new that the paint had been scarcely dry when he had read himself in, a frigate of the finest design, fast and powerful. He glanced at the dark stern windows, as if he were still in the old *Hyperion*'s great cabin, his life suddenly changed. And by one man.

He touched his pockets without even noticing it, ensuring that he had all he needed. He would go on deck, where the officer-of-the-watch would be anxiously waiting to gauge his mood, more nervous at the prospect of disturbing his captain than at the threat of the wind.

He knew it was mostly his own fault; he had remained apart and aloof from his officers since taking command. It must not, could not continue.

He turned away from the stern windows. The rest was just a dream. His uncle was dead, and only the ship was reality. And he, Captain Adam Bolitho, was quite alone.

1

A Hero Remembered

Lieutenant Leigh Galbraith strode aft along the frigate's maindeck and into the shadows of the poop. He was careful not to hurry, or to show any unusual concern which might create rumour amongst the groups of seamen and marines working at their various forenoon tasks.

Galbraith was tall and powerfully built, and had learned the hard way to accustom himself to low deckhead beams in one of His Britannic Majesty's ships of war. He was *Unrivalled*'s first lieutenant, the one officer who was expected to maintain order and discipline as well as oversee the training of a new ship's company. To assure his captain that she was in all respects an efficient unit of the fleet, even to assume command at any time should some disaster befall him.

The first lieutenant was twenty-nine years old, and had been in the navy since the tender age of twelve like many of his contemporaries. It was all he had known, all he had ever wanted, and when he had been promoted to acting commander and given a ship of his own he had thought himself the luckiest man alive. A senior officer had assured him that as soon as convenient he would take the next step, make the impossible leap to full captain, something which had once seemed like a dream.

He paused by an open gunport and leaned on one of the frigate's thirty eighteen-pounders, and stared at the harbour and the other anchored ships. Carrick Roads, Falmouth, glittering in the May sunshine. He tried to contain the returning bitterness, the anger. He might have had a command like this fine ship. *Could. Might.* He felt the gun's barrel warm under his fingers, as if it had been fired. Like all those other times. At Camperdown with Duncan, and at Copenhagen following Nelson's flag. He had been commended for his coolness under fire, his ability to contain a dangerous situation when his ship was locked in battle with an enemy. His last captain had put his name forward for a command. That had been the brig *Vixen*, one of the fleet's workhorses, expected with limited resources to perform the deeds of a frigate.

Just before he had been appointed to *Unrivalled* he had seen his old command lying like a neglected wreck, awaiting disposal or worse. The war with France was over, Napoleon had abdicated and been sent into exile on Elba. The impossible had happened, and with the conflict in North America being brought thankfully to a close by Britain and the United States alike, the prospect of peace was hard to accept. Galbraith was no different; he had never known anything but war. With ships being paid off, and men discharged with unseemly haste with neither prospects nor experience of anything but the sea, he was lucky to have this appointment. More than he deserved, some said behind his back.

He had been pulled around the ship an hour earlier in the jolly boat, to study the trim as she lay motionless above her own reflection. She had been in commission for five months, and with her rigging and shrouds blacked-down, each sail neatly furled to its yard, she was a perfect picture of the shipbuilder's art. Even her figurehead, the naked body of a beautiful woman arched beneath the beakhead, hands clasped behind her head, breasts thrust out in a daring challenge, was breathtaking. *Unrivalled* was the first to carry that name on the Navy List, the first of the bigger frigates which had been hastily laid down to meet the American threat, which had cost them dearly in a war neither side could win. A war which was already becoming a part of history.

Galbraith plucked his uniform coat away from his chest and tried to push the resentment aside. He *was* lucky. The navy was all he knew, all he wanted. He must remember that at all times.

He heard the Royal Marine sentry's heels click together as he approached the screen door to the aftermost cabins.

'First lieutenant, *sir!*'

Galbraith gave him a nod, but the sentry's eyes did not waver beneath the brim of his leather hat.

A servant opened the door and stood aside as Galbraith entered the captain's quarters. Any man would be proud, honoured to have her. When Galbraith had stood watching with the assembled ship's company and guests as the ship's new captain, her *first* captain, had unrolled his commission to read himself in and so assume command, he had tried to banish all envy and accept the man he was to serve.

After five months, all the training and the drills, the struggle to recruit more landmen to fill the gaps once the pressed hands had been discharged, he realised that Captain Adam Bolitho was still a stranger. In a ship of the line it might be expected, especially with a new company, but in frigates and smaller vessels like his *Vixen* it was rare.

He watched him warily. Slim, hair so dark it could have been black, and when he turned away from the stern windows and the reflected green of the land, the same restlessness Galbraith had noticed at their first meeting. Like most sea officers, he knew a lot about the Bolitho family, Sir Richard in particular. The whole country did, or seemed to, and had been stunned by the news of his death in the Mediterranean. Killed by a marksman in the enemy's rigging, the very day Napoleon had stepped ashore in France after escaping from Elba. The day peace had become another memory.

Of this man, Sir Richard Bolitho's nephew, he had heard only titbits, although nothing remained secret for long in the fleet. The best frigate captain, some said; brave to a point of recklessness, others described him. He had been given his first command, a brig like Galbraith's, at the age of twenty-three; and later lost his frigate *Anemone* fighting a vastly superior American force. Taken prisoner, he had escaped, to become flag captain to the man who was now Flag Officer, Plymouth.

Adam was looking at him now, his dark eyes revealing strain, although he was making an effort to smile. A youthful, alert face, one which would be very attractive to women, Galbraith decided. And if some of the gossip was to be believed, that was also true.

Galbraith said, 'The gig is lowered, sir. The crew will be piped at four bells, unless . . .'

Adam Bolitho moved to the table and touched the sword which was lying there. Old in design, straight-bladed, and lighter than the new regulation blades. It was part of the legend, the Bolitho sword, worn by so many of the family. Worn by Richard Bolitho when he had been marked down by the enemy.

Galbraith glanced around the cabin, the eighteen-pounders intruding even here. When cleared for action from bow to stern *Unrivalled* could present a formidable broadside. He bit his lip. Even if they were so badly undermanned. There were cases of wine waiting to be unpacked and stowed; he had seen them swayed aboard earlier, and knew they had come from the Bolitho house here in Falmouth, which would be the captain's property now. Somehow it did not seem to fit this youthful man with the bright epaulettes. He noticed, too, that the cases were marked with a London address, in St James's Street.

Galbraith clenched his fist. He had been there once. When he had visited London, when his world had started to collapse.

Adam forced his mind into the present. 'Thank you, Mr Galbraith. That will suit well.' He waited, saw the questions forming in the first lieutenant's eyes. A good man, he thought, firm but not impatient with the new hands, and wary of the old Jacks who might seek favours from an unknown officer.

He could feel the ship moving very gently beneath his feet. Eager to move, to be free of the land. *And what of me, her captain?*

He had seen Galbraith looking at the wine; it was from Catherine. Despite all that had happened, her despair and sense of loss, she had remembered. Or had she been thinking of one who had gone?

'Is there something else?' He had not meant to sound impatient, but he seemed unable to control his tone. Galbraith had not apparently noticed. Or had he simply become accustomed to the moods of his new lord and master?

Galbraith said, 'If it is not an imposition, sir, I was wondering . . .' He hesitated as Adam's eyes settled coldly on him. Like someone watching the fall of shot, he thought.

Then Adam said, 'I am sorry. Please tell me.'

'I should like to pay my respects, sir. For the ship.' He did not flinch as a voice on deck yelled obscenely at a passing bumboat to stand away. 'And for myself.'

Adam dragged out the watch from his pocket and knew Galbraith had noticed it. It was heavy and old, and he could recall exactly the moment when he had seen it in the shop in Halifax. The ticking, chiming clocks all around him, and yet it had seemed a place of peace. Escape, so many times. At the change of duties on deck, reefing or making sail, altering course, or entering harbour after a successful landfall . . . The old watch which had once belonged to another 'seafaring officer'. One thing had made it different, the little mermaid engraved on the case.

He said, 'If you think we can both be spared from the ship?' It was not what he had meant to say. It was the mermaid which had distracted him, the girl's face, so clear, as in the shop. *Zenoria*.

Then he said, 'I would take it kindly, Mr Galbraith.' He looked at him steadily and thought he could see a momentary warmth, something he had tried not to encourage. 'Impress on the others, extra vigilance. We are under orders. I don't want any deserters now. We'd not have enough to work ship, let alone fight.'

'I shall deal with it, sir.' Galbraith moved towards the door. It was not much, but it was the closest they had yet been.

Adam Bolitho waited for the door to close, then walked to an open quarter window and stared down at the water rippling beneath the counter.

A beautiful ship. Working with the local squadron, he had felt the power of her. The fastest he had known. Soon the anonymous faces would become people, individuals, the strength and the weakness of any ship. *But not too close. Not again.* As if someone had whispered a warning.

He sighed and looked at the cases of wine. How would Catherine manage, what would she do without the man who had become her life?

He heard three bells chime faintly from the forecastle.

It was going to be hard, even harder than he had imagined. People watching him, as they had watched his beloved uncle, with love, hatred, admiration and envy, none of them ever far away.

He knew Galbraith's background, and what had smashed his chance of promotion to the coveted post rank. It could happen to anybody. *To me.* He thought of Zenoria again, and of what he had done, but he felt no shame, only a deep sense of loss.

He was about to walk beneath the open skylight when he heard Galbraith's voice.

'When the Pendennis battery fires one gun, you will dip the flag and ensign, Mr Massie, and all hands will face aft and uncover.'

Adam waited. It was like an intrusion, but he felt unable to move. Massie was the second lieutenant, a serious young man who held the appointment because his father was a vice-admiral. He was, as yet, an unknown quantity.

Massie said, 'I wonder if Sir Richard's lady will be there.'

He heard their feet move away. An innocent remark? And who did he mean? Catherine, or Belinda, Lady Bolitho?

And there would be spite to bring out the worst. Shortly after *Unrivalled* had commissioned, the news of Emma Hamilton's death had been released. Nelson's lover and inspiration and the nation's darling, but she had been allowed to die alone in Calais, in poverty, abandoned by so-called friends and those who had been entrusted with her care.

The ship moved slightly to her cable and he saw his reflection in the thick glass.

Brokenly he said, 'I'll never forget, Uncle!'

But the ship moved again, and he was alone.

Bryan Ferguson, the Bolitho estate's one-armed steward, stared at the two ledgers on his table. Both had remained unopened. It was late evening but through the window he could still see tall trees silhouetted against the sky, as if the day was reluctant to end. He stood up and walked to the cupboard, pausing as the creeper outside the window rustled slightly. A wind, freshening from the south-east at last, as some of the fishermen had said it would. After all that stillness. Ferguson opened the cupboard and took out a stone bottle and one glass. *After all that sadness.*

There was another glass in there, too, kept especially for

the times when John Allday came over on some pretext or other from the little inn at Fallowfield on the Helford River. The Old Hyperion: even the name had a deeper significance this day.

It might be a while yet before John Allday came here. The *Frobisher*, Sir Richard Bolitho's flagship, was coming home to be paid off. Or maybe not, now that Napoleon was in France on the rampage again. And it was only last year that the town had gone wild at the news: the allied armies were in Paris, Bonaparte was finished. Exile in Elba had not been enough; he had heard Lady Catherine say that it was like putting an eagle in an aviary. Others were of the opinion that Boney should have been hanged after all the misery and murder he had caused.

But Allday would not remain on board the ship where Sir Richard had fallen. Only when he was back, perhaps sitting here with a wet between those big hands, would they know the real story. Unis, his wife, who ran the Old Hyperion, often received letters from him, but Allday himself could not write, so his words came through George Avery, Bolitho's flag lieutenant. Theirs was a rare and strange relationship within the rigid bounds of the navy, and Allday had once remarked that it seemed wrong that while the flag lieutenant read and wrote his letters for him, he never received any himself. And from the moment when the dreadful news had broken in Falmouth, Ferguson had known that Allday would never entrust that moment to anyone, or share it, or commit it to paper. He would tell them himself, in person. If he could.

He coughed; he had swallowed a measure of rum without noticing that he had poured it. He sat down again and stared at the unopened ledgers. Above his head he could hear his wife Grace moving about. Unable to rest, unable even to deal with her usual duties as housekeeper, a position of which she was very proud. As he was.

He gripped the glass tightly with the one hand which was now able to do so much. Once he had believed he would be useless, just another piece of human flotsam left behind in this seemingly endless war. But Grace had nursed him through all of it. Now he found himself recalling the moment mostly at times like these, in the shadows, when it was easier to picture the towering pyramids of sails, the lines of French ships, the deafening crash and roar of broadsides as the two fleets had joined in a bloody embrace. It had seemed to take all day for them to draw together, and all the while the sailors, especially the new ones, pressed men like himself, had been forced to watch the enemy's topsails rising like banners until they had filled the horizon. One officer had later described the awesome sight as resembling the armoured knights at Agincourt.

And all the while, aboard the frigate *Phalarope*, so puny she had seemed against that great line of battle, he had seen their young captain, Richard Bolitho, urging and encouraging, and once, before Ferguson himself had been smashed down, he had seen him kneel to hold the hand of a dying sailor. He had never forgotten his face on that terrible day, never would forget it.

And now he was the steward of this estate, its farm and its cottages, and all the characters who made it a good place to work. Many of them were former sailors, men who had served with Bolitho in so many ships and in every part of the world where the flag had been hoisted. He had seen many of them at the church today, for Sir Richard Bolitho was one of them, and Falmouth's most famous son. Son of a sailor, from generations of sea officers, and this house below Pendennis Castle was a part of their history.

Across the yard he could see lights now in some of the rooms, and imagined the line of portraits, including the painting of Sir Richard as the young captain he had known. His wife Cheney had commissioned it while Bolitho had been away with the fleet. Bolitho had never seen his wife again; she had been killed with their unborn child when her carriage had shed a wheel and overturned. Ferguson himself had carried her, seeking help when it was already too late. He smiled sadly, reminiscently. *And with only one arm.*

The Church of King Charles the Martyr, where the lives and deaths of other Bolithos were commemorated, had been filled to capacity, servants from the house, farm workers, strangers and friends pressed close together to pray and to remember.

He allowed his mind to dwell on the family pew near the pulpit. Richard Bolitho's younger sister Nancy, who had not yet come to terms with her own husband's death. Roxby, 'the

King of Cornwall', would not be an easy man to lay aside. Next to her Catherine, Lady Somervell, tall and very erect, all in black, her face covered by a veil, and only the diamond pendant shaped like an opened fan which Bolitho had given her moving on her breast to betray her emotion.

And, beside her, Adam Bolitho, his eyes upon the altar, his chin lifted. Defiant. Determined. And, like the moment when he had come to the house after his uncle's death, and had read Catherine's note and clipped on the old family sword, so like the young, vanished sea officer who had grown up here in Falmouth.

There had been another officer with him, a lieutenant, but Ferguson had noticed only Adam Bolitho and the beautiful woman beside him.

It had reminded him painfully of the day in that same church when a memorial service had been conducted following the news that Sir Richard and his mistress had been lost in the wreck of the *Golden Plover* off the African coast. Many of the same people had been there, as well as Bolitho's wife. Ferguson could remember her look of utter disbelief when one of Adam's officers had burst in with the revelation that Bolitho and his companions were alive, and had been rescued against all odds. And when Lady Catherine's part had become known, how she had given hope and faith to the survivors in that open boat, she had been taken to their hearts. It had seemed to sweep aside the scandal, and the outrage which had been previously voiced at their liaison.

Together or alone, Ferguson could see them clearly. Catherine, her dark hair streaming unchecked in the wind while she walked on the cliff path, or paused by the stile where he had seen them once, as if to watch some approaching ship. Perhaps hoping . . .

Now there was no hope, and her man, her lover and the nation's hero, was buried at sea. Near his old *Hyperion*, where so many had died, men Ferguson had never forgotten. The same ship Adam had joined as a fourteen year old midshipman. Nancy, Lady Roxby, would be remembering that too, Adam in a captain's uniform, but to her still the boy who had walked from Penzance when his mother had died. The name 'Bolitho' written on a scrap of paper was all he had had. And now he was the last Bolitho.

There were to be other, grander ceremonies in the near future, in Plymouth, and then at Westminster Abbey, and he wondered if Lady Catherine would go to London and risk the prying eyes and the jealous tongues which had dogged her relationship with the nation's hero.

He heard a step in the yard and guessed it was Young Matthew, the senior coachman, making his rounds, visiting the horses, his dog Bosun puffing slowly behind him. Old now, the dog was partly deaf and had failing eyesight, but no stranger would ever pass him without his croaking bark.

Matthew had been in church also. Still called 'young', but a married man now, he was another part of the family, *the little crew* as Sir Richard had called them.

Buried at sea. Perhaps it was better. No aftermath, no false display of grief. Or would there be?

He thought of the tablet on the wall of the church beneath the marble bust of Captain Julius Bolitho, who had fallen in battle in 1664.

> The spirits of their fathers
> Shall start from every wave;
> For the deck it was their field of fame,
> And ocean was their grave.

It said it all, especially to those assembled in the old church in this place of seafarers, the navy and the coastguard, fishermen and sailors from the packets and traders which sailed on every tide throughout the year. The sea was their life. It was also the enemy.

He had sensed it when the church had resounded at the last to *The Sailors' Hymn*.

He had heard the bang of a solitary gun, like the one which had preceded the service, and seen Adam turn once to look at his first lieutenant. People had parted to allow the family to leave. Lady Catherine had reached out to touch Ferguson's sleeve as she had passed; he had seen the veil clinging to her face.

He went to the window again. The lights were still burning.

13

He would send one of the girls to deal with it, if Grace was too stricken to do it.

He thought of the shipwreck again. Adam had come to the house when Vice-Admiral Keen's young wife had been there; Keen, too, had been aboard the *Golden Plover*.

Zenoria, from the village of Zennor. He knew Allday had suspected something between them, and he himself had wondered what had happened that night. Then the girl lost her only child, her son by Keen, in an accident, and had thrown herself off the cliff at the notorious Trystan's Leap. He had been with Catherine Somervell when they had brought the small, broken body ashore.

Adam Bolitho had certainly changed in some way. Matured? He considered it. No, it went far deeper than that.

Something Allday had said stood out in his mind, like the epitaph.

They looked so right together.

Captain Adam Bolitho sat in one of the high-backed chairs by the open hearth and half-listened to the occasional moan of the wind. It was freshening, south-easterly; they would have to keep their wits about them tomorrow when *Unrivalled* weighed anchor.

He shifted slightly in the chair, which with its twin was amongst the oldest furniture in the house. It was turned away from the dark windows, away from the sea.

He stared at the goblet of brandy on the table beside him, catching the candlelight which brought life to this room, the grave portraits, the paintings of unknown ships and forgotten battles.

How many Bolithos had sat here like this, he wondered, not knowing what the next horizon might bring, or if they would ever return?

His uncle must have thought it on that last day when he had left this house to join his flagship. Leaving Catherine outside where there was only darkness now, except for Ferguson's cottage. His lights would remain until the old house was asleep.

He had been surprised by Lieutenant Galbraith's request to join him at the church; he had never met Richard Bolitho as far as Adam knew. But even in *Unrivalled* he had felt it. Something lost. Something shared.

He wondered if Catherine was able to sleep. He had pleaded with her to stay, but she had insisted on accompanying Nancy back to her house on the adjoining estate.

He stood, and looked at the stairway where she had said farewell. Without the veil she had looked strained and tired. And beautiful.

'It would be a bad beginning – for you, Adam. If we stayed here together there would be food for rumour. I would spare you that!' She had spoken so forcefully that he had felt her pain, the anguish which she had tried to contain in the church and afterwards.

She had looked around this same room. Remembering. 'You have your new ship, Adam, so this must be your new beginning. I shall watch over matters here in Falmouth. It is yours now. *Yours by right.*' Again, she had spoken as if to emphasise what she herself had already foreseen.

He walked abruptly to the big family Bible, on the table where it had always lain. He had gone through it several times; it contained the history of a seafaring family, a roll of honour.

He opened it at the page with great care, imagining the faces watching him, the portraits at his back and lining the stairway. A separate entry in the familiar, sweeping handwriting he had come to know, to love, in letters from his uncle, and in various log books and despatches when he had served him as a junior officer.

Perhaps this was what troubled Catherine, the subject of his rights and his inheritance. The date was that upon which his surname of Pascoe had been changed to Bolitho. His uncle had written, *To the memory of my brother Hugh, Adam's father, once lieutenant in His Britannic Majesty's Navy, who died on 7th May 1795.*

The Call of Duty was the Path to Glory.

His father, who had brought disgrace to this family, and who had left his son illegitimate.

He closed the Bible and picked up a candlestick. The stair creaked as he passed the portrait of Captain James Bolitho, who had lost an arm in India. *My grandfather.* Bryan Ferguson

15

had shown him how, if you stood in the right place and the daylight favoured you, you could see where the artist had overpainted the arm with a pinned-up, empty sleeve after his return home.

The stair had protested that night when Zenoria had come down to find him weeping, unable to come to terms with the news that his uncle, Catherine, and Valentine Keen had been reported lost in the *Golden Plover*. And the madness which had followed; the love which he could not share. It was all contained, so much passion, so much grief, in this old house below Pendennis Castle.

He pushed open the door and hesitated as if someone was watching. As if she might still be here.

He strode across the room and opened the heavy curtains. There was a moon now, he could see the streaks of cloud passing swiftly across it like tattered banners.

He turned and looked at the room, the bed, the candlelight playing over the two portraits, one of his uncle as a young captain, in the outdated coat with its white lapels which his wife Cheney had liked so much, and one of Cheney on the same wall, restored by Catherine after Belinda had thrown it aside.

He held the candles closer to the third portrait, which Catherine had given to Richard after the *Golden Plover* disaster. Of herself, in the seamen's clothing with which she had covered her body in the boat she had shared with the despairing survivors. 'The other Catherine', she had called it. The woman few had ever seen, he thought, apart from the man she had loved more than life itself. She must have paused here before leaving with Nancy; there was a smell of jasmine, like her skin when she had kissed him, had held him tightly as if unable or unwilling to break away.

He had taken her hand to his lips but she had shaken her head, and had looked into his face, as if afraid to lose something. He could still feel it like a physical force.

'No, dear Adam. Just hold me.' She had lifted her chin. 'Kiss me.'

He touched the bed, trying to keep the image at bay. *Kiss me.* Were they both so alone now that they needed reassurance? Was that the true reason for Catherine's departure on this terrible day?

16

He closed the door behind them and walked down the stairs. Some of the candles had gone, or had burned so low as to be useless, but those by the hearth had been replaced. One of the servant girls must have done it. He smiled. No secrets in this old house.

He swallowed some brandy and ran his fingers along the carvings above the fireplace. The family motto, *For My Country's Freedom*, worn smooth by many hands. Men leaving home. Men inspired by great deeds. Men in doubt, or afraid.

He sat down again.

The house, the reputation he must follow, the people who relied on him, it would all take time to accept or even understand.

And tomorrow he would be the captain again, all he had ever wanted.

He looked at the darkening stairs and imagined Bolitho coming down to face some new challenge, to accept a responsibility which might and did finally destroy him.

I would give everything I have just to hear your voice and take your hand again, Uncle.

But only the wind answered him.

The two riders had dismounted and stood partly sheltered by fallen rock, holding their horses' heads, staring out at the whitecapped waters of Falmouth Bay.

'Reckon she'll come, Tom?'

The senior coastguard tugged his hat more securely over his forehead. 'Mister Ferguson seemed to think so. Wanted us to keep an eye open, just in case.'

The other man wanted to talk. ''Course, you *knows* her ladyship, Tom.'

'We've had a few words once or twice.' He would have smiled, but his heart was too heavy. His young companion meant well enough, and with a few years of service along these shores he might amount to something. Know Lady Catherine Somervell? How could he describe her? Even if he had wanted to?

He watched the great span of uneasy water, the serried ranks of short waves broken as if by some giant's comb, while the wind tested its strength.

17

It was noon, or soon would be. When they had ridden up from town along the cliff path he had seen the small groups of people. It was uncanny, like some part of a Cornish myth, and there were plenty of those to choose from. A town, a port which lived off the sea, and had lost far too many of its sons to have no respect for the dangers.

Describe her? Like the time he had tried to prevent her from seeing the slight, battered corpse of the girl who had committed suicide from Trystan's Leap. He had watched her hold the girl in her arms, unfasten her torn and soaking clothes to seek a scar, some identifying mark, when all features had been destroyed by the fall and the sea. On that little crescent of beach in the dropping tide after they had dragged her through the surf. It was something he would never forget, nor wanted to.

At length he said, 'A beautiful lady.' He recalled what one of Ferguson's friends had said of her. 'A sailor's woman.'

He had been in the church with all the others, had seen her then, so upright, so proud. *Describe her?*

'Never too busy or too important to pass the time o' day. Made you feel like you *was* somebody. Not like a few I could mention!'

His companion looked at him and thought he understood.

Then he said, 'You was right, Tom. She's comin' now.'

Tom removed his hat and watched the solitary figure approaching.

'Say nothing. Not today.'

She was wearing the faded old boat cloak she often used for these clifftop walks, and her hair was unfastened and blowing freely in the wind. She turned and faced the sea at the place where she often paused on her walks; the best view of all, the locals said.

The young coastguard said uneasily, 'You don't think she . . .'

Tom turned his head, his eye trained to every movement and mood of the sea and these approaches.

'*No.*' He saw the fine edge of the ship as she tacked around Pendennis Point and its brooding castle, close-hauled and hard over, clawing into the wind before standing towards St Anthony Head. She carried more canvas than might be expected, but he

18

knew what the captain intended, to weather the headland and those frothing reefs before coming about to head into open waters for more sea-room, with the wind as an ally.

A tight manoeuvre, well executed if *Unrivalled* was as short-handed as was rumoured. Some might call it reckless. Tom recalled the dark, restless young captain in the church and all those other times. He had seen him grow from midshipman to this moment in his life, which must be the greatest challenge of all.

He saw the woman unfasten her shabby boat cloak and stand unmoving in the blustery wind. Not in black, but in a dark green robe. Tom had seen her waiting on this same path for the first sign of another ship. So that he would see her, sense her welcome.

He watched the frigate heeling over and imagined the squeal of blocks and the bang of wild canvas as the yards were hauled round. He had seen it all so many times before. He was a simple man who did his duty, peace or war.

What ship did *she* see, he wondered. What moment was she sharing?

Catherine walked past the two horses but did not speak.
Don't leave me!

2

No Longer A Stranger

Adam Bolitho rested one hand on the quarterdeck rail and watched the misty horizon tilt as if to dislodge the entire ship. For most of the forenoon they had been engaged in sail drill, an exercise made even more uncomfortable than usual by the blustery wind. It was directly from the north, and strong enough to force *Unrivalled* to lean until the sea spattered against the sealed gunports and drenched the men working aloft and on deck like a tropical storm.

Three days since the rugged Cornish coastline had vanished astern, and each one had been put to good use.

The hands were sliding down to the deck now, the landsmen and others less confident holding tightly to the ratlines when the ship heeled over to leeward, so that the sea appeared to be directly beneath them. There was a smell of rum even in the wind, and he had already noticed a thin trail of greasy smoke from the galley funnel.

He saw the first lieutenant waiting by the starboard ladder, his face giving nothing away.

'That was better, Mr Galbraith.' He thought he saw Galbraith's eyes drop to the pocket where he carried the old timepiece and wondered what it must be like to take orders as a lieutenant again, instead of being in command. 'Dismiss the watch below.' He heard the seamen running from their stations, glad to be spared further discomfort, and to curse their captain over a tot of rum.

He knew the sailing master was watching him from his usual position, near his helmsmen whenever the ship was altering course or changing tack.

Adam walked to the weather side and wiped spray from his face, his body angled to the deck as the sails filled out like breastplates again. The sea was lively with cruising white horses, although it was calmer than when they had been in Biscay. There was too much spray to make out the lie of the land, but it was there, a long, purple hump, as if a bank of cloud had dropped from the sky. Cape St Vincent. And despite all the drills, the alterations of course to test the topmen and new hands alike, this was the exact landfall. He had seen the sailing master's calculations and his daily estimates of distance covered.

His name was Joshua Cristie, and he had a face so weathered and creased that he looked like the Old Man of the Sea, although Adam knew he was in his forties. He had served in almost every size and class of vessel from schooner to second-rate, and had been a sailing master for some ten years. If the senior warrant officers were the backbone of any man-of-war, the sailing master must surely be her rudder. *Unrivalled* was lucky to have him.

Adam joined him and said, 'Gibraltar tomorrow, eh?'

Cristie regarded him impassively. 'I see no problems, sir.' He had a clipped, matter-of-fact manner, and did not waste words.

Adam realised that Galbraith had come aft again, this time with one of the ship's five midshipmen. He tested his memory. Sandell, that was his name.

Galbraith was saying, 'I was observing you, Mr Sandell. *Twice*, I've warned you before. Discipline is one thing, force another!'

The midshipman retorted, 'He was doing it on purpose, sir. Hanging back so that my party was delayed.'

It was unusual for Galbraith to reveal such anger, especially with some of the watchkeepers close enough to hear. He seemed to calm himself with an effort.

'I know you must control the men in your charge. If you are to become a King's officer that is all a part of it. Inspire them, persuade them if you like, but *do not abuse them*. I'll not remind you again!'

The midshipman touched his hat and retreated. Adam caught only a glimpse of his profile. Galbraith had made an enemy there, as was the way of first lieutenants everywhere.

Galbraith walked up the sloping deck and said, 'Young ruffian! Too ready with his starter by far. I know his part of the drill was held up by the man in question, I saw it myself. But with sixty hands short, and some of those aboard little better than bumpkins, it needs more care.'

It was like mist clearing from a telescope. Adam suddenly remembered hearing that a midshipman had been put ashore to await a court martial after a sailor had been accidentally killed at sea. The matter had never come to court martial and the midshipman had been sent to another vessel. He had been an admiral's son. It had been about the time when Galbraith had seen his promised promotion cancelled. Nobody could prove there was a connection; few would even care. Except Galbraith. And he was here, second-in-command of one of the navy's most powerful frigates. Would he remain content, or would he be too afraid for what was left of his career to show the spirit which had once earned him a command of his own?

'Any orders, sir?'

Adam glanced at the nearest eighteen-pounders. Another difference. *Unrivalled*'s armament consisted mainly of such guns, and they made up the bulk of her topweight. The designers had insisted that these eighteen-pounders, usually nine feet in length, be cast a foot shorter in an effort to reduce some of the weight.

A frigate was only as good as her firepower and her agility, and he had taken careful note of the sea creaming almost as high as the ports on the lee side. In a fierce ship-to-ship action, a captain could no longer rely on supremacy merely by taking and holding the wind-gage.

He said, 'We shall exercise the larboard battery this afternoon, Mr Galbraith. I want our people to know their guns like their own minds. As you remarked, we are short-handed, and if required to engage on both sides at once we shall be busy indeed.' He saw the slight frown. 'I know we may not be called to fight. The war might be over already for all we know.' He touched his arm and felt him flinch at the contact. 'But *if* we fight, I intend this ship to be the victor!'

Galbraith touched his hat and walked away, no doubt to face the questions and displeasures of the wardroom.

Adam walked to the dripping hammock nettings and steadied himself as the deck lurched to another strong gust. The land was almost gone from view. Cape St Vincent, the scene of one of the war's greatest engagements, where Nelson had scorned the rigidity of Fighting Instructions and attacked the Spanish flagship *Santissima Trinidad* of one hundred and thirty guns, the largest warship in the world. So like his uncle, he thought. Sir Richard Bolitho had never allowed the conventional rules of battle to preclude initiative and personal daring. It seemed wrong that the admirals so admired and so loved by those they had led had never met face to face.

He ran a sodden handkerchief over skin streaming now with spray. Identical to the handkerchief he had given Catherine in the church, knowing she had used it to dry her eyes behind the veil. Galbraith had seen that too . . .

He shook himself angrily and walked to the rail. A few of the hands were splicing and repairing; as in any frigate, the miles of cordage needed constant attention. Some of them raised their eyes and immediately looked away. Men who could make or break any ship. He smiled grimly. *Any captain.* Some of them were from the assize courts, debtors and thieves, tyrants and cowards. The alternatives were transportation or the rope. He watched spray bursting through the beakhead, making the beautiful figurehead shine like a nymph rising from the sea itself.

Unrivalled would draw them together, as a team, as one company.

And when they reached Gibraltar, what orders would he find waiting? To return to England, or be redirected to some other squadron in a different ocean? If nothing had changed he would continue on to Malta, to join the new squadron under the flag of Vice-Admiral Sir Graham Bethune. He was dismayed by the return of the pain. Bethune had been sent to relieve Sir Richard Bolitho, but Fate had decided otherwise. But for that, it might have been Bethune who had died, and Richard Bolitho would have been reunited with his Catherine. *Kate.*

Like himself, Bethune had been one of Bolitho's midshipmen, in his first command, the little *Sparrow*. As Valentine Keen had been a midshipman when Sir Richard had been captain of a frigate. So many missing faces. *We Happy Few.* Now there were hardly any.

He saw two of the 'young gentlemen' dodging along the slippery maindeck, calling to one another above the bang of canvas and the sluice of water, apparently without a care in the world.

Here there were only five of them. He would make an effort to get to know each one. Galbraith's sharp comment about inspiration and leadership cut both ways; it always had. In larger ships, which carried broods of midshipmen, there was always the risk of bullying and petty tyranny. He had discovered it soon enough for himself, like so many things which had taught him to defend himself and stand up for those less able to do so.

Today, his reputation with both blade and pistol would end any trouble before it could begin. But it had not been easy. How slow he had been to understand, to come to terms with it. The regular lessons with a local teacher, and later, when he had learned to handle a sword, the intricacies of defence and attack. Slow? Or had he merely decided that he did not want to know how it was all paid for? Until he heard his teacher in the next room, in bed with his mother. And the others.

It was different now. They could think what they liked, but they dared not slander her name in his presence.

But the memory remained, like an unhealed wound.

He saw the midshipman of the watch, Fielding, writing something on his slate, his lip pouting with concentration. The same midshipman who had called him one morning when he had been powerless to break that same dream.

He thought of Catherine again, that last desperate kiss before she had left the house. *To protect my reputation.* There was no defence against dreams. Just as, in those same dreams, she had never resisted him.

He heard a slight cough behind him. That was Usher, the captain's clerk, who had once been the purser's assistant, a small, nervous man who seemed totally out of place in a ship of war. O'Beirne, the ruddy-faced surgeon, had confided that the man was dying, 'a day at a time', as he had put it. His lungs were diseased, only too common in the confines of a ship. He thought of Yovell, the clerk who had become

24

his uncle's secretary. A scholar who was never without his Bible. He would have been there when . . . He turned away and closed his mind to it.

'Yes, Usher?'

'I've done copies of the lists, sir. Three of each.' He always found it necessary to explain every detail of his work.

'Very well. I shall sign them after I have eaten.'

'Deck there! Sail on the larboard quarter!'

Everyone looked up. The voice of the masthead lookout had been heard only rarely on this passage.

The master tugged down his hat and said, 'Shall I send another man aloft, sir?'

Adam glanced at him. Cristie was a professional; he would not be here otherwise. It was not an idle comment. And here was Wynter, the third lieutenant and officer-of-the-watch, hurrying from the chart room, but with biscuit crumbs on his coat to betray his other activities. Young, efficient and keen, when required he could put on such a blank expression that it was impossible to know what he was thinking, which was unusual for a junior lieutenant. But his father was a member of Parliament, so perhaps that might explain it.

Adam said, 'Your glass, Mr Fielding. I shall go up directly.' He thought he saw Cristie's deepset eyes sharpen. 'I shall not shorten sail. Yet.' He wedged his hat inside the companion way and felt his hair wet against his forehead. 'A trader seeking the company of a frigate?' He shook his head as if someone had answered. 'I think not. I know a few King's officers who would not be slow to press a few prime hands, no matter what the Admiralty directs us to do!'

Cristie gave a rare grin. He would know. Even sailors with the genuine Protection, the document which should have defended them against the demands of a hungry fleet, had been pressed. It would take months for someone to find out and do something about it.

Cristie said, 'If she holds up to wind'rd we'll never be able to reach her.'

Adam looked up at the towering masts. *Why?* Was it a demonstration of something? Bravado, perhaps?

He slung the big telescope over his shoulder and strode forward to the main chains before gazing up again at the

25

swaying crosstrees, where the lookout would be perched like a sea bird, uncaring, or indifferent to the other world far beneath his dangling legs.

The others watched until Lieutenant Wynter exclaimed, 'What ails him, Mr Cristie? How can he know anything more than the rest of us?'

'The Cap'n don't miss much, Mr Wynter.' He gestured to the biscuit crumbs. 'Your little pleasures, for instance!'

A seaman murmured, 'First lieutenant's comin' up, sir!'

'*Damn!*' Wynter stared at the captain's slim figure, leaning back and outwards above the creaming water surging from the finely raked stem. Wynter was twenty-two years old and could remember the congratulations and the envy alike when he had been appointed to *Unrivalled*. The first of her class, the kind of frigate which had been denied them when they had needed them most in the war against the new American navy. With the fleet being cut down and officers as well as seamen being discharged or put on half-pay without any visible prospects, he had been fortunate. Like Galbraith, the senior, who seemed old for his rank when compared with most lieutenants; he must have seen this appointment as a last chance rather than a new beginning.

A new ship, and commanded by one already proclaimed a brave and resourceful officer. The name alone was enough, part of the legend, and now of the mourning for the admiral who had inspired and shocked the nation.

Wynter had been serving in an elderly third-rate when his appointment had been posted. He still had no idea why he had been selected. His father, a rising member of Parliament and one well known for his outspoken criticism of naval and military affairs, was certainly not behind it. Even when he had first gone to sea as a midshipman, his father had offered little encouragement.

'A good regiment would have been preferable. I could have bought you a comfortable living where you would have served with gentlemen, not uncouth ruffians! Don't come to me for pity when you lose an arm or a leg through some captain's hunger for glory!'

And Wynter had never been in a sea fight, mainly because the old seventy-four had been too slow to chase an enemy, and was often left far behind the rest of the squadron. She would doubtless be hulked, like so many of the other worn-out ships which had stood between England and her natural enemies for so many years. He saw Bellairs, the senior midshipman, in charge of *Unrivalled*'s signals and with any luck the next in line for lieutenant's examination, talking to the sailing master, ready to muster his men if something unusual happened. Even *he* had seen action, several times if he was to be believed, when he had served with the Channel Fleet in a small thirty-two gun frigate.

Wynter stared up at the captain again. He was almost there now, apparently untroubled by the height, and the unnerving shake and quiver of the masts under their great weight of spars and cordage.

He knew something of Captain Adam Bolitho's past. A command at twenty-three, and a list of successes against the Americans and the French, with prize money to show for it. Nobody spoke of the other matter, the disgrace to his family when his father had changed sides to command a privateer against his own country during the American War of Independence. But everybody knew about it. How must he feel? He turned away as a shaft of watery sunlight lanced into his eyes. *How would I feel?*

He heard Cristie telling the first lieutenant about the mast-head's sighting. He did not hear any reply or comment, but Galbraith was like that. Easy to talk to in the wardroom, on matters relating to shipboard duties or the watch bill. Ready to give advice about the suitability of certain men for the various parts of ship. On a personal level, or when asked to offer an opinion about the course of the war or the reliability of the higher command, he would close up like a clam. Unlike some of the others. Captain Louis Bosanquet, the officer in charge of the ship's Royal Marines, was the complete opposite. Like a steel blade to his men, he was outspoken about almost everything in the mess, especially when he had had too much to drink. His second-in-command, Lieutenant John Luxmore, on the other hand, went by the book, and seemed to live only for the drilling and betterment of his 'bullocks'. O'Beirne, the surgeon from Galway, who knew more jokes than any-one Wynter had ever met, and Tregillis the purser were easy enough to share a mess with, no better or worse than men in any other ship of this size. The exception was Vivian Massie, the swarthy second lieutenant, who had seen plenty of action and did not bother to hide a driving ambition. Beyond that he could be withdrawn, almost secretive, as if any personal revelation might be considered weakness. Good in a battle, but a bad enemy, Wynter had decided.

He stiffened as Galbraith joined him by the rail.

Captain Bolitho had almost reached the crosstrees. But even he could make a mistake. If he slipped and fell, if he missed hitting a spar or the ship herself, the fall would knock him senseless. It would take far too long to heave to and lower a boat. He glanced at Galbraith's strong profile. Then *he* would be in command. Perhaps only temporarily, but it would offer him the recognition he needed and must crave. It happened in battle, just as it had struck down the captain's uncle. *Dead men's shoes.* Nobody mentioned it, but it was on most people's minds when it came to promotion.

Wynter shaded his eyes and peered up again through the maze of rigging and flapping canvas.

Why should the captain do it? Did he trust no one? He had heard Bosanquet remark once that he knew the captain no better than when he had stepped aboard. Galbraith had been present, and had answered, 'I could say the same about you, sir!' That had ended it. That time.

A figure moved from the gundeck and paused, gazing at the sea. It was Jago, the captain's coxswain, the only man aboard who had actually served with Adam Bolitho before. He had a lean, darkly tanned face and hair tied in a neat, old-fashioned queue, like the gunner's mate he had been. A man with a past, he had been flogged in another ship, wrongly it was said, by a sadistic captain, and there was still a certain anger about him, a contained defiance. Wynter had seen him stripped and sluicing his body at the washdeck pump; the scars had been familiar enough, but Jago carried them differently, almost with pride. Bloody arrogance, Massie had called it.

Whatever the truth of it, he would know their captain better than any of them. He had been with him when they had stormed a battery during an attack by the combined forces on the dockyards and principal buildings in Washington. Some

28

claimed that raid was revenge for the American invasion of Canada and the attack on York; others said it was a final show of strength in a war no one could win.

Luke Jago knew the officers on the quarterdeck were watching him and could make a fair bet as to their thoughts. He, too, was surprised to find himself here, in his new station, when all he had wanted was to quit the navy, with only bitterness in his soul.

He could recall exactly when Captain Bolitho had asked him to be his coxswain; could remember his refusal. Bolitho was one of only a few officers Jago had ever liked or trusted, but his mind had been made up. Determined. Until that last battle, the deck raked by the enemy's fire, men crying out and falling from aloft. When the commodore had pitched on to his side, already beyond aid. He knew the rumours like all the rest of them, that the commodore had been shot by somebody aboard their own ship, but he had heard no more about it. He gave a quick grin. He couldn't even remember the bloody man's name any more.

Unlike the boy John Whitmarsh, the captain's servant, who had survived when *Anemone* had gone down. He remembered him well enough. The smile faded. The Yankees had hanged Bolitho's old coxswain for ensuring that *Anemone* would not live to become their prize.

Captain Bolitho had taken a liking to the boy; maybe he had seen something of himself in him. He had wanted to sponsor him with his own money, so he could finish his education and wear the King's coat some day. Jago could remember the boy showing him the dirk the captain had given him, probably the only gift he had ever received. Without a tremor in his voice, he had told Jago that he wanted to stay with his captain. It was all he wanted, he said.

He had watched Adam Bolitho's face when he had told him Whitmarsh had been killed. A ball had shattered against one of the guns, and the iron splinter had ended his young life instantly; he had died without a trace of pain or terror.

And the exact moment when he had made up his mind, or had it made up for him. He was still uncertain, unwilling to believe it was not his decision alone. They had shaken hands on it with the smoke still hanging in the air, when the enemy

29

frigate had broken off the action. 'A victory, sir,' he had heard himself say. 'Or as good as.' He had thought himself mad then. Until they had buried their dead, including the boy John Whitmarsh, with the beautiful dirk still strapped to his side.

One hundred and sixty feet above their heads and oblivious to their thoughts, Adam Bolitho eased himself into position and looked down at the ship, which seemed to pivot from side to side as if his perch in the crosstrees was motionless. He had never tired of the sight since he had made his first dash aloft as a midshipman in his uncle's old *Hyperion*. Even when he had been mastheaded for some prank or indiscretion, he had always managed to marvel at what he saw. The ship, far beneath his shoes, the little blue and white shapes of the officers and master's mates, the clusters of seamen and scarlet-coated marines. *His ship*, all one hundred and fifty feet of her, over a thousand tons of weapons, masts and spars, and the men to serve and fight her.

His uncle had confided that he had always hated heights, had feared going aloft when his ship had made or reefed sails. Another lesson Adam had learned, that fear could be contained if it seemed more dangerous to reveal it.

He glanced at his companion. A leathery face and a pair of the keenest eyes he had seen, like polished glass.

He hesitated. 'Sullivan, isn't it?'

The seaman showed his uneven teeth. 'Thass me, sir.' He smiled slightly as Adam unslung the telescope.

'Where away?' It was strange: despite his attempt to stay at arm's length, the ship was closing in. A face he could barely recall. A typical Jack, some would say. Hard, rough, and, in their way, simple men.

'Same bearin', sir.'

He steadied the glass, raising it very carefully as breaking crests leaped into view, magnified into small tidal waves in the powerful lens.

He felt the spar quiver and shake against his body, mast upon mast, down to the ship's keelson. He could remember the genuine pleasure and pride of the men who had built her when he had insisted they come aboard for her commissioning.

And there she was, rising and dipping, her canvas dark against the scudding clouds.

The lookout said, 'Square-rigged at the fore, sir.'

Adam nodded and waited for the glass to steady again. A brigantine, handling well in the offshore wind, almost bows-on. When he lowered the glass she seemed to drop away to a mere sliver of colour and movement. It never failed to surprise him that men like Sullivan, who would scorn a telescope, or trade it for a new knife or fresh clothing, or drink if it was offered, could still see and recognise another vessel when a landsman might not even notice it.

'Local, d' you think?'

Sullivan watched him with sudden interest. 'Spaniard, I'd say, sir. I seen 'em afore, as far to the south'rd as Good Hope. Handy little craft.' He added doubtfully, 'Rightly 'andled, er course, sir!'

Adam took another look. The master was right. They would never catch her with the wind against them. And why should they care? Lose more time and distance when tomorrow they should lie in the shadow of the Rock?

It was like yesterday. He had been returning to Plymouth and it had been reported that a boat had been heading out to meet them. Not merely a boat: an admiral's barge, the flag officer himself coming to tell him, to be the first to prepare him for the news of his uncle's death. Vice-Admiral Valentine Keen. His uncle's friend. He felt the same stab of guilt; he would never lose it. Zenoria's husband. After her death he had married again. But like that moment alone in the silence of the house, he had thought only of Zenoria. What he had done.

Keen had told him what he knew, the circumstances of Bolitho's death and of his burial at sea. Nothing was definite, except that his flagship had engaged two frigates, manned by renegades and traitors who, with others, had aided Napoleon's escape from Elba; he had marched on Paris almost before the allies had recovered from the shock.

Bethune would know more of the details by now, where the frigates had taken refuge prior to their unexpected meeting with *Frobisher*, who was involved, how it had been planned. He found he was gripping the telescope so tightly that his knuckles were almost white. Spain was an ally now. And yet a Spaniard had been involved.

He repeated quietly, 'Spaniard, you say?'

31

The man regarded him thoughtfully. Sir Richard Bolitho's nephew. A fire-eater, they said. A fighter. Sullivan had been at sea on and off for most of his forty years, and had served several captains, but could not recall ever speaking to one. And this one had even known his name.

'I'd wager a wet on it, sir.'

A wet. What John Allday would say. Where was he now? How would he go on? The old dog without his master.

Adam smiled. 'A wager it is then. A wet you shall have!' He seized a stay and began to slide towards the deck, heedless of the tar on his white breeches. Instinct? Or the need to prove something? When he reached the deck the others were waiting for him.

'Sir?' Galbraith, poised and guarded.

'Spanish brigantine. He's a damned good lookout.'

Galbraith relaxed slowly. 'Sullivan? The best, sir.'

Adam did not hear him. 'That vessel is following us.' He looked at him directly. It was there. Doubt. Caution. Uncertainty. 'I shall not forget that craft, Mr Galbraith.'

Wynter leaned forward and said eagerly, 'An enemy, sir?'

'An assassin, I believe, Mr Wynter.'

He swung away; Jago was holding his hat for him. 'See that the wardroom mess provides a double tot for Sullivan when he is relieved.'

They watched him walk to the companion way, as if, like the two midshipmen he had seen earlier, he did not have a care in the world.

Midshipman Fielding stood examining the telescope which the captain had just returned to him. He would put it in the next letter to his parents, when he got round to it. How the captain had spoken to him. No longer a stranger . . . He smiled, pleased at the aptness of the phrase. That was it.

He recalled the time he had gone to waken the captain when Lieutenant Wynter had been concerned about the wind. He had dared to touch his arm. It had been hot, as if the captain had had a fever. And he had called out something. A woman's name.

He would leave that out of the letter. It was private.

But he wondered who the woman was.

It was like sharing something. He thought of the captain's easy confidence when he had slithered down to the deck like one of the topmen. Perhaps the others had not noticed it.

He smiled again, pleased with himself. *No longer a stranger.*

Vice-Admiral Sir Graham Bethune walked to the quarter window of the great cabin and observed the activity of countless small craft in the shadow of the Rock. He had visited Gibraltar many times throughout his career, never thinking that one day his own flagship would be lying here, with himself at the peak of his profession. Although a frigate captain earlier in the war, he had been surprised and not a little dismayed to discover how his post at the Admiralty had softened him.

He glanced at the dress coat with its heavy gold-laced epaulettes which hung on one of the chairs, the measure of the success which had brought him to this. He was one of the youngest flag officers on the Navy List. He had always told himself that he would not change, that he was no different from that young, untried captain in his first serious encounter with the enemy, with only his own skills and determination to sustain him.

Or from the midshipman. He stared at the shadowed side of the Rock. Aboard the little sloop-of-war *Sparrow*, Richard Bolitho's first command.

He still could not come to terms with it. He could remember the signal being brought to his spacious rooms at the Admiralty, the writing blurring as he had read and understood that the impossible had happened: Napoleon had surrendered. Abdicated. It had ended. A release for so many, but for him like a great door being slammed shut.

He stared around the cabin, the rippling reflections of water on the low deckhead. It had seemed so small, so cramped after his life in London. He *had* changed.

He could hear the movement of the men on the upper deck, the creak of tackles as stores sent across from one of the supply vessels from England were hoisted inboard.

His thoughts returned to Catherine Somervell, from whom they were never far away. That night at the reception at Castlereagh's home, when Admiral Lord Rhodes had stunned the guests by calling Bolitho's wife to join him and share the applause for her absent husband. When Bethune had begged to be allowed to escort Catherine to her Chelsea house, she had refused. She had been composed enough to consider him; there was enough scandal. Later he had heard of the attack at her home, a disgusting attempt to rape her by a Captain Oliphant, apparently a cousin of Rhodes. After that, things had moved quickly. Rhodes had not become First Lord as he had hoped and expected, and his cousin had not been heard of since.

He looked at the heavy coat again. *And I was ordered here.* In command of a small group of frigates entrusted with patrol and search operations, too late to relieve Sir Richard Bolitho at Malta, nor even in England when the news of his death had broken. No wonder he had changed. He had once imagined himself comfortably, if not happily, married to a woman who suited his role and shared his ambitions. Now even their life together had been soured by those events, and he suspected his wife had been a willing partner in Rhodes' attempt to humiliate and insult Catherine at that reception for Wellington.

He crossed to the opposite quarter and shaded his eyes against the glare to gaze at the mainland. Spain. It was hard not to think of it as the enemy; in Algeciras there had always been eyes watching for the arrival of a new sail, with riders ready to gallop to the next post where the message could be relayed. *Another ship from England. Where bound? For what purpose?*

And there were many who still believed Spain harboured enemies who had already taken advantage of Napoleon's downfall to settle old scores in these waters, to resume piracy and the running of slaves to a ready market in America and the Indies, despite the laws so piously passed to forbid it. The new allies. Would it last? Could they ever forget?

A cutter pulled strongly past the counter and the crew tossed oars in salute, a midshipman in charge rising to remove his hat within the shadow of the flagship. His Britannic Majesty's Ship *Montrose* of forty-two guns was little different from any other frigate to the casual observer, but Bethune knew that his blue command flag at the fore made her unique.

He heard voices beyond the screen door. His flag captain, Victor Forbes, was a brisk, no-nonsense man who was very aware that this was no longer a private ship, and that flag had made all the difference to him in particular; he had even had to vacate these quarters for his admiral. Bethune had seen the seamen and marines glancing at him when he took his regular walks up and down the quarterdeck. A far cry from the Thames Embankment or the London parks, but it was better than nothing. He touched his stomach. He would not let himself go to seed like some of the flag officers he knew. In case . . . *In case what?*

Tomorrow *Montrose* would weigh and return to Malta, unless new orders came to direct otherwise. It was becoming ever more difficult to keep a part of his mind in the world of the Admiralty, to assess or disregard the next possible strategy, which had once been so clear to him. Even to know the true deployment of the allied armies, or whether Napoleon was indeed fighting a rearguard action.

Today he might receive fresh information. That was the irony of it. The ship which had been sighted just an hour ago was *Unrivalled*. He had felt a certain involuntary shock when he had seen his flag lieutenant's report in the log, *Unrivalled (46). Captain Bolitho.* Not like a step forward; rather, looking back. The names, the faces . . .

And now Adam Bolitho was here. In a new ship. *At least I was able to send word of that before he was struck down.*

He clenched his fists. He had heard one of the seamen saying to his mate when they had been splicing below the quarterdeck:

'I tell 'ee, Ted. We'll ne'er see his like again, an' that's God's truth!'

The sailor's simple tribute, shared by so many. And yet, like so many, that unknown sailor had never laid eyes on Richard Bolitho.

The door opened and he saw Captain Forbes looking around the cabin, probably to ensure his admiral had not changed it out of all recognition.

'What is it, Victor?'

The reflected sunlight was too strong for him to see the captain's expression, but he sensed it was one of uncertainty, if not actual disapproval.

We are about the same age, and yet he behaves like my superior officer. He tried to smile, but it would not come.

35

Captain Forbes said, '*Unrivalled* has anchored, sir.' Then, as an afterthought, 'She's big. We could have done with a few more like her when . . .'

He did not go on. There was no need.

'Yes. A fine ship. I envy her captain.'

That did surprise Forbes, and this time he was unable to conceal it. His vice-admiral, who was both liked and respected, and would no doubt rise to some even more exalted post when the Admiralty directed, lacked for nothing. He could use favour or dislike as he chose, and no one would question him. To profess envy was unthinkable.

'I shall make the signal, sir.'

'Very well. *Captain repair on board*.' How many times he had seen it break out at the yard, for himself and for others. And now for Adam Bolitho. Every new meeting like this one would be an additional strain. *For us both*.

Forbes was still here, hand on the screen door.

'I was thinking, sir. Perhaps we might entertain *Unrivalled*'s captain. I'm sure the wardroom would be honoured.' He hesitated under Bethune's stare. 'You know the way of it, sir. Word from home.' He added warily, 'You would be our guest too, of course, sir.'

'I am certain Captain Bolitho would be delighted.' He looked away. 'I would also be pleased. None of us should ever forget how or why we are here.'

He heard Forbes marching across the quarterdeck, calling for the midshipman of the watch. Bethune had not even seen him leave the cabin.

Unrivalled was joining his squadron. This was the best way. He thought of Bolitho again. *No show of favouritism*.

But they would have a glass together first, while he read his despatches from that other world. He smiled again, and it was very sad. *No looking back*.

Adam Bolitho sat in one of the cabin chairs and crossed his legs, as if the action would force him to relax. He had been greeted very correctly when he had climbed up *Montrose*'s tumblehome, amid the twitter of boatswain's calls, the slap and crack of muskets being brought to the present under a cloud of pipeclay. All due respects to a captain, and he wondered why

36

it surprised him. He had been so received aboard many ships large and small, and in all conditions. When it had been hard to prevent his hat from being blown away, or with a boat cloak tangling around his legs. He had never forgotten a story his uncle had told him about a captain who had tripped over his own sword and pitched back into his barge, to the delight of the assembled midshipmen.

Perhaps, like the vice-admiral sitting opposite him, turning over the pages of his despatches with practised speed, he too had changed. On his way across to the flagship he had glanced astern at his own command. Above her reflection, sails neatly furled, all boats in the water to seal their seams, she would make any would-be captain jealous. *And she is mine.* But as of this moment she would be a part of a squadron, and, like her, he would have to *belong.* He watched Bethune's bowed head, the lock of hair falling over his brow. More like a lieutenant than a Vice-Admiral of the Blue.

It had been an awkward meeting, which even the din of the reception could not hide or cover. Friends? They were hardly that. But they had always been a part of something. Of someone.

He had mentioned the brigantine and his suspicions to Bethune. It would be in his report, but he felt he should use it to dispel the lingering stiffness between them. Instead of dismissing it, the vice-admiral had seemed very interested.

'It is the kind of secret war we are fighting out here, Adam. Algerine pirates, slavers – we are sitting on a powder keg.'

Bethune looked up suddenly. 'It seems the lords of the Admiralty are as much in the dark as we are!'

Adam said, 'You would know better than most, sir.' They both laughed, the tension all but gone.

He liked what he saw. Bethune had an open, intelligent face, a mouth which had not forgotten how to smile. He knew from Catherine's letters that she had trusted him. He could understand why.

Bethune said, 'I almost forgot. When we reach Malta I should have more information to act upon.' He was making up his mind. 'There is a Lieutenant George Avery at my headquarters there. You will know him?'

'Sir Richard's flag lieutenant, sir.' He felt his muscles tense,

37

but made another attempt. 'They were very close, I believe. I thought he had returned to England in *Frobisher*.'

'I did not force him to stay, but his knowledge is very valuable to me – to us. He was with Sir Richard when he dealt with the Algerines. And with a certain Spanish connection.' He smiled slightly. 'I see that interests you?' He turned as muffled thuds came from the direction of the wardroom. Adam knew of the invitation, and that *Montrose*'s captain would be there also. As a guest, as was the custom, although Adam had never known any captain refused entry to a wardroom in his own ship.

Bethune said, 'In any case, I did not have to press Lieutenant Avery. It seems he has nothing for which to return.'

I have a ship. George Avery has nothing.

'I look forward to meeting him again. My uncle,' he hesitated, 'and Lady Somervell spoke highly of him. As a friend.'

Bethune picked up his untouched glass of wine.

'I give you a sentiment, Adam. "To absent friends."' He drank deeply and grimaced. 'God, what foul stuff!'

They both knew it was to hold at bay something far deeper, but when Captain Forbes and his first lieutenant arrived to escort them to the wardroom, they sensed nothing unusual.

Adam saw Forbes' eyes rest briefly on the old Bolitho sword, which lay beside Bethune's.

Why had he not seen it for himself? How could he have doubted it? It was still there, like a hand reaching out.

The lifeline.

A Matter of Pride

Sir Wilfred Lafargue waited while Spicer, his clerk, gathered up a bulky file of documents, and then folded his hands on the empty desk.

'I foresee several problems, perhaps serious ones, arising in the near future. But insurmountable? I think not.'

Normally, such a comment would leave a client hopeful, if not entirely satisfied. But Lafargue, as a lawyer and the senior partner of this prestigious firm which bore his name, was conscious only of its lack of substance.

He knew it was because of his visitor, standing now by the far window in this vast office. It was Lafargue's favourite view of the City of London, and the dome of St Paul's, a constant reminder of its power and influence.

Lafargue was always in command; from the moment the tall doors were opened to admit a client, potential or familiar, his routine never varied. There was a chair directly opposite this imposing desk, forcing the client to face the full light of the windows, more like a victim than one who would eventually be charged a fee which might make him blanch and reconsider before returning. Except that they always did return.

But this one was different. He had known Sillitoe for a good many years; Baron Sillitoe of Chiswick, as he now was. The Prince Regent's Inspector-General, and a man of formidable connections long before that. Feared, hated, but never ignored. Those who did regretted it dearly.

Sillitoe was a man of moods, and this again unsettled Lafargue; it broke the pattern of things and was disconcerting.

Restless, unable to remain still for more than a few minutes, he seemed disturbed by something which had not yet been revealed.

Lafargue, as usual, was expensively dressed, his coat and breeches cut by one of London's leading tailors, but the clothing could not completely disguise the signs of good living which made him appear older than his fifty-eight years. Sillitoe on the other hand had never changed; he was lean, hard, as if anything superfluous or wasteful had long since been honed away. A good horseman, he was said to exercise regularly, his secretary panting beside him while he outlined one or another of his schemes. He was also a swordsman of repute. For Lafargue it made the comparison even more difficult to accept. Sillitoe was the same age as himself.

Sillitoe was motionless, watching something below, perhaps the carriages wending their way towards Fleet Street, perhaps merely waiting for something. Lafargue saw that the doors were once more closed; Spicer had departed. As senior clerk he was invaluable, and although he appeared to be very dull he never missed the slightest nuance or inflection. Even here, at Lincoln's Inn, which Lafargue considered the very centre of English law, there were some things which should and must remain private. This conversation was one of them.

He said, 'I have studied all the deeds available. Sir Richard's nephew Adam Bolitho, once known as Pascoe, is deemed the legal heir to the Bolitho estate and adjoining properties as listed . . .' He stopped, frowning, as Sillitoe said, 'Get on with it, man.' He had not raised his voice.

Lafargue swallowed hard. 'However, Sir Richard's widow and dependant, the daughter, will have some rights in the matter. They are supported by the trust instituted by Sir Richard. It may well be that Lady Bolitho will want to install herself at Falmouth where she did, in fact, enjoy a conjugal residency at one time.'

Sillitoe rubbed his forehead. What was the point? Why had he come? Lafargue was a celebrated lawyer. *Otherwise neither of us would be here.* He controlled his impatience. Lafargue would act when the time came. If it did . . .

He looked across at the other buildings, the small green expanses of parks and quiet squares, and saw St Paul's. Where the nation, or a select few, would gather to pay homage to a hero. Some with genuine grief, others there only to be seen and admired. Sillitoe had never understood why any sane man would volunteer to spend his life at sea. To him, a ship was only a necessary form of transport. Like being caged, unable to move or act for himself. But he had accepted that others had different views, his nephew George Avery among them.

When they had last met he had offered him a position, one both important and, in time, lucrative. Sillitoe never threw money to the winds without proof of ability, and his nephew was a mere lieutenant, who had been passed over for promotion after being taken prisoner by the French; he had been freed only to face a court martial for losing his ship.

Any other man would have jumped at the opportunity, or at least shown some gratitude. Instead, Avery had returned to his appointment as Sir Richard Bolitho's flag lieutenant, and must have been with him when he had been killed.

He said flatly, 'And what of Viscountess Somervell?' He did not turn from the window, although he heard the intake of breath. Another lawyer's ploy.

'In the eyes of the law, she has no rights. Had they been at liberty to marry . . .'

'And the people? What will they say? The woman who inspired their hero, who displayed courage when most would fall back in despair? What of her part?'

He knew Lafargue would think he was referring to Catherine's bravery and strength in the open boat after the shipwreck; he was intended to. But Sillitoe was seeing something very different, something which had preyed on his mind and had never released him since he and his men had burst into the house by the river. Bruised and bleeding, stripped naked and with her wrists tied cruelly behind her back, she had fought her attacker. Sillitoe had held her against his body and covered her with a sheet or curtain, he could not remember what it had been or the exact order of things. His men beating her attacker, dragging him down the stairs, and then those moments alone with her, her head against his shoulder, her hair beautiful in disarray.

A nightmare. And he had wanted her. Then and there.

'The people? Who listens to the *people*?' Lafargue was regaining his self-control. His old arrogance.

Sillitoe turned his back on the city, his face in shadow.

'In France they listened. Eventually!'

Lafargue watched him, sensing the bitterness, the anger. And something else. He recalled Catherine Somervell coming here to consult him, at Sillitoe's suggestion, on a matter of purchasing the lease of a building where Bolitho's estranged wife lived, at her husband's expense. Belinda Bolitho had been horrified to discover that her home was owned by the woman she most hated. A woman scorned.

Lafargue's eyes sharpened professionally. No, there was far more to it than that. He watched Sillitoe, dressed all in grey as was his habit, move swiftly to the opposite side of the room. He had the ear of the Prince Regent, and when the King, drifting in madness, eventually died, who could say to what heights he might not rise?

Lady Somervell . . . he had thought of her as Catherine just now, which showed that he was unusually overwrought . . . was the key. Lafargue remembered her entering this room. She had walked straight towards him, her eyes never leaving his. To call her beautiful was an understatement. But a symbol could be soiled, and envy and spite were well known to Lafargue in the world of law.

They had praised Nelson to the skies, and those who had cried out the loudest had been the biggest hypocrites. A dead hero was safe, and could be remembered without anxiety or inconvenience.

Edward Berry, Nelson's favourite flag captain, had once quoted, *God and the navy we adore, when danger threatens but not before.*

Napoleon was said to be in retreat; it might soon be over. Not like the last time. Truly over . . .

How soon after that would those same people turn on the woman who had defied society and protocol for the man she loved?

He ventured, 'If Lady Somervell were to remarry . . . Her husband was killed in a duel, I understand.'

Sillitoe sat down abruptly. Everyone knew about Somervell, a gambler and a waster who had used much of Catherine's money to extricate himself from debt. A man who had plotted with Bolitho's wife to have his mistress imprisoned and transported as a common thief. One of Bolitho's officers had called him out and had mortally wounded him. He had paid for it with his own life.

I would have killed him myself.

How much did Lafargue really know?

He would know, for instance, that the post of Inspector-General had once been Viscount Somervell's. Another bitter twist.

'I think it unlikely.' He tugged out his watch. 'I must leave now.'

Lafargue asked, too casually, 'And how goes the war?'

Sillitoe glanced around the room. 'I shall see the Prince Regent this afternoon. He is more concerned with the army than the fleet at this moment. As well he might be.'

Lafargue stood. He felt unusually drained and could not explain it. He said, 'I have received an invitation to the memorial service at St Paul's. The cathedral will be crowded to the full, I have no doubt.'

It was a question. Sillitoe said, 'I shall be there.'

'And Lady Somervell?'

Sillitoe saw the double doors open silently. Perhaps there was a hidden bell, some sort of secret signal.

'She has been invited.' Their eyes met. 'Privately.'

It told Lafargue nothing. He took his hat from the clerk, and sighed. It told him everything.

Unis Allday walked slowly around the small parlour, making certain that everything was as it should be. She knew she had already done it several times, but she could not help it. Beyond the open door she could hear voices, the only two customers at the Old Hyperion inn. Auctioneers from the sound of them, on their way to Falmouth for tomorrow's market.

Everything looked neat. There was a smell of freshly baked bread, and new casks of ale on their trestles, each with its own clean towel. She paused, and with her hands on her hips stared at her reflection in the looking-glass. She did not smile, but examined every feature as she would a new girl applying for work in the kitchen.

She shivered, staring at herself. As he would see her. His friend Bryan Ferguson had brought the news. The man-of-war

Frobisher which had taken her man away from her last year was at Plymouth. John Allday was back, and coming home. She looked around the parlour again. Coming home. She allowed her mind to explore it. Never to leave her.

She could hear her brother, also named John, chopping wood for the kitchen. She had told him not to, with only one leg, but he was doing it for her. Allowing her this time to be alone.

She walked through the outer parlour. The auctioneers were still there but one was counting out money, and their horses were already at the door. She walked past them into the afternoon sunshine. Almost June, the summer of 1815. Where had it all gone, and so quickly?

She gazed down the empty road, the hedgerows rippling slightly under the breeze off Falmouth Bay, campion and foxglove splashing colour against the many shades of green. She turned and looked at the inn. She could not have done it without her brother. He had lost his leg in the line while serving with the Thirty-First regiment of foot, the Old Huntingtonshires. If it had been her, she thought, she would have given up. Now, freshly painted, the inn sign with the ship which had become so important in their lives was moving restlessly, as if the old *Hyperion* was remembering also.

Unis was well acquainted with the ways of the sea, its demands and its cruelties. Her first husband had been a master's mate in that same old ship and had died aboard her, like so many others. John Allday had burst into her life not far from here, when she had been attacked by two footpads while on her way to this very inn.

Big, shambling, but there was no man like him. As he had dealt with her attackers she had realised that he was in pain; he was suffering from an old wound, which she knew now had been a sword-thrust to the chest. She had seen the scar many times. She wiped her eyes. *He was coming home.* Bryan Ferguson had said it would be today or tomorrow. She knew it was today. How could she? But she knew.

The two auctioneers were leaving, heaving themselves into their saddles, well filled with rabbit pie and the vegetables she grew behind the inn. They waved to her, and cantered away.

She was small, pretty and neat, but customers did not take liberties with her. Not more than once.

She smiled. Anyway, she was a foreigner, from over the border in Devon, the fishing port of Brixham where she had been born and had lived until her man had been reported killed. *Discharged dead*, the navy termed it.

She pushed some hair from her eyes and looked at the hillside, which was alive with young lambs either grazing or frolicking in the pale sunshine. Foreigner maybe, but she would be in no other place.

Bryan Ferguson had warned her, or had tried to; her brother had also done his best. It would be difficult, most of all for John Allday. She thought of that last visit, when Bryan had brought the news that Sir Richard Bolitho was ordered to sea again. Even Unis had been angry; he had been back in England no time at all. The house below Pendennis was empty now, except for the Fergusons and the servants.

She recalled the young Captain Bolitho at the church. So erect, brave in his dress uniform, with the old sword at his hip which had been pointed out to her. All that was left of the man they were remembering.

And Lady Catherine. She had come here to the inn whenever she had wanted a friend, and Unis ventured to call herself that, when Sir Richard was away at sea. She had been in the parlour that night Squire Roxby had died, and had gone from here to comfort his widow. A family, but it was more than that. In the room where John had finally found himself able to tell her about his son John Bankart, who had died in battle, how he had carried him himself, and had put him over the side for his burial.

She glanced at the narrow stairway. And together they had had Kate. That would be different this time, too. She nodded firmly. *From now on.* She had seen the hurt on the strong, weathered features when he had returned from sea, and his own child had run from him to Unis's brother.

Little Kate was upstairs now in the beautiful cot John had made for her. Like the toys, and the perfect ship models; his big, clumsy-looking hands could perform miracles.

Her brother had said, 'When I got back from the war, a pin missing and all, I was grateful. I was thankful to be spared, crippled or not. When things were bad I remembered, or tried to, all those lines of men. Friends I'd known, lying out in the field, bleeding to death, calling out with nobody to hear. Waiting to die, quickly, to be spared the crows and the scum who rob the likes of poor soldiers after a battle. What I hated most was pity, well meant or otherwise. All I had left was my pride.' He had looked at the old tattoo on his arm and had managed to smile. 'Even in the old bloody regiment!'

Unis knew what John's standing as the admiral's coxswain had meant to him. How he had belonged. That was what he had said, right here, just before he had left. Not merely the personal coxswain of England's most famous sailor, but his friend. And he had been there. Bryan Ferguson had told them about it after Adam Bolitho's return, and he had heard it from the admiral at Plymouth. John had been at Richard Bolitho's side when he had been shot down.

Horses' hooves and the rattle of wheels startled her from her thoughts, but the sounds went on, and were lost around the curve of the road.

She stared at the hand pressed under her heart. Was it fear? John was safe. He would never go back to sea. She knew he and Bryan Ferguson had discussed it, talked about the point at which a man was reckoned too old to fight for King and country. It was like a red rag to a bull for John Allday.

She thought of his letters; how she had waited for them, yearned for them. And had often wondered about the officer who had written them on John's behalf. George Avery was a good man, and had stayed at the Old Hyperion. She had often thought of him reading her letters aloud to John, a little like having letters from home for himself, although John had told her he never received any.

How long would it take? What would he do? He had often said he would never become just another old Jack, yarning and 'swinging the lamp'.

But it would be hard, perhaps for all of them. Bryan Ferguson had told her that he and her John had been pressed together here in Cornwall, and taken to a King's ship in Falmouth. Bolitho's ship. What had grown from that unlikely meeting was stronger than any rock.

Here on the edge of the little village of Fallowfield, it was not like Brixham or Falmouth. Farm workers and passing tradesmen were more common than men of the sea. But there would still be talk. Everyone knew the Bolitho family. And Catherine was in London, they said. There would be more ceremonies there; how could she endure it? There was gossip enough in any town or village. How much worse it must be in the city.

She heard her brother descending the stairs, the regular thump of his wooden leg. His spar, John Allday called it.

'Little Kate's fast asleep.' He limped towards her. 'Still thinking on it, Unis love? We'll make it right for him, see?'

'Thank you for that, John. I don't know what I'd have done –' She looked into his face and froze, unable to move. She whispered, 'Oh, dear God, make my man happy again!'

The sound of Bryan Ferguson's pony and trap seemed louder than it had ever been.

She tugged at her skirt and pushed some hair from her face again.

'I can't! I can't!'

Nobody moved, nobody spoke. He was suddenly just there, filling the entrance, his hat in one hand, his hair shaggy against the sunlight.

She tried to speak, but instead he held out his arms, as though unable to come forward. Her brother remembered it for a long time afterwards. John Allday, who had rescued and won his only sister, was in the room, as if he had never been away.

He was wearing the fine blue coat with the gilt buttons bearing the Bolitho crest, which had been made especially for him, and nankeen breeches and buckled shoes. The landsman's ideal of the English sailor, the Heart of Oak. So easily said by those who had not shared the horrors of close action at sea or on land.

John Allday held her close against him, but gently, as he would a child or some small animal, and touched her hair, her ears, her cheek, afraid he might hurt her in some way, unable to let go of her.

He thought he heard a door close, very quietly. They were alone. Even his best friend Bryan was silent, out there with his fat little pony named Poppy.

'You're a picture, Unis.' He tilted her chin with the same care. 'I've thought about this moment for a long time.'

She asked, 'The officer, Mister Avery?'

47

Allday shook his head. 'Stayed with the ship. Thought he was needed.' He held her away from him, his big hands cupping her shoulders, his eyes moving over her, as if he was only now realising what had happened.

She stood quite still, feeling the strength, the warmth of his hard hands. So strong and yet so unsure, so wistful.

'You're here. That's all I care about. I've missed you so much, even when I tried to be with you over the miles . . .' She broke off. She was not reaching him even now.

Suddenly he took her hand in his, and led her like a young girl to the nook where his model, his first gift to her, was carefully mounted.

'I was there, y' see. All the while. Comin' home, we was. We'd got the orders. I never seen such a change in the man.' He looked at her with something like anguish. 'Comin' home. What we both wanted.'

They sat down on a scrubbed wooden bench, side by side, like strangers. But he held her hand, and spoke so quietly that she had to put her head against his arm to hear him.

'He often asked about you an' little Kate.' The sound of the child's name seemed to unsteady him. 'Is she safe? An' well?'

She nodded, afraid of breaking the spell. 'You'll see.'

He smiled, something faraway. Perhaps another memory.

He said, 'He knew, y' see. When we went up on deck. He knew. I felt it.'

She heard her brother by the door, and thought she saw Bryan Ferguson's shadow motionless in a shaft of light. Sharing it. As they had every right.

She found she was gripping his hand more tightly, and said, 'I want you as my man again, John Allday. I'll give you the love you need. I'll help you!'

But when he turned his face to hers there was no pain, no despair.

He said, 'I was with him to the end, love. Just like we always was, from the first broadside at the Saintes.'

He seemed to realise that they were no longer alone. 'I held him.' He nodded slowly. Seeing it. Confronting it. 'He said, *easy, old friend*. Just to me, like he always did. *No grief. We always knew.*' He looked at her and smiled, perhaps truly

48

aware of her for the first time. 'Then he died, an' I was still holdin' him.'

She stood up and put her arms around him, sharing his loss, feeling such love for this one man.

She murmured, 'Let it go, John. Later we shall lie together. It's all that matters now.'

Allday held her for several minutes.

Then he said, 'Get the others, eh?'

She shook him gently, embracing him, her heart too full for words.

A life was gone. Hers was complete.

Brush . . . brush . . . brush . . .

Catherine, Lady Somervell, sat facing the tilted oval mirror, her hand rising and falling without conscious thought, her long hair spilling over one shoulder. In the candlelight it looked almost black, like silk, but she did not notice.

The hour was late and beyond the windows the evening had darkened, the Thames revealed only by the light of an occasional lantern, a wherryman, or some sailor on his way to one of the riverside taverns.

But here in the Walk, there were very few people, and the air was heavy, as if with storm. She saw the candles beside the mirror shiver and stared at the reflection of the bed behind her. There were far too many candles in the room; they were probably the cause of the stuffiness. But there were always too many, had been since that night of raw terror. *In this room. On that bed.* She had overcome it. But it had never left her.

She continued to brush her hair, pausing only at the sound of a fast-moving carriage. But it did not slow or stop.

She thought of the housekeeper, Mrs Tate, who was somewhere downstairs. Even she had changed her way of life since that night, when she had been visiting her sister in Shoreditch as had been her habit. Now she never left the house unattended, and watched over her with a tenderness Catherine had never suspected. And she had never once mentioned it. Her own thoughts had been too full, too chaotic in those first weeks after the attack. Even then it had been like witnessing the horrific violation of someone else, not herself. A stranger.

Except on nights like these. Warm, even clammy, the thin

gown clinging to her body like another skin, despite the bath she had taken before coming upstairs.

She hesitated, and then pulled open a drawer deliberately and took out the fan. Richard had given it to her after his ship had called at Madeira. So long ago.

She looked at the diamond pendant which hung low on her breast. It, too, was shaped like a fan. So that she would not forget, he had said. The pendant the intruder had turned over in his fingers while she had been helpless, her wrists pinioned behind her. She looked involuntarily at the nearest window. He had used the cord. He had struck her, so that she had almost lost her senses, when she had called him a thief. Outraged, like a madman. And then he had begun to torment her, to strip her there, on that bed.

She touched her breast and felt her heart beating against her hand. But not like then, or all those other times, when the memory had returned.

And afterwards . . . The word seemed quite separate from her other thoughts. Sillitoe and his men had burst into the room, and he had held her, protected her while her attacker had been dragged away. It had been like a sudden calm after a terrible storm.

She thought of Malta, her brief visit in an Indiaman, which had been on government business and bound for Naples. Sillitoe had arranged for her to be landed at Malta, even though she knew he would once have done anything to keep her from Richard, and he had made no attempt to gain any advantage either on the passage out or on the journey back to England. If anything, he had been withdrawn, perhaps at last understanding what it had cost her to leave the man she loved behind in Malta.

Forever.

She had seen him only twice since Richard's death. He had offered his condolences, and assured her of his readiness to help in any way he could. As with the lawyer, Lafargue, he had understood immediately her concern for Adam. He had been correct in every way, and had made it his business to begin enquiries of his own.

Catherine thought she understood men, had learned much out of necessity.

But after Richard, how could she survive? Where would be the point?

She recalled the exact moment when they had been reunited, at English Harbour over ten years ago. She had been married to Somervell, the King's Inspector-General.

Dazed and yet on guard because of the unexpectedness of the meeting, and the danger she had known it would offer. Telling him he needed love, *as the desert craves for rain.*

Or was I speaking of myself? My own desires?

And now he is dead.

And tomorrow, another challenge. All those staring eyes. Not those of the men who had stood with him and had faced death a hundred times, or the women who had loved and welcomed them when they had returned home. Without limbs. Without sight. Without hope.

No. They would be the faces and the eyes she had seen that evening at the celebration of Wellington's victory. Rhodes, who had been championed as the new First Lord of the Admiralty. Richard's wife, bowing to applause she would never earn or deserve. And the unsmiling wife of Graham Bethune. Unsmiling until the moment of insult, as if she had been a part of it. All enemies.

She had turned her back on them. Had come here, half blind with anger and humiliation. She stood up quickly and stared at the bed. *And he was waiting for me.*

Tomorrow, then. The bells would toll, the drums echo through the empty streets. They would be remembering her Richard, her dearest of men, but they would be looking at her. *At me.*

And what would they see? The woman who had inspired a hero? The woman who had endured a shipwreck, and fought the danger and misery so that they might all hope to live, when most of them had already accepted a lingering death. The woman who had loved him. *Loved him.*

Or would they see only a whore?

She faced the mirror again and unfastened her gown, so that it fell and was held until she released it and stood naked, the hair warm against her spine.

As the desert craves for rain.

She sat again and recovered the brush. She heard a step on

51

the stairs, quick and light. It would be Melwyn, her maid and companion. Cornish, from St Austell, a fair girl with an elusive, elfin prettiness. She was fifteen.

She stared unwaveringly at the mirror. Fifteen. *As I was when I was with child. When my world began to change.* Richard had known of that; Sillitoe also knew.

She heard a tap at the door and pulled the gown up to her shoulders. Melwyn entered the room and closed the door.

'You've not eaten, m' lady.' She stood her ground, quietly determined. 'Tesn't right. Cook thought . . .'

She stood quite still as Catherine twisted round to look at her. Then she said simply, 'You'm so beautiful, m' lady. You must take more care. Tomorrow d' be so important, and I can't be with you. No room for servants . . .'

Catherine clasped her round the shoulders and pressed her face into the fair hair. Richard's sister had told her that Melwyn meant *honey-fair* in the old Cornish tongue.

'You're no mere servant, Melwyn.' She embraced her again. 'Tomorrow, then.'

The girl said, 'Sir Richard will expect it.'

Catherine nodded very slowly. She had nearly given in, broken down, unable to go through with it. She lifted her chin, felt the anger giving way to pride.

She said, 'He will, indeed,' and smiled at a memory the girl would never know or understand. 'So let's be about it, then!'

52

4

New Beginning

Captain Adam Bolitho ran lightly up the companion ladder
and paused as the bright sunshine momentarily dazzled him.
He glanced around the quarterdeck, fitting names to faces,
noting what each man was doing.

Lieutenant Vivian Massie had the afternoon watch, and
seemed surprised by his appearance on deck. Midshipman
Bellairs was working with his signals party, observing each
man to see if he was quick to recognise every flag, folded
in its locker or not. It was hard enough with other ships in
company, but alone, with no chance to regularly send and
receive signals, there was always a danger that mistakes born
out of boredom would be made.

Four bells had just chimed from the forecastle. He looked
up at the masthead pendant, whipping out half-heartedly in a
wind which barely filled the sails. He walked to the compass
box. East-by-south. He could feel the eyes of the helmsmen
on him, while a master's mate made a business of examining
a midshipman's slate. All as usual. And yet . . .

'I heard a hail from the masthead, Mr Massie?'

'Aye, sir.' He gestured vaguely towards the starboard bow.
'Driftwood.'

Adam frowned and looked at the master's log book. Eight
hundred miles since leaving Gibraltar, in just under five days.
The ship was a good sailer despite these unreliable winds,
conditions which might be expected in the Mediterranean.

No sight of land. They could be alone on some vast,
uncharted ocean. The sun was hot but not oppressively so,

and he had seen a few burns and blisters amongst the seamen.

'Who is the lookout?'

He did not turn, but guessed Massie was surprised by what seemed so trivial a question.

He did not recognise the name.

'Send Sullivan,' he said.

The master's mate said, 'He's off watch below, sir.'

Adam stared at the chart. Unlike those in the chart room, it was stained and well used; there was even a dark ring of something where a watchkeeper had carelessly left a mug.

'Send him.' He traced the coastline with his fingers. Fifty miles or so to the south lay Algiers. Dangerous, hostile, and little known except by those unfortunate enough to fall into the hands of Algerine pirates.

He saw the seaman Sullivan hurrying to the main shrouds, his bare feet hooking over the hard ratlines. His soles were like leather, unlike some of the landsmen, who could scarcely hobble after a few hours working aloft, although even they were improving. He heard Partridge, the ship's barrel-chested boatswain, call out something, and saw Sullivan's brown face split into a grin.

He knew that Cristie, the master, had arrived on deck. That was not unusual. He checked his log at least twice in every watch. His entire world was the wind and the currents, the tides and the soundings; he could probably discover the exact condition of the seabed merely by arming the lead with tallow and smelling the fragment hauled up from the bottom. Without his breed of mariner a ship was blind, could fall a victim to any reef or sandbar. Charts were never enough. To men like Cristie, they never would be, either.

Adam shaded his eyes and peered up at the mainmast again.

'Deck, there!'

Adam waited, picturing Sullivan's bright, clear eyes, like those of a much younger man peering through a mask.

'Wreckage off the starboard bow!'

He heard Massie say irritably, 'Could have been there for months!'

Nobody answered, and he sensed that they were all looking at their captain.

54

He turned to the sailing master. 'What do *you* think, Mr Cristie?'

Cristie shrugged. 'Aye. In this sea it could have been drifting hereabouts for quite a while.'

He was no doubt thinking, *why*? To investigate some useless wreckage would mean changing tack, and in this uncertain wind it might take half a day to resume their course.

The master's mate said, 'Here's Sullivan, sir.'

Sullivan walked from the shrouds, gazing around the quarter-deck as if he had never seen it before.

'Well, Sullivan? A fool's errand this time?'

Surprisingly, the man did not respond. He said, 'Somethin's wrong, sir.' He looked directly at his captain for the first time. Then he nodded, more certain, knowing that the captain would not dismiss his beliefs, his sailor's instinct.

He seemed to make up his mind. 'Gulls, sir, circlin' over the wreckage.'

Adam heard the midshipman of the watch suppress a snigger, and the master's mate's angry rebuke.

A shadow fell across the compass box. It was Galbraith, the first lieutenant.

'Trouble, sir? I heard what he said.'

Gulls on the water meant pickings. Circling low above it meant they were afraid to go nearer. He thought of the boy John Whitmarsh, who had been found alive after *Anemone* had gone down.

'Call all hands, Mr Galbraith. We shall heave to and lower the gig.' He heard the brief, almost curt orders being translated into trilling calls and the responding rush of feet. *What's the bloody captain want this time?*

He raised his voice slightly. 'Mr Bellairs, take charge of the gig.' He turned to watch the hands rushing to halliards and braces. 'Good experience for your examination!' He saw the midshipman touch his hat and smile. *Was it so easy?*

He saw Jago by the nettings and beckoned him across. 'Go with him. A weather eye.'

Jago shrugged. 'Aye, sir.'

Galbraith watched the sails thundering in disorder as *Unrivalled* lurched unsteadily into the wind.

55

He said, 'I would have gone, sir. Mr Bellairs is not very experienced.'

Adam looked at him. 'And he never will be, if he is protected from such duties.'

Galbraith hurried to the rail as the gig was swayed up and over the gangway.

Did he take it as a slight because one so junior had been sent? Or as a lack of trust, because of what had happened in his past?

Adam turned aside, angry that such things could still touch him.

'Gig's away, sir!'

The boat was pulling strongly from the side, oars rising and cutting into the water as one. A good boat's crew. He could see Jago hunched by the tiller, remembered shaking hands with him on that littered deck after the American had broken off the action. And John Whitmarsh lay dead on the orlop.

'Glass, Mr Cousens!' He reached out and took the telescope, not noticing that the name had come to him without effort.

The gig loomed into view, up and down so that sometimes she appeared to be foundering. No wonder the frigate was rolling so badly. He thought of Cristie's comment. *In this sea.*

He saw the oars rise and stay motionless, a man standing in the bows with a boathook. Jago was on his feet too, but steadying the tiller-bar as if he was calming the boat and the movement. The hard man, and a true sailor, who hated officers and detested the navy. But he was still here. *With me.*

Bellairs was trying to keep his footing, and was staring astern at *Unrivalled*. He held up his arms and crossed them.

Massie grunted, 'He's found something.'

Cristie barely spared him a glance. 'Somebody, more like.'

Adam lowered the glass. They were pulling a body from the sea, the bowman fending off the surrounding wreckage with his boathook. Midshipman Bellairs, who would sit for lieutenant when the admiral so ordered, was hanging over the gunwale vomiting, with Jago holding his belt, setting the oars in motion again as if all else was secondary.

'Fetch the surgeon.'

'Done, sir.'

'Extra hands on the tackles, Mr Partridge!' The boatswain was not grinning now.

He thought again of Whitmarsh, the twelve year old who had been 'volunteered' by a so-called uncle. He had told him how he had drifted from the sinking frigate, holding his friend's hand, unaware that the other boy had been dead for some while.

He turned to speak to Sullivan but he had gone. He handed the telescope to the midshipman of the watch; he did not need to look again to know the gulls were swooping down once more, their screams lost in distance. The spirits of dead sailors, the old Jacks called them. Scavengers fitted them better, he thought. He heard O'Beirne giving instructions to two of his loblolly boys. A good surgeon, or another butcher? You might never know until it was too late.

Adam walked to the side, two marines springing out of his way to allow him to pass. The gig was almost here, and he noticed that Bellairs was on his feet again.

Why should it matter? We all had to learn. But it did matter.

A block squeaked, and he knew Partridge's mates were lowering a canvas cradle to hoist the survivor inboard. It would probably finish him, if he was not dead already.

Other men were running now to guide the cradle over the gangway, clear of the boat-tier.

Adam said, 'Secure the gig and get the ship under way, if you please. Take over, Mr Galbraith.' He did not see the sudden light in Galbraith's eyes, but he knew it was there. He was being given the ship. *Trusted.*

The surgeon was on his knees, sleeves rolled up, his red face squinting with concentration. Large and heavy though he was, he had the small hands and wrists of a very much younger person.

'I cannot move him far, sir.'

To the sickbay, the orlop. There was no time.

'Carry him aft, to my quarters. More room for you.'

He leaned over and looked at the man they had pulled from the sea. From death.

One bare arm showed a faint tattoo. The other was like raw meat, a bone protruding through the blackened flesh. He was

57

so badly burned it was a marvel he had lived this long. A fire, then. Every sailor's most dreaded enemy.

Someone held out a knife. ''E were carryin' this, sir! English, right enough.'

O'Beirne was cutting away the scorched rags from the body. He murmured, 'Very bad, sir. I'm afraid . . .' He gripped the man's uninjured wrist as his mouth moved, as if even that were agonising.

Perhaps it was the sound of the ship coming about, her sails refilling, slapping and banging as the great yards were braced hard round, or the sense of men around him again. A sailor's world. His mouth opened very slightly.

''Ere, matey.' A tarred hand with a mug of water pushed through the crouching onlookers, but O'Beirne shook his head and put a finger to his lips.

'Not yet, lad.'

Jago was here, on his knees opposite the surgeon, lowering his dark head until it seemed to be touching the man's blistered face.

He murmured, 'He's *here*, mate. Right here with us.' He looked up at Adam. 'Askin' for the Captain. You, sir . . .' He broke off and lowered his face again. 'Ship's name, sir.' He held the man's bare shoulder. 'Try again, mate!'

Then he said harshly, 'No good, sir. He's goin'.'

Adam knelt and took the man's hand. Even that was badly burned, but he would not feel it now.

As his shadow fell across the man's face he saw the eyes open. For the first time, as if only they lived. What did he see, he wondered. Someone in a grubby shirt, unfastened, and without the coat and the gold lace of authority. Hardly a captain . . .

He said quietly, 'I command here. You are safe now.'

It was a lie; he could feel his life draining away like sand in an hourglass, and even the unwavering eyes knew it.

He was using all his strength. The eyes moved suddenly to the shrouds and running rigging overhead.

Who was he? What did he remember? What was his ship? It was no use. He heard Bellairs say, 'There were four others, sir. All burned. Tied together. He must have been the last one left alive . . .' He could not continue.

Adam felt the man's hand tighten very slightly in his. He watched his mouth, saw it forming a word, a name.

O'Beirne said, '*Fortune*, sir.'

Someone else said, 'Probably a trader. They was English anyway, poor devils!'

But the hand was moving again. Agitated. Desperate.

Adam leaned closer, until his face was only inches from the dying man's. He could smell his agony, his despair, but he did not release his hand.

'Tell me, *what is it*?'

Then, with great care, he lowered the hand to the deck. The sand had run out. It was as if only one thing had kept him alive, long enough. For what? Revenge?

He rose and stood for a few moments looking down at the dead man. An unknown sailor. Then he looked around at their intent faces. Troubled, curious, some openly distressed. It was perhaps the closest he had been to them since he had taken command.

He said, 'Not "fortune". He got it out, though.' The man's eyes were still open, as if he were alive, and listening. 'It was *La Fortune*. A Frenchman who sank his ship.'

Jago said, 'Shall I have him put over, sir?'

He was still on his knees, and glanced at Adam's hand as it rested briefly on his shoulder.

'No. We shall bury him during the last dog watch. It is the least we can do.'

He saw Bellairs, deathly pale despite his sunburn, and said, 'That was well done, Mr Bellairs. I shall enter it in your report. It will do you no harm.'

Bellairs tried to smile but his mouth would not move.

'That man, sir –'

But the deck was empty, and the sailmaker's crew would soon be stitching up the nameless sailor for his last journey on earth.

'I intend to find out. And when I do, I shall see that he does not leave us unavenged!'

The sun stood high in a clear sky, so that the reflected glare from the anchorage was almost a physical presence. *Unrivalled*, with all sails clewed up except topsails and jib, seemed to be gliding towards the sprawled panorama of battlements and sand-coloured buildings, her stem hardly causing a ripple.

Adam Bolitho raised a telescope and examined the other vessels anchored nearby. *Montrose*, the forty-two gun frigate which Sir Graham Bethune had chosen for his flagship, was surrounded by boats and lighters. She had left Gibraltar two days ahead of *Unrivalled*, but from the activity of storing and watering ship it seemed she had arrived in Malta only today, more evidence of their own fast passage despite the contrary winds.

Adam was still not sure what he thought of Bethune's decision to sail separately. In company they might have exercised together, anything to break the day-to-day routine.

He did not know the vice-admiral very well, although what he had seen of him he had liked, and had trusted. He had been a frigate captain himself, and a successful one, and in Adam's book that rated very high. Against that, he had spent several years employed ashore, latterly at the Admiralty. *Something I could never do.* It might make an officer over cautious, more aware of the risks and the perils of responsibility in a sea command. He had even heard Forbes, *Montrose*'s captain, question the need for such caution. It was unlike the man to criticise his admiral, but they had all had too much to drink.

He moved the glass further and saw three other frigates anchored in line, flags barely moving, windsails rigged to provide a suggestion of air in the crowded quarters between decks.

Not a large force, something else which would weigh heavily on Bethune's mind. With Napoleon at large on the French mainland again, no one could predict the direction the conflict might take. The French might drive north to the Channel ports, and seize ships and men to attack and delay vital supplies for Wellington's armies. And what of the old enemies? There would still be some who were prepared and eager to renew their allegiance to the arrogant Corsican.

'Guardboat, sir!'

Adam shifted the glass, and beyond the motionless launch saw other buildings which appeared to merge with the wall of the nearest battery.

Catherine had been here. For a few days, before she had been forced to take passage back to England.

The last time, the last place she had seen his uncle. He tried to turn aside from the thought. The last time they had been lovers.

Cristie called, 'Ready, sir!'

Adam walked to the rail and stared along the length of his command. The anchor swaying slightly to the small movement, ready to let go, men at halliards and braces, petty officers staring aft to the quarterdeck. To their captain. He saw Galbraith on the opposite side, a speaking trumpet in his hands, but his eyes were on Wynter, the third lieutenant, who was up forward with the anchor party. Galbraith had intended to take charge himself, and Adam had been surprised by this discovery, more so because he had not noticed it earlier. A strong, capable officer, but he could not or would not delegate, as in the matter of Bellairs and the wreckage, the pathetic corpses, the screaming gulls.

He said, 'Carry on, Mr Galbraith!'

'Lee braces, there! Hands wear ship!'

'Tops'l sheets! Tops'l clew lines!'

Galbraith's voice pursued the seamen as they hauled and stamped in unison on the sun-dried planking, waiting to belay each snaking line of cordage.

'Helm a'lee!'

Adam stood very still, watching the land pass slowly across the bowsprit and the proud figurehead.

'Let go!' Galbraith nodded curtly and the great anchor hit the water, flinging spray over the bustling seamen.

The Jack broke from the bows almost immediately, and he saw Midshipman Bellairs turn to smile at one of his signals party. But he had not forgotten the man they had plucked from the sea, only to surrender him again. Adam had seen the boy when they had cleared lower deck for the ceremony. Even the wind had dropped.

It had been strangely moving for new hands and old Jacks alike. Most of them had seen men they knew, and had shared their meagre resources with in one messdeck or another, pitched outboard like so much rubbish after a battle. But for some reason the burial of this unknown sailor had been different.

He had known Galbraith was watching him as he had

61

read from the worn and salt-stained prayer book. He smiled. His aunt Nancy had given it to him before he had joined *Hyperion.*

Take good care of it, Adam. It will take good care of you.

It was the only thing he still possessed from that day, a lifetime ago.

He looked up now at the monkey-like figures of seamen securing sails, and freeing the boat tackles. How long this time? What orders? His mind refused to submit. *And what of a ship named* La Fortune*?*

The dying man might have been mistaken, his reeling mind betraying him, clinging perhaps to a memory which, like him, was now dead.

But suppose? There had been many French ships at sea when Napoleon had abdicated. The two frigates which had engaged *Frobisher* on the day of his uncle's death had not come from nowhere.

'Orders, sir?'

'Post sentries, Mr Galbraith. I don't want any unlawful visitors. And have a boat prepared for the purser – he'll need to go ashore to look for fruit.'

Even a man-of-war invited attention when she lay at anchor. With gunports left open to afford some relief to men off watch, there was easy access for dealers and women, too, given half a chance. He smiled again, privately. *Especially a man-of-war.*

A boatswain's mate called, 'Guardboat coming alongside, sir!'

Galbraith seemed to come abruptly out of his habitual reserve.

'Letters from home, maybe, sir? We might learn what's happening!'

Adam glanced at him, this Galbraith who was still unknown to him.

'Passenger on board, sir!' He thought Bellairs sounded disappointed. 'A lieutenant, sir!'

Adam walked to the entry port, and saw the officer in question shaking hands with the Royal Marine lieutenant who was in charge of the boat. A tall man, dark hair streaked with grey. Adam clenched his fist without realising it. It had to come. But not now, not like this. He was unprepared. Vulnerable.

Perhaps Bethune had been trying to warn him at Gibraltar.

Galbraith said uncertainly, 'I do not recognise him, sir.'

'Why should you?' He touched his arm, aware of the sharp sarcasm. 'Forgive me. My rank does not afford me a licence to insult you.' He stared at the entry port. 'He is – was – my uncle's flag lieutenant. And friend.'

Then he walked to meet his visitor, and all he could feel was envy.

Lieutenant George Avery seated himself in a high-backed chair and watched as the cabin servant placed two goblets of wine on a table. The chair felt hard, unused, like the ship herself.

Strange how it became with ships, he thought. In a King's ship you always expected to see a familiar face, catch a name you had once known. The navy was a family, some said; you were always a part of it.

He had been introduced to the senior lieutenant, a powerfully built man with an honest face and a firm handshake. But he was a stranger.

He studied the captain. He had been prepared for this meeting, although he guessed Adam Bolitho had been disconcerted by it.

But it was not that. He observed him now, in profile as he wrote briefly on a pad for a small, sickly-looking man who must be a clerk.

They had met several times, and Avery had always remembered his quick, observant approach to his work and the people he met, in retrospect always youthful, always restless. *Like a young colt*, Richard Bolitho had once said.

The resemblance was there, to the portraits in the house in Falmouth. And, above all, to the man he had served, and had loved.

We are about the same age, but whereas he has his career and his future ahead like a beacon, I have nothing. Adam Bolitho and his uncle had been kept apart far more than they had been together, and yet, in his mind, Avery had always thought of one as being in the mould of the other. It was not so. Adam had changed in some way, matured as was inevitable for any man of his rank and responsibility. But it went far deeper. He was guarded, withdrawn. Perhaps still unable or unwilling

63

to accept that the cloak, the guardian presence, was gone, that there was not even a shadow.

Adam was looking at him now, holding out the goblet.

'You will like this.'

But he was not telling him; he was asking him to share something.

Avery held up the goblet, and thought of the wines she had sent aboard for Richard Bolitho.

'I am told that you saw Lady Somervell when you were in England, sir? Before you sailed.'

'Aye. She was concerned that I would not care enough to order some wine for myself!' Then he did smile, and, only briefly, he was the young, headstrong officer Avery had first met.

Avery said, 'She never forgets,' and the smile faded. Like sunlight dying even as you watched, he thought.

'We were at Falmouth . . . I pray to God she is able to come to terms with this terrible loss.' He changed tack swiftly, in the manner Avery remembered. 'And what of you? Shall you remain here in Malta?'

Avery put down the goblet. It was empty, and he could taste the wine on his lips, but he did not recall drinking it.

'I am able to elaborate on the information already to hand, sir.' He hesitated. 'Sir Richard had cause to meet Mehmet Pasha, the man who commands and governs in Algiers. I was with him, and was privileged to share the intelligence we gained there. If I may be of help?'

He moved his shoulder and Adam saw him wince: the old wound which had brought him down and had cost him his ship. *We have so much in common.* He had seen his own flag cut down in surrender when, like Avery, he had been too badly wounded to resist. And he also had been a prisoner of war, before making his escape. A court martial had cleared and had praised him. The verdict could just as easily have destroyed him.

He said, 'I would be grateful. Sir Graham Bethune has very little on which to proceed.'

Above and around them the anchored frigate was alive with shipboard sounds, and once during their conversation he got up and closed the cabin skylight against them. As if, for these moments, he wanted to share it with nobody else.

Avery spoke evenly and without any obvious emotion, but Adam understood what it was costing, and what it meant to him. At last, here was someone who had been there. Had seen what had happened.

Avery said simply, 'I saw him fall.' The tawny eyes were distant. He almost smiled. 'Allday was with me.'

Adam nodded, but dared not speak or interrupt. For Avery's sake, but mostly for his own.

Avery was looking at the sloping stern windows, and the anchored ships beyond.

'He was the bravest and the most compassionate man I ever served, ever knew. When I was pulled out to your ship just now, I almost asked to be taken ashore. But I had to come. Not out of duty or respect – they are mere words. Not even because it was your right to be told. Above all, I thought I would feel resentment, because you are here and he is not. I now know that I did the right thing. He spoke of you often, even on the day he fell. He was proud of you, of what you had become. *More like a son*, he said.'

Adam said, quietly, 'Did he suffer?'

Avery shook his head.

'I think not. He spoke to Allday. I could not hear what he said, and I had not the heart to question him afterwards.'

Afterwards.

Avery's eyes moved to the table, and the envelope which was addressed to Vice-Admiral Bethune.

'I shall take it to him when I leave, sir.'

Duty, so often used as an escape from tragedy. Adam had learned it the hard way, better than most.

He said, 'You could return later. We might sup together. Nobody else.' He felt like a hypocrite, but was glad when Avery declined. 'Tomorrow, then. There will be a conference, I believe?'

Avery glanced down, and almost unconsciously plucked a solitary gold thread from his coat. Where he had once worn a twist of gold lace to distinguish him as an admiral's aide, his flag lieutenant.

Bethune would already have one of his own, as Valentine Keen had had at Halifax. There could be resentment.

Avery said, 'If you so requested, I should be pleased . . .' He smiled again, faintly, as though his mind were somewhere else. 'Honoured to accompany you. I can still stand a fair watch, and I have nothing to go home for as yet.'

Adam recalled that Avery was the nephew of Sillitoe, that man of power whose name was rarely out of the newssheets. Another nephew. Another coincidence.

He held out his hand. 'I'm glad you came. I'll not forget.'

Avery took a small package from his pocket and unwrapped it with great care.

The locket. He had seen his uncle wearing it whenever he had been on deck with his shirt unfastened. *As I do.* He took it and held it to the sunlight, the perfect likeness, Catherine's bare shoulders and high cheekbones. He was about to turn it over to examine the inscription when he saw the broken clasp and severed chain. As clean a cut as if done by a knife. His fingers closed tightly upon it. No knife. The marksman's shot must have done it.

Avery was watching him.

'I have been unable to find a local craftsman with skill enough to repair it. I would have sent it to her . . . Now, I think it better that you should be the one, sir.'

They faced one another, and Adam understood. In his way Avery had been in love with her also. Now that she needed help, there was no one.

'Thank you for saying that. Perhaps I shall be able to return it myself.'

Avery picked up his hat, knowing he would do nothing of the kind. Suddenly he was pleased at what he had done. He looked at Adam, and for a fleeting moment he saw the other face. He smiled. *Like a good flag lieutenant.*

Galbraith was at the entry port when they came on deck, and saw them shake hands, as if each was reluctant to break the contact. He noticed, too, that the visitor paused and glanced almost involuntarily at the mainmast truck, as if he still expected to see a flag there.

In his cabin once more, Adam took out the locket and read

66

the inscription, and her voice seemed to speak to him as it did whenever he received a letter from her.

> *May Fate always guide you.*
> *May love always protect you.*

She must have remembered those words when she had watched *Unrivalled* standing out into Falmouth Bay. As she would always look for the ship which would never come.

He turned as Galbraith appeared by the open screen door.

'Concerning tomorrow, sir?'

It was the only way. Perhaps Galbraith understood, and in time might share it.

'Take a glass with me first, eh?'

He slipped the locket into his pocket, out of sight. But the voice still persisted.

'There is something we must discuss, before I meet the vice-admiral tomorrow. You see, I have a plan . . .'

It was a new beginning for all of them.

5

A Contest

Lieutenant Leigh Galbraith strode across the quarterdeck and reported, 'The watch is aft, sir!' Like his unerring steps over and past ringbolts and other obstacles, it was part of an unchanging routine at sea. He even touched his hat to the shadowy shape of Lieutenant Massie, whom he was about to relieve.

It was still quite dark, but when his eyes eventually became accustomed he would see the approach of dawn in the fading stars, the hardening of the horizon. Massie stifled a yawn.

'West-by-south, sir.' He stared up at the pale outlines of the sails, filling only occasionally with the wind across the starboard quarter.

Galbraith glanced at the helmsmen, eyes flickering in the shaded light from the compass. Other shapes were moving into position: the morning watch, when the ship would come alive again.

Galbraith looked at the tiny glow from the cabin skylight. Was the captain awake, or was it a ploy to keep the watch on its toes?

He thought of Captain Bolitho's return from his meeting with the vice-admiral. Galbraith had no idea what had been said, but the captain had come back on board barely able to conceal his anger.

Galbraith tried to dismiss it. At first light they would sight and resume contact with another frigate, *Matchless* of forty-two guns. She had been in the Mediterranean for three years attached to one squadron or another, and would therefore be very familiar with shipping movements and the lurking danger of pirates. Corsairs.

Matchless was commanded by a senior post-captain named Emlyn Bouverie, a man who came from a proud naval family, and was thought likely for promotion to flag rank in the near future. Galbraith did not know him, but those who did apparently heartily disliked him. Not a tyrant or martinet like some he had known, but a perfectionist, who was quick to reprimand or punish anyone who fell below his own high standards.

He said, 'You are relieved, sir.' He lifted the canvas hood from the master's chart table and peered at the log with the aid of a tiny lantern. They would sight land before noon, according to Cristie. He had never known him to be wrong.

He steadied the light with care. The coast of North Africa: to most sailors a place of mystery and strange superstitions, and best avoided.

He studied Cristie's fine handwriting. *6th June, 1815.* What would this day bring?

Captain Bolitho had called his officers and those of senior warrant rank together in his cabin. Galbraith straightened his back and glanced at the skylight again. Remembering it.

The captain had described the mission. A visit to Algiers, to investigate. Their intentions were peaceful, but guns' crews would exercise twice a day all the same. It was said that Algiers was protected by some six hundred guns. It would not be much of a contest if the worst happened.

The captain had looked at their faces and had said, 'There was a French frigate named *La Fortune* in the Western Mediterranean before Napoleon's surrender. Others too, and it is known that the Dey of Algiers and the Bey of Tunis have offered sanctuary to such men-of-war in exchange for their services. The prisons are still filled with Christians, people snatched from passing vessels, and held on no more serious charge than their religious beliefs. Torture, slavery, and open acts of aggression against merchantmen sailing under our protection – the list is endless. With our "allies" . . .' he had made no effort to conceal his contempt '. . . we had a chance to put paid to this piracy once and for all. Now with Napoleon at the head of his armies again, the Dey in particular may use our predicament to gain even more control of these waters, and beyond.'

Somebody, Galbraith had thought Captain Bosanquet of the Royal Marines, had asked about the sailor they had rescued and later buried at sea.

Captain Bolitho had answered shortly, 'Probably one of many.' And again something like bitterness had crept into his voice. 'Which is why Captain Bouverie intends to make a peaceful approach. Vice-Admiral Bethune's squadron is hard pressed as it is. He sees no alternative.'

Bouverie was the senior captain, as he reminded them often enough by hoisting signals at every opportunity. Galbraith half-smiled. He would make a good admiral one day.

The master's mate of the watch said softly, 'Cabin light's out, sir.'

'Thank you, Mr Woodthorpe. I am glad *you* are awake!' He saw the man's teeth in the dimness.

How would it be this time? He thought of the moment when they had shared wine together; it had shown him another side of Adam Bolitho. He had even touched on his early days at sea as a midshipman, and had spoken of his uncle, his first captain. Opening out, demonstrating a warmth which Galbraith had not suspected.

After his visit to the flagship, he had shut that same door. At first Galbraith thought that he had expected some priority, a preference because of his famous surname, and had resented Bouverie's slower, more cautious approach. But Adam Bolitho was a post-captain of some fame, and had not come by it easily. He would be used to Bouveries in the navy's tight world.

It was deeper than that. Driving him, like some unstoppable force. Something personal.

Like the brigantine, which might or might not be following *Unrivalled*. Twice on this passage they had sighted an unknown sail. The lookouts had not been certain; even the impressive Sullivan could not swear to it. But Captain Bolitho had no such doubts. When he had signalled Bouverie for permission to break company and give chase, the request had been denied with a curt *negative*.

Galbraith had heard him exclaim, 'This is a ship of war! I'm no grocery captain, damn his eyes!'

Galbraith recognised the light step now, and heard his passing comment to the master's mate. Then he saw the open shirt, rippling in the soft wind, and remembered the savage scar he had seen above his ribs when he had found him shaving in his cabin. He was lucky to be alive.

Bolitho had seen his eyes, and said, 'They made a good job of it!' And had grinned, and only for a second or so Galbraith had seen the youth override the experience and the memories.

A good job. Galbraith had heard the surgeon mention that when Adam Bolitho had been captured, more dead than alive, he had been operated on by the American ship's surgeon, who had in fact been French.

'Good morning, Mr Galbraith. Everything is as it was, I see?' He was looking up at the topsails. 'I could make her *fly* if I got the word!'

Pride? It was stronger than that. It was more like love.

He moved to the compass box and nodded to the helmsmen, and their eyes followed him further still, to the canvas-covered table.

'We shall exercise the main battery during the forenoon, Mr Galbraith.'

Galbraith smiled. That would go round the ship like a fast fuse. But it had to be said that the gun crews were improving.

'And call the hands a quarter-hour earlier. I expect a smart ship today. And I want our people properly fed, not making do with muck!'

Another side. Captain Bolitho had already disrated the cook for wasting food and careless preparation. Many captains would not have cared.

He was holding the same little lamp, but did not seem to be looking at the chart, and Galbraith heard him say quietly, 'June sixth. I had all but forgot!'

'May I share it, sir?'

For a moment he thought he had gone too far. But Adam merely looked at him, his face hidden in shadow.

'I was thinking of some wild roses, and a lady.' He turned away, as if afraid of what he might disclose. 'On my birthday.' Then, abruptly, 'The wind! By God, *the wind*!'

71

It was as though the ship had sensed his change of mood. Blocks and halliards rattled, and above their heads the main topsail boomed like a drum.

Adam said, 'Belay my last order! Call all hands directly!' He gripped Galbraith's arm as if to emphasise the importance of what he was saying. 'We shall sight land today! Don't you see, if we *are* being followed it's their last chance to outreach us!'

Galbraith knew it was pointless to question his sudden excitement. At first light they should be changing tack to take station on *Matchless* again. There was not a shred of evidence that the occasional sightings of a far-off sail were significant, or connected in any way. But the impetuous grip on his arm seemed to cast all doubt to the rising wind.

He swung round. 'Pipe all hands, Mr Woodthorpe! And send for the master, fast as you can!'

He turned back to the indistinct outline. 'Captain Bouverie may not approve, sir.'

Adam Bolitho said quietly, 'But Captain Bouverie is not yet in sight, is he?'

Men rushed out of the shadows, some still dazed by sleep, staring around at the flapping canvas and straining rigging until order and discipline took command.

The master, feet bare, stumped across the sloping deck, muttering, 'Is there no peace?' Then he saw the captain. 'New course, sir?'

'We will wear ship, Mr Cristie! As close to the wind as she'll come!'

Calls shrilled and men scrambled aloft, the perils of working in darkness no longer a threat now to most of them.

Blocks squealed, and someone stumbled over a snaking line, which was slithering across the damp planking as if it were truly alive.

But she was answering, from the instant that the big double-wheel was hauled over.

Galbraith gripped a backstay and felt the deck tilting still further. In the darkness everything was wilder, louder, as if the ship were responding to her captain's recklessness. He dashed spray from his face and saw pale stars spiralling around the masthead pendant. It was all but dawn. He looked towards the captain. Suppose the sea was empty? And there was no other vessel? He thought of Bouverie, what might happen, and knew, without understanding why, that this was a contest.

Unrivalled completed her turn, water rushing down the lee scuppers as the sails refilled on the opposite tack, the jib cracking loudly, as close to the wind as she could hold.

Cristie shouted, 'Steady as she goes, sir! East-by-south!'

Afterwards, Galbraith thought it was the only time he had ever heard the master either impressed or surprised.

'Make fast! *Belay!*'

Men ran to obey each command; to any landsman it would appear a single, confused tangle of canvas and straining cordage.

Adam Bolitho gripped the rail and said, 'Now she *flies*! Feel her!'

Galbraith turned, but shook his head and did not speak. The captain was quite alone with his ship.

'Hands aloft, Mr Lomax! Get the t'gallants on her and put more men on the maincourse! They're like a pack of old women today!'

Lieutenant George Avery stood beneath the mizzen mast, where the marines of the afterguard had been mustered for nearly an hour. He had heard a few whispered curses when the galley fire had been doused before some of the watchkeepers had managed to snatch a quick meal.

He felt out of place aboard *Matchless*, alien. Everything worked smoothly enough, as might be expected in a frigate which had been in commission for over three years. But he had sensed a lack of the companionship he himself had come to recognise and accept. Every move, each change of tack or direction, seemed to flow from one man. No chain of command as Avery knew it, but a single man.

He could see him now, feet apart, hand on his hip, a square figure in the strengthening daylight. He considered the word; it described Captain Emlyn Bouverie exactly. Even when the ship heeled to a change of tack, Bouverie remained like a rock. His hands were square too, strong and hard, like the man.

Bouverie said, 'Attend the lookouts, Mr Foster, you should know my orders by now!' His voice always carried without any apparent effort, and Avery had never seen him deign to use a speaking trumpet, even in the one patch of wind they had encountered after leaving Malta.

He heard a lieutenant yelling out names, and thought he knew why. Soon now *Unrivalled* would be sighted, provided Adam Bolitho had kept on station as instructed. He recalled the meeting aboard the flagship. Bouverie had vetoed the suggestion that Avery should sail with *Unrivalled* instead of 'the senior officer's ship', and Bethune had concurred. Looking back, Avery still wondered if it was because he had truly agreed, or if he had simply needed to demonstrate that no favouritism would be shown Sir Richard Bolitho's nephew.

He gazed aloft as the topgallant sails broke free from their yards and filled to the wind, the topmen spread out on either side, all aware of their captain's standards.

Pride, jealousy? It was difficult to have one without the other. *Matchless* had been in these waters for more than three years, and despite her coppered hull was heavy with weed and marine growths. *Unrivalled* had been forced to shorten sail several times during the day to remain on station, while at night they must be almost hove to. He could imagine Adam Bolitho's frustration and impatience. *And yet I hardly know him.* That was the strangest part. Like handing over the locket. *When I wanted it for myself.*

He realised that Bouverie had joined him by the mizzen. He could move swiftly when it suited him.

'Bored, Mr Avery? This may seem a mite tame after your last appointment!'

Avery said, 'I feel like a passenger, sir.'

'Well spoken! But I cannot disrupt the running of my command with a wrong note, eh?'

He laughed. In fact, Bouverie laughed frequently, but it rarely reached his eyes.

'All secure, sir!' Somebody scuttled past; nobody walked in *Matchless*.

Bouverie nodded. 'I've read the notes and observations on your last visit to Algiers. Could be useful.' He broke off and shouted, 'Take that man's name, Mr Munro! I'll have no damned laggards this day!'

That man. After three years in commission, a captain should have known the name of every soul aboard.

Again, the ambush of memory. How Richard Bolitho had impressed upon his officers the importance of remembering men's names. *It is often all they can call their own.*

He turned, startled, as Bouverie said, 'You must miss the admiral,' as if he had been reading his thoughts.

'I do indeed, sir.'

'I never met him. Although I too was at Copenhagen, in *Amazon*, Captain Riou. My first stint as a lieutenant. A real blooding, I can tell you!' He laughed again, but nobody turned from his duties to watch or listen. Not in *Matchless*.

Bouverie's arm jerked out once more. 'Another pull on the weather forebrace and belay! *Far too slow!'*

He changed, just as suddenly. 'Did you have much to do with Lady Somervell? Turn a man's heart to water with a glance, I'm told. A true beauty – caused more than a few ripples in her time!'

'A woman of courage also, sir.'

Bouverie was studying him in the gloom. Avery could feel it, like the stare of a prosecuting officer at a court martial. As he could feel his own rising resentment.

Bouverie swayed back on his heels. 'If you say so. I'd have thought –' He broke off and almost lost his balance. 'What the *hell* was that?'

Someone shouted, 'Gunfire, sir!'

Bouverie swallowed hard. 'Clod!' He strode to the opposite side. 'Mr Lomax! *Where away?'*

Avery licked his lips, tasting the brine. A single shot. It could only mean one thing, a signal to heave to. He stared at the horizon until his eyes throbbed. Every morning since leaving Malta it had been like this. As soon as *Unrivalled* was sighted Bouverie would make a signal, as if he was always trying to catch them out. Without looking he knew that the first signal of the day was already bent on, ready to soar up to the yard, when most ships would have been content to remain in close company. He shivered, from more than the rising wind, recalling Adam Bolitho's impatience at the meeting when doubts had been voiced about the brigantine. Only some ridiculous obsession, something to command attention, to impress. *Not any more.*

He heard the first lieutenant say, '*Unrivalled* must be off her station, sir!'

'I know that, God damn it! We are to alter course when . . .' He turned towards Avery. 'Well, what do you think? Or do "passengers" have no opinions?'

Avery felt very calm.

'I believe *Unrivalled* has found something useful, sir.'

'Oh, *very* diplomatic, sir! And what of Captain Adam Bolitho? Does he truly believe he is above obeying orders, and beyond the discipline that binds the rest of us?'

An inner voice warned him, *take care.* Another insisted, *you have nothing more to lose.*

He said, 'I was with Sir Richard Bolitho at Algiers, sir. Things have changed since then. If we attempt to enter without permission . . .' He glanced round, seeing the first touch of gold spill over the horizon. The moment he had always loved. But that, too, was past. 'This ship will be destroyed. Your ship, sir, will be blasted apart before you can come about. I have seen the anchorage, and the citadel, and some of the fanatics who control those guns.'

'I have faced worse!'

Avery relaxed. He had always been able to recognise bluster.

'Then you will know the consequences, sir.'

Bouverie stared at him. 'God damn you for your impertinence!' Then, surprisingly, he grinned. 'But bravely said, for all that!' He looked at the clearing sky as a voice yelled, 'Sail on the starboard quarter!' The merest pause. '*Two* sail, sir!'

Bouverie nodded slowly. 'A prize, then.'

The first lieutenant climbed down from the shrouds with a telescope.

'She's a brigantine, sir.'

Avery looked at his hands. They were quite still, and warm in the first frail sunlight. They felt as if they were shaking.

Bouverie was saying, 'No, not that signal, Mr Adams.' He took a glass from the signals midshipman and steadied it with care. He was studying *Unrivalled*'s topsails, like pink shells in the clear light, although the sun had not yet revealed itself.

'When she is on station again, make *Captain repair on board.*'

Avery turned away. How many times would Adam Bolitho read that signal with different eyes from other men? When his uncle had called him to his flagship to tell him of the death of Zenoria Keen. *We Happy Few . . .* It had been their secret.

Bouverie said, 'Breakfast, I think. Then we shall hear what our gallant Captain Bolitho has to say.' The good humour seemed even more volatile than his usual mood. 'I hope it pleases me!'

But, out of habit or memory, Avery was watching the signals party bending on the flags.

Bouverie sat squarely in a broad leather chair, hands gripping the arms as if to restrain himself.

He said, 'Now, Captain Bolitho. In your own words, of course. Share your discoveries with me, eh?' He glanced towards his table where Avery was sitting with a leather satchel and some charts, while beside him the ship's clerk was poised with his quill at the ready. 'For both our sakes, I think some record of this conversation should be kept. Sir Graham Bethune will expect it.'

Adam Bolitho walked to the stern windows and stared at his own ship, her sheer lines and shining hull distorted in the weathered glass. Hard to believe that it had all happened so quickly, and yet it was exactly as he had imagined when he had ordered *Unrivalled*'s change of course. They had all thought him mad. They were probably right.

He could recall the calm, professional eye of old Stranace, the ship's gunner, when he had explained what he required. Stranace was more used to the deadly quiet of the magazine and powder store, but like most of his breed he had never forgotten his trade, or how to lay and train an eighteen-pounder.

It must have taken the brigantine's people completely by surprise. Day in, day out, following the two frigates, knowing almost to the minute when they would reduce sail for the night, then to see one of the quarry suddenly looming out of the last, lingering darkness with every sail set, on a converging tack with no room for manoeuvre and no time to run . . .

One shot, the first *Unrivalled* had fired in anger.

Adam had watched the splash, the succession of jagged fins of spray as the ball had skipped across the water no more than a boat's length from her bows. He had touched the gunner's shoulder; it had felt like iron itself. No words were needed. It was a perfect shot, and the brigantine, now seen to be named *Rosario*, had hove to, her sails in confusion in the wind which had changed everything.

He heard the quill scratching across the paper and realised he had been describing it. He looked again and saw the brigantine's outline, more like a blurred shadow than reality. *Unrivalled* had put down two boats, and they had done well, he thought, with the lively sea, and their movements hampered by their weapons. Jago had been with him. Amused, but deadly when one of *Rosario*'s crew had raised a pistol as the boarders had flung their grapnels and swarmed aboard. He had not even seen Jago move, his blade rising and falling with the speed of light. Then the scream, and the severed hand like a glove on the deck.

Lieutenant Wynter had been in the second boat, and with his own party had put the crew under guard. After Jago's example there was no further resistance.

Rosario was Portuguese but had been chartered repeatedly, at one time by the English squadron at Gibraltar. The master, a dirty, unshaven little man, seemed to speak no English, although he produced some charts to prove his lawful occasions. The charts, like *Rosario*, were almost too filthy to examine. As Cristie later remarked, 'By guess an' by God, that's how these heathen navigate!'

A sense of failure then; he had sensed it in the restlessness of the boarding party, the apparent confidence of *Rosario*'s master. Until Wynter, perhaps the least experienced officer in the ship, had commented on the brigantine's armament, six swivel guns mounted aft and near the hold. And the smell . . .

Adam had ordered the hatches to be broached. Only one cargo had a stench like that, and they found the chains and the manacles where slaves could be packed out of sight, to exist, if they could, in terror and their own filth until they were shipped to a suitable market. There had been blood on one set of irons, and Adam guessed that the wretched prisoner had been pitched overboard.

He had seen Wynter's eyes widening with shocked surprise when he had said coldly, 'A slaver then. Worthless to me. Fetch a halter and run this bugger up to the main yard, as an example to others!'

Wynter's expression had changed to admiring comprehension when the vessel's master had thrown himself at Adam's feet, pleading and sobbing in rough but completely adequate English.

'I thought he might remember!'

Confident and less gentle, they had continued their search. There was a safe, and the gibbering master was even able to produce a key.

Adam turned now as Avery opened the satchel.

'*Rosario* had no papers as such. That alone makes her a prize.' He smiled faintly. 'For the moment.'

Avery laid out the contents of the satchel. A bill of lading, Spanish. A delivery of oil to some garrison, Portuguese. A log book, crudely marked with dates and what could be estimated positions. Some shadowed *Unrivalled*.

Bouverie said abruptly, 'Many such men are paid to spy and inform their masters of ship movements, theirs and ours.' He gave the characteristic nod. 'But I'll give you this, Bolitho. You did not imagine it!'

Adam felt the sudden surge of excitement. *The first time since* . . . He said, 'And there is a letter. I do not speak French, but I recognise it well enough.'

Avery was holding it. 'For the captain of the frigate *La Fortune*.' He gave a grave smile. 'I learned my French the hard way. As their prisoner.'

Bouverie rubbed his chin. 'So she is in Algiers. Under a great battery, you say.'

Adam said, 'The bait in the trap, sir. They will not expect us to ignore it.'

It was as if some invisible bonds had been cut. Bouverie almost sprang out of the chair.

'Out of the question! Even if we hold *Rosamund* –'

Avery heard himself correcting gently, '*Rosario*, sir,' and cursed himself. Always the good flag lieutenant . . .

Adam persisted, 'No, sir, we use her. To spring the trap. They know we are trailing our cloaks, and they will be

79

expecting the brigantine. I am sure she is a regular visitor there.'

He was aware of the tawny eyes on him, Avery watching but not seeing him. As if he were somewhere else . . . He was suddenly deeply moved. *With my uncle.*

'*Rosario* appears to be an agile vessel, sir. It would seem only fair if we were to "chase" her into Algiers?'

Bouverie swallowed. 'A cutting-out expedition? I'm not at all certain –' Then he nodded again, vigorously. 'It might work, it's daring enough. Foolhardy, some will say.'

Adam returned to the stern windows. One of the *Rosario*'s crew had told him that they had often carried female slaves, some very young girls. The master had delighted in abusing them.

He thought of Zenoria, her back laid open by a whip. Keen had rescued her, and she had married him. Not out of love. Out of gratitude.

The mark of Satan, she had called it.

He heard himself say, 'Time is short, sir. We cannot delay.'

'The authority for such an act, which might provoke another outbreak of war . . .'

'Is yours, sir.'

Why should it matter? Bouverie would not be the first or the last officer to await a decision from a higher authority. But it did matter. It had to.

He said, 'I can take *Rosario*. I am short-handed, but we could share the burden between us. Then so would the laurels be equally divided.'

He saw the shot go home. Like one of old Stranace's.

'We'll do it. I'll send you some good hands within the hour.' Bouverie was thinking fast, like a flood-gate bursting open. 'Will you take the *Rosario*'s master with you, in case . . . ?'

Adam picked up his hat and saw blood on his sleeve. Jago's cutlass.

'I shall take him. Later, I shall see him hang.' He looked at Avery. 'By the authority vested in *me*!'

Adam Bolitho lowered his telescope and moved into the shadow of the brigantine's foresail. There would be hundreds of eyes watching from the shore. One mistake would be enough to betray them.

Bang.

He saw a waterspout burst from the sea. Close. But was it near enough to deceive their audience?

He had seen *Matchless* leaning over as she had changed tack for her final approach, and he had seen the citadel, all and more than Avery had described. It looked as if it had been there for centuries, since time began. Avery had told him about a secret, cave-like entrance to which they had been taken in a large galley. You could lose an army trying to storm such a place. Or a fleet.

He glanced at the *Rosario*'s master. Once aboard and in command of his own vessel again, he seemed to have grown in stature, as if all the pathetic pleading and whimpering for his life had been forgotten. Slumped by the bulwark, Jago sat with both legs outthrust, his eyes never leaving the man's face.

Nothing was certain. The master had intended to hoist some sort of recognition signal as they had tacked closer to the protective headland. Adam had said, 'No. They will know *Rosario*. They will not expect a signal when she is being chased by an enemy!'

Somebody had even laughed.

He turned to look at the swivel guns, all loaded and primed. And the hatch covers. He could imagine the extra seamen and marines crammed in the holds, listening to the occasional bang of *Matchless*'s bow-chaser, sweating it out. Captain Bosanquet was down there with them, apparently more concerned with the state of his uniform in the filthy hold than the prospect of being dead within the next hour.

He stepped into the shadow again and held his breath, and carefully raised his glass and trained it on the citadel, and the main wall which Avery had remembered so clearly. A movement. He watched, hardly daring to blink. Guns, an entire line of them, thrusting their muzzles through the embrasures, the menace undiminished by distance. He could almost hear their iron trucks squeaking over the worn stone.

He felt the hull shiver. Whatever else he was, *Rosario*'s master knew these waters well. They were in the shallows now, heading for the anchorage. Avery was right. He felt

81

almost light-headed. *Right.* The great guns would not depress enough to endanger the brigantine. Like the batteries he had seen at Halifax, carefully sited on the mainland and on a small island in the harbour, so that no enemy ship could slip past them undetected.

But here there was no island.

He saw the first gun fire and recoil, smoke writhing above the old walls like a ragged spectre. Then, one by one, the others followed. The sound seemed to be all around them, like an unending echo. Probably bronzed guns. They were just as deadly to a wooden hull.

He thought of *Unrivalled* outside, somewhere around the headland and still out of sight. Galbraith and Cristie, and all the others who despite his own attempts to remain detached were no longer strangers to him.

Could he never accept it? Like the moment when Galbraith had picked men for the *Rosario*'s raiding party. It had been difficult for him; almost everybody, even the green hands, had volunteered. Madness, then. What would Galbraith be thinking now? Feeling pride at having been left in command? Or seeing a chance of permanent promotion if things went badly wrong?

A seaman called, 'One o' them galleys headin' this way, sir! Starboard bow!'

Matchless was firing again, a broadside this time; it was impossible to tell where the shots were falling. There were more local vessels in evidence. Lateen sails and elderly schooners, with dhows etched against the water like bats.

He felt his mouth go dry as splashes burst around *Matchless*'s bows. Close. Too damned close. He bit his lip and scrambled to the opposite side.

When he lifted his head again, it was all he could do to stop himself from shouting aloud.

Directly across the larboard bow, and framed against the citadel's high walls, was the frigate. He tried to take it in, to hold it in his mind, like all those other times. The range and the bearing, the point of embrace. To see the frigate lying at her anchor, brailed-up sails filling and emptying in the offshore wind the only suggestion of movement, was unnerving. Unreal.

He cleared his throat. 'Ready about! Warn all hands, Mr Wynter!'

He groped for the short, curved fighting sword and loosened it. He could hear Jago's voice in his thoughts. 'Take the old one, sir. *The* sword!'

And his own reply. Like somebody else. 'When I've earned it!'

The *Rosario*'s ragged seamen were hauling on halliards and braces, their bare feet gripping the deck like claws, without feeling.

It only needed one of them to shout, to signal. He found his fingers clenched on the hilt of the hanger. They must not be taken. There would be no quarter. No pity.

He moved around the mast and watched the helmsman putting down the wheel, one of *Unrivalled*'s topmen at his side, a dirk in his fist.

'*Matchless* 'as gone about, sir!' The man breathed out noisily. 'They're best off out o' this little lot!'

Adam stared at the frigate. Old but well maintained, her name, *La Fortune*, in faded gilt lettering across her counter. Thirty guns at a guess. A giant to the local craft on which she preyed in the name of France. There were faces along her gangway and poop, but no muzzles were run out. Adam felt his body trembling. Why should they be? Those great guns had seen off the impudent intruder. He could hear some of them cheering, laughing. Not too many of them, however; the rest were probably ashore, evidence of their security here.

Rosario's master jumped away from the helmsman and cupped his hands, staring wild-eyed as the frigate's masts towered over them. The dirk drove into his side and he fell without even a murmur.

Even at the end he must have realised that nothing Adam could do would match the horror his new masters would have unleashed on those who betrayed them.

It was already too late. With the helm hard over and the distance falling away, *Rosario*'s bowsprit mounted the frigate's quarter like a tusk and splintered into fragments, cordage and flapping canvas shielding Wynter's boarding party as they swarmed up and over the side.

Adam drew his hanger and waved it.

'At 'em, lads!' Hatches were bursting open and men ran, half blinded by the sunlight, carried forward by their companions, reason already forgotten.

Adam grasped a dangling line and dragged himself over the frigate's rail, slipping and almost falling between the two hulls.

An unknown voice rasped, 'Don't leave us *now*, sir!' And laughed, a terrible sound. Matched only by the scarlet-coated marines, somehow holding formation, bayonets like ice in the sun's glare, Captain Bosanquet shouting, 'Together, Marines! *Together!*'

Adam noticed that his face was the colour of his fine tunic.

A horn or trumpet had added its mournful call to the din of shouting, the clash of steel, the screams of men being hacked down.

The boarding party needed no urging. Beyond the smoke and the scattering sailing craft was open water. *The sea.* All they had. All that mattered.

Adam stopped in his tracks as a young lieutenant blocked his way. He was probably the only officer left aboard.

'Surrender!' It had never left him. Not at moments like this. 'Surrender, damn your eyes!'

The lieutenant lowered his sword but drew a pistol from inside his coat. He was actually grinning, grinning while he took aim, already beyond reach.

Jago lunged forward but halted beside Adam as the French officer coughed and staggered against the gangway. There was a boarding axe embedded in his back.

Adam stared up at the masthead pendant. The wind was still with them.

'Hands aloft! Loose tops'ls!'

How could they hope to do it? To cut out a ship from a protected harbour?

'Cut the cable!' He wiped his mouth and tasted blood on his hand, but could recall no contest. Men were surrendering, others were being thrown over the side, dead or alive it did not matter.

La Fortune was free of the ground, her hull already moving as the first topsails and a jib steadied her against the thrust of wind, the demands of her rudder.

Guns were firing, but *La Fortune* moved on, untouched by the battery which could not be brought to bear.

He saw the *Rosario* drifting away, an oared galley already attempting to grapple her.

Wynter was shouting, 'She's answering, sir!' Not so blank and self-contained now, but wild-eyed, dangerous. His father the member of Parliament would scarcely have recognised him.

Jago said, 'Lost three men, sir. Another'll go afore long.'

He winced as iron hammered against the hull, grape or canister from *Rosario*'s swivels, and licked his parched lips. A Froggie ship. There would be wine on board. He turned to mention it to the captain.

Adam was watching a Royal Marine hoist a White Ensign to the frigate's gaff. Without surprise that they had done it. That they had survived.

But he said, 'For you, Uncle! For you!'

6

None Braver

Adam Bolitho closed his small log book and leaned his elbows on the cabin table. For a moment he watched the dying light, the shadows moving evenly across the checkered deck as *Unrivalled* tilted to a steady wind across the quarter. A fine sunset, the thick glass and the cabin skylight the colour of bronze.

He massaged his eyes and tried to thrust aside the lingering disappointment, and accept what he had perceived as unfairness. Not to himself, but to the ship.

They had done what many would have considered foolhardy, and, having cut out a valuable prize from under the noses of the Dey's defenders, they had joined the other ships outside the port in an atmosphere of triumph and excitement.

Now *Unrivalled* sailed alone. At any other time Adam would have welcomed this, the independence beloved of frigate captains.

But he had sensed the resentment when Captain Bouverie had decided to return to Malta with the captured *La Fortune*, and, as senior officer, to reap the praise and the lion's share of any reward which might be forthcoming. From what Adam had managed to glean from the French frigate's log, it seemed that her captain had been employed along the North African coast, snatching up or destroying local shipping with little or no opposition. The circumstances of war must have changed his role to that of a mercenary, under French colours now that Napoleon was back in Europe, but living off whichever ally found his services most useful when there was no other choice.

Adam had known nothing but war all his life, and even while he had been at sea he had been well aware of the constant threat of invasion. He thought of *La Fortune*'s captain and others like him. *How would I feel, if England was overrun by a ruthless enemy? Would I continue to fight? And for what?*

He felt the rudder shudder beneath the counter. The glass was steady, but Cristie insisted that the wind which had given them *Rosario* and their one chance to cut out the frigate was the forerunner of stronger gusts. It was not unknown in the Mediterranean, even in June.

Two of the cutting-out party who had died of their wounds had been from *Unrivalled*, and they had been buried immediately. But it was another source of grievance, and then open protest, now that the prize had disappeared with *Matchless*. There had been an outbreak of violence in one of the messes, and a petty officer had been threatened when he had intervened. So there would be two men for punishment tomorrow.

Adam disliked the grim ritual of flogging. It too often broke a man who might have made something of himself had he been properly guided. He recalled Galbraith's words to the midshipman. *Inspired.* The hard man would only become harder and more unruly. But until there was an alternative . . .

He frowned as the cabin servant entered and walked down the tilting deck towards him. One of the ship's boys, his name was Napier, and he had been trained originally to serve the officers in the wardroom. He took his duties very seriously and wore an habitual expression of set determination.

Galbraith had made the choice himself, no doubt wondering why a post-captain did not have a servant of his own.

Click . . . click . . . click. Napier wore ill-fitting shoes for this new employment, probably bought from one of the traders who hung around the King's ships, and the sound grated on Adam's nerves.

'Napier!' He saw the youth stiffen, and changed his mind. 'No matter. Fetch me some of that wine.' He curbed his impatience, knowing he himself was at fault. *What is the matter with me?* The boy he was going to sponsor for midshipman, the boy he had been trying to fashion in his own image, if he was honest enough to admit it, was dead.

Napier hurried away, pleased to be doing something. *Click*

. . . click . . . click. He thought of the state of the French frigate's stores. *La Fortune* had been down to her last resources when she had been seized, her powder and shot, salted meat, and even the cheese the Frenchmen took as a part of life almost finished.

He recalled Jago's remarks about wine, and smiled. There had indeed been plenty of that, under lock and key until Bosanquet of the Royal Marines had shattered it with a well-aimed pistol shot.

Napier brought the bottle and a glass and placed them with great care beside the log book.

Adam could feel the eyes on him as he poured a glass. *The Captain.* Who lived in this fine cabin and was oblivious to the cramped conditions and brutal humour of the messdecks. Who wanted for nothing.

The wine was cool, and he imagined Catherine selecting it for him. Who else would care about such things? He would eke it out. Like the memory: hold on to it.

The glass almost broke in his fingers as he exclaimed, *'Hell's teeth*, boy!' He saw Napier cringe, and said urgently, 'No! Not you!' Like calming a frightened animal; he was ashamed that it was always so easy. For the Captain.

He said evenly, 'Tell the sentry to fetch the first lieutenant, will you?'

Napier twisted his hands together, staring at the glass.

'Did I do somethin' wrong, sir?'

Adam shook his head.

'A bad lookout is the one who sees only what he expects to see, or what others have told him to expect.' He raised his voice. *'Sentry!'* When the marine thrust his head around the screen door he said, 'My compliments to the first lieutenant, and would you ask him to come aft.' He looked back at the boy. 'Today, I am that bad lookout!'

Napier said slowly, 'I see, sir.'

Adam smiled. 'I think not, but fetch another bottle, will you?'

It was probably only a flaw in his memory. Something to cover his anger at Bouverie's arrogant but justified action over the prize.

And what of *La Fortune*? Were there still people who did not know or believe that ships had souls? She was not a new vessel, and must have seen action often enough against the flag which the marine had hoisted at her peak. Now she would probably be sold, most likely to the Dutch government. Another old enemy. Several prizes had already been disposed of in that manner, and yet, as the vice-admiral himself had pointed out, the fleet was as short of frigates as ever.

Galbraith entered the cabin, his eyes taking in the wine, and the anxious servant.

'Sir?'

'Be seated. Some wine?'

He saw the first lieutenant relax slightly.

'The Frenchman we took – she was short of everything, especially powder and shot.'

Galbraith took time to pick up and examine the glass. 'We were saying as much earlier, sir.'

So they had been discussing it in the wardroom, and most of all, he had no doubt, the prize money which might eventually be shared out.

'And yet there was a letter, which Lieutenant Avery translated.' Remembering his bitterness. 'To *La Fortune*'s captain. Supposedly from a lady.' He noted the immediate interest, and then the doubt. 'I can see you think as I did.' He grinned ruefully. 'Eventually!'

Galbraith said, 'It seems strange that anyone would be able to send a letter to a ship whose whereabouts were largely unknown.'

Adam nodded, his skin ice-cold in spite of the cabin's warmth.

'To promise the delivery of the one thing they did not need. Wine!'

Galbraith stared past him. 'Daniel . . . I mean, Mr Wynter made a note of the dates in *Rosario*'s log, sir.'

'Did he indeed? We may have cause to thank him for his dedication.'

He was on his feet, his shadow angled across the white-painted timbers, as if the hull was leaning hard over.

'My orders are to remain on this station and to await instructions. That I must do. But we shall be *seen* to be here. There are those who might believe that *Matchless* has

89

gone to obtain assistance, and that time is now more precious than ever.'

Galbraith watched him, seeing the changing emotions, could almost feel him thinking aloud.

He ventured, 'They are expecting supplies, above all powder and shot. If there are other ships sheltering in Algiers . . .'

Adam paused and touched his shoulder. 'And they still have *La Fortune*'s captain to help matters along, remember?'

'And we are alone, sir.'

Adam nodded slowly, seeing the chart in his mind. 'The Corsican tyrant once said, "Wherever wood can swim, there I am sure to find this flag of England."' The mood left him as quickly. 'The truest words he ever spoke.' He realised for the first time that the servant, Napier, had been in the cabin the whole time, and was already refilling the glasses. With the wine from St James's Street in London. He said, 'We have no choice.'

He walked to the stern windows, but there was only a fine line to separate sky from sea. Almost dark. *My birthday.*

He thought of her, whom he had loved and had lost, and when he looked at the old sword hanging from its rack, reflecting the lantern light, he thought of another who had helped him and was rarely out of his thoughts. Neither had been his to lose in the first place.

He said suddenly, 'How did it feel today, having a command of your own again?'

Galbraith did not appear to hesitate.

'Like me, sir, I think the ship felt uneasy without her captain.'

Their eyes met, and held. The barrier was down.

There was nothing else. For either of them.

The carriage with its perfectly matched greys wheeled sharply into the drive and halted at the foot of the steps. Sillitoe jumped down with barely a glance at his coachman.

'Change the horses, man! Quick as you can!'

He knew he was allowing his agitation to show itself, but he was powerless against it. He left the carriage door open, the watery sunlight playing on its crest. Baron Sillitoe of Chiswick.

A servant was sweeping the steps but removed the broom and averted his eyes as Sillitoe ran past him and threw open the double doors before anyone could be there to greet him.

He was late. Too late. And all because he had been delayed by the Prime Minister: some errand for the Prince Regent. It could have waited. *Should* have waited.

He saw his minute secretary, Marlow, coming towards him from the library. A man who knew all his master's moods but had remained loyal to him, perhaps because of rather than in spite of them, Marlow recognised his displeasure now, and that there was no point in attempting to appease him.

'She is not here, m' lord.'

Sillitoe stared up and around the bare, elegant staircase. There were few paintings, although the portrait of his father, the slaver, was a notable exception, and fewer objets d'art. Spartan, some called it. It suited him.

'Lady Somervell was to wait here for me! I told you exactly what I intended –' He stopped abruptly; he was wasting more time. 'Tell me.'

He felt empty, shocked that it had been so simple to deceive him. It had to be the case. No one else would dare, dare even to consider it.

Marlow said, 'Lady Somervell *was* here, m' lord.' He glanced at the open library door, seeing her in his mind. All in black but so beautiful, so contained. 'I tried to make her comfortable, but as time passed she became . . . troubled.'

Sillitoe waited, controlling his impatience, and surprised by Marlow's concern. He had never thought of his small, mild-mannered secretary as anything but an efficient and trustworthy extension of his own machinations.

Another door opened soundlessly and Guthrie, his valet, stood watching him, his battered features wary. More like a prizefighter than a servant, as were most of the men entrusted with Sillitoe's affairs.

'She wanted a carriage, m' lord. I told her there would be great crowds. Difficulties. But she insisted, and I knew you would expect me to act in your absence. I hope I did right, m' lord?'

Sillitoe walked past him and stared at the river, the boats, the moored barges. Passengers and crews alike always pointed to this mansion on the bank of the Thames. Known to so many, truly known by none of them.

'You did right, Marlow.' He heard horses stamping on flagstones, his coachman speaking to each by name.

He considered his anger as he would a physical opponent, along the length of a keen blade or beyond the muzzle of a duelling pistol.

He was the Prince Regent's Inspector-General, and his friend and confidential adviser. On most matters. On expenditure, the manipulations of both army and naval staffs, even on the subject of women. And when the King finally died, still imprisoned in his all-consuming madness, he could expect an even greater authority. *Above all, the Prince Regent was his friend.*

He attempted to look at it coldly, logically, as was his way with all obstacles. The Prince, 'Prinny', knew better than most the dangers of envy and spite. He was quick to see it among those closest to him, and would do what he could to preserve what he called 'a visible stability'. Perhaps he had already tried to warn him what might become of that stability, if his inspector-general were to lose his wits to a woman who had openly scorned and defied that same society for the man she loved.

And I did not realise. He could even accept that. But to believe that the future King had betrayed him, had given him a mission merely to keep him away and safe from slander and ridicule, was beyond belief. Even as he knew it was true. It was the only explanation.

Marlow coughed quietly. 'The horses have been changed, m' lord. Shall I tell William to stand down now?'

Sillitoe regarded him calmly. So Marlow knew too, or guessed.

He thought of Catherine, in this house or around the river's sweeping bend in Chelsea. Of the night he had burst in with Guthrie and the others and had saved her. *Saved her.* It was stark in his mind, like blood under the guillotine during the Terror.

He thought of Bethune's stupid, conniving wife, and Rhodes, who had expected to be created First Lord of the Admiralty. Of Richard Bolitho's wife; of so many who would be there today. Not to honour a dead hero, but to see Catherine shamed. Destroyed.

Now he could only wonder why he had hesitated.

He said curtly, 'I am ready.' He brushed past his valet without seeing the cloak which was to conceal his identity. 'That fellow from the *Times*, the one who wrote so well of Nelson . . .' He snapped his fingers. 'Laurence, yes?'

Marlow nodded, off guard only for a moment.

'I remember him, m' lord.'

'Find him. Today. I don't care how, or what it costs. I believe I am owed a favour or two.'

Marlow walked to the entrance and watched Sillitoe climb into the carriage. He could see the mud spattered on the side, evidence of a hard drive. No wonder the horses had been changed.

The carriage was already wheeling round, heading for the fine gates on which the Prince Regent himself had once commented.

He shook his head, recalling without effort the grand display of Nelson's procession and funeral. A vast armada of boats which had escorted the coffin by barge, from Greenwich to Whitehall, and from the Admiralty to St Paul's. A procession so long that it reached its destination before the rear had started to move.

Today there would be no body, no procession, but, like the man, it would be long remembered.

And only this morning he had heard that the end of the war was imminent. No longer merely a hope, a prayer. Could one final battle destroy so monstrous, so immortal an influence? He smiled to himself, sadly. Strange that on a day like this it seemed almost secondary.

Sillitoe pressed himself into a corner of the carriage and listened to the changing sound of the iron-shod wheels as the horses entered yet another narrow street. Grey stone buildings, blank windows, the offices of bankers and lawyers, of wealthy merchants whose trade reached across the world. The hub, as Sir Wilfred Lafargue liked to call it. The coachman, William, knew this part of London, and had managed to avoid the main roads, most of which had been filled with aimless crowds, so different from its usual bustle and purpose. For this was Sunday, and around St Paul's it would be even worse. He felt for his watch but decided against it. Half an hour at the most. But for the delay with the Prime Minister, he would have had ample time in hand, no matter what.

He leaned forward and tapped the roof with his sword.

'What is it now? Why are we slowing down, man?'

William hung over the side of his perch.

'Street's blocked, m' lord!' He sounded apprehensive; he had already had a taste of Sillitoe's temper on the drive to Chiswick House.

Sillitoe jerked a strap and lowered the window. So narrow here. Like a cavern. The smell of horses and soot . . .

He could see a mass of people, and what appeared to be a carriage. There were soldiers, too, and one, a helmeted officer, was already trotting towards them. Young, but lacking neither intelligence nor experience, his eyes moved swiftly to take in Sillitoe's clothing and the bright sash of the order across his chest, and then the coat of arms on the door.

'The way is blocked, sir!'

William glared down at him.

'"My lord"!'

The officer exclaimed, 'I beg your pardon, my lord, I did not know . . .'

Sillitoe snapped, 'Must get through to St Paul's. I do not have to explain why, I trust.' He could feel the anger rising again; this was only the calm before the storm. He studied the officer coldly. 'Fourteenth Light Dragoons. I know your agent, at Gray's Inn, I believe?'

He saw the shot go home.

'A vehicle has lost a wheel, my lord. It could not have happened in a worse place. I have already had to turn back one carriage – a lady –'

'A lady?' It was Catherine. It had to be. He glanced at the shining helmets and restless horses, and said sharply, 'I suggest you dismount those pretty warriors and remove the obstruction.'

'I – I am not certain. My orders –'

Sillitoe leaned back. 'If you value your commission, Lieutenant.'

It took only minutes for the dragoons to drag the vehicle to one side, and for William to drive the length of the street.

Deliberate? An accident? Or was it what Richard Bolitho had always called Fate?

He thought of her. On foot, hemmed in by gaping, curious faces. He looked out again and saw St Paul's. Close to, it dominated everything, so that the silence was all the more impressive.

'Stop now!'

He knew William was against it, and was probably wishing the massive Guthrie was here with him, but he climbed down to calm the horses before they became troubled by the slow-moving crowds, and the unnatural silence.

What might they have done? Would they have dared to turn her back at the cathedral's imposing entrance, on some paltry excuse, perhaps because there was no record of her invitation? Catherine, of all people. On this damnable day.

He quickened his pace, used to staring eyes and peering faces, beyond their reach, or so he believed now.

A hand plucked at his coat. 'Would you buy some flowers to honour his memory, sir?'

Sillitoe thrust him aside with a curt, 'Out of my way!'

Then he stopped, as if he had no control of his limbs. It explained the silence, the complete stillness, the like of which this place had never witnessed.

Catherine, too, stood quite still, and erect, surrounded by people and yet utterly detached from them.

Across the cathedral steps was an uneven rank of men. Sailors, or they had been before they had been cut down in battle. Men without arms, or hobbling on wooden stumps. Men with burned and scarred faces, victims of a hundred different battles and as many ships, but today joined as one. Sillitoe tried to reason with it, coldly, as was his habit. They were probably from the naval hospital at Greenwich and must have come upriver for this occasion, as if they had been drawn to it by the same power which had stopped him in his tracks. All wore scraps of uniform, some displayed tattoos on their arms; one, in a sea officer's uniform, was wearing his sword.

Sillitoe wanted to go to her. Not to speak, but only to be beside her. But he did not move.

Catherine was aware of the silence; she had even seen the mounted dragoons ordered to remove the wrecked vehicle. But it was all somewhere else. Not here. Not now.

She stood, unmoving, watching the man in the officer's uniform as he stepped slowly forward from the watching barrier of crippled sailors. The ones with wooden spars. Half-timbered Jacks, as Allday called them. She trembled. But he always said it without contempt, and without pity, for they were himself.

The officer was closer now, and she realised that his uniform was that of a lieutenant. Clean and well-pressed, but the careful stitching and repairs were evident. He had one hand on another man's shoulder, and when she saw his eyes she knew that he was blind, although they were clear and bright. And motionless.

His companion murmured something, and he removed his cocked hat with a flourish. His grey hair and threadbare uniform did not belong to this moment; he was the young lieutenant again. And these were his men.

He held out his hand and for an instant she saw him falter, until she reached out to him and took it in hers.

'You are welcome here.' Very gently, he kissed her hand. Still no one spoke or moved. As if this vignette were caught in time, like these ragged, proud reminders who had come to honour her.

Then he said, 'We all knew Sir Richard. Some of us served with or under him. He would have wished you to be so met today.'

She heard a step beside her and knew it was Sillitoe.

She murmured, 'I thought . . . I thought . . .'

He slipped his hand beneath her elbow and said, 'I know what you thought. What you were intended to think.'

Without looking above or beyond the watching figures, he knew that the great doors had opened.

He said, 'Thank you, gentlemen. No admiral's lady could ever have a braver guard of honour!'

There were smiles now, and one man reached out to touch Catherine's gown, muttering something, beaming at her while tears streamed down his cheeks. She removed her black veil, and stared up the steps.

96

'I do not have the words, Lieutenant. But later . . .' But there was no grey-haired officer, or perhaps her eyes were too blurred to see. A ghost, then. Like those who lay with Richard.

'Take me in, please.'

She did not hear the stir of surprise that ran through that towering place like a sudden wind through dry leaves, nor see the admiration, or outrage, or the angry disappointment, as Sillitoe guided her to his pew, which otherwise would have been empty.

She gripped her left hand in her right, feeling the ring her lover had placed there on Zenoria Keen's wedding day.

In the eyes of God, we are married.

She could not look ahead, and dared not think of what was past, that which she could never regain.

It was a proud day, for Richard, and for all those who had loved him.

And, only for this moment, they would be together.

It was just before dawn that the full force of the wind made itself known. Joshua Cristie, *Unrivalled*'s taciturn sailing master, found no comfort in the fact that his predictions had proved right, for this was the enemy. Others might fear the cannon's roar and the surgeon's knife, but Cristie was a sailor to his fingertips, like most of his forebears, and saw the weather's moods as his foes. As he gripped a stanchion to steady himself on the lurching deck he watched the sky, burning like molten copper, with long, dark clouds scudding beneath it as if they were already ashes.

They had shortened sail during the middle watch; he had heard the captain giving orders as he had hurried to the chart room to collect his precious instruments.

The captain seemed well able to make his immediate demands understood. On the face of it, *Unrivalled* was a smart and disciplined ship. *On the face of it.* But Cristie knew that it was only on the surface. Until men were truly tested to the limit, they would not know. She was still a new ship, and like any other was only as strong as the men who served her, and the chain of command which directed them as surely as any rudder. *Unless.*

The captain was here now, his old seagoing coat flapping in the wind, the dark hair pressed against his face by the flying spray. Even that looked like droplets of copper in the strange light.

'Let her fall off a point, Mr Cristie! Steer south-west-by-south!'

More men ran across to halliards and braces, some only half-dressed after the urgent call for all hands.

Cristie shouted, 'Still backing a piece, sir! She'll not hold this close to the wind for much longer!'

The captain seemed to hang on to his words, then swung round to face him. Cristie tested the moment, as he would a sounding or a compass bearing.

'We could come about and run with it, sir.' He hesitated, his mind grappling with the crack and thunder of canvas, the drone of straining rigging. 'Or we could lie-to under close-reefed main tops'l!'

Galbraith was yelling for more hands, and a few anonymous figures were in the mizzen top, cutting away broken cordage.

Cristie heard the captain say, '*No*. We'll hold as close as we can.' He was staring up at the swaying yards, the sickening motion making each plunge seem as if the ship were out of control.

But there were two more men on the big double-wheel, and as a solid curtain of spray burst over them and the quartermasters, they looked like survivors clinging to a capsizing wreck.

Adam Bolitho watched a party of seamen securing the hammock nettings. It was not vital. Seamen had slept in sodden hammocks before, and they would again. But it gave them a sense of purpose, kept them occupied when, even now, fear might be striding amongst them.

Unrivalled was leaning hard over, her lee bulwark almost awash, water spurting past the forward carronades and knocking men off their feet like skittles.

He held his breath, counting seconds as the bows dipped yet again, the hull quivering as it smashed into solid water, as if she had driven ashore.

He cupped his hands. 'Fore t'gan's'l's carried away!' He

saw Galbraith staring at him. '*Leave it!* Not worth risking lives!'

He watched the sail destroy itself, being ripped apart as if by giant, invisible hands until there were only shreds.

Men were clambering across the boat-tier now, urged on by the boatswain's powerful bellow. If a boat came adrift it would run amok on the deck, maiming and killing if not secured.

He heard Partridge shout, 'Make a bloody seaman of ye yet, damned if I don't!'

Old Stranace would be down there too. Dragging himself from gun to gun, checking each breeching rope, making sure that *his* equipment was not being lost or damaged.

Adam shivered, and felt the icy water exploring his spine and buttocks. But it was not that. It was a wildness, an elation he had not felt since he had lost *Anemone*.

The ship's backbone, the professionals. They never broke.

Midshipman Fielding was knocked sideways by a block swinging from a severed halliard. A seaman caught his arm and pulled him to his feet. Adam recognised the man as one of those due to be flogged. *Today* . . . He even saw the man grin. Like Jago. Amused. Contemptuous.

He seemed to hear John Allday's voice, when they had served together. His summing up of a ship's ability or otherwise.

Aft the most honour, mebbe, but forrard the better men!

He could see the horizon now, blurred with spray, writhing in the fierce light. Men's faces, bodies soaked and bruised, some with nails torn out by the tormented canvas they had fisted and kicked into submission, their world confined to a dizzily swaying yard, their strength that of the men up there with them.

But was it worth it? To risk so much, everything, on a frail belief?

A boatswain's mate ran past him, one arm outthrust, his mouth a soundless hole as the wind's fury increased to an insane scream. Adam thought he had seen something fall, probably from the main topsail yard, hardly making a splash as it hit the sea and was swamped by the water surging back from the stem.

Not even a cry. The fall had probably killed him. But

99

suppose he lived long enough to break surface and see his ship already fading into the storm?

It happened often enough, something which landsmen never considered when they saw a King's ship passing proudly at a safe distance.

Midshipman Bellairs wiped his face with his sleeve and gasped, 'It can't go on!'

Cristie heard him, and exclaimed harshly, 'Later on you'll remember this, my lad! When you're striding your own deck and making poor Jack's life a bloody misery! Leastways I hope you'll remember, for all our sakes!'

He watched the captain, his body angled to the quarterdeck, his voice carrying above the wild chorus of wind and sea.

'It's what *you* want to be, right?' He liked Bellairs; he would make a good officer, given the chance. He glanced at the captain again. *And the example.* Cristie had seen the best and the worst of them in his day. His own family had grown up in Tynemouth, in the next street to Collingwood, Nelson's friend and second-in-command at Trafalgar.

He heard Lieutenant Massie say, 'I'll not answer for the jib if we try to come about!'

Cristie nudged the midshipman and repeated, '*Remember it*, see!'

He moved away as the captain strode towards him.

'What say you, Mr Cristie? Do you think me mad to drive her so?'

Cristie did not know if Bellairs was listening, nor did he care. It was nothing he could mark on his chart, or record in the log. And nobody else would understand. The captain, the one who drove himself and everybody else, who had not hesitated to lead his own men on a cutting-out raid which had seemed an almost certain disaster, had *asked* him. Not told him, as was every captain's right.

He heard himself say, 'There's your answer, sir!' He watched his face as he looked at the widening bank of blue sky as it spread from horizon to horizon. The wind had lessened, so that the rattle of broken rigging and the flapping tails of torn canvas intruded for the first time. Soon the sun would show above the retreating cloud, and steam would rise from these wet, treacherous decks.

100

Men were pausing to draw breath, to peer around for messmates or for a special friend, as they might after action. Two of the younger midshipmen were actually grinning at one another and shaking hands with a kind of jubilant triumph.

Adam saw all and none of it. He was staring up, at the first lookout to risk the perilous climb aloft.

'Deck there! Sail on th' weather bow!'

He turned to Cristie and said quietly, 'And *there*, my friend, lies the enemy.'

7

A Bad Ship

Lieutenant Galbraith pivoted round on his heels and stared up to the quarterdeck rail, eyes slitted against the first hard sunshine.

'Ship cleared for action, sir!'

Adam did not take out his watch; he had no need to. From the moment the small marine drummer boys had begun the staccato rattle of beating to quarters, he had watched the ship come alive again, the savage wind almost forgotten. Only fragments of canvas and snapped cordage, flapping 'Irish pennants', as the old hands called them, gave any hint of the storm which had passed as quickly as it had found them.

Seven o'clock in the morning: six bells had just chimed from the forecastle. It was all routine, normal, and yet so different.

Adam had stood by the rail, feeling the ship preparing for whatever challenge she might meet within the next few hours. Screens torn down, hutchlike cabins folded away and stowed in the holds with furniture and all unnecessary personal belongings. A bad moment, when some might pause to reflect that their owners might not need them after this day was past.

It had taken ten minutes to clear the ship from bow to stern. Even his cabin, the largest he had ever occupied and a place which still lacked personality, was open, so that gun crews and powder monkeys could move unhindered if the shot began to fly.

The galley fire had been doused at the beginning of the storm, and there had been no time to relight it. Men fought better on a full belly, especially when they had already been contesting wind and sea for most of the night.

He stared along the maindeck, at the gun crews standing by their charges, the long eighteen-pounders which made up the bulk of *Unrivalled*'s artillery. Most of them were stripped to the waist, new hands and landsmen following the example of the seasoned men who had seen and done it all before. Any clothing was precious to a working sailor, and costly to replace out of his meagre pay. Fabric also attracted gangrene, and hampered treatment should a man be wounded.

Adam thought he could smell the rum even from the quarterdeck. The purser had been quietly outraged by the extra issue he had ordered, a double tot for every man, as if the cost would be extracted from his own pocket.

But it had bridged the gap, and would do no harm at all.

Six seamen to each gun, including its captain, but hauling the heavy cannon up a tilting deck if the ship was to leeward of an enemy would require many more. An experienced crew should be able to fire a shot every ninety seconds, at the outset of battle in any case, although Adam had known some gun captains prepared and ready to fire three shots every two minutes. It had been so in *Hyperion*, an exceptional ship; a legend, like her captain.

He smiled, but did not see Galbraith's quick answering grin.

The ship was moving steadily and, apparently, unhurriedly, with courses and staysails clewed up or furled. It seemed to open up the sea on either beam, and Adam had seen several of the unemployed seamen clambering up to seek out the enemy. To watch and prepare themselves as best they could. He considered it. *The enemy.* There were two of them, one large, a cut-down man-of-war by her appearance, the other smaller, a brig.

It was still so peaceful. So full of quiet menace.

Who were they? What had prompted their mission to Algiers?

He saw Lieutenant Massie by the foremast, ready to direct the opening shots, his own little group of midshipmen, messengers and petty officers waiting to pass his orders, and to close their eyes and ears to all else around them.

103

He turned away from the rail and saw the Royal Marines stationed across the deck, scarlet ranks moving evenly to the ship's motion. Cristie, and Lieutenant Wynter, Midshipman Bellairs and his signals party, the helmsmen and master's mates. A centre. The ship's brain. He glanced at the tightly packed hammock nettings, slight protection for such a prize target.

He raised his eyes and saw more marines in the fighting tops. He had always thought of it when facing an action at sea. The marksmen, one of whom he knew had been a poacher before enlisting, not out of patriotism but rather to avoid prison or deportation. They were all first-class shots.

He looked at the horizon again, the tiny patches of sails against the hard blue line. He would think even more of it now, since Avery had described those final moments, so quietly, so intimately. He bit his lip, controlling it. All these men, good and bad, would be looking to him. *Aft, the most honour.* He touched the old sword at his hip, remembering the note she had left with it. *For me.* He had seen Jago's searching glance when he had come on deck. The old sword, the bright epaulettes. What had he thought? Arrogance, or vanity?

Jago was climbing the quarterdeck ladder now, his dark eyes barely moving, but missing nothing. A man he might never know, but one he did not want to lose.

Jago joined him by the rail and stood with his arms folded, as if to show his contempt for some of those watching. Like Lieutenant Massie, or the sulky midshipman named Sandell. San*dell*, as he insisted on being called.

Jago said, 'The first ship, sir. Old Creagh thinks he knows her.'

So casually spoken. *Testing me?*

The face formed in his mind. Creagh was one of the boatswain's mates, and would have been carrying out a flogging if *Unrivalled* had turned back instead of forcing her passage into the teeth of the storm. A lot of people might be thinking that, and cursing their captain for his stubborn refusal to give way.

'One of Mr Partridge's mates.' He did not see Jago's quiet smile, although he sensed it.

'He swears she's the *Tetrarch*. Served in her some years back.'

Adam nodded. Like a family. Like the men who served them, there were bad ships too.

Tetrarch was a fourth-rate, one of a rare breed now virtually erased from the Navy List. Classed as ships of the line, they had been rendered obsolete by the mounting savagery and improved gunnery of this everlasting war. The fourth-rate was neither one thing nor the other, not fast enough to serve as a frigate, and, mounting less than sixty guns, no match for the battering she must withstand in the line of battle. Ship to ship. Gun to gun.

Tetrarch had been caught off Ushant some three years ago. Attacked and captured by two French frigates, she had not been heard of since.

Now she was back. And she was here.

Jago said, 'Cut down, she is.' He rubbed his chin, a rasping sound like an armourer's iron. 'But still, she could give a fair account of herself. And with that other little bugger in company.'

Adam tried to put himself in the enemy's position, assessing the distant vessels as if he were looking down on them. Like impersonal markers on an admiral's chart. The brig would be sacrificed first. She had to be, if the bigger ship was indeed loaded with supplies and powder for others still sheltering in Algiers, enjoying what Bethune had called the Dey's one-sided neutrality. After losing *La Fortune* to such a calculated trick, they would be doubly eager to even the score.

On a converging tack, both close-hauled, but the enemy would have the wind's advantage. And there was not enough time to replace the fore topgallant sail.

Galbraith had joined him, his face full of questions.

Adam asked, 'How long, d' you think?'

Galbraith looked up at the masthead pendant, flapping and drooping. How could the wind change so completely?

He answered, 'An hour. No more.' He hesitated. 'She has the wind-gage, sir.'

'It's the little terrier which concerns me. We shortened sail in time last night. But our lady will be hard put to lift her skirts in a hurry!' He studied the set of each sail, the yards braced round. The wind would decide it. 'I want to hit them before they can do too much damage.'

The men at the quarterdeck nine-pounders glanced at one another. *Too much damage.* Not just timber and cordage, but flesh and blood.

Adam walked to the compass box and back again. 'Our best shots must be all about today, Mr Galbraith.' He smiled suddenly. 'A guinea for the man who marks down the captain. Theirs, not ours!'

Some of those same men actually laughed aloud. Captain Bouverie would not approve of such slack behaviour aboard *Matchless.*

He turned aside. 'Be watchful of powder. The decks will soon be bone dry. One spark . . .' He did not need to continue.

He took a glass and held it to his eye; it was already warm against his skin.

Three ships, drawing together as if by invisible warps. Soon to be close, real, deadly.

I must not fail. Must not.

But his voice sounded flat and without emotion, betraying nothing of his thoughts.

'Load in ten minutes, Mr Galbraith. But do not run out. Let the people take their time. Gunnery is god today!'

If I fall. He had his hand on his pocket and could feel the locket there, carefully wrapped. *Who would care?*

He thought suddenly of the old house, empty now, except for the portraits. Waiting.

They would care.

It was time.

Galbraith glanced quickly at his captain and then leaned over the quarterdeck rail.

The final scrutiny. There was always the chance of a flaw in the rigid pattern of battle.

Decks sanded, particularly around each gun, to prevent men from slipping in the madness of action on blown spray or blood. Nets had been spread above the deck to protect the gun crews and sail-handling parties from falling debris, and impede any enemy reckless enough to try and board them.

The gunner and his mates had already gone to the magazine to prepare and issue charges to the powder monkeys, most of whom were mere boys. With no experience to plague them, they were less concerned than some of the older hands, who would look for reassurance at familiar faces around them, every man very aware of the two pyramids of sail, so much nearer now, although seemingly motionless on the glistening water.

Galbraith shouted, '*All guns load*!'

Each eighteen-pounder was an island, its crew oblivious to the rest. Just as during the constant drills when they had roundly cursed every officer from the captain downwards, they were testing the training tackles, casting off the heavy breeching ropes, freeing the guns for loading. That too was a routine, a ritual, the bulky charge taken by the assistant loader from the breathless powder monkey, to be eased into the waiting muzzle and tamped home by the loader. No mistakes. Two sharp knocks to bed it in, and a wad tamped in to secure it.

Experienced gun captains had already selected their shots from the garlands, holding each ball, weighing it, feeling it, making sure it was a perfect shape, for the opening roar of battle.

It had all been done deliberately and without haste, and Galbraith knew why the captain had ordered them to take their time, for this first attempt at least. Now there was a stillness, each crew grouped around its gun, every captain staring aft at the blue and white figures of discipline and authority. As familiar as the guns which were their reason for being, in the company of which they greeted every dawn, and which were constant reminders of a ship's hard comradeship.

And yet despite the toughness of such men, Galbraith knew the other side of the coin. Like the seaman who had been lost overboard, without even a cry. Later there would be a sale of his few possessions, before the mast, as they called it, and messmates and others who had barely known him would dip into their purses and pay exorbitant prices so that money could be sent to a wife or mother somewhere in that other world.

He turned and looked at his captain, speaking quietly with the master, gesturing occasionally as if to emphasise something. He gazed at the oncoming vessels. The moment of embrace. There would be more possessions to bargain for if today turned sour on them.

He blinked as a shaft of sunlight glanced down between the braced yards. The smaller vessel had tacked, widening the distance from her consort. The terrier, the captain had called her. Ready to dart in and snap at *Unrivalled*'s vulnerable stern and quarter. One shot could do it: a vital spar, or worse, damage to the rudder and steering gear would end the fight before *Unrivalled* had bared her teeth. He looked at the captain again. *He would know.* His first command had been a brig. He had been twenty-three, someone had said. He would know . . .

The enemy had the advantage of the wind, and yet Captain Adam Bolitho showed no sign of anxiety.

'We will load both broadsides and engage first at full range, gun by gun. Tell the second lieutenant to sight each one himself. We will then luff, and if the wind is kind to us we can rake the enemy with the other full broadside.'

Galbraith dragged his mind back to the present. Extra hands at the foremast ready to set the big forecourse, until now brailed up like the others. With the fore topgallant sail missing, they would need every cupful of wind when they came about. And even then . . .

Adam called, *'Open the ports!'*

He imagined the port lids lifting along either beam, could see the water creaming past the lee side. *Unrivalled* was leaning over, and she would lean still further when they set the forecourse. He had guessed what Galbraith was thinking. If the wind deserted them now, the enemy ships could divide and outmanoeuvre him. He touched his pocket again. If not, the long eighteen-pounders on the weather side, at full elevation, would outrange the others. He smiled. So easily said . . .

Cristie had told him something about the *Tetrarch* which he had not known. She had been in a state of near mutiny when she had been attacked by the French frigates. Another bad captain, he thought, like *Reaper*, in which the company had mutinied against their captain's inhuman treatment and had joined together to flog him to death. *Reaper* was back with the fleet now, commanded by a good officer, a friend of Adam's, but he doubted that she would ever entirely cleanse herself of the stigma.

And *Tetrarch* might be the same. Her armament had been

reduced in order to allow for more hold space, but she could give a good account of herself.

He looked up at the black, vibrating shrouds, the soft underbelly of the main topsail, seeing it in his mind even now. *Anemone* torn apart by the American's heavy artillery. Men falling and dying. *Because of me.*

He squared his shoulders, and felt his shirt drag against the ragged scar where the iron splinter had cut him down.

It was enough.

He said, 'Run out!'

Every spare man, even the Royal Marines were on the tackles, hauling the guns up the tilting deck to thrust their black muzzles through the ports. The enemy was faceless, unknown. But it would be madness to show *Unrivalled*'s shortage of hands from the outset. After that . . .

There were a few hoarse cheers as the crouching gun crews saw the enemy angled across each port, and he heard Lieutenant Massie's sharp response.

'Keep silent, you deadheads! Stand to your guns! I'll have none of it!'

Adam walked to the rail and watched the nearest vessel, the brig. Like his old *Firefly*. Well handled, leaning over while she changed tack. Probably steering south-east. He thought of Cristie. *By guess and by God.* He measured the range, surprised still that he could do it without hesitation. The *Tetrarch* had taken in her fore and main courses and was preparing to await her chance, poised across the starboard bow as if nothing could prevent a collision.

There was a dull bang, and seconds later a hole appeared in the main topsail. A sighting shot. He clenched his fists. *Not yet, not yet.* Another shot came from somewhere, sharper, one of the brig's bow-chasers probably. He saw the feathers of spray dart from wave to wave, like flying fish. Still short.

'Forecourse, Mr Galbraith!' He strode to the opposite side. 'Lay for the mainmast, Mr Massie! On the uproll!'

The enemy might be expecting a ragged broadside, and be waiting for a chance to close the range before *Unrivalled* could reload.

Adam heard Massie yell, 'Ready! *Fire!*'

He kept his eyes fixed on the other ship. Massie was

managing on his own, pausing at each breech, one hand on the gun captain's shoulder, the trigger-line taut, ready, the target framed in the open port like a painting come to life.

'*Fire!*'

Gun by gun, the full length of *Unrivalled*'s spray-dashed hull, each one hurling itself inboard on its tackles to be seized, sponged out and reloaded, the men racing one another to run out again, whilst on the opposite side the crews waited their turn, with only the empty sea to distract them from the regular crash of gunfire.

Someone gave a wild cheer.

'Thar goes 'er main topmast! B' Jesus, look at 'er, mates!'

But the other ship was firing now, iron hammering into *Unrivalled*'s lower hull, a stray ball slamming through a port and breaking into splinters.

Adam tore his eyes from the spouting orange tongues of fire, feeling the blows beneath his feet like wounds to his own body. Men were down, one rolling across the deck, kicking and coughing blood, another crouched against a gun, fingers interlaced across his stomach, his final scream dying as he was dragged aside and the gun run up to its port again.

Galbraith yelled, 'He's standing off, sir!' He flinched as a powder monkey spun round, his leg severed by another haphazard shot. Adam saw another run and snatch up the fallen charge, eyes terrified, and averted from someone who had probably been his friend.

He turned. 'Wouldn't you? If you were full to the gills with powder and shot?' He shut them from his mind. 'Stand by on the quarterdeck!' There was smoke everywhere, choking, stinging, blinding.

He could no longer see the other ship; the forecourse was filled to the wind, blotting out the enemy's intentions.

'Put the helm down!' He dashed his wrist across his eyes and thought he saw the ship's head already answering the helm, swinging bowsprit and flapping jib across the wind.

'Helm's a' lee, sir!'

Adam heard someone cry out and knew a ball had missed him by inches.

Come on! Come on! If *Unrivalled* was caught aback across

110

the eye of the wind she would be helpless, doomed. He felt the deck planking jump again and knew the ship had been hit.

'*Off tacks and sheets!*' He walked level with the quarterdeck rail, his hand brushing against the smooth woodwork. Without seeing, he knew the forward sails were writhing in confusion, spilling the wind, allowing the bows to swing still further, unhampered.

'*Fores'l haul! Haul, lads!*'

One man slipped on blood and another dragged him to his feet. Neither spoke, nor looked at one another.

She was answering. Adam gripped the rail, and felt her standing into the opposite tack, sails filling and booming, the yards being hauled round until to an onlooker they would appear almost fore-and-aft.

'*Hold her!* Steer east-by-south!' Adam glanced swiftly at Cristie. Only a second, but it was enough to see a wild satisfaction. The pride might come later.

'Starboard battery!' Massie was there now, his sword in the air, his face a mask of concentration as he watched the brig swinging away, caught and unprepared for *Unrivalled*'s change of tack.

'*Fire!*'

It must have been like an avalanche, an avalanche of iron. When the whirling smoke, swept aside by the wind, laid bare the other vessel it was hard to recognise her, almost mastless, her shattered stumps and rigging dragging outboard like weed. She was a wreck.

Adam took a telescope from Midshipman Fielding, and felt the youth's hand shaking. *Or is it mine?*

'Again, Mr Cristie! Man the braces and stand by to wear ship!' He tried to calm himself and steady the glass.

The terrier was dead. The real target could never outpace them.

'All loaded, sir!'

He watched the other ship. Saw the scars left by *Unrivalled*'s first controlled broadside, the holes punched in her darkly tanned canvas.

Galbraith called, 'Ready, sir!' He sounded hoarse.

'Bring her about and lay her on the starboard tack.' He

glanced up at the forecourse, at scorched holes which had not been there earlier. *Earlier? On my birthday.*

Galbraith's voice again. 'We could call on him to strike, sir.'

'*No*. I know what that feels like. We will open fire when we are in position.' The smile would not come. 'The wind will not help him now.' He saw Midshipman Bellairs watching him fixedly, and said, 'Signal the brig to lie-to. We will board her presently.'

Bellairs beckoned to his signals party. 'A prize, sir?' Like Galbraith he sounded parched, as if he could scarcely speak.

'No. A trophy, Mr Bellairs.' He looked at Galbraith. 'Bring her about and take in the t'gallants. We shall commence firing.' He measured the distance again. 'A mile, would you say? Close enough. Then we will see.'

He watched the sudden activity on deck, the shadows swinging across the flapping sails while the frigate continued to turn, the grim faces of the nearest gun crews.

It was neither a contest nor a game, and they must know it.

He saw Massie pointing with his sword and passing his orders, the words lost in the din of canvas and tackles.

Unless that flag came down, it would be murder.

Using the wind across his quarter to best advantage, *Tetrarch*'s captain had decided to wear ship, not to close the range but to outmanoeuvre and avoid *Unrivalled*'s challenge.

Adam observed it in silence, able to ignore the bark of commands, the sudden protesting bang of canvas as his ship came as close to the wind as she could manage.

He raised his telescope again and trained it on the other vessel as she began to come about; he could even discern her figurehead, scarred and rendered almost shapeless by time and weather, but once a proud Roman governor with a garland of laurel around his head. Her captain might try to elude his adversary until nightfall. But there was little chance of that. It would only prolong the inevitable. He stared at the other ship's outline, shortening, the masts overlapping while she continued to turn.

He could sense Galbraith and some of the others watching him, all probably full of their own ideas and solutions.

If they came too close and the other ship caught fire, her lethal cargo could destroy all of them. Adam had done it himself. Jago had been there then, also.

He said sharply, 'Stand by to starboard as before, Mr Massie! Gun by gun!'

He wiped his eye and looked again. The enemy was bows-on, and in the powerful lens it looked as if her bowsprit would parry with *Unrivalled*'s jib boom.

'*As you bear!*'

He saw the *Tetrarch*'s canvas billow and fill, the bright Tricolour showing itself briefly beyond the braced driver. What did the flag mean to those men, he wondered? A symbol of something which might already have been defeated.

He thought of *Frobisher*, the cruel twist of fate which had brought her and her admiral to an unplanned rendezvous with two such ships as this one.

'*Fire!*' He watched the first shots tearing through the enemy's forecourse and topsails, and felt although he could not hear the sickening crash of falling spars and rigging.

Like *Anemone* . . .

But she continued to turn, exposing her broadside and the bright flashes from her most forward guns. Some hit *Unrivalled*'s hull, others hurled waterspouts over the side, where gun crews were working like fiends to sponge out and reload.

He heard Lieutenant Luxmore of the Royal Marines yelling a name as one of his marksmen in the maintop fired his Brown Bess at the enemy without waiting for the order. At this range, it was like throwing a pike at a church steeple. *The madness.* No one could completely contain it.

There was a wild cheer as with tired dignity *Tetrarch*'s fore topmast appeared to stagger, held upright only by the rigging. Adam watched, unable to blink, as the mast seemed to gain control, tearing shrouds and running rigging alike as if the stout cordage were made of mere twine, the sails adding to the confusion and destruction until the entire mast with upper spars and reeling foretop spilled down into the smoke.

Only a part of his mind recorded the shouts from the gun captains, yelling like men possessed as each eighteen-pounder slammed against its open port. Ready to fire.

He moved the glass very slightly. There was a thin plume of smoke from the maindeck of the other ship. Any fire was dangerous, in a fight or otherwise, but with holds full of gunpowder it was certain death. He glanced at *Unrivalled*'s upper yards and the whipping masthead pendant.

'Fall off a point!'

He saw Massie staring aft towards him, his sword already half raised.

There was no room for doubt, less for compassion. *Because that captain could be me.*

Tetrarch was still turning, her bows dragging at the mass of fallen spars and cordage. There were men too, struggling in the water, calling for help which would never come.

The next slow broadside would finish her. At almost full range, high-angled to the rise of the deck, it would smash through the remaining masts and canvas before *Tetrarch*'s main battery could be brought to bear.

'*As you bear!*' It was not even his own voice. He thought he saw the sun lance from Massie's upraised blade, and somehow knew that the gun crews on the larboard side had left their stations to watch, their own danger forgotten.

He stiffened and steadied the glass again. This time, he knew it was his own hand shaking.

'*Belay that order!*'

There was too much smoke, but certain things stood out as clearly as if the enemy had been alongside.

The forward guns were unmanned, and there were figures running across the ship's poop and halfdeck, apparently out of control. For an instant he imagined that the fire had taken control, and the ship's company were making a frantic attempt to escape the imminent explosion.

And then he saw it. The French flag, the only patch of colour on that broken ship, was falling, seemingly quite slowly, until somebody hacked the halliards apart so that it drifted across the water like a dying sea bird.

Cristie grunted, 'Sensible man, I'd say!'

Someone else said harshly, 'A lucky one too, God damn his eyes!'

Tetrarch was falling downwind, her maincourse and mizzen already being brailed up, as if to confirm her submission.

Adam raised the glass again. There were small groups of men standing around the decks; others, dead or wounded it was impossible to tell, lay unheeded by the abandoned guns.

Midshipman Bellairs called, 'White flag, sir!' Even he seemed unable to grasp what was happening, even less that he was a part of it.

'Heave to, if you please!' Adam lowered the glass. He had seen someone on that other deck watching him. With despair, hate; he needed no reminding. 'Take the quarter-boat, Mr Galbraith, and pick your boarding party. If you find it safe for us to come alongside, then signal me. At any sign of treachery, you know what to do.'

Their eyes held. *Know what to do.* *Unrivalled* would fire that final broadside. Any boarding party would be butchered.

Galbraith said steadily, 'I shall be ready, sir!'

'A close thing.'

'We would have run them down, sir. The way you handled her . . .'

Adam touched his sleeve. 'Not that, Leigh. I wanted them dead.'

Galbraith turned away, beckoning urgently to one of his petty officers. Even when the quarter-boat had been warped alongside and men were clambering down the frigate's tumble-home, he was still reliving it.

The Captain had called him by his first name, like an old and trusted friend. But more, he remembered and was disturbed by the look of pain on the dark features. Anguish, as if he had almost betrayed something. Or someone.

'Bear off forrard! Give way all!'

They were dipping and rising over the choppy water, the boat's stem already clattering through drifting flotsam and lolling corpses. Galbraith shaded his eyes to look up at the other vessel, huge now as they pulled past her bows, seeing the damage which *Unrivalled*'s guns had inflicted.

'Marines, take the poop! Creagh, put your party below!' He saw the boatswain's mate nod, his weatherbeaten face unusually grim. He was the man who had first recognised *Tetrarch*, and perhaps remembered the blackest moment in her life, when she had been surrendered to the enemy.

Sergeant Everett of the marines called, 'Watch yer back, sir! I'd not trust a one of 'em!'

Galbraith thought of the captain again. *It might have been us.* Then he lurched to his feet, one hand on the shoulder of an oarsman in this overcrowded boat, his mind empty of everything but the grapnel thudding into the scarred timbers and the hull grating alongside.

'With me, lads!'

Within a second he might be dead, or floating out there with the other corpses.

And then he was up and over the first gunport lid, tearing his leg on something jagged but feeling nothing.

There were more people on deck than he had expected. For the most part ragged and outwardly undisciplined, the sweepings of a dozen countries, renegades and deserters, and yet . . . He stared around, taking in the discarded weapons, the sprawled shapes of men killed by *Unrivalled*'s slow and accurate fire. It would need more than greed or some obscure cause to weld this rabble into one company, to stand and fight a King's ship which for all they knew might have been expecting support from other men-of-war.

He thought of the hand on his sleeve, and pointed with his hanger.

'Where is your captain?' He could not recall having drawn the blade as he had scrambled aboard.

A man stepped or was pushed towards him. An officer of sorts, his uniform coat without facings or rank.

He said huskily, 'He is dying.' He spread his hands. '*We* pulled down the flag. It was necessary!'

One of Creagh's seamen shouted, 'Fire's out!' He glared at the silent figures below the poop as if he would have cut each one down himself. 'Lantern, sir! Knocked over!'

The ship was safe. Galbraith said, 'Run up our flag.' He glanced at *Unrivalled*, moving so slowly, the guns like black teeth along her side. Then he looked up at the squad of Royal Marines with their bayoneted muskets. They had even managed to depress a swivel gun towards the listless men who were now their prisoners. A blast of canister shot would deter any last-minute resistance.

Sergeant Everett called, 'Captain's up here, sir!'

Galbraith sheathed his hanger. It would be useless in any case if some hothead tried to retake the ship. The groups of men parted to allow him through, and he saw defeat in their strained features. The will to fight was gone, if it had ever been there. Apathy, despair, fear, the face of surrender and all it represented.

Tetrarch's captain was not what he had expected. Propped between one of his officers and a pale-faced youth, he was at a guess about Galbraith's age. He had fair hair, tied in an old-style queue, and there was blood on his waistcoat, which the officer was attempting to staunch.

Galbraith said, 'M'sieur, I must tell you . . .'

The eyes opened and stared up at him, a clear hazel. The breathing was sharp and painful.

'No formalities, Lieutenant. I speak English.' He coughed, and blood ran over the other man's fingers. 'I suppose I *am* English. So strange, that it should come to this.'

Galbraith stared around. 'Surgeon?'

'None. So many shortages.'

'I will take you to my ship. Can you manage that?'

What did it matter? A renegade Englishman; there was a slight accent, possibly American. Perhaps one of the original privateers. And yet he did not seem old enough. He stood up; he was wasting time.

'Rig a bosun's chair. You, Corporal Sykes, attend this officer's wound.' He saw the doubt in the marine's eyes. 'It is important!'

Creagh shouted, '' Nother boat shovin' off, sir!'

Galbraith nodded. Captain Bolitho had seen or guessed what was happening. A prize crew, then. And there was still the dismasted brig to deal with. He needed to act quickly, to organise his boarding party, to have the prisoners searched for concealed weapons.

But something made him ask, 'What is your name, Captain?'

He lay back against the others, his eyes quite calm despite the pain.

'Lovatt.' He attempted to smile. 'Roddie – Lovatt.'

'Bosun's chair rigged, sir!'

Galbraith said, 'We have a good surgeon. What is the nature of your wound?'

He could hear the other boat hooking on, voices shouting to one another, thankful that reinforcements had arrived. All danger forgotten, perhaps until the night watches, when there would be thoughts for all men.

Lovatt did not conceal his contempt as he said bitterly, 'A pistol ball. From one of my gallant sailors yonder. When I refused to haul down the flag.'

Galbraith put his hand on the shoulder of the boy, who had not left the wounded man.

'Go with the others!'

His mind was full. An English captain who was probably an American; a ship which had been handed to the enemy after a mutiny; and a French flag.

The boy tried to free himself and Lovatt said quietly, 'Please, Lieutenant. Paul is my son.'

Two seamen carried him to the hastily rigged boatswain's chair. Once, Lovatt cried out, the sound torn from him, and reached for his son's hand. His eyes moved to the newly hoisted flag at the peak, the White Ensign, so fresh, so clean above the pain and the smell of death.

He whispered, '*Your* flag now, Lieutenant.'

Galbraith signalled to the waiting boat's crew and saw Midshipman Bellairs peering up at him. He would learn another lesson today.

Lovatt was muttering, 'Flags, Lieutenant . . . We are all mercenaries in war.'

Galbraith saw blood on the deck and realised it was his own, from the leg he had cut when climbing aboard.

The chair was being hoisted and then swayed out over the gangway.

He said, 'Go with him, boy. Lively now!'

Creagh joined him by the side as the chair was lowered into the boat, where Bellairs was waiting to receive it.

'Found this, sir.' He held out a sword. 'Th' cap'n's, they says.'

Galbraith took it and felt the drying blood adhering to his fingers. A sword. All that was left of a man. Something to be handed on. He thought of the old Bolitho blade, which today his captain had worn. *Or forgotten.*

He studied the hilt. One of the early patterns, with a five-ball

118

design, which had been so resented by sea officers when it had been introduced as the first regulation sword. Most officers had preferred their own choice of blade.

Deliberately, he half-drew it from its leather scabbard and read the engraving. He could even picture the establishment, in the Strand in London, the same sword-cutlers from whom he had obtained the hanger at his hip.

He stared across at his own ship, and at the boat rising and dipping in the swell on its errand of mercy.

Better he had been killed, he thought. A King's officer who had become a traitor: if he lived through this, he might soon wish otherwise.

He sighed. Wounded to be dealt with, dead to be put over. And a meal of sorts. After that . . . He felt his dried lips crack into a smile.

He was alive, and they had won the day. It was enough. It had to be.

8

No Escape

Denis O'Beirne, *Unrivalled*'s surgeon, climbed wearily up the quarterdeck ladder and paused to recover his breath. The sea was calmer, the sun very low on the horizon.

The ship's company was still hard at work. There were men high in the yards, splicing a few remaining breakages, and on the maindeck the sailmaker and his crew were sitting cross-legged like so many tailors, their palms and needles moving in unison, ensuring that not a scrap of canvas would be wasted. Apart from the unusual disorder, it was hard to believe that the ship had exchanged fire on this same day, that men had died. Not many, but enough in a small, self-contained company.

O'Beirne had served in the navy for twelve years, mostly in larger vessels, ships of the line, always teeming with humanity, overcrowded and, to a man of his temperament, oppressive. Blockade duty in all weathers, men forced aloft in a screaming gale, only to be recalled to set more sail if the weather changed in their favour. Bad food, crude conditions; he had often wondered how the sailors endured it.

A frigate was something else. Lively, independent if her captain was ambitious and able to free himself from the fleet's apron strings, and imbued with a sense of companionship which was entirely different. He had observed it with his usual interest, seen it deepen in the few months since *Unrivalled* had commissioned on that bitterly cold day at Plymouth, and the ship's first captain had read himself in.

As surgeon he was privileged to share the wardroom with

120

the officers, and during that period he had learned more about his companions than they probably knew. He had always been a good listener, a man who enjoyed sharing the lives of others without becoming a part of them.

A surgeon was classed as a warrant officer, his status somewhere between sailing master and purser. A craftsman rather than a gentleman. Or as one old sawbones had commented, neither profitable, comfortable, nor respectable.

In recent years the Sick and Hurt Office had worked diligently to improve the naval surgeon's lot, and to bring them into line with army medical officers. Either way, O'Beirne could not imagine himself doing anything else.

He was entitled to one of the hutch-like cabins allotted to the lieutenants, but preferred his own company in the sickbay below the waterline. His world. Those who visited him voluntarily came in awe; others who were carried to him, like those he had left on the orlop deck, or had seen being put over the side in a hasty burial, had no choice.

He glanced around the quarterdeck. Here, in this place of authority and purpose, the roles were reversed.

Unrivalled was rolling steeply despite the sea's calmer face, lying to as she had for the entire day, with the battered *Tetrarch* under her lee, the air alive with hammers and squealing blocks as the boarding party had used every trick and skill known to seamen to erect a jury-rig, enough for *Tetrarch* to get under way again, and be escorted to Malta.

The little brig had capsized and vanished even before many of her wounded could be ferried to safety. He had heard few regrets from anyone, and even the loss of potential prize money had seemed insignificant.

Two ships, and the sun already low above its reflection. He saw the captain staring up at their new fore topgallant sail, while Cristie, the master, pointed out something where the topmen were still working.

O'Beirne thought of his latest charge, *Tetrarch*'s captain. He had borne up well, considering the angle of the pistol shot and a great loss of blood. The ball had been fired point-blank, and his waistcoat had been singed and stained with powder smoke. Only one thing had saved his life: he had been wearing one of the outdated crossbelts which some officers had still been using when O'Beirne had first gone to sea. It had a heavy buckle, like a small horseshoe. The ball had been deflected by it, and had broken in half.

They had stripped him naked and the loblolly boys had held him spreadeagled on the makeshift table, already ingrained with the blood of those who had gone before him.

O'Beirne could shut his ears and concentrate on the work in hand, but his mind was still able to record the inert shapes which lay in the shadows, or propped against the frigate's curved timbers. There had been no time to separate or distinguish the living from the dead. He had become accustomed to it, but still liked to believe he had not become hardened by it. He remembered the powder monkey who had lost a leg: it had been a challenge not to watch his face, his eyes so filled with terror as the knife had made its first incision. He had died on the table before the saw could complete the necessary surgery.

O'Beirne had seen his surgeon's mate scribble in a dog-eared log book. The powder monkey had been ten years old.

O'Beirne came from a large family, seven boys and three girls. Three brothers had entered the Church, two had donned the King's coat in a local regiment of foot, another had gone to sea in a packet ship. His sisters had married honest farmers and were raising families of their own. The brother who had gone to sea was no more; neither were the two who had 'gone for a soldier'.

He smiled to himself. There was something to be said for the Church after all.

He realised that the captain was looking at him. He seemed clear-eyed and attentive while he listened to what Cristie had to say, and yet O'Beirne knew he had been on deck or close to it since dawn.

Adam walked away from the rail and stared down at the sailmaker's crew.

'What is it?'

'The captain, sir.' He hesitated as the dark eyes met his. 'Captain Lovatt.'

'The prisoner, you mean. Is he dead?'

O'Beirne shook his head. 'I've done what I could, sir.

There is some internal bleeding, but the wound may heal, given time.'

He had not considered the man a prisoner, or anything but a wounded survivor. He had fainted several times, but had managed to smile when he had finally come to his senses. O'Beirne had prevented him from moving his arms, telling him it might aggravate the inner wound, but they all did it, usually after they had been rendered incapable of thought or protest by liberal helpings of rum. Just to make certain their arms were still there, and not pitched into the limbs and wings tub like so much condemned meat.

He saw a muscle tighten in the captain's jaw. Not impatience, but strain. Something he was determined to conceal.

He said, 'He asked about you, sir, while I was dressing the wound. I told him, of course. It helps to keep their minds busy.'

'If that is all . . .' He turned away, and then back abruptly. 'I am sorry. You are probably more tired than all the rest of us!'

O'Beirne observed him thoughtfully. It was there again, a kind of youthful uncertainty, so at odds with his role as captain, of this ship and all their destinies.

He knew Lieutenant Wynter and a master's mate were trying to catch the captain's eye; the list of questions and demands seemed endless.

He said, 'He knew your name, sir.'

Adam looked at him sharply.

'Because of my uncle, no doubt.'

'Because of your father, sir.'

Adam returned to the rail and pressed both palms upon it, feeling the ship's life pulsating through the warm woodwork. Shivering, every stay and shroud, halliard and brace, extensions of himself. Like hearing his first sailing master in *Hyperion*, so many years ago. *An equal strain on all parts and you can't do better.*

And now it was back. Was there no escape? No answers to all those unspoken questions?

Midshipman Bellairs called, 'Signal from *Tetrarch*, sir! *Ready to proceed!*'

He stared across the water, purple now with shadow, and saw

123

the other ship angled across the dying sunlight, pale patches of new canvas marking the extent of Galbraith's efforts.

'Thank you, Mr Bellairs. Acknowledge.' He looked at the portly surgeon without seeing him. 'Make to Mr Galbraith, *With fair winds. Good luck.*' Then, aware of the lengthening shadows, 'Roundly does it!'

O'Beirne was surprised, that this youthful man should take the time to send a personal message when he had so many urgent matters demanding his attention, and more so that he himself could be moved by it.

Adam was very conscious of the scrutiny, and moved away from it to the rail again and stood watching the greasy smoke rising from the galley funnel. The working parties were fewer, and some of the old hands were loitering, looking on as *Tetrarch* tested her jury-rig for the first time.

Men had died this day, and others lay in fear of living. But there was a smell of pitch and tar in the air, spunyarn and paint, *Unrivalled* shaking off the barbs of war, and her first sea fight.

'I shall get the ship under way.' He saw the surgeon turn, and knew he thought his visit had been in vain. 'After that, I shall come below and see the prisoner, if that is what you desire.'

Calls shrilled and men ran once more to halliards and braces: the sailors' way, exhausted one minute, all energy the next.

O'Beirne lowered himself carefully down the steep ladder, his mind lingering on the captain's last remark.

Half aloud, he said, 'What *you* need, more like, if I'm any judge.'

But it was lost in the hiss and boom of canvas as *Unrivalled* once again responded to those who served her.

They faced one another, the moment intensified by the stillness of O'Beirne's sickbay below the waterline. Adam Bolitho seated himself in the surgeon's big leather chair, which seemed to dominate this private place like a throne.

He looked at the other man, who was propped in a kind of trestle, one of O'Beirne's own inventions. It helped to ease the breathing, and lessened the risk of the lung filling with blood.

Two captains. He could not think of them as victor and vanquished. *We are only two men.*

Lovatt was not what he had expected. A strong but sensitive face, with hair as fair as Valentine Keen's. The hands, too, were well shaped, one clenching and unclenching against the throbbing pain of his wound, the other resting as if untroubled against the curved timbers of the hull.

Lovatt spoke first.

'A fine ship, Captain. You must be proud to have her.' He gazed at the nearest frame. 'Grown, not cut by saw. Natural strength, rare enough in these hard times.'

Adam nodded. It was indeed rare, with most of the oak forests hacked down over the years to supply the demands of the fleet.

He thought of Galbraith's hastily written message, and said, 'What did you hope to achieve?'

Lovatt almost shrugged. 'I obey orders. Like you, Captain. Like all of us.' The fist opened and closed again as if he had no control over it. 'You will know that I was expecting to be met, to be escorted the remainder of the passage to Algiers.'

Adam said quietly, '*La Fortune* was taken. She is a prize, like *Tetrarch*.' Half his mind was still with the scene he had left on deck. A lively breeze, a steadier motion with the wind almost across the taffrail. A soldier's wind, the old hands called it. It would help Galbraith's jury-rig, and it allowed *Unrivalled* to hold up to windward in case they required assistance.

He glanced around O'Beirne's domain, at the piles of well-thumbed books, the cupboards, and racks of bottles and jars clinking occasionally with the vibration of the rudder-head.

The smell here was different too. Potions and powders, rum and pain. Adam hated the world of medicine and what it could do to a man, even the bravest, under knife and saw. The price of victory. He looked at his companion again. And defeat.

'You asked to see me?' He curbed his impatience. His was the need.

Lovatt regarded him with calm eyes.

'My father fought alongside yours in the struggle for independence. They knew one another, although I did not know about you, the son.'

Adam wanted to leave, but something compelled him to remain. 'But you were a King's officer.'

'When I am handed over to the right authority I shall be

125

condemned as one. No matter – my son is all I have now. He will forget.'

Adam heard boots scrape outside the door. A marine sentry. O'Beirne was taking no chances. *On either of us.*

Lovatt was saying, 'I left America and returned to England, to Canterbury, where I was born. I had an uncle who sponsored my entry as midshipman. The rest is past history.'

'Tell me about *Tetrarch*.'

'I was third lieutenant in her . . . a long time ago. She was a fourth-rate then, but past her best. There was bad feeling 'twixt the captain and the senior lieutenant, and the people suffered because of it. When I spoke up on their behalf I discovered I had stepped into a trap. Because of my father, an Englishman *on the wrong side*, I was left in no doubt as to how my future would be destroyed. Even the second lieutenant, whom I had thought a friend, saw me as a threat to his own advancement.' He gave a sad smile. 'Not unknown to you perhaps, sir?'

Midshipman Fielding peered around the door. 'Mr Wynter's respects, sir, and he wishes to take in another reef.' His eyes were fixed on Lovatt.

'I shall come up.' Adam turned back, and saw something like desperation in the hazel eyes.

'There was no mutiny. They simply refused to stand to their guns. I agreed to remain aboard until their case had been put to the French.' The eyes were distant now. 'Most of them were exchanged, I believe. I was branded a traitor. But an American privateer came into Brest . . . Until then I had been a trusted prisoner of the French navy. On parole, *on my honour.*' It seemed to amuse him. 'And I had met a girl there. Paul is our son.'

Adam stood, his hair brushing the deckhead. 'And now you are a prisoner again. Did you think your mention of my father could buy you privilege? If so, then you do not know me.' It was time to go. *Now.*

Lovatt sank back against the trestle. 'I knew your name, what it has come to mean to sailors of all flags. My wife is dead. There is only Paul. I was planning to obtain passage to England. Instead, I was given command of *Tetrarch*.' He shook his head. 'That damned, wretched ship. I should have forced you to fire on us. Finished it!'

126

The deck moved slightly. They would all be up there waiting for him. The chain of command.

Adam stopped, his hand on the door. 'Canterbury? You have people there still?'

Lovatt nodded. The effort of conversation was taking its toll. 'Good friends. They will care for Paul.' He looked away, and Adam saw the despair in his clenched fist. 'But he will come to hate me, I think.'

'He is still your son.'

Again the faint smile. 'Be content, Captain. *You* have your ship.'

O'Beirne filled the doorway, his eyes everywhere.

Adam said, 'I have finished here.' He regarded Lovatt coldly. *The enemy*, no matter which flag he served or for what reason.

But he said, 'I shall do what I can.'

O'Beirne opened a cupboard and took out a bottle of brandy, which he had been saving for some special occasion although he had not known what. He recalled the even, Cornish voice as the captain had spoken a simple prayer before the corpses were put over the side. Most of the dead were unknown. Protestant, Catholic, pagan or Jew, it made no difference to them now.

He found two glasses and held them up to the light of the gently spiralling lantern to see if they were clean, and noticed the dried blood, like paint, on his cuff.

Lovatt cleared his throat, and said, 'I believe he meant it.'

O'Beirne pushed a glass towards him. 'Here – kill or cure. Then you must rest.'

He lingered over the glass. Some special occasion . . . He saw the brandy tilting with the rhythm of the sea, and imagined Captain Bolitho with his men, watching the stars, holding station on this man's ship.

He said, 'Of course he meant it.' But Lovatt had fallen into an exhausted sleep.

From somewhere aft he heard the sound of a fiddle, probably in the junior warrant officers' mess. Badly played, and out of tune.

To Denis O'Beirne, ship's surgeon, it was the most beautiful sound he had heard for a long time.

*   *   *

127

Vice-Admiral Sir Graham Bethune walked across the tiled floor and stood by one of the tall windows, careful to remain in the shadows, but feeling the heat of the noon sun like something physical. He shaded his eyes to stare at the anchored ships, his ships, knowing what made each distinct from the others, just as he now knew the faces and characters of each of his captains, from his bluff flag captain Forbes in *Montrose*, out there now with her awnings and windsails shimmering in the harsh glare, to the young but experienced Christie in the smaller twenty-eight gun *Halcyon*. It was something he could now accept, as he had come to accept the responsibility of his rank, one of the youngest flag officers on the Navy List.

The sense of loss was still there, as strong as ever, and if anything he felt even more impatient, conscious of a certain disappointment which was new to him.

Whenever he was at sea in *Montrose* he felt this same restlessness. He had confided to Sir Richard Bolitho more than once his discomfort at commanding, but not being in command, of his own flagship. Each change of watch or unexpected trill of a bosun's call, any sound or movement would find him alert, ready to go on deck and deal with every kind of incident. To leave it to others, to wait for the respectful knock on the screen door, had been almost unbearable.

Bethune had grasped at the chance of a seagoing appointment, having imagined that the corridors of the Admiralty were not for him.

He had been wrong, but it was hard to come to terms with it.

He watched the small boats pulling around the captured French frigate, *La Fortune*. A prize indeed. It had been a risk, and he had seen Adam Bolitho's face clearly in his mind as he had read the report. But a risk skilfully undertaken. If their lordships required any further proof that the Dey of Algiers was intent on even more dangerous escapades, this was it.

He recalled Bouverie's description of the cutting-out expedition. It was wrong to take sides, and Bethune had always despised senior officers who did so, but Bouverie had given the impression that the capture of the frigate had been entirely his own idea.

He turned his back on the grand harbour and its crumbling

backdrop of ancient fortifications, and waited for his eyes to become accustomed to the dimness of this room which was a part of his official headquarters. Once owned by a wealthy merchant, it was almost palatial. There was even a fountain in the small courtyard, and a balcony. In this house was the room where Catherine Somervell had made her final visit to her beloved Richard.

Bethune had ordered that it be kept locked, and could guess what his staff thought about it. He had visited the room only once. So still, so quiet, and yet when he had thrown open the shutters the din and turmoil of Malta seemed to swamp the place. It was uncanny.

There was a bell on a table. He had only to ring it and a servant would appear. Wine, perhaps? Or something stronger? He almost smiled. That was not like him, either; he had seen the results of over-indulgence only too often at the Admiralty.

He walked to another window. When he thought of his wife in England, and of their two young children, he could feel only guilt. Because he had been glad to leave, or because he had not trusted his own feelings for Richard Bolitho's mistress? It seemed absurd out here. He turned as someone tapped on the door.

Or was it?

It was his flag lieutenant, Charles Onslow. Young, eager, attentive. And dull, so dull. He was a distant cousin, and the appointment had been a favour to his wife.

Onslow stood just inside the door, his hat beneath his arm, his youthful features set in a half-smile.

'I am sorry to interrupt you, Sir Graham.' He usually prefaced any remark to Bethune with an apology, not like the Onslow he had heard barking at his subordinates. Favour or not, he would be rid of him.

'I welcome it!' Bethune stared at the heavy dress coat which was hanging carelessly on the back of a chair. So many officers envied him, and looked to him in hope of their own advancement.

I do not belong here.

'What is it?'

'A report from the lookout, Sir Graham. *Unrivalled* has been

129

sighted. She will enter harbour in late afternoon if the wind prevails.'

Bethune dragged his thoughts into the present. *Unrivalled* had quit her station. Adam must have had good reason. If not . . .

Onslow added helpfully, 'She has a ship in company. A prize.'

Another from Algiers, perhaps, although it seemed unlikely. He was reminded of Richard Bolitho's insistence that, unpopular though it might be with some senior officers, the bare bones of the written Fighting Instructions were no substitute for a captain's initiative.

Always provided that the end justified the methods.

'You may signal *Unrivalled* when she enters harbour, *Captain repair here when convenient.*'

Onslow frowned; perhaps he thought it too leisurely. Slack.

He was turning in the doorway. 'I all but forgot, Sir Graham.' He dropped his eyes. 'A lieutenant named Avery desires an audience with you.'

Bethune plucked his shirt from his ribs. 'How long has he been waiting?'

'The secretary brought word an hour back. I was dealing with signals at the time. It was an unusual request, I thought.'

He was enjoying it. He, more than any, would know that Avery had been flag lieutenant to Sir Richard Bolitho. He would also know that Avery had volunteered to remain at Malta to offer his assistance and the experience he had gained when he had visited the lion's den, Algiers.

'Ask him to come up. I shall apologise to him myself.'

It was almost worth it to see the rebuke go home like the sounding-shot before a broadside.

He made to pick up his heavy coat but decided against it.

He heard Avery in the corridor; he had come to recognise the uneven, dragging step.

Avery paused and gazed almost uncertainly around the room, like so many sea officers out of place on dry land. He would have to get used to it, Bethune thought.

He offered his hand, smiling.

'I regret the delay. It was unnecessary.' He gestured to

130

the envelope on the table. 'Your orders. You are free to leave Malta, and take passage in the next available vessel. Go home. You háve done more than enough here.' He saw the tawny eyes come finally into focus, as if Avery's mind had been elsewhere.

'Thank you, Sir Graham. I was ready to leave.' The eyes searched him. 'I came to see you because . . .' He hesitated.

Bethune tensed, anticipating it. Avery would know this place. The room. Where there was now only silence.

Avery said, almost abruptly, 'I heard that *Unrivalled* has been sighted. With a prize.'

Bethune did not question how he knew, although he himself had only just been told. It was something beyond explanation: the way of sailors, he had heard an old admiral call it.

He said, 'Forgive me. I spoke of home. It was thoughtless.'

Avery regarded him without emotion, vaguely surprised that he should remember, let alone care. He had no home. He had lived at Falmouth. As Allday had put it often enough, 'like one of the family'. Now there was no family.

He shrugged. 'I might be needed here. I have a presentiment about this prize, something Captain Bolitho and I discussed. He is a shrewd man – his uncle would be proud of him.'

Bethune said gently, 'And of you, I think.' He swung round as another tap came from the door. *'Come!'*

It was Onslow again, his eyes moving quickly from the envelope on the table to his admiral's dishevelled appearance, coatless in the presence of a junior officer. He avoided looking at Avery completely.

'I beg your pardon, Sir Graham. Another report from the lookout. The schooner *Gertrude* has been sighted.'

Bethune spread his hands. 'We are busy, it seems!' Then he turned on his flag lieutenant, his mind suddenly clear. *'Gertrude*? She is not due for several days, surely, wind or no wind. Send a messenger to the lookout immediately.'

Onslow added unhappily, 'And Captain Bouverie of *Matchless* is here, Sir Graham.'

Avery said, 'I shall leave, sir.'

Bethune held out his hand.

'Sup with me tonight. Here.' He knew Avery disliked Bouverie, mainly, he suspected, because he had brought him back to Malta with the French frigate, when Avery would have preferred Adam's company. The same bond which held them all together. He allowed himself to explore the thought. *And Catherine, who has touched us all.*

Avery smiled. 'I would relish that, sir.' And meant it.

Bethune watched him leave, and heard the uneven step retreating. There were many things to deal with: *Unrivalled*'s unexpected return, and the early arrival of the courier schooner *Gertrude*. Despatches. Letters from England, orders for the ships and men under his command. It could all wait. He would ask Adam to join them, and, out of courtesy, his flag captain as well. Show no favouritism . . .

There would be others here tonight. He looked across at the empty balcony and the sealed shutters. Invisible, perhaps, but they would be very close.

He realised that Onslow was still there.

'I will see Captain Bouverie now. After that, I shall discuss the wine for this evening.' He pulled on the heavy coat with its bright epaulettes and silver stars. It seemed to make a difference to everyone else around him, but he was the same man underneath.

Poor Onslow; it was not entirely his fault. He caught him at the half-open door.

'You are invited too, of course.'

For once, Onslow was unable to control his pleasure. Bethune hoped he would not regret the impulse.

He thought of Avery, wanting to leave this place, but afraid of the life he might find waiting for him.

He smiled to himself and faced the door, ready to perform.

Catherine had visited him once at the Admiralty, privately, if not actually in secret. She had removed her glove so that he could kiss her hand. The knowledge hit him like a fist. Adam, George Avery, and one of the youngest flag officers on the Navy List . . . they were all in love with her.

The night was warm, but a soft breeze from the sea had driven away the day's clinging humidity.

Three officers stood side by side at an open window, watching the lights, boats bobbing like fireflies on the dark water. There were a few pale stars, and from the narrow streets they could hear singing and cheering. Earlier there had been a raucous ringing of bells, until some drunken sailors had been chased out of the church.

Captain Forbes had made his excuses and had remained in his ship, the captured *Tetrarch* needing his full attention. She looked larger in harbour against the sloops and brigs, and her valuable cargo of powder, shot and supplies, to say nothing of the vessel herself, would fetch a substantial reward in the prize court.

But even that seemed secondary, especially in this cool room with its banks of flickering candles.

It had been a boisterous meal, interspersed with countless toasts and good wishes for absent friends. Lieutenant Onslow had been fast asleep for most of it, and even the servants had been surprised by the amount of wine he had swallowed before sliding on to the floor.

The little schooner *Gertrude* had carried overwhelming news: the British and allied armies under the Duke of Wellington had met and fought Napoleon at a place called Waterloo. When *Gertrude* had weighed anchor to carry her despatches around the fleet there had been little more information than that, except that there had been horrific casualties in a battle fought in mud and thunderstorms, and victory had more than once hung in the balance. But it had been reported that the French army was in retreat. To Paris perhaps, although even as they waited there might still be a reverse in fortune.

But out there in the harbour aboard ships of every size and type men were cheering, men who had known nothing but war and sacrifice. Bethune remembered that day in London when the news of Napoleon's defeat had been brought to the Admiralty; he himself had been the one to interrupt the First Lord's conference and announce it. Fourteen months ago, almost to the day. And since then, the chain of events which had freed the tyrant from Elba, and had set his feet once more on the march for Paris . . .

He glanced at Adam's profile, knowing that he was remembering also. When England's hero, their beloved friend, had fallen to the enemy's marksman.

Tomorrow he must draft new orders to his captains and commanders, for no matter how the war was waged ashore the requirements for this squadron, like the whole fleet, were unchanged. To show the flag, to protect, to fight, and if need be, to intimidate, and maintain mastery of the sea which had been won with so much blood.

Adam felt the scrutiny but kept his eyes on the dark harbour, and the place where he knew *Unrivalled* was lying. Thinking of them all . . . Galbraith, quietly proud one moment, openly emotional the next. The imposing surgeon, O'Beirne, forgetting himself and capering in a little jig to the shantyman's fiddle. And the others, faces he had come to know. Faces he had once attempted to hold at a distance.

And the prisoner, Roddie Lovatt, delirious, but reaching out for his son, speaking in both English and French with equal intensity. Adam had seen the boy, and had recalled Lovatt's words to him. If there had been any name for the expression on the face of one so young, it could only be hatred.

A servant had brought yet another tray of filled glasses, one of which he placed carefully with the rest where Onslow still lay snoring loudly.

Bethune called, 'To our special friends! They will live forever!'

Adam felt the locket in his pocket, and shared the moment. And the guilt.

The three glasses clinked together and a voice said, 'To Catherine!'

Across the darkened courtyard Bethune thought he heard her laugh.

9

Luckier Than Most

Unis Allday paused and brushed a stray hair from her eyes and listened to some of the customers in the 'long room', as her brother called it, laughing and banging their tankards on the scrubbed tables. The Old Hyperion had been busy today, busier than she could remember for some months.

She scraped the slices of apple into a dish and stared out of the kitchen window. Flowers everywhere, bees tapping against the glass, the sun warm across her bare arms. The news of the great battle 'over there' had been brought to Falmouth by courier brig and had gone through the port and surrounding villages like wildfire, eventually reaching this little inn which nestled on the Helford River at Fallowfield.

It was not a rumour this time, it was far beyond that. The people who worked on the farms and estates in the area could only speak of victory, and no longer *when* or *if*. Men could go about their affairs without fear of being called to the Colours or snatched up by the hated press gangs. The war had levied a heavy toll; there were still very few young men to be seen in the lanes or around the harbours, unless they held the precious Protection. Even then, they could never be certain how some zealous lieutenant, desperate for recruits and fearful of what his captain might say if he returned to his ship empty-handed, might interpret his duty if the chance offered itself. And there were cripples a-plenty to remind anyone who might believe that the war had kept its distance from Cornwall.

She thought of her brother John, who had lost a leg when he had been serving with the Thirty-First regiment of foot.

135

She could not have managed without him, when she had taken this inn and had made it prosper. Then her other John, Allday, had come into her life, and they had been wed here in Fallowfield.

Her brother had said very little since the news of the French collapse had been shouted around the villages, and had seemed to distance himself from the customers. Perhaps he despised the lively banter and the steady sale of cider and ale which kept it close company, remembering now more than ever what the war had cost him, and all those who had stood shoulder to shoulder with him on the right of the line.

Maybe he would get over it, she thought. He was a kindly man, and had been so good with little Kate when she had been born, with John away at sea. She inspected a pot on its hook without seeing it, and then turned to look at the model of the *Hyperion* which John Allday had made for her. The old ship which had changed and directed the lives of so many, hers among them. Her first husband had served in *Hyperion* as a master's mate and had been killed in battle. John Allday had been pressed in Falmouth and put aboard a frigate commanded by Captain Richard Bolitho; *Hyperion* had later become their ship. She would always think of them together, although she knew little of men-of-war, except those which came and left on the tide. It had seemed only right that this inn should now bear *Hyperion*'s name.

John Allday was not very good at hiding things from her, neither his love for her and their child, nor his grief.

People who did not understand always wanted to know, were always asking him, despite her warnings, about Sir Richard Bolitho. What he was like, truly like as a man. And always asking about his death.

Allday had tried, and was still trying, to fill every day, as if that was the only way he could come to terms with it. As his best friend Bryan Ferguson had confided, 'Like the old dog losing his master. No point any more.'

And Unis knew that the old wound was troubling him, although if she had asked him he would have denied it. Ferguson had said that he should have quit the sea long ago, even as he had known, better than anyone, that John

136

Allday would never leave the side of his admiral, his friend, while they were both still needed.

Unis saw the pain in his face more frequently now, as he made himself useful about the inn, especially when he was lifting barrels of ale on to their trestles. She would get some of the other men to do it in future, if she could manage it without Allday finding out.

She knew that he went occasionally across to Falmouth, and this was something she could not share, nor attempt to. The ships, the sailors, and the memories. Missing being a part of it, not wanting to become just another old Jack, 'swinging the lamp', as he put it.

Unis often thought of the ones who had become close to her. George Avery, who had stayed here several times, and who wrote her husband's letters at sea for him, and read hers to him. John had told her that Avery never received any letters himself, and it had saddened her in some way.

And Catherine, who had called here when she had needed *to be with friends*. Unis had never forgotten that, nor would she.

Nothing was the same, even at the big grey house below Pendennis Castle. Ferguson had said little about it, but she knew he was deeply concerned. Lawyers had been to the house from London, pursuing the matter of a settlement, he had said. The estate had been left to Captain Adam Bolitho; it had been signed and sealed. But there were complications. Sir Richard's widow and his daughter Elizabeth had to be considered. No matter what Sir Richard had wanted, nor what Catherine had meant to him.

Where would she go now? What would she do? Bryan Ferguson would not be drawn on the possibilities. He was worried about his own future; he and his wife had lived and worked at the estate for many years. How could lawyers from London know anything about such things as trust and loyalty?

She thought, too, of the memorial service at Falmouth. She had heard of the grander services at Plymouth and in the City of London, but she doubted they could match the united bond of pride and love, as well as sorrow, that day in the crowded church.

Her brother walked into the kitchen, his wooden leg thumping heavily on the flagstones.

137

He reached for his long clay pipe. 'Just spoke with Bob, the farrier's son.' He took a taper from the mantel and held it to the flames, careful not to look at her. 'There's a frigate in Carrick Roads. Came in this morning.' He saw her fingers bunch into her apron, and added, 'Don't fret, lass, none of her people will come this far out.'

She looked at the old clock. 'He'll be down there, then. Watching.'

He studied the smoke from his pipe, almost motionless in the warm air. Like that day when he had been struck down. All in a line, like toy soldiers. The smoke had lingered there too. For days. While men had called out, and had eventually died.

'He's got you, and young Kate. He's lucky. Luckier than most.'

She put her arms round him. 'And we've got *you*, thank God!'

Someone banged his tankard on a table and she dabbed her face with her apron.

'There now, no rest for the wicked!'

Her brother watched her bustle out of the kitchen, and heard her call out to somebody by name.

Hold fast there, John. He did not know if he had spoken aloud, or to whom he had been speaking, himself, or the sailor home from the sea.

He heard a gust of laughter and was suddenly proud of his neat little sister, and even perhaps ashamed that he had given way to his bitter memories. It had not always been so. He squared his shoulders and tapped out his pipe in the palm of his hand, carefully, so as not to break it. Then he strode in to the adjoining room and picked up an empty tankard. Like the old Thirty-First. *Stand together, and face your front.*

He was back.

Catherine Somervell gripped a tasselled handle and leaned forward as the carriage with its matching greys turned into the imposing gateway. The sky over the Thames was clear, but after several days of thunderstorms and heavy rain nothing seemed certain.

She was alone, and had left her companion Mèlwyn to pay the men who were repairing the front door of her Chelsea house. Sillitoe had sent his carriage to collect her, and she had seen several people in the Walk turn to watch, some to smile and wave.

It was still hard to accept. To come to terms with. To understand.

Some had left flowers for her; one had even placed an expensive arrangement of roses on her doorstep with the simple message, *For the Admiral's Lady. With admiration and love.*

And by contrast, last night, probably during the thunderstorm, someone had scratched the word *whore* on the same door. Melwyn had been outraged, the affront sitting strangely on one so young. Because she felt a part of it.

She watched the horses' ears twitching as the carriage rolled to a halt. She could see the Thames again. The same river, but a world apart.

As speculation about the war had hardened into fact, she had wondered how the news would affect Adam. She had written to him, but she knew from bitter experience that letters took their time reaching the King's ships.

Once, when she had been passing the Admiralty, she had realised how complete her isolation from Richard's world had become. She knew no one in those busy corridors, or even 'by way of the back stairs', as he had called it. Bethune was in the Mediterranean, in Richard's old command, and Valentine Keen was in Plymouth. She thought of Graham Bethune's concern for her, and his furious estrangement from his wife. He was an attractive man, and good company. It was probably for the best that he was so far away.

A boy in a leather apron had opened the door and was lowering the step. He, at least, should be spared the suffering and the separation of war.

She climbed down and looked up at the coachman.

'Thank you, William. That was most comfortable.' She sensed his surprise, that she had remembered his name, or because she had spoken at all. She saw his eyes move to her breast and the diamond pendant there, and just as swiftly move away. Like the men painting the front door. She had seen their expressions. Their curiosity.

Then she thought of the blind lieutenant and the crippled

sailors at the cathedral. It made the others seem lower than the dust.

A servant opened the doors for her, a man she did not know. He gave a quick bow.

'If you will wait in the library, m' lady. Lord Sillitoe will join you presently.'

She walked into the room and saw the chair where she had sat, waiting for Sillitoe on the day of the memorial service. Only two weeks ago. A lifetime.

And now she was here again. Sillitoe had taken it upon himself to deal with the legal complications; she had seen another carriage in the drive, and somehow knew it was that of the City lawyer, Sir Wilfred Lafargue. Sillitoe seemed to know everyone of consequence, friend or enemy. Like the private article someone had shown her in the *Times* newssheet, a very personal appraisal, a dedication to the one man she had loved.

Sir Richard practised total war, and inspired others to seek a total victory. To the Navy, his will remain an abiding influence. We shall never forget him, nor the woman he loved to the end.

Her name had not been mentioned. There was no need.

Sillitoe had said nothing about it. There had been no need for that, either.

The door opened and he strode into the room, his quick, keen glance taking in the dark green gown, the wide-brimmed straw hat with its matching ribbon. Perhaps surprised to see her out of mourning; the hooded eyes gave little away, but she recognised approval in them.

He kissed her hand, and half-turned as horses clattered across the drive.

'Lafargue can make even a single word into an overture.' He waited for her to sit and arrange her gown. 'But I think the way has become clear.'

She felt the eyes upon her, the power of the man. An intensity which so many had found cause to fear.

She had only once seen him off guard, that day at the cathedral, when he had pushed through the silent crowd to be at her side. As if he believed he had failed her in some way, something which he was unable to conceal.

And other times. When he had arranged passage for her to Malta . . . *For that last time.* She clenched her fist around her

140

parasol. She must not think of it. She had often found him watching her, like this moment, in this great, silent house overlooking the Thames. Perhaps remembering yet again the night he had burst into her room, and had held her, shielded her, as his men had dragged away the madman who had attempted to rape her.

He had made no secret of his feelings for her. Once, in this house, he had even mentioned marriage. But after that terrible night, how did he really regard her?

She thought of the lightning over the river last night, probably while the unknown pervert had been scratching his poison on the door. It had all come back to her. Melwyn had felt it too, and had climbed into bed with her, holding her hand, a child again, until the storm had abated.

Sillitoe said, 'Lady Bolitho will have the right to visit Falmouth. A lawyer acceptable to Lafargue,' he almost smiled, 'and, of course, to me, will be present. Certain items . . .' He broke off, suddenly tired of evasion. 'It would not be advisable for you to be present. Captain Bolitho is the accepted heir, but in his absence we may have to make allowances.'

She said quietly, 'I had no intention of returning to Falmouth.' She raised her chin and regarded him steadily. 'There would be some who would say that the mare was hasty to change saddles!'

Sillitoe nodded. 'Bravely spoken.'

'Time will pass. I shall become a stranger there.'

'Adam will ask you to visit or take up residence, whichever you choose. When he eventually returns.'

She was on her feet without knowing that she had left the chair. She looked down at the river: people working on barges, a man walking his dog. Ordinary things. She bit her lip. Beyond her reach.

She said, 'I think that might be dangerous.'

She did not explain. She did not need to.

And she spoke the truth. What would she do there? Watch the ships, listen to the sailors, torture herself with memories they had shared with no one?

Sillitoe waited, watched her turn, framed against the sun-dappled window, her throat and shoulders as brown as any country lass working in the fields, the pendant glittering

141

between her breasts. The one woman he truly wanted; he had never considered it as a need before. And the only one he could never have.

He said abruptly, 'I have to leave London. Tomorrow or the next day.' He saw her hand close into a fist again. What was troubling her? 'To Deptford. I was going to suggest that you stay here. You would be well taken care of, and I would feel safer.'

She looked at the river once more. 'That would do your reputation injury, surely?'

'It is of no consequence.' He was standing beside her, like that day at St Paul's. 'After this *duty* I shall be spending more time in the pursuit of my own affairs, unless . . .'

She turned towards him, unnerved by the realisation that this was the true reason for asking her here. 'Unless?'

'The Prince Regent seems to feel that my work as Inspector-General has run its course.' He shrugged. 'He is probably right.'

She could feel the beat of her heart, like a hammer, and said again, 'Unless what?'

'I think you know, Catherine.'

'Because of me. What they will say. How it would look. They would pillory you, just as they tried to destroy Richard.' She repeated, 'Because of me.'

'And do you think I care what people say about me? What they have always been careful to conceal to my face? Power is like a fine blade – you must always use it with care, and for the right purpose!'

A bell was ringing somewhere, another visitor. But she could not move.

It had been wrong, stupid, to allow herself to become dependent on this hard, remote man. And yet she had known it was there. As at St Paul's, when he had risked the stares and the condemnation.

She said softly, 'You should have married someone suitable.'

He smiled. 'I did. Or I thought she suited. But she went with another. Greener pastures, I believe it is called.'

He said it without anger or emotion, as though it were something forgotten. Or was that, too, another form of defence?

There were voices now, probably the secretary Marlow or one of his burly servants.

He put his hand on her arm and held it, and she watched, detached, as if she were watching someone else.

She said, 'Would you have me as your mistress, my lord?'

She lifted her eyes and looked at him. Angry, wanting to hurt this unreachable man.

He took her other arm and turned her towards him, holding her only inches away.

'As I said before, Catherine. As my wife. I can give you the security you need and deserve. I loved you at a distance, and sometimes I fought against it. So now it is said.'

She did not resist as he pulled her against him, did not even flinch when he touched her hair and her skin. A voice was screaming, *what is the matter with you*? But all she could see was the damaged door. *Whore.*

She whispered, 'No. Please don't.'

He held her away and studied her face, feature by feature.

'Come with me on this last duty, Catherine. Then I will know.' He tried to smile. 'And so will the Prince Regent!'

Again it came to her. When she had met Richard at Antigua, so long ago, it seemed, she had told him that he needed love, *as the desert craves for rain.* She had been describing herself.

She thought of all the rare, precious times they had spent together. As one. And the endless waiting in between. And the finality.

Don't leave me.

But there was no reply.

John Allday rested against the iron railings at the top of the jetty, so well-worn throughout the years that they were quite smooth, and stared across the crowded anchorage. One of the local carriers had given him a ride into Falmouth; he would doubtless be calling at the inn later on for some free ale.

Allday was glad he had come. It was something he could not explain to Unis, to anybody. It was probably bad for him, holding on to the past. Was it that . . . ?

She was a frigate of some thirty-eight guns, although he had noticed that some of her ports were empty, as if her main armament had been cut down for some reason. She was named

143

Kestrel, and even without a glass he had seen her figurehead, the spread wings and curved beak. As if it were alive. He did not know the ship, and that troubled him. Before long, there would be many more ships coming and leaving which were strangers to him, in name and reputation. No reminders.

He studied the frigate with a critical eye. A fine-looking vessel, freshly painted, and her furled or brailed-up canvas all new from the sailmakers. There were few local craft around her, so she was not in Falmouth to take on stores. He had heard someone say that *Kestrel* was already armed and provisioned, in readiness for a long voyage. Not Biscay or the Mediterranean this time; somewhere far away, perhaps. There were scarlet uniforms at the gangways and forecastle; her captain was taking no chances on last-minute desertions. A change of heart caused by the news of more advances across the Channel, the end finally in sight.

But the navy would still be needed. And there would always be deserters.

He heard some old sailors discussing the ship, their voices loud, as if they wanted to be noticed. In a moment they would try to draw him into it.

He moved a few paces along the jetty, and looked down at the water lapping over the stone stairs which had seen so many thousands arrive and depart. It was as if his life had begun here, when he had been taken aboard Bolitho's frigate *Phalarope*. With Bryan Ferguson, and some others who had not been quick enough to avoid a landing party. An unlikely way to begin something so strong. It was not as if he had been a green recruit; he had served in the fleet before. He frowned and glanced down at his good blue coat with the buttons which Bolitho had had made for him. The Bolitho crest, for an admiral's coxswain. He sighed. *And friend.*

Unis was doing all she could to make his life comfortable. She gave him encouragement, and she gave him love. And there was little Kate. He recalled how pleased Lady Catherine had been when she had heard their decision to name her Kate. The same name Sir Richard used for her.

And now she was gone from the old grey house. It seemed so empty without her; even his best friend Bryan had said as much. He went there when he could, if only to share a wet with him, or to yarn about old times.

There was talk that Sir Richard's widow might return. No one seemed to know anything for certain. Lawyers and snotty clerks, what did they understand about this place and its people? Even the smell of it. Paint and tar, fishing nets hung to dry in the June sunshine, and the sounds. Winches and hammers, local dealers haggling with some of the fishing skippers who had come into the harbour earlier than usual. And always the sea.

He touched his chest, but the pain hesitated, like a warning at the door. Fallowfield was quiet, and usually peaceful. He knew that Unis got worried when sailors came so far out to the Old Hyperion. He had seen her watching, caring.

'Oars!'

The order rang out sharply, but a little too shrill for the occasion. Allday turned as a jolly-boat thrust around the jetty, the bowman scrambling to his feet to seize a boathook. There was a smart-looking midshipman by the tiller, his hat tilted against the sunlight.

'Up!'

The oars rose as one, like white bones, while the midshipman brought the hull against the wooden piles with barely a shudder.

Allday nodded. Rakishly done. So far. You never knew with the young gentlemen, ready to listen and learn one minute, tyrants the next.

One of the old sailors on the jetty cackled, 'Look at *'im*! Proper little 'ero, eh, lads?'

Allday frowned. The speaker would not be saying that if he was back in the *perfect* navy he was usually describing in one of the local taverns.

The midshipman was clattering up the stone steps, a shining new dirk pressed against his side. Allday made to move aside, but the boy, and he was little more than that, blocked his way.

'Mister Allday, sir?' He was gazing at him anxiously, while the boat's crew looked on with interest.

Very new and very young. Calling him 'mister' and 'sir'. He would have to learn quickly, otherwise . . . It hit him like

145

the pain in his chest. His was a different world now. He did not belong any more.

'That's me.' The midshipman reminded him of someone . . . A face formed in his mind. Midshipman Neale of the *Phalarope*, who had eventually become captain of a frigate himself. Neale had died after being taken prisoner of war. With Richard Bolitho. He felt it again. *And me.*

The midshipman breathed out with relief. 'My captain saw you, sir.' It was as if he were afraid to turn towards the anchored ship, in case he was being watched.

'He sends his respects, sir.'

Allday shook his head, and corrected roughly, 'Compliments!'

The midshipman was equally firm. '*Respects*, sir. And would you come aboard, if you have the time?'

Allday touched his arm. 'Lead on.' It was worth it just to see the idlers on the jetty staring down at them. The loud-mouthed one could put that in his pipe and smoke it!

He threw his leg over the gunwale and said, 'So long as I'm not being pressed!'

Some of the oarsmen grinned. *Because they think I'm too bloody old.*

'Bear off forrard! Out oars! Give way together!'

Then the midshipman turned to stare at him, and said, 'Never fear, sir, they'll be up to your standard soon!' And he was proud of it.

Allday looked around, avoiding the eyes as the seamen lay back on their looms, unable to accept it. The midshipman knew who he was. *Knew him.*

Eventually he managed to ask, 'And who is your captain?'

The boy looked surprised, and almost misjudged the tug of the tiller-bar.

'Why, Captain Tyacke, sir! Sir Richard Bolitho's flag captain!'

Allday looked up at the fierce kestrel with its spread wings, at a seaman using a marlin spike but pausing in the middle of a splice to peer down at him. Captain James Tyacke. A face from yesterday. Or half a face, with that terrible disfigurement, his legacy from the Nile.

And the midshipman stood and removed his hat as the boat hooked on to the main chains, and Allday climbed up the

146

'stairs' to the entry port. His mind was too crowded to record that he did it with ease and without pain.

It was like one of those things you think about, in a dream or a part-remembered story from someone else. A lieutenant greeted him, older than most for his rank, so probably from the lower deck. *Come up the hard way.* He had heard Tyacke speak of others like that. From him, with his qualities of seamanship and professional skill, there was no higher praise.

Beneath the quarterdeck, his mind trying to take in everything. Neat stands of pikes, and smartly flaked lines. The smell of fresh paint and new cordage. Just months since he had seen Bolitho fall, had caught and held him to the last. Tyacke had been there, too, but because of the close action he had been prevented from leaving his men. He nodded to himself, as if someone had spoken. *Yesterday.*

A Royal Marine sentry drew his boots together as the lieutenant tapped on the screen door. She could have been any ship . . . He almost expected Ozzard to open the door.

But it was Captain Tyacke. He shook his hand, waved aside all formality and guided him into the great cabin. Through the broad, sloping stern windows Allday was aware of Carrick Roads, stationary masts and moving patches of sails. But, in truth, he saw none of it.

Tyacke seated him by a table, and said, 'I called at Falmouth in the hope that I might see Lady Somervell. But when I sent word to the house I was told that she is in London.' He looked at the skylight, and made no attempt, as he had used to do, to turn aside to hide the hideous scars.

Allday said, 'She would have wanted to see you, sir.'

Tyacke held up his hand. 'No rank here. I shall write to her. I am under orders for the West African station. But when I saw you through the glass just now, I had to speak with you. Chance, like happiness, does not come so easily.'

Allday said, awkwardly, 'But we thought . . .' He tried again. 'My wife Unis was certain that you were to be married, if and when *Frobisher* was paid off. I thought you might spend some time ashore.' He tried to grin. 'You've earned it more 'n most!'

Tyacke glanced at the adjoining sleeping cabin, glad that his

147

big sea chest had at last been taken below. His companion for so many years. Thousands and thousands of miles logged, icy gales and blistering heat. Guns and death. The chest had been standing near the door of Marion's house, waiting for men to come and take it to his new command. This ship.

He said, 'I always thought I'd like to return to Africa. Their lordships were good to me, and granted my request.' He looked up at the skylight again; maybe he could see the mainmast truck from there. No admiral's flag any more. A private ship. His own.

Allday heard someone bringing glasses. He thought of Unis, how lucky he was to have her.

Tyacke was speaking again, with no discernible emotion in his voice.

'It would not have worked, you see. The two children . . .' He touched his scarred face, reliving it. 'I can understand how they felt about it.'

Allday watched him sadly. *No, you don't.*

Tyacke gestured to the unknown servant.

'Nelson's blood, am I right?'

Allday saw the servant give him a quick glance, and was glad he had put on his best coat today. As if he had known.

'It will do me good to get away from all of it. There's nothing for me here. Not any more.' Tyacke took a full goblet. 'It's something we shared, were a part of. Nothing can alter that.' He swallowed some of his drink, his blue eyes very clear.

Then he said, after a silence, 'He gave me back my *pride*, my hope, when I had thought them gone forever. I'll never forget him, and what he gave to me.' He smiled briefly. 'It's all we can do now. Remember.'

He poured another generous measure of the rum and thought of Marion, her face when he had left the neat house, the children hiding in another room. Another man's home, another man's children.

Then he stared around the cabin and knew it was what he wanted. It was the only life he knew, or could expect.

Back to the anti-slavery patrols where he had been serving when he had first met Richard Bolitho. The trade was more extensive and more lucrative than ever despite all the treaties and promises; the slavers would have the pick of the ships as soon as this war was finally ended. Like the ones which had been there that day. When he had seen him fall, and this big, shambling man with the goblet almost lost in one of his hands had held him with a tenderness which few could imagine. Unless they had shared it. Been there. *With us.*

He smiled suddenly. And he never had told Marion about the yellow gown which he had always carried in that old sea chest.

Later in the afternoon they went on deck. There was a hint of mist below Pendennis Castle, but the glass was steady and the wind was fair. *Kestrel* would clear harbour before most good people were awake and about their business.

Allday stood by the entry port, feeling the ship stir slightly beneath his fine shoes. He was surprised that he could accept it, without pain and without pity. He would never lose it, any more than the tall captain with the burned and melted face would forget.

The jolly-boat was already coming alongside, and the same midshipman was at the tiller. For some reason Allday was glad of it.

They faced one another and shook hands, each somehow knowing they would not meet again. As was the way with most sailors.

Tyacke waved to the boat, and asked, 'Where to now, old friend?'

Allday smiled. 'Goin' home, Cap'n.'

Then he walked to the entry port, and paused and touched his forehead to the quarterdeck, and to the great ensign curling lazily from aft. For John Allday, admiral's coxswain, it would never end.

He climbed down into the boat and grinned at the young midshipman. The worst part was behind him.

The midshipman eased over the tiller-bar and said shyly, 'Will you, sir?'

Allday nodded, and waited for the bowman to cast off.

'Bear off forrard! Out oars! Give way *together*!'

It would never end.

10

Captain To Captain

Luke Jago made his way unhurriedly aft, his lean body angled easily to the deck. *Unrivalled* was heading west again, steering close-hauled on the starboard tack under topsails and topgallants, the wind light but enough to hold her steady.

Here on the ship's messdeck the air was heady with rum, and the smell of the midday meal. Unlike a ship of the line, there were no guns on this deck. Each mess was allotted a scrubbed table and bench seats, with hooks overhead where the hammocks would be slung when the ship piped down for the night. In larger vessels the guns were a constant reminder to seamen and marines alike, when they swung themselves into their hammocks, and when they were piped on deck for any emergency. Their reason for being.

Jago glanced at the tables as he passed. Some of the men looked at him and nodded, others avoided his eye. It suited him well enough. He recalled that the captain had said he could use the little store which adjoined the cabin pantry for his meals, but he had declined. He had been surprised by Captain Bolitho's offer, and that he should even care about it.

He half-listened to the loud murmur of voices and the clatter of plates. The forenoon watchkeepers were already tucking into their boiled meat, and what looked like oatmeal. The new cook was far better than his predecessor; at least he was not so mean with his beef and pork. And there was bread, too. The captain had sent a working party to one of the garrisons in Malta: the army always seemed to live well when it was not in the field. And there was butter, while it lasted. When the purser had supervised the issue to all the messes, you would have thought he was parting with his own skin. But they were always like that.

To these men, experienced or raw recruits, such small items, taken for granted by those ashore, were luxuries. When they were exhausted it would be back to iron-hard ship's biscuits, with slush skimmed off the galley coppers to make them edible. He grinned inwardly. A sailor's lot.

He saw the glint of metal and scarlet coats, marine sentries, and, crowded together while the food was ladled out, the prisoners from the ill-fated *Tetrarch*. Jago had seen them eating so voraciously when they had been brought aboard that it seemed they had not been properly fed for years. Now some were even working with the various parts of ship, under supervision of sorts. But Jago thought that no matter what lay ahead for these men, they were somehow glad to be back in the world which had once been their own.

The admiral at Malta, Bethune, had wanted to get rid of them as quickly as possible, the British ones at any rate. Someone else would have to decide their fate. Would anybody bother to investigate the circumstances, he wondered? Mutineers, deserters, or men who had been misled? The end of a rope was the usual solution.

He thought of the captain again. He had given orders that these men were to receive the same rations as the ship's company. Troublemakers would be punished. *Instantly*. He could see Bolitho's face as he had said it. Jago knew that most captains would have kept these men on deck in all weathers, and in irons. As an example. As a warning. And it was cheaper, too.

He paused by one of the tables and studied a finely carved model of a seventy-four. *Unrivalled* had been in commission for only six months, and during that time he had watched this superb carving take on meaning and life.

The seaman raised his head. It was Sullivan, the keen-eyed lookout.

'Almost done, 'Swain.'

Jago rested one hand on his shoulder. He knew the history of the model: she was the *Spartiate*, a two-decker which had been in Nelson's Weather Division at Trafalgar. Sullivan kept to himself, but was a popular man by any standard. Trafalgar: even the word gave him a sort of presence. He had been there, in the greatest naval battle of all time, had cheered with all the others when they had broken through the French line, only to be stunned by the signal that Lord Nelson, 'Our Nel', had fallen.

When Jago had watched the captain he had found himself wondering if he ever compared the death of his uncle, Sir Richard Bolitho, a man who had been as well liked and respected as Nelson, but had been killed in what might have been an accidental engagement. In the end, it was the same for both of them.

He looked over Sullivan's head at the next mess, where the ship's boys were quartered. Signed on by parents who wanted to be rid of them, and others like Napier, who had been appointed the captain's servant, living in the hope of outside sponsorship, and the eventual chance of a commission. He remembered the captain's face when he had told him that the boy John Whitmarsh had been killed. He had intended to sponsor the boy as midshipman, and all the while Whitmarsh had wanted only to remain with him.

There was another boy at the mess table, the one called Paul, son of the *Tetrarch*'s renegade captain. Had he continued the fight and faced one of *Unrivalled*'s broadsides with his holds filled to the deckhead beams with powder . . . at least it would have been a quick death, Jago thought.

Sullivan did not look up, but said, 'What'll they do with 'im?'

Jago shrugged. 'Put him ashore, maybe.' He frowned, angry without knowing why. 'War is no game for children!'

Sullivan chuckled. 'Since when?'

Jago glanced around the partly filled messdeck, the swaying rays of sunlight probing down through the gratings and an open hatchway.

This was his world, where he belonged, where he could catch the *feel* of the ship, something which would be denied him if he accepted the captain's offer.

His eyes fell on the burly seaman named Campbell, who had been sentenced to a flogging for threatening a petty officer. There had been two men brought aft for punishment,

152

but the other had been killed during the opening shots of the engagement, and the captain had ordered that Campbell's punishment should be stood over. He was sitting there now, his face blotchy with sweat from too much rum. Wets from others, for favours done, or perhaps the need to keep on the good side of this seemingly unbreakable troublemaker.

One of the hard men, Campbell had received a checkered shirt at the gangway several times. Jago knew what it was like to be flogged; although the punishment had been carried out unjustly, and despite the intervention of an officer on his behalf, he would carry the scars to the grave. No wonder men deserted. He had nearly run himself, twice, in other ships, and for reasons he could scarcely remember.

What had held him back? He grimaced. Certainly not loyalty or devotion to duty.

Again he recalled the day he had shaken hands with Captain Bolitho after they had driven off the big Yankee. A bargain, something done on the spur of the moment while the blood was still pounding with the wildness of battle. It was something new to him, which he did not understand. And that, too, troubled him.

Campbell looked at him. 'This is an unexpected honour, eh, lads? To 'ave the Cap'n's cox'n amongst the likes of us!'

Jago relaxed. Men like Campbell he could handle.

'Far enough, Campbell. I'll take no lip from you. You've been lucky, so make the best of it.'

Campbell seemed disappointed. 'I never meant nuthin'!'

'*One foot*, just put one foot wrong and I shall drag you aft myself!'

Somebody asked, 'Why are we goin' to Gib again, 'Swain?'

Jago shrugged. 'Despatches, to land *Tetrarch*'s people –'

Campbell said harshly, 'Run 'em up to the mainyard, that's what I'd do!' He pointed at the boy in the other mess. ''*Is* bloody father for a start!'

Jago smiled. 'That's more like it, Campbell. A ten year old boy. A fair match, I'd say!'

Sullivan said softly, 'Officer on the deck, 'Swain!'

Someone else murmured, 'Bloody piglet, more like!'

It was Midshipman Sandell, striding importantly past the messes, chin in the air and not bothering to remove his hat, a courtesy observed by most officers. Jago ducked beneath one of the massive deckhead beams and realised that the midshipman was still able to walk upright, even wearing the hat. Sandell was carrying a gleaming, and, Jago guessed, very expensive sextant, probably a parting gift from his parents. Earlier he had seen the midshipmen assembled on the quarter-deck taking their noon sights, watched critically by Cristie, the master, as they had tried to estimate the ship's position for their logs.

Cristie missed very little, and Jago had heard him give Sandell the rough edge of his tongue more than once, to the obvious glee of the others.

Jago faced him calmly. It made upstarts like him dangerous.

'Oh, you're here, are you?' Sandell peered around, as if he had never set foot on the lower deck before. 'I want the boy, Lovatt. He is to lay aft, *now*.'

'I'll fetch him, Mr Sandell.'

'How many times do I have to tell people?' He was almost beside himself. 'San*dell*! That's easy enough, surely?'

Jago murmured, 'Sorry, sir.' It had been worth it just to see the shot go home. As he had intended it would.

He beckoned to the boy, and asked, 'The captain wants him, sir?'

Sandell stared at him, as if astonished that anyone should dare to question him. But, angry or not, some inner warning seemed to prevent another outburst. Jago's demeanour, and the fine blue jacket with gilt buttons, appeared to make him hesitate.

He said loftily, 'The captain, yes.' He snapped his fingers. 'Move yourself, boy!'

Jago watched them leave. Sandell would never change. He had shown no sign of fear during the fight, but that meant little; his kind were usually more afraid of revealing their fear to others than of fear itself. He winked at Sullivan. But if Sandell wanted to climb the ladder of promotion, he would be wise not to turn his back.

Unrivalled's wardroom, which was built into the poop structure on the gundeck, seemed spacious after other frigates George Avery had known. Unlike the lower deck, the ship's officers shared the cabin and dining space with six eighteen-pounders, three on either side.

The midday meal had been cleared away, and Avery sat by an open gunport watching some gulls diving and screaming alongside, probably because the cook had pitched some scraps outboard.

Two days out of Malta, on passage for Gibraltar, as if everything else was unreal. The dinner with Vice-Admiral Bethune and Adam Bolitho, then the excitement at being a part of something which he had begun with Sir Richard, had all been dashed by the arrival of another courier vessel. *Unrivalled* would take Bethune's despatches to the Rock and pass them on to the first available ship bound for England. Whatever Bethune really thought about it, he had made himself very clear. His latest orders were to contain the activities of the Dey's corsairs, but to do nothing to aggravate the situation until more ships were put under his flag.

Adam had been quietly resentful, although *Unrivalled* was the obvious choice: she was faster and better armed than any other frigate here or anywhere else in the fleet. There had been reports of several smaller vessels being attacked, taken or destroyed by the corsairs, and communications between the various squadrons and bases had never been so important. There was still no definite news of a total victory over Napoleon's army. Waterloo had broken his hold over the line, and it seemed as if all French forces were in full retreat. Even Marshal Ney's formidable cavalry had been defeated by the red-coated squares of infantry.

And he, Lieutenant George Avery, had received orders which countermanded all others. He was to return to England and present himself to their lordships, perhaps to add his report to all those which must have gone before. He laid his hand on the gun, warm, as if it had been recently fired. Perhaps he was too close. It was not another report they wanted. It was a post-mortem.

He looked around at his companions. It was a friendly enough wardroom, and he was after all a stranger, a temporary member of their small community.

And it was always in the air. It was only natural, and he

knew he was being unreasonable to expect otherwise. *I was there. When he fell.*

Galbraith, the first lieutenant, understood, and confined his questions to the subject of Avery's visit to the Dey's stronghold, and if there was any real risk that the attacks on shipping and the seizure of Christians would spark off a bigger confrontation. The war with France would soon be over; it probably already was. Galbraith would be thinking of his own future, thankful that he was at least in a stronger position than many, in a new and powerful frigate, with a captain whose name was known because of his famous uncle as well as his own past successes.

Massie, the second lieutenant, remained scornful, if not openly critical of Bethune's change of direction.

'When Boney surrenders this time, their lordships will cut the fleet to the bare bones! We'll have less chance than ever to topple these would-be tyrants!' To recover from such a costly war every nation, former friends and enemies alike, would be seeking fresh trade routes, and would still need the ships and men to protect them.

He saw Noel Tregillis, the purser, poring over one of his ledgers. He rarely stopped work even in here.

Captain Bosanquet of the Royal Marines was asleep in his chair, an empty goblet still clasped in his fingers, and his second-in-command Lieutenant Luxmore had gone to share a drink with his sergeant.

The portly surgeon, O'Beirne, had made his excuses and had gone aft to the great cabin, leaving his food untouched. The prisoner, Lovatt, was unwell; the wound was not healing to O'Beirne's satisfaction.

He had said sharply, 'He should have been put ashore in Malta. All this is quite unnecessary.' The severity of the comment was uncharacteristic of this generally quiet, affable man, who Avery knew took his work very seriously.

Even O'Beirne had touched on the subject, on their first night at sea. He had known Lefroy, *Frobisher*'s bald surgeon. It was to be expected: the fraternity of fleet surgeons was even more close-knit than the family of sea officers.

But once more it had all come back. The surgeon rising from his knees, from the bloodstained deck where Allday had held

156

his admiral with such terrible anguish, and saying, 'He's gone, I'm afraid.' In so few words.

Through a skylight he heard someone laugh. It was young Bellairs, sharing the afternoon watch with Lieutenant Wynter. What must it be like to be seventeen again, with the examination for lieutenant anticipated with every despatch satchel? A boy to a man, midshipman to officer, and Bellairs would deserve it. Avery thought of Adam, and how he had changed, confidence and maturing tempering him like the old sword he now wore. He smiled. A man of war. Perhaps . . .

And me? A passed-over luff with memories but no prospects.

He thought of Sillitoe, his energy, his manipulations, and of the last time they had met and parted. He had never believed that he could have felt something like pity for him.

Feet scraped outside the screen door, and Galbraith looked up from an old and much handled newssheet.

'What is it, Parker? D' you want me?'

The boatswain's mate nodded towards Avery and said, 'The cap'n's compliments, zur, an' 'e'd like you to step aft, directly.'

Galbraith stood up. 'The prisoner?'

The boatswain's mate gazed curiously around the wardroom. Just another part of the same ship. But so different.

He said, 'Dyin', I thinks, zur.'

The purser glanced up from his ledger, his face trained to give nothing away. *One less mouth to feed.*

Galbraith reached out and took the empty goblet from Bosanquet's limp hand. He said, 'If you need me . . .'

Avery picked up his hat. 'Thank you. I know.'

He walked into the deeper shadows of the poop and saw the Royal Marine sentry standing outside the screen door of the great cabin. The seat of command, which he himself would never know. Also the loneliest place in any King's ship.

The sentry straightened his back and tapped his musket smartly on the deck.

'Flag lieutenant, *sir*!'

Avery glanced at him. A homely, unknown face.

'Not any more, I'm afraid.'

157

The marine's eyes did not even flicker beneath his leather hat.

'You always will be to us, sir!'

Afterwards, he thought it was like a hand reaching out to him.

So let's be about it.

Adam Bolitho put a finger to his lips as Avery began to speak.

He said quietly, 'Come aft,' and led the way to the sloping stern windows. With the sun directly overhead, the panorama of blue water and cloudless sky was like some vast painting.

'Thank you for coming so quickly.' He turned his head as he heard Lovatt's rambling voice again. More like a conversation than one man. Questions and answers, and, just once, a tired laugh. And coughing. 'He's dying. O'Beirne's done all he can. I've been with him, too.'

Avery watched the dark profile, the strain around the eyes and mouth. He could feel the energy too, refusing to submit. When he had entered the cabin, his mind still clinging to the sentry's words, he had taken in the coat tossed carelessly on to a chair, one of Cristie's charts weighed down on a table by the bench seat, some brass dividers, the master's notebook. An untouched cup of coffee and an empty glass beside it. The captain was driving himself again; perhaps in truth he did resent the change of orders. Avery knew well enough that there were few bonds as strong as the one he had enjoyed with Richard Bolitho anywhere in the navy. Rank and responsibility did not allow it.

Or did he blame himself in some way? What captain would tolerate a prisoner, even a wounded one, in his own quarters?

Adam said, 'He's delirious for much of the time. Young Napier's in there with the surgeon – he's a good lad.' He added with some bitterness, 'Lovatt believes he's his son!'

Avery had seen Lovatt's son on the way here, waiting with one of the midshipmen as escort. He could guess the rest.

When Adam turned, he was calm again.

'I asked you to come here because I think you can help me.'

Why had he sent for him, and not the first lieutenant?

Adam said, 'In your original report to Sir Graham Bethune, you made mention of a Captain Martinez, whom you described as adviser to Mehmet Pasha, the governor and commander-in-chief in Algiers. Spanish . . .'

He broke off as Lovatt shouted, 'Helm *a-lee*, man! Are you blind, damn you!' It was followed by a bout of coughing, and Avery heard O'Beirne's resonant voice for the first time.

Adam continued, 'A renegade, you said?'

Avery forced himself to think, aware of the controlled urgency in the captain's tone.

'Yes, sir. He changed sides several times, but is useful to the Dey. He has or had connections in Spain when we met him. But the Dey is a hard man to serve, and Martinez will be very aware of it.'

Adam said, 'Lovatt spoke of him this morning. He said that the powder and shot, and other supplies not listed, were provided by Spanish sources, the whole of *Tetrarch*'s cargo to be exact.'

Avery tried to shut his ears to the pitiful muttering and retching from the sleeping compartment. This was important, it had to be, and yet it made no sense.

Adam said, 'He also told me that a second supply ship was to follow *Tetrarch*.' He gestured impatiently to the chart. 'Tomorrow we shall be north of Bona. The hornets' nest, eh?' He almost smiled. 'You will doubtless remember it well?'

Avery was silent for a moment, seeing it in his mind, as he had done in the past.

'It would make sense, sir. Our patrols, such as they are, would be less likely to sight them, and even then . . .'

Adam touched his sleeve. 'And *even then*, supporting ships would be required, and the admiral would have to be informed, and consulted – it is an old and familiar story!'

So he was bitter about Bethune's change of heart. Avery said, 'News travels fast in these waters, sir. *Tetrarch*'s capture, and your cutting out of *La Fortune*, will put an edge on things.'

The louvred door opened slightly, and O'Beirne peered into the cabin.

'If you still wish it, sir, I think this might be the time.'

159

Adam acknowledged it. He meant, *the only time*.

'So be it.' He looked briefly at his coat, hesitated and then slipped his arms into the sleeves. Then, to Avery, he said softly, 'Captain to captain, remember?'

To Avery the scene was nightmarish. Lovatt was propped up in the surgeon's makeshift trestle, one hand gripping it as if it was moving, his arm around the waist of the boy called Napier. O'Beirne was wedged into a corner, fingers interlaced on his knees, as if he had to force them to stay still.

'Aha, Captain! No urgent matters to keep you occupied?'

Lovatt's voice was stronger again, but that was all. His face seemed sunken, and his hazel eyes very bright, like somebody else looking out from a feverish mask.

Avery saw his hand tighten around the boy's body, and noticed that Napier had removed the noisy shoes, and his feet were bare on the checkered deck covering.

'Young Paul here is a comfort!' He contained another cough, and Napier dabbed his forehead with a damp cloth, gently and without hesitation, as if he had been trained for it.

But he was nothing like Lovatt's son in appearance, being taller and about four years older. Was Lovatt really deceived? Or perhaps it was a need, a desperate need.

Adam rested his hands on the trestle. 'You spoke earlier of the other supply ship, Captain Lovatt?'

Lovatt twisted his head from side to side, as if he could hear something. Or someone.

'Mercenaries! War makes us all hunger for something!' He was quiet again as the cloth moved gently over his brow. 'I could not offer my men a reason for dying, you see? It was a gesture. A final conceit!'

He seemed to see Avery for the first time.

'*Who is this?* A spy? A witness?'

O'Beirne moved as if to restrain him but Adam shook his head.

'This is George Avery. He is a friend.'

'Good.' Lovatt closed his eyes and O'Beirne gestured quickly to another basin. It contained a folded dressing, soaked in blood.

Avery watched a thin tendril drip from Lovatt's mouth, like red silk against his ashen skin. The boy dabbed it away, frowning with concentration as Avery had seen him do when he had poured the captain's wine.

'Thanks, Paul. I – I'm so *sorry* . . .'

Avery had seen many men suffer, and had endured great pain himself. And yet still he thought, with immense bitterness, why did death have to be so ugly, so without dignity?

Pain, suffering, humiliation. A man who had once hoped and loved, and lost.

'Where lies the land, Captain?' Stronger again.

Adam said quietly, 'We are nor'-east of Bona. Ship's head, west-by-south.'

The eyes found and settled on his face. 'You *will* see to his safety, Captain?'

'I will do what I can.' He hesitated. *Where was the point?* 'You have my word on it, Captain Lovatt.'

Lovatt let his head fall back and stared at the white deckhead. Adam saw the boy Napier show fear for the first time, and guessed that he thought Lovatt had died.

He must not leave it now. Could not.

'There were two other frigates in harbour.' He repeated the question, and saw the hazel eyes focus again.

'Two. Did I tell you that?' He looked at Napier and tried to smile. 'So like your mother, you know? *So . . . like . . . her.*'

Adam leaned over the trestle, hating it, the despair, the pain, the surrender. The very stench of death.

He asked sharply, '*Will they sail?*'

He could feel O'Beirne's disapproval, his unspoken objections. Avery was very still, a witness; it was impossible to guess what he was thinking.

Something thudded on the deck overhead, and there were sounds of tackle being hauled through the blocks. Normal, everyday shipboard noises. And there were men up there too. *Who depend on me.*

I must not care what others think.

He persisted, '*Will they sail?*'

'Yes.' Lovatt seemed to nod. 'So run while you can, Captain.' His voice was failing, but he tried once more. '*But promise me . . .*' He gave one small cry and more blood choked the words in his throat. This time it did not stop.

O'Beirne dragged the dead man's arm from Napier's waist

161

and pushed him away, knowing that any show of sentiment would make a lasting impression.

Adam laid his hand on the boy's shoulder.

'That was well done. I am proud of you.'

Napier was still staring at Lovatt's contorted, bloodied face. Although he seemed quite calm, his body was shaking uncontrollably.

Adam said, 'Send for the first lieutenant.'

He kept his hand on Napier's shoulder. *For his sake or for mine?*

O'Beirne said, 'I shall have my people clean up in here, sir.' He studied the captain, as if he was discovering something he had previously missed. 'He should be buried soon, I think.'

'Tell the sailmaker. Did he have any possessions?' *Did.* Already in the past. Not a man any more. A thing.

As if reading his thoughts, O'Beirne said bluntly, 'It were better he had been killed outright!'

Galbraith was already in the great cabin, grim-faced, reassuring.

Adam said, 'We shall bury him at dusk.'

Avery listened intently, afraid something had eluded him. Some seamen were here now, accustomed to death, and to concealing their feelings in its presence.

Galbraith said, 'He had nothing but the sword, sir.'

Adam looked at him, his eyes distant. *But promise me . . .* What had he been going to say? He turned and saw the dead man's son standing just inside the door, his eyes wide and unblinking. He stared at the trestle bed, and may have seen Lovatt's face before one of the seamen covered it with a piece of canvas. The same boy who had refused to come to his father's side when he was dying, even at the last . . . His anger faded as quickly as it had flared. The boy was quite alone. *As I once was. As I am now.* He had nothing left.

He turned away, aware that Avery was watching him. There was so much to do. Lovatt had called it a final conceit. Was that all it meant?

The boy said, 'I would like the sword, *capitaine*.' His voice was very controlled, and clear, so that even his mother's French inflection was noticeable.

Adam said to Napier, 'Take him forrard and report to my cox'n. He will tell you what to do.'

Then, to the boy, he said, 'We will speak of the sword later.'

He walked to the stern windows and stared at the sky, feeling the ship around him. *Second to none.*

Galbraith was back. 'Orders, sir?' Once again, the lifeline. To normality. To their world.

'Sail drill, Mr Galbraith. See if the topmen can improve their timing.'

Galbraith smiled.

'And tomorrow I thought we might exercise the eighteen-pounders, sir.'

Adam looked back at the sleeping compartment. It was bare but for his own cot, which he had been unable to use. There was only Lovatt's sword leaning against the hanging wardrobe. Final.

He recalled Galbraith's remark.

'I think not, Leigh.' He saw Avery clench his fist. So he already knew. 'I fear that tomorrow it will be in earnest.'

11

The Last Farewell

Galbraith stifled a yawn and walked up to the weather side of the quarterdeck. Another morning watch, when a ship came alive again and found her personality. A time for every competent first lieutenant to delegate work, and to discover any flaws in the pattern of things before his captain drew his attention to them.

He felt a growing warmth on his cheek, and the ship sway to a sudden gust of wind. He saw the helmsmen glance from the flapping driver to the masthead pendant, licking out now across the larboard bow, easing the spokes with care to allow for it.

It would be hot today, whatever the wind decided. The decks had been washed down at first light, and were now almost dry, and some of the boatswain's crew were filling the boats with water to prevent the seams opening when the sun rose to its zenith. His eye moved on. Hammocks neatly stowed, lines flaked down ready for instant use, without the danger of tangling and causing an infuriating delay.

A brief glance aloft told him that more men were out on the yards, searching for breaks and frayed ends, another daily task.

He saw the cabin servant, Napier, making his way aft, a covered dish balanced in one hand, and recalled the burial, Lovatt's body sliding over the side after the captain had spoken a few words. A seaman, one of Lovatt's, tugged off his tarred hat: respect or guilt, it was hard to tell. Napier had been there also, standing in the dying light beside Lovatt's son. As the body had been tipped on a grating Napier had put his arm around the other boy's shoulder.

Galbraith saw another gust crossing the heaving water, ruffling it like a cat's fur. The large ensign was standing out from the peak, and beyond the naked figurehead the hazy horizon tilted to a steeper angle. *In for a blow* . . . He smiled. As the master had predicted. The wind had shifted, veered overnight, north-easterly across the starboard quarter.

He walked to the opposite side again and looked at the compass, the helmsman's eyes noting every move. Due west. Gibraltar in three days, less if the wind increased. He watched a seaman on the gundeck splicing a rope's end, his face stiff with concentration. Another, who had been applying grease to a gun truck, reached out and took it from him. The strong, tarred fingers moved like marlin spikes, there was a quick exchange of grins, and the job was done. One of the prisoners, helping a new hand still mystified by the intricacies of splicing and rope work. *If only they were not so undermanned.* He paced impatiently up the tilting deck. There was still half the morning watch to run, and a hundred things he needed to supervise.

The lookouts had sighted a few distant sails, doubtless fishermen. It was as well they were not hostile. What would happen if they could get no more men at Gibraltar? He looked towards the cabin skylight, imagining Captain Adam Bolitho down there, alone with his thoughts. No matter what orders the vice-admiral had given him, or any other flag officer for that matter, he had nothing with which to rebuke himself. So short a time in commission, and together they had welded a mixed collection of hands into one company, had cut out a frigate and had taken a supply ship. It could have gone against them if *Tetrarch* had fought to the finish; they might both have been destroyed. And yet, despite all this, Galbraith still found his captain impossible to know. Sometimes almost bursting with spirit and enthusiasm, and then suddenly remote, as if he were afraid to draw too close to any one person. He thought of Lovatt, and the captain's determination to extract all available intelligence, even though the man was dying. What *was* Lovatt after all? A traitor, most would say; an idealist at best. Yet there had been compassion in the captain's voice when he had buried that unhappy man.

He heard a step on the companion ladder and saw Lieutenant Avery staring at the sea and the sky.

165

'No breakfast, then?'

Avery grimaced and joined him by the compass. 'Too much wine last night. It was stupid of me.' He peered aft. 'The captain about yet?'

Galbraith studied him. Avery sounded depressed, and he guessed it had nothing to do with the wine.

'Once or twice. Sometimes I think he never sleeps.' Then, 'Walk with me. Blow away the cobwebs, eh?'

They fell into step together. They were both tall men, and like most sea officers who cared to take regular exercise they were able to walk without difficulty among watchkeepers and working parties alike, their feet avoiding ringbolts and gun tackles without conscious effort, when any one of those obstacles would have sent a landsman sprawling.

Galbraith said, 'You've known Captain Bolitho for a long time, I gather.'

Avery glanced covertly at him. '*Of* him. We have not met very often.'

Galbraith paused as a halliard snaked past his thigh. 'I should think he'd be a hellish fine target for women, but he's not married.'

Avery thought of the girl who had killed herself. He sensed that Galbraith was not merely seeking gossip to pass it on elsewhere. He wanted to know his captain, perhaps to understand him. *But not from me.*

Galbraith continued to walk, aware of Avery's unwillingness to discuss it, and changed the subject.

'When all this is over, what do you intend for yourself?'

Avery winced at the pain in his head. 'On the beach. There will be too many officers in better positions than mine for me to compete any more.' *Like you.*

Galbraith said, 'You have a very famous uncle, I hear. If I were in your shoes –'

Avery halted abruptly and faced him. 'I hope you never are, my friend!' He thought of the locket the admiral had been wearing when he had been shot down, which he had given to Adam. What would become of Catherine?

Midshipman Fielding said, 'The captain's on his way, sir.' He had been trying very hard not to look as if he had been eavesdropping.

Galbraith touched Avery's arm. 'I did not mean to pry, George. but I need to understand this man. For all our sakes.'

Avery smiled, for the first time. 'One day, when he is down there in his cabin, the *man* without the bright epaulettes, ask him. Just ask him. His uncle taught me that, and so much more.'

Adam Bolitho walked from the companion way and nodded to the master's mate of the watch.

'A promising start to the day, Mr Woodthorpe.' He looked up at the braced yards, the canvas full-bellied now, cracking occasionally in the breeze. Seeing the ship as Galbraith had this morning, but viewing it so differently.

'We shall set the maincourse directly, Mr Galbraith.' He shaded his eyes to look at the compass as it flashed in reflected sunlight. 'Then bring her up a point. She can take it. Steer west-by-north.' He gestured at the midshipman. 'And, Mr Fielding, after you have brushed the crumbs off your coat, you will note the change in the log and inform Mr Cristie!'

One of the helmsmen glanced at his mate and grinned. So little, Adam thought, and yet it was infectious. He walked to the rail and pressed his hands on it. Hot, bone-dry already. He looked at the boats on their tier, the trapped water slopping over the bottom boards as *Unrivalled* dipped her stem into a trough, and spray pitched over the bowsprit.

A wind. Please God, a wind.

He saw some seamen splicing, and one he did not recognise showing another how to twist and fashion the strands into shape. The man must have sensed it and stared up at the quarterdeck. Where might his loyalty lie? Perhaps like Jago, it was *just another officer.*

He said suddenly, 'You have a key to the strongbox, Mr Galbraith?' He turned his back to watch a solitary bird, motionless above the mizzen truck. 'Use it as you will. Any letters, documents and the like.'

Galbraith seemed uncertain, and shook his head.

'None, sir.'

Adam saw the master's head and shoulders hesitate in the companion hatch. Cristie's eyes were already on the masthead pendant.

Adam joined Avery by the nettings, sensing his isolation from the others. Knowing the reason for it.

'Think, George, it will be full summer when you walk ashore in England.'

Avery did not respond. He had thought of little else since his change of orders. He gazed at the working parties on deck, the sure-footed topmen moving like monkeys in the shrouds; even the greasy smell from the galley funnel was like a part of himself.

And the letters he had written for Allday, and the replies he had read from his wife. *Belonging*.

He tried to think of London, of the Admiralty, where there would be polite interest or indifference to what he had to say. And he did not care. That was almost the worst part.

Had he really lain in bed in that gracious house, with the tantalising Susanna Mildmay? Beautiful Susanna . . . beautiful and faithless.

Adam said, 'Is there something I can do?'

Avery studied him, memories stirring and fading like ghosts. 'When I reach England . . .'

They stared up as the lookout's voice turned every head.

'Deck there! Sail, fine on the starboard bow!'

Galbraith shouted, 'Mr Bellairs, aloft with you! Take your glass, man!'

Avery smiled, and reached out as if to take Adam's hand. 'I shall think of you.' The rest was lost in the sudden rush of feet and another cry from the masthead.

He said softly, 'No matter.'

The moment was past.

Midshipman Bellairs' voice carried easily above the sounds of sea and flapping canvas.

'Deck there! Square-rigger, sir!'

Adam folded his arms and looked along the length of his command. The forenoon watch had not been piped, but the deck and gangways seemed to be crowded with men. And yet there was hardly a sound. Some stared ahead to the darker line of the horizon, others inboard at the ship, at one another.

Cristie muttered, 'No fisherman this time, then.'

Adam waited, feeling the uncertainty. The doubt.

He said, 'Frigate.'

Galbraith was peering up at the mainmast crosstrees, as if willing Bellairs to confirm or deny it.

'Beat to quarters, sir?' Even his voice seemed hushed.

'Not yet.' Adam held out his hand, remembering Avery's despair. 'There'll be another out there somewhere.' He watched the low banks of cloud. 'They will have had plenty of time to prepare. We've had the sun behind us since first light – a blind man could see us.'

Galbraith moved closer, excluding all the others.

'We still have time, too, sir.'

Adam looked at him.

'To run?'

'We shall be hard put to stand and fight.'

Adam touched his arm, and felt it tense as if he had been expecting a blow.

'That was well said, Leigh. I respect you for it.'

He could see the two ships in his mind, as if they were within range instead of miles distant, visible only to the masthead lookout and Bellairs. He would learn something today. If he lived through it.

'How many extra hands do we have aboard?'

'Fifty-five, and two injured. I'll clap the whole lot in irons if you think –'

What had Lovatt called it? *A gesture. But too late.*

He said suddenly, 'Clear lower deck, and have all hands lay aft.' He attempted to smile, but his mouth refused. 'Though it would seem they are already here!'

He walked to the compass once more, hearing the sound of his shoes on the deck, like that day at his court martial at Portsmouth. So impossibly long ago. He heard the trill of calls below decks, and a few idlers running to join the mass of figures already on deck.

Galbraith said, 'Lower deck cleared, sir.'

Adam touched the compass box, remembering the brief moments of clarity before Lovatt had died.

I could not offer them a reason for dying.

He could have been speaking at this very moment.

Adam turned and strode to the quarterdeck rail and looked out across the sea of upturned faces. The others he had already seen, the afterguard, and the swarthy Lieutenant Massie who was responsible for the gunnery of this ship. And young Wynter, whose father was a member of Parliament. And the two scarlet-coated marine officers, standing a little apart from the others; the midshipmen and the master's mates; men and faces which had become so familiar within six months.

'You will know by now that two ships are standing to the west'rd of us.'

There were some quick, uncertain glances, and he sensed the sudden understanding as Bellairs' clear voice called, 'Second ship, starboard bow! Square-rigged, sir!'

'They are not there by accident. It is their intention to engage, seize, or destroy *Unrivalled*.'

He saw some of them looking at the black eighteen-pounders, perhaps already considering the hazards – the older men would call it folly – of engaging two frigates at once. Heeling to the wind, it would require brute force to haul the guns back to their ports on the weather side once they had been fired.

'The war with Napoleon has likely been over for some time. We shall be told eventually. *I hope.*'

He saw old Stranace, the gunner, offer a dour grin. It was little enough, but it was all he had.

Adam pointed at the empty sea.

'These ships will respect no treaty, no pieces of paper applauded by old men in government. They are already out-laws!' He let his arm drop and recalled Lovatt's words. *We are all mercenaries in war.*

He laid both hands on the rail and said deliberately, 'I need trained men today.' He saw some of *Unrivalled*'s people looking at those who had been thrust amongst them. None had forgotten the days, so recently passed, when men had been seized and dragged aboard King's ships by the hated press gangs with no less severity.

'I can promise you nothing, but I can offer the chance of a new beginning. If we lose the day, our fate at the hands of the enemy will be prolonged and terrible. If we win, there is the possibility of freedom.' He thought of Avery, and said, 'Of England. You have my word upon it.' What he had said to Lovatt . . .

Galbraith pointed. 'That man! Speak up!'

170

It was a seaman who would not have seemed out of place in any ship, any port.

'An' if we refuse, Cap'n? If we stands by our rights?'

There was a growl of agreement.

'Rights?' Adam patted a quarterdeck nine-pounder by his knee. 'Speak to me of those rights when these are silent, eh?'

He nodded to Galbraith. He had made a mistake; the gesture had misfired. Galbraith joined him by the rail.

'Show of hands!'

The silence was physical. Crushing. Far worse than if they had jeered at his inability to reach them.

Then he heard Partridge, the massive boatswain, bawling out as if it were a part of normal routine.

'Right, then, you lot over 'ere. Lively, lads! Creagh, take their names, if you still knows 'ow to write!'

And somebody laughed. *Laughed.*

Adam turned towards them again. The crowd was breaking into groups, pushed and sorted into small parties, the blues and whites of warrant officers moving amongst them, taking control. He tried to remember; how many had Galbraith mentioned? Over fifty: not an army, but it might make the difference. Men who had been cheated, lied to and ill-treated for most of their lives, when loyalty to one another carried far more weight than flag or country, they had decided.

Galbraith was beside him again.

'I would never have believed it, sir.' He hesitated. 'Would you tell me? How did you do it?'

Adam saw the one man who had challenged him. Their eyes met across the bustling figures and frantic petty officers, and then the man gave a shrug. Resignation, or was it trust after all?

He murmured, 'Perhaps I offered them a reason for living.'

He felt spray dash across his cheek. The wind was still rising. The *chance*.

But all he heard was Lovatt's mocking laugh.

He turned on his heel and said, 'Now you may beat to quarters, and clear for action, Mr Galbraith.' He saw the boy Napier watching from beside the capstan, and called, 'Fetch my coat, will you. My sword, too.' But Jago was already there, the old sword held casually, almost indifferently.

'Here, sir.'

Adam held out his arms and felt him clip the sword into place. Was this, too, a final conceit?

Jago stood back. 'Scum they may be, sir, but fight they will. Like me, they don't know nothing else!'

At that moment the drums began their staccato roll to beat to quarters.

Adam stared at the sea until his eyes misted over. He felt no fear. If anything, it was pride.

Adam Bolitho brushed a lock of loose hair from his eyes and used his sleeve as a shield against the glare from a lively sea, broken now by the strengthening wind.

One bell chimed from forward, and he saw Midshipman Fielding apparently jerk out of his thoughts and turn the half-hour glass before someone rebuked him.

So little time since the first hint of danger; two hours, or less. It was hard to remember, but it would all be noted in the log. He licked his dry lips. For posterity.

Even the ship had changed in that time. Cleared for action, *Unrivalled* was stripped, like the gun crews who had discarded their shirts but retained their neckerchiefs to tie over their ears against the roar of battle, of her main and mizzen courses and staysails, so that the deck felt open and vulnerable. Under topsails and topgallants, with the big forecourse loosely brailed, she was making a fair speed through the water, spray constantly breaking over the beakhead and forecastle. Nets had been rigged to protect the gun deck from falling wreckage. Adam faced each possibility like a challenge, the margin between winning and losing. And lastly the boats. He did not move from his place on the weather side of the quarterdeck but could see the boat-tier, each hull already bailed and steaming in the hot sunshine.

It was always a bad moment when the boats were lowered and cast adrift on a sea-anchor, to await collection by the victors. Even seasoned sailors never accepted or became accustomed to it. The boats were their last hope of survival. Adam had seen some of them watching Partridge's crew rigging the tackles in readiness for hoisting and then swinging each boat outboard. Abandoned . . .

But Adam had seen hideous casualties caused by splinters ripped from tiered boats, like flying razors when they cut into human flesh. It was the last task.

He took a telescope from its rack and trained it across the nettings. It was no longer a suspicion, or a flaw on the dawn horizon, but brutal reality. The enemy.

Two ships. Frigates, their hazy silhouettes overlapping as if joined, a common illusion. They were probably some five miles away; he could see each sail, braced so hard round that they were almost fore-and-aft. Another trick perhaps, but each captain was hard put to hold his ship up into the wind, as close-hauled as any professional officer could manage.

Who were they? What did they hope for today, apart from victory? Perhaps it was better not to know your enemy, to see his face. You might recognise yourself in him.

He gazed across the deck. They were all present, the Royal Marines at the barrier of packed hammocks, extra hands on the big double-wheel, Lieutenant Wynter with the afterguard, his midshipman, Homey, close by. Cristie and his senior master's mate, and Avery, arms folded, hat tilted over his eyes, observing. As he must have done so many times with . . .

Adam swung away. 'Very well, Mr Galbraith, cast off the boats!'

He saw faces turn away from the guns to watch. This was the worst moment. Especially for newcomers.

Galbraith returned to the quarterdeck and waited for the gap left in the nets to be sealed. He did not look astern at the drifting cluster of boats.

'If I might make a suggestion, sir.'

Adam said, 'I know. My coat, it troubles you.'

'You have me all aback, sir. But any marksman will be looking for the chance to mark down the captain. You know that well enough!'

Adam smiled, touched by the concern. Genuine, like the man.

'The enemy will know *Unrivalled* has a captain, Leigh. I want our people to know it, too!'

He raised the glass again. The frigate astern of her consort had hoisted a signal of some kind. Two flags, nothing more. A private signal, perhaps? It could also be a ruse, to make

173

him believe it was the senior ship. He recalled Francis Inch, his first lieutenant in *Hyperion*, telling the midshipmen that in ship-to-ship actions beyond the control of the ponderous line of battle a good captain often survived by trickery as much as agility.

He considered it. Two frigates, neither as powerful as *Unrivalled*, but, used aggressively and with determination, they were formidable.

He said, almost to himself, 'They will try to divide our strength. Tell Mr Massie to point each gun himself, no matter which side we engage first. The opening shots will decide.' He paused, and repeated, '*Must* decide.'

He walked from one side of the deck to the other, hearing Galbraith calling to Massie. If *Unrivalled* altered course away from those ships, they would gain the advantage from the wind. He imagined the two frigates, like counters on an admiral's chart. From line ahead to line abeam, they would have no choice, nor would they want one.

He heard the spray pattering over the lee side, and thought, *no, Captain Lovatt, not running away.*

When Galbraith returned he found his captain by the compass, his shirt and coat opened to the hot wind. There was no sign of the strain he had glimpsed earlier. He found himself thinking of the woman again, the one Avery so pointedly had not discussed. What had happened, he wondered. What would she feel if she could see him now on this bright, deadly forenoon?

Adam said, 'Pass the word to load. Single-shotted to starboard, double-shotted to larboard, but do not run out. At the turn of the glass, we shall alter course and steer south-west.' He almost smiled. 'What the enemy intended, I believe. A lively chase with the wind under their coattails without too much risk to themselves, and if all else fails they will hope to run us ashore on the African coast. What say you?'

Galbraith stared up at the rippling masthead pendant. 'It would make sense, sir.' He sounded doubtful, surprised.

Adam said, 'We will luff at the right moment and rake the nearest one. Tell Massie, each ball must make its mark.'

'I did tell him, sir.'

But Adam was not listening; he was seeing it. 'We must get

174

to grips, it's our only way out. So get all spare hands off the upper deck. We are short-handed, remember? And they will know it!'

Galbraith saw him turn away and gesture urgently to the cabin servant, Napier.

'You! Over here!'

Napier hurried across, past grim-faced seamen and marines, a cutlass thrust through his belt, his shoes clicking on the sun-dried planking and bringing some unexpected grins from the crew of a nine-pounder. One called, 'Look, boyos! We've nowt to fear now! We're all in good hands!'

Adam said gently, 'Your place is below. You know what to do.'

Napier faced him anxiously, with something like desperation.

'My place is here, sir, with you.'

There was no laughter now, and Cristie looked away, perhaps remembering somebody.

Adam said, 'Do as I ask. I shall know where you are. I mean it.'

Jago heard it, too, feeling the handshake again, the strange sense of sharing what he could not contain or understand.

Galbraith watched the boy return to the companion way, head high, the cutlass almost dragging along the deck.

Adam raised the glass once more, and remembered that Midshipman Bellairs was still at the masthead.

'Carry on, Mr Galbraith. Bring her about. Let's see her fly today!' His hand was raised and Galbraith waited, remembering every phase, and each mood, like pictures in a child's most treasured book.

And saw his captain suddenly give a broad grin, teeth very white against his tanned skin.

'And be of good heart, my friend. We shall win this day!'

Cristie's voice was harsh, his Tyneside accent even more pronounced as he shouted, 'Steady as she goes, sir! Sou'-west-by-south!'

Another bang echoed across the choppy water, the second gun to be fired. Adam clenched his knuckles against his thighs, counting seconds and then feeling the ball smash into *Unrivalled*'s lower hull. He did not need the glass; he had seen the smoke from the nearest pursuer before it was shredded in the wind. The second shot, and both had come from the frigate on *Unrivalled*'s starboard quarter. Not because the other, on almost exactly the opposite quarter, could not bear but, he suspected, because the ship which had fired was the senior, and probably mounted heavier bow-chasers.

The ship which had made that brief signal. No trick, then; she was the main danger. *Unrivalled*'s stern was vulnerable to any shot, no matter how badly aimed. The rudder, the steering tackles . . . He shut his mind to it.

'*Stand by to come about, Mr Galbraith!*' He strode to the rail again, and shaded his eyes. Two shots; it was enough. He dared not risk it any further. Disabled, *Unrivalled* would be destroyed piecemeal.

As he turned he saw the staring eyes of those at the gun tackles along the starboard side, muzzles pointing at the empty sea. The breechings were cast off, the guns were loaded, and men with sponges, worms and rammers were already poised for the next order, their bodies shining with sweat, as if they had been drenched by a tropical rain.

'*Stand by on the quarterdeck!*'

Massie would be ready with his gun captains. All those drills . . . it was now or not at all.

'*Put the helm down!*'

Feet skidded on wet gratings as the three helmsmen hauled over the spokes. With her topsails filled to the wind *Unrivalled* began to respond immediately, her head swinging even as more men freed the headsail sheets, spilling out the wind, to allow the bows to thrust unimpeded into and across the eye. Sails flapped and banged in confusion, and as the deck tilted hard over the nearest enemy ship appeared to be charging towards the concealed broadside.

It must have taken the other captain completely by surprise. From a steady, unhampered chase to this: *Unrivalled* pivoting round, revealing her full broadside, and none of his own guns yet able to bear.

'Open the ports! *Run out!*'

All order had gone. Men yelled and cursed with each heave

176

on the tackles until every port was filled, and there was no longer an empty sea for a target.

Massie strode past the empty boat-tier. *'Fire!'* A slap on a man's tense shoulder. 'As you bear, *fire!*'

As each trigger line was jerked an eighteen-pounder thundered inboard to be seized and sponged out, charge and ball tamped home.

Adam shouted, 'Hold her now! Steer north-west!'

There were more yells, and he imagined that he heard the splintering crack of a falling spar, although it was unlikely above the din of canvas and straining rigging, and the last echoes of a full broadside.

The other frigate was falling downwind, her bowsprit and jib boom shot away, the tangle of severed cordage and wildly flapping sails dragging her round.

Adam cupped his hands. 'On the uproll! *Fire!'*

It was a ragged broadside, some of the guns had not yet run out, but he saw the iron smash home, and bulwarks and planking, broken rigging and men being flung like flotsam in a high wind.

It might have been us.

Galbraith was shouting, 'The other one's coming for us, sir!'

The second frigate seemed so near, towering above the larboard quarter, stark in the hard sunlight. He could even see the patches on her forecourse, and the pointing sword of a once-proud figurehead.

He winced as more iron smashed into the hull, feeling the deck lurch beneath his feet, and hearing the heavy crash of a ball ripping into the poop. The enemy's jib boom was already overreaching the larboard quarter.

He dashed the smoke from his eyes and saw a man fall on the opposite side, his scream lost in the report of a solitary gun.

He waved to Cristie. *'Now!'*

The wheel was moving again, but one of the helmsmen was sprawled in blood. *Unrivalled* turned only a point, so that it appeared as if the other ship must ride up and over her poop. The jib boom was above the nettings now, men were firing, and through the swirling smoke Adam saw vague figures swarming out on the other frigate's beakhead and bowsprit, cutlasses glinting dully in the haze of gunfire.

Going to board us. It was like another voice.

'Clear lower deck, Mr Galbraith!' Suppose it failed? He thrust the thought away and dragged out his sword, conscious of Avery beside him, and Jago striding just ahead, a short-bladed weapon in his fist.

Adam raised the sword. 'To me, *Unrivalled*!'

She was a well-armed ship. He could remember the admiration, the envy. Apart from her two batteries of eighteen-pounders, she also mounted eight thirty-two pound carronades, two of which were almost directly below his feet.

It happened within seconds, and yet each moment remained separate, stamped forever in his memory.

Midshipman Homey slipping and falling to his knees, then being hit in the skull by a heavy ball even as he struggled to his feet. Flesh, blood and fragments of bone splashed across Adam's breeches. The carronades roared out together, crashing inboard on their slides and hurling their massive balls, packed with grape and jagged metal, directly into the enemy forecastle.

Avery turned and stared at him, shook his sword, shouted something. But the stare did not waver, and he fell face down, and the packed mass of boarders surged across his body and on to the other ship's deck.

It was useless to hesitate. There were too many who depended . . . But for only a second Adam halted, looking for the man who had been his uncle's friend.

Jago was dragging at his arm.

'Come *on*, sir! We've got the bastards on the run!'

A dream, a nightmare; scenes of desperate brutality, all mercy forgotten. Men falling and dying. Others dropping between the two hulls, the only escape. A face loomed out of the yelling, hacking mob: it was Campbell, the hard man, waving a flag and screaming, 'The flag! They've struck!'

Now there were different faces, and he realised that, like Avery, he had fallen and was lying on the deck. He felt for the sword, and saw Midshipman Bellairs holding it; it must have been knocked out of his hand.

And then the pain reached him, a searing agony, which

punched the breath from his lungs. He groped for his thigh, his groin; it was everywhere. A hand was gripping his wrist and he saw it was O'Beirne, and understood that he was on *Unrivalled*'s gun deck; he must have lost consciousness, and he felt something akin to panic.

He said, 'The orlop! You belong with the wounded, *not here*, man!'

O'Beirne nodded grimly, his face sliding out of focus like melting wax. Then it was Jago's turn. He had torn down the front of Adam's breeches and was holding something in the hazy sunlight. No blood. No gaping wound. It was the watch, which he always carried in the pocket above his groin. A shot had smashed it almost in two pieces.

He was losing control again. The shop in Halifax. The chiming chorus of clocks. The little mermaid . . .

Jago was saying, 'Christ, you were lucky, sir!' He wanted to lessen it, in his usual way. But the levity would not come. Then he said, *'Just hold on.'*

Men were cheering, hugging one another, the marines were rounding up prisoners . . . so much to do, the prizes to be secured, the wounded to be tended. He gasped as someone tried to lift him. And Avery. Avery . . . *I shall have to tell Catherine. A letter. And the locket.*

Somehow he was on his feet, staring up at the flag as if to reassure himself. But all he could think of was the little mermaid. Perhaps it was her way; the last farewell.

Then he fainted.

12

Aftermath

Like an unhurried but purposeful beetle, *Unrivalled*'s gig pulled steadily around and among the many vessels which lay at anchor in Gibraltar's shadow.

It was a time of pride, and of triumph, climaxing when they had entered the bay with one prize in tow and the other in the hands of a prize crew. To the men of the fleet, hardened by so many years of setbacks and pain, it had been something to share, to celebrate. Ships had manned their yards to cheer, boats from the shore had formed an unofficial procession until the anchors had splashed down, and order and discipline was resumed.

And the war was over. Finally over. That was the hardest thing to confront. Napoleon, once believed invincible, had surrendered, and had placed himself under the authority of Captain Frederick Maitland of the old *Bellerophon* in Basque Roads, to be conveyed to Plymouth.

The officer of the guard who had boarded *Unrivalled* within minutes of her dropping anchor had exclaimed, 'When you fought and took the two frigates, *we* were at peace!'

Adam had heard himself answer shortly, 'It made no difference.'

He thought of the men who had fallen in that brief, savage action. Of the letters he had written. To the parents of Midshipman Thomas Homey, who had been killed even as the second frigate had surged into their quarter. Fourteen years old, not even begun.

And to Catherine, a long and difficult letter. Seeing

Avery's shocked and unwavering gaze, like an unanswered question.

Midshipman Bellairs was sitting behind him, beside Jago at the tiller.

'Flagship, sir!'

Adam nodded. He had taken a calculated risk, and had won. It was pointless to consider the alternatives. *Unrivalled* might have been caught in stays, taken aback as she tried to swing through the wind. The two frigates would have used the confusion to cross her stern and rake her, each broadside ripping through the hull. A slaughterhouse.

He stared at the big two-decker which lay directly across their approach, His Britannic Majesty's Ship *Prince Rupert* of eighty guns, a rear-admiral's flag rising and drooping at her mizzen truck.

He made to touch his thigh and saw the stroke oar's eyes on him, and controlled the impulse. He had examined his body in the looking-glass in his cabin, and found a great, livid bruise, showing the force of the impact. A stray shot perhaps, fired at random as his men had hacked their way on board the enemy. Even now, four days after the engagement, the pain was almost constant, and caught him unaware, like a reminder.

The surgeon, rarely at a loss for words, had been strangely taciturn. Perhaps when he had fallen unconscious again he had said something, revealed the despair which had tormented him for so long.

O'Beirne had said only, 'You are in luck, Captain. Another inch, and I fear the ladies would have been in dire distress!'

He looked up now and saw the flagship towering above them, the gig's bowman already standing with his boathook, and prepared himself for the physical effort of boarding. Seeing his eyes on the ship's massive tumblehome, the 'stairs' up to the gilded entry port, Jago said quietly, 'Steady she goes, sir!'

Adam glanced at him, remembering his face when he had torn open his breeches to deal with the wound. Poor Honey's blood and brains had made it look worse than it

ized the handrope, gritting his teeth as he took the first step.

An unknown voice sang out, 'Cap'n comin' aboard! Stand by . . . *pipe*!'

Adam climbed, step by step, each movement bringing a shaft of pain to his thigh.

The calls shrilled, and as his head rose above the sill he saw the scarlet-coated guard, the seemingly vast area of the flagship's impeccable deck.

The guard presented arms, and a duplicate of Captain Bosanquet brought down his blade with a flourish.

The flag captain strode to greet him. Adam held his breath. Pym, that was his name. The pain was receding, playing with him.

'Welcome aboard, Captain Bolitho! Your recent exploits had us all drained with envy!' He looked at him more closely. 'You were wounded, I hear?'

Adam smiled. It seemed so long since he had done that. 'Damaged, sir, nothing lasting!'

They walked together into the poop's shadow, so huge after *Unrivalled*. He allowed his mind to stray. *Or* Anemone . . .

The flag captain paused. 'Rear-Admiral Marlow is still studying your report. I have had your despatches transferred to a courier – she will leave this afternoon. If there is anything else I can do to assist you while you are here, you have only to ask.' He hesitated. 'Rear-Admiral Marlow is newly appointed. He still likes to deal with things at first hand.'

It was as good as any warning. Captain to flag rank; he had seen it before. *Trust nobody.*

Rear-Admiral Elliot Marlow stood with his back to the high stern windows, hands beneath his coattails, as if he had been in the same position for some time. A sharp, intelligent face, younger than Adam had expected.

'Good to meet you at last, Bolitho. Take a chair. Some wine, I think.' He did not move or offer his hand.

Adam sat. He knew he was strained and tired, and unreasonable, but even the chair seemed carefully placed. Staged, so that Marlow's outline remained in silhouette against the reflected sunlight.

Two servants were moving soundlessly around the other side of the cabin, each careful not to look at the visitor.

Marlow said, 'Read your report. You were lucky to get the

better of two enemies at once, eh? Even if, the perfectionists may insist, you were at war with neither.' He smiled. 'But then, I doubt that the Dey of Algiers will wish to associate himself with people who have failed him.' He glanced at his flag captain, and added, 'As to your request respecting the son of that damned renegade, I suppose I can have no objection. It is hardly important . . .'

Pym interrupted smoothly, 'And Captain Bolitho has offered to pay all the costs for the boy's passage, sir.'

'Quite so.' He gestured at the nearest servant. 'A glass, eh?'

Adam was glad of a chance to regain his bearings.

He said, 'With regard to the prizes, sir.'

Marlow subjected his glass to a pitiless scrutiny. 'The prizes, yes. Of course, their role may also have changed in view of the French position. I have heard it said that frigate captains sometimes see prize money as the price of glory. A view I find difficult to comprehend.'

Adam realised that his glass was empty, and said bluntly, 'The Dey of Algiers had three frigates at his disposal, sir. With the re-opening of trade routes, those ships could have been a constant threat. That threat was removed, and at some cost. I think it fair enough.'

Captain Pym adroitly changed the subject.

'How long will your repair take, d' you think?'

Adam looked at him and smiled thinly.

'We did much of it after the fight.' He considered it, seeing the dangling cordage, the limping wounded, the canvas bundles going over the side. 'A week.'

Marlow waved one hand. 'Give him all the help you can . . .' He pointed at the table. 'That despatch from the Admiralty, where is it?'

Adam relaxed very slowly. The real reason for his visit. Not to congratulate or to crucify him. That was Bethune's domain. Marlow had not even mentioned his use of the prisoners to fill the gaps in *Unrivalled*'s company.

Marlow put his glass down with great care and took some papers from his flag captain.

'You are instructed to take passengers when you return to Malta. Sir Lewis Bazeley and his party, of some importance, I gather. It is all explained in the orders.'

Captain Pym said hastily, 'Because of the danger from corsairs and other renegades, a man-of-war is the only safe option.' He gave a tight smile. 'As your own recent fight against odds has proved. I am sure that Vice-Admiral Bethune would have chosen your ship, had he been consulted.'

Adam found he could return the smile. He could understand why Pym was a flag captain.

'Anything else?' Marlow stared at him. 'Now is the time to ask.'

'I have a midshipman named Bellairs, sir. He is due for examination shortly, but in the meantime I would like to rate him acting-lieutenant, and pay him accordingly. He has done extremely well during this commission.'

He had not seen Marlow all aback before, and neither, he suspected, had Pym.

'Bellairs? Has he family? Connections?'

'He is my senior midshipman, sir. That is all that concerns me.'

Marlow seemed vaguely disappointed.

'You deal with it.' He turned away, dismissing him. 'And, er – good fortune, Captain Bolitho.'

The door closed behind them.

Pym grinned widely. 'That was damned refreshing! Leave it with me!'

He was still grinning when the calls trilled again, and Adam lowered himself into the waiting gig.

'Bear off forrard! Give way all!'

Bellairs stood to watch a passing trader, ready to warn them away if they came too near.

Adam said, 'By the way, Mr Bellairs, you will be moving shortly.'

Bellairs forgot his poise in the captain's gig, and said, '*Move*, sir? But I hoped to . . .'

Adam watched Jago's face over the midshipman's shoulder. 'To the wardroom.'

It was only a small thing, after all. But it made it seem very worthwhile.

Catherine, Lady Somervell, moved slightly in her seat and tilted her wide-brimmed straw hat to shade her eyes from the sun. With the windows all but closed it was hot, and her gown was damp against her skin.

The City of London had never featured largely in her life, and yet in the past few months she had come here several times. It was always busy, always teeming. The carriage could have been open, but she was constantly aware of the need for discretion, and had noticed that the coachman never seemed to use the same route; today, as on those other visits, the vehicle was unmarked, never the one Sillitoe had been using on the day of the service at St Paul's. She had seen the cathedral this morning, dominating its surroundings as it had on that day, which she would never forget nor wanted to relinquish.

She looked at the passing scene; the carriage was moving slowly in the congestion of the road. Grey-faced offices, one of which she had visited with Sillitoe when he had kept an appointment with some shipping agent; she had been politely entertained in another room.

There were stalls here, flowers and fruit, someone elsewhere making a speech, another drawing a crowd with a performing monkey.

Now they were returning to Sillitoe's house in Chiswick. Never once had he forced his presence on her, but he was always ready to help her, to escort her, or if necessary to give his opinion on her decisions for the immediate future.

She glanced at him now, on the seat opposite, frowning slightly as he leafed through yet another sheaf of papers. His mind was ever agile, ever restless. Like their last visit to Sir Wilfred Lafargue at Lincoln's Inn. He was a lawyer of repute, but when he and Sillitoe were together they were more like conspirators than legal adviser and client.

She thought of the letter she had received from Captain James Tyacke, a concise, unemotional account of why marriage to the woman he had once loved had proved impossible. It had saddened her, but she had understood his reasons, and the sensitivity he would never reveal. A man who had been utterly withdrawn, almost shy, when he had been forced to leave the only world he understood; she was proud to call him her friend, as he had been Richard's. Perhaps for him the sea was the only solution, but it was not, and never could be, an escape.

She realised that Sillitoe was looking at her, as he often did, when he believed she did not know.

'I have to go to Spain.' Calmly said, as was his habit, but not the same. This was a mood she had not seen or sensed before.

'You said that it was possible.'

He smiled. 'And I asked you if you would come with me.'

'And I told you that there has been enough damage done already because of me. And you know that is true.'

She averted her eyes to look at a passing vehicle, but saw only her reflection in the dusty glass.

Sillitoe's sphere of influence encompassed both politics and trade, although he was no longer Inspector-General. The Prince Regent, who was notorious for his infidelities, had feared whatever stain a liaison between his adviser and confidante and the admiral's whore might cast on his reputation as the future monarch. She felt the old, familiar bitterness. The men in power with their mistresses and their homosexual lovers were forgiven if their affairs were kept separate from rank and authority, and were not conducted where they might offend the royal eye.

She had rarely seen Sillitoe reveal anger. A week ago, a cruel cartoon had appeared in the *Globe*. It had depicted her standing nude and looking at ships below in a harbour. The caption had been, *Who will be next?*

She had seen his anger then. There had been apologies. Someone had been dismissed. But it was there all the same. Hate, envy, malice.

Perhaps even the Prince's courtiers had had a hand in it.

She recalled Lafargue's advice on Belinda, Lady Bolitho. *Never underrate the wrath of an unloved woman.*

Sillitoe said, 'You need security, Catherine. And protection. I can offer you both. My feelings remain unchanged.' He glanced round, frowning as a gap appeared in the buildings and the river was revealed. Masts and loose, flapping sails. Arriving and departing; sailors from every corner of the world. She wondered briefly if the coachman, who seemed to know London like the back of his own hand, had been ordered to avoid ships and sailors also.

She looked at him again. His face was tense, his mind obviously exploring something which troubled him.

He said, 'You could stay at my house. You would not be molested by anything or anybody, my staff would see to that.' As he had said when someone had carved the word *whore* on the door of her Chelsea house.

He said abruptly, 'There is always danger. I see it often enough.'

'And what would people say?'

He did not answer her directly, but the hooded eyes seemed calmer.

'If you come to Spain, you may be yourself again. I go first to Vigo, where I must see some people, and then on to Madrid.' He laid the papers aside and leaned forward. 'You like Spain, you speak the language. It would be a great help to me.' He reached out and took her hand. 'I should be a very proud man.'

She gently withdrew the hand, and said, 'You are a difficult man to refuse. But I must confront whatever future remains for me.'

She heard the coachman making his usual clucking sounds to the horses, a habit she had noticed whenever they were approaching the Chiswick house. The journey had passed, and now she must do something, say something; he had done so much to help, to support her in the aftermath of Richard's death.

There was another vehicle in the drive. So he had known she would refuse; the carriage was waiting to take her to Chelsea, a lonely place now without her companion Melwyn, whom she had sent back to St Austell temporarily to help her mother with work for a forthcoming county wedding.

They would surely notice the change in the girl. She had become confident, almost worldly. *As I once was at that age.*

She was aware now of Sillitoe's expression; ever alert, he seemed suddenly apprehensive, before he regained his habitual self-assurance. She followed his eyes and felt the chill on her spine. The carriage door bore the fouled anchors of Admiralty, and there was a sea officer standing beside it, speaking with Sillitoe's secretary.

So many times. Messages, orders, letters from Richard. But always the dread.

'What is it?'

He waited for a servant to run up and open the door for her. Afterwards, she thought it had been to give himself time.

He said, 'I shall not keep you. The Admiralty still needs me, it would appear.' But his eyes spoke differently.

Marlow accompanied her into the house and guided her to the library, where she had always waited for Sillitoe.

'Is something wrong?'

The secretary murmured, 'I fear so, m' lady,' and withdrew, closing the tall doors.

She heard voices, the sound of hooves; the visitor had departed without partaking of hospitality. Sillitoe drank little, but always remembered those to whom the gesture was welcome.

He came into the library and stood looking at her without speaking, then, without turning his head, he called, 'Some cognac.'

Then he crossed the room and took her hand, gently, without emotion.

'The Admiralty has just received news on the telegraph from Portsmouth. There has been a fight between one of our frigates and two pirates.'

Without being told, she knew it was *Unrivalled*, and that there was something more.

Sillitoe said, 'Lieutenant George Avery, my nephew and Sir Richard's aide, was killed.' He remained silent for a moment, then said, 'Captain Adam Bolitho was injured, but not badly so.'

She stared past him, at the trees, the misty sky. The river. The war was over. Napoleon was a prisoner, and probably even now being conveyed to some other place of internment. And yet, although it was over, it was not yet over; the war was here, in this quiet library.

Sillitoe said, 'George Avery was your friend also.' And then, with sudden bitterness, 'I never found the time to know him.' He gazed at the window. 'I see him now, leaving to rejoin Sir Richard when I wanted him to stay with me. I do believe that he felt sorry for me.' He waved his hand, and the gesture seemed uncharacteristically loose and vague. 'All this – and his loyalty came first.'

The door opened and Guthrie placed a tray and the cognac on a table, glancing at Catherine. She shook her head, and the door closed again.

Sillitoe took the glass, and sat in one of the uncomfortable chairs.

'He was coming home, damn it. It was what we both needed. What we both *fought*!'

She looked around, feeling the silence, as if the great house were holding its breath.

Adam was safe. There would be a letter from him as soon as it was possible. In the meantime, he was at sea, in the one element he knew and trusted. Like James Tyacke.

She walked past the chair, her mind suddenly quite clear, with that familiar sensation of detachment.

She put her hand on his shoulder and waited for him to turn his head, to look at the hand, and then at her.

As she had been, defenceless.

She said softly, 'My Spanish is not so perfect, Paul.' She saw the light returning to his eyes, and did not flinch as he took both her hands and kissed them. 'Perhaps . . . we can both find ourselves again.'

He stood, and then held her fully against his body, for the first time.

He said nothing. There were no words.

Eventually there was a gentle tap on the door, and Marlow's voice. Unreal.

'Is there anything I can do, m' lord?'

She answered for him. 'Tell William to put away the carriage, please. It will not be required again today.'

It was done.

Bryan Ferguson hurried into the kitchen and all but slammed the door behind him.

He looked at his friend, seated in the chair he always occupied when he visited them, the familiar stone bottle on the table.

'Sorry to have left you so long, old friend. I'm bad company today.' He shook his head as Allday pushed the bottle towards him. 'I think not, John. Her ladyship might think badly of the "servants" having a wet!'

Allday watched him thoughtfully.

'She changed much?'

Ferguson walked to the window and stared at the stable yard, giving himself time to consider it. The smart carriage was as before, and Young Matthew was talking to the coachman. He smiled sadly. *Young* Matthew, the Bolitho household's senior coachman. Filling out now, and a little stooped. But he had always been called 'young', even after his father had died.

He said, 'Yes. More than I thought.' It stuck in his throat. Like a betrayal.

Allday said it for him. 'High an' mighty, is she? Thought so, when I last seen her.'

Ferguson said, 'She walks from room to room with that damned lawyer, making notes, asking questions, treating my Grace like she's a kitchen maid! Can't understand it!'

Allday sipped the rum. It, at least, was good. 'I can remember when Lady Bolitho was no more'n a paid companion to the wife of some bloody-minded old judge! She may have *looked* like Sir Richard's wife, but it went no deeper. That's it an' all about it!'

Ferguson only partly heard. 'As if she owns the place!'

Allday said, 'Young Cap'n Adam's away, Bryan, an' there's only the lawyers to fight over it. It's nothin' to them.'

Ferguson touched his empty sleeve, as he often did when he was upset, although he was not aware of it.

'She asked about the sword.' He could not stop himself now. 'When I told her that Lady Catherine had given it to Captain Adam, like Sir Richard had intended, all she said was, *she had no right*!' He looked at his oldest friend. 'Who had any better right, eh? God damn them, I wish she was back in the house where she belongs!'

Allday waited. It was worse than he thought, worse than Unis had warned him it might be. 'She done the right thing to stay away while this is goin' on, an' you knows it. How would it look, that's what a lot of people would say. A sailor's woman, but she got pride too, an' that's no error! Look what happened to Lady Hamilton. All the promises and the smiles came to naught. Our Lady Catherine's not like any of 'em.

I know, I seen her in that damned boat after the wreck, an' other times, the two o' them laughin' and walkin' together, just like you have. We'll not see the likes o' them again, you mark me well!'

Ferguson felt the empty sleeve again. 'Seemed to think I was getting past my duties here. That's how it sounded to me anyway. God damn it, John, I don't *know* anything else!'

'It's all written down. Your position here is safe. Sir Richard took care o' that, like he did for everyone else.' He looked away suddenly. ''Cept for himself, God rest him.'

Ferguson sat at the table. Sir Richard had always called Allday his oak, and suddenly he understood, and was grateful for it.

He said in a calmer voice, 'An' then she went into the big room, *their* room.' He gestured towards the house. 'She told the lawyer that Sir Richard's picture should be down with all the others of the family. The ones of Cheney and Catherine she said could be removed as far as she was concerned.'

Allday asked, 'She stayin' overnight?'

'No. Plymouth. With Vice-Admiral Keen.'

Allday nodded sagely, his head shaggy in the reflected sunshine. He enjoyed his visits here. One of the family, he had always described it, until good fortune had offered him Unis, and the little inn in Fallowfield.

'I hopes that one'll be on the lookout for squalls!'

A stable boy thrust his head around the door, but hesitated when he saw Allday, who had become something of a legend around Falmouth since Sir Richard Bolitho's last battle.

Ferguson said, 'What is it, Seth?'

'They'm comin' now, Mister Ferguson!'

Ferguson stood up and took a deep breath.

'I won't be long.'

Allday said, 'We done a lot worse together, Bryan, remember?'

Ferguson opened the door, and smiled for the first time.

'That was then, old friend.'

He walked across the yard, so familiar underfoot that he would have known every cobble in the dark.

He considered Allday's question. *Has she changed much?* He saw her now, on the broad steps leading up to the entrance, elegant in a dark red gown, a hat which he guessed was fashionable in London shading her face. In her late forties, with the same autumn-coloured hair, like the young wife she had replaced when Cheney Bolitho had been killed in a carriage accident. It was hard to believe that he himself, with only one arm, had carried her, seeking help, when she and her unborn child were already dead.

It was one of fate's cruellest ironies that Richard Bolitho and his 'oak' had found Belinda in almost exactly the same circumstances after an accident on the road.

Her face was unsmiling, the mouth tighter than he remembered it. He tried not to think of Allday's pungent summing-up. *High and mighty.*

She was speaking to the lawyer, a watchful, bird-like man, while Grace waited to one side, her bunch of keys in her hand.

Ferguson saw her expression, and felt his own anger rising again. Grace, the finest housekeeper anyone could wish for, and a wife who had nursed him through pain and depression after losing his arm at the Saintes, hovering like a nobody.

'There you are, Ferguson. I shall be leaving now. But I expect to return on Monday, weather permitting.' She walked across the yard, and paused. 'And I should like to see a little more discipline among the servants.'

Her eyes were amused, contemptuous. Ferguson said, 'They are all trained and trustworthy, m' lady. Local people.'

She laughed softly. 'Not foreigners like me, you mean? I think that quaint.'

He could smell her, too. Heady, not what he might have expected. He thought of the delicate scent of jasmine in his estate office.

She said, 'Are all the horses accounted for among the other livestock?'

Ferguson saw her eyes move to the nearest stall, where the big mare Tamara was tossing her head in the warm sunlight.

He said, 'That one was a gift from Sir Richard.'

She tapped his arm very gently. 'I am aware of it. She will need exercise, then.'

Ferguson was suddenly aware of the hurt, like that which he had seen in Grace's eyes.

'No, m' lady, she was ridden regularly, until . . .'

She smiled again; she had perfect teeth. 'That has an amusing ring, don't you think?' She glanced towards the carriage, as though impatient. 'I might take her for a ride myself on Monday.' She was looking at the house again, the windows where the room faced the sea. 'You have a suitable saddle, I trust?'

Ferguson felt that she knew, that she was enjoying it, mocking him.

'I can get one if you intend . . .'

She nodded slowly. '*She* used a saddle like a man, I believe? How apt!'

She turned away abruptly and was assisted into the carriage. They watched it until it was out on the narrow road, and then walked together to their cottage.

Ferguson said, 'I'll take John back to Fallowfield presently.'

Grace took his arm and turned him towards her. She had seen his face when they had been in the room with the three portraits, and the admiral's bed. Lady Bolitho had got rid of Cheney's portrait before; it had been Catherine who had found and restored it. Bryan was a good man in every way, but he would never understand women, especially the Belindas of this world. Catherine would always be an enemy to Belinda, but Cheney's love she could never usurp.

Allday made to rise from his chair as they entered, but Grace waved him down.

'Bad?' was all he said.

Ferguson answered sharply, 'We shall have no say in things, that's certain.'

Grace put down another glass. 'Here, my love. You deserve it.' She looked from them to the empty hearth, the old cat curled up in one corner. Home. It was everything; it was all they had.

She remembered how Bryan had described those moments of Adam's first visit here after his uncle's death, when he had picked up the old sword and read the letter Catherine had left for him.

Like rolling back the years, he had said, like seeing the young Captain Bolitho again. Surely nothing could destroy all that.

She said with soft determination, 'I must lock up,' and looked at them both, saddened rather than angered by one woman's petty spite. 'God will have His say. I shall have a word with Him.'

It was Tom, the coastguard, who found her body. A year or so ago, he would have done so earlier. He had been riding loosely in the saddle, his chin tucked into his neckcloth, his mind only half aware. Like his horse, he was so familiar with every track and footpath along this wild coastline that he had always taken it for granted. Behind him, his young companion was careful not to disturb him or annoy him with unnecessary questions and observations; he was a good fellow, inexperienced though he was, and should make a competent coastguard. He had been thinking, *and he is replacing me next week.* It had been hard to accept, even though he had known to the day when his service was to be ended, and he had already been offered employment with the mail at Truro. But after all he had seen and done on these lonely and often dangerous patrols, it would be something unknown, and perhaps lacking in a certain savour.

He had heard all about the comings and goings at the old grey house, the Bolitho home for generations. Lawyers and clerks, officials, all Londoners and strangers to him. What did they know of the man and the memory? Tom had been there at the harbour when news of the admiral's death had arrived. He had been at the old church for the memorial service, when the flags had been dipped to half-mast, and young Captain Adam Bolitho had taken his place with Lady Somervell. He had thought of the times he had met her along this same coast, walking or riding, or just watching for a ship. *His* ship, which would never come any more.

And at first he had thought that it *was* her, that patch of colour, a piece of clothing moving occasionally in the breeze off Falmouth Bay. It was one of her favourite places.

Like that other time when she had joined him in the cove below Trystan's Leap and had cradled the small, broken body of the girl named Zenoria. All those times.

He had found himself dropping from the saddle, running the last few yards down the slope where the old broken wall stood half-buried in gorse and wild roses.

And then he had seen her horse, Tamara, another familiar sight on his lonely patrols above the sea.

But it had not been Catherine Somervell. He had thrust his hand into her clothing, cupping her breast, aware of her eyes watching him through the veil over her hat. But the heart, like the eyes, had been still.

He should have known; the angle of the head told him some of it, the riding crop on its lanyard around the gloved, clenched hand and the bloody weals on the mare's flank told the rest.

Tamara would have known. Would have pulled back, even if beaten, from jumping the old wall. She would have known . . .

'What is it, Tom?'

He had forgotten his companion. He stared up at the dark outline of the old house, just visible above the hillside.

'Fetch help. I'll stay here.' He glanced at the side-saddle, which had slipped when the woman had been thrown.

'It's got a lot to answer for.' He had been describing the house. But his companion was already riding hard down the slope, and there was no sound but the wind off the bay.

13

Envy

Eight days after her arrival at Gibraltar, *Unrivalled* was to all intents once more ready for sea. Pym, the rear-admiral's flag captain, had been true to his word, and had supplied as much as he could to speed repairs and replace standing and running rigging which was beyond recovery.

But it went far deeper than that. Adam Bolitho had seen and felt it from the first day. There was a new stubbornness in the men, and a kind of resentment that anyone should think *Unrivalled*'s own ship's company could not manage without outside help or interference.

Some of the wounded who had been transferred ashore to more comfortable surroundings had returned on board, eager to help, unwilling to be separated from the faces and voices they knew.

Adam had imagined that he would be able to weigh and sail unimpeded by the passenger Rear-Admiral Marlow had described. The written orders had explained little, merely emphasising the need for haste and, above all, safety. As Pym had said, 'No more battles, Bolitho!'

Curiously, it had been the third lieutenant, Daniel Wynter, who had been able to supply more information. Sir Lewis Bazeley was well known in the political circles frequented by Wynter's father. A hard-headed businessman who had been largely responsible for designing and building defences along England's south coast from Plymouth to the Nore when a French invasion had seemed a very real possibility, he had been knighted for his efforts, and it was suggested that his next appointment was Malta, where the fortifications had altered little since the first cannon had been mounted. If there had been any lingering doubts about Malta's future, they had been dispersed. A fortress in the Mediterranean's narrows, who commanded it held the key to Gibraltar and the Levant.

But Adam's hopes were dashed by the arrival at the Rock of the *Cumberland*, a stately Indiaman; he had been with Galbraith the previous morning when she had dropped anchor. Like most of John Company's ships she was impressively armed, and, he had no doubt, equally well manned. The H.E.I.C. paid generously, and offered other financial benefits to officers and seamen alike. Adam's thoughts on that score were shared by most sea officers: if as much money and care had been lavished on the King's navy, the war might have ended in half the time.

There was to be no ceremony, he had been told; the great man would transfer to the more spartan comforts of the frigate and be on his way.

The sooner the better, Adam thought.

He had visited the flagship this morning, and Pym had congratulated him on the appearance of his ship, and the speed with which the scars of battle had been hidden, if not removed. Tar, paint and polish could work wonders, and Adam was proud of the men who had done it.

The severe bruising to his groin had been given little opportunity to improve, and inevitably the pain returned when he most needed all his energy and patience.

The greater, and far more pleasant, surprise had been at the twenty or so seamen who had volunteered to sign on, after his promise to do what he could for anyone who would fight for *Unrivalled*. Galbraith had not shared the surprise, and said only that he thought the whole lot should have put their names down without question. Ten of those same men had been killed or wounded in the fight.

Adam wondered what Lovatt would have made of it.

As he had written in his report to the Admiralty, *'I gave them my word. Without them, my ship would have been lost.'* It might blow a few cobwebs away from that place. He also wondered what Bethune might have done, given the same choice. A man between two separate roles. The one he had known as a young captain. The one he was living now.

Unrivalled's gig was turning in a wide arc as she returned from the flagship. Adam leaned forward, his eyes slitted against the glare, studying the line and the trim of his command. He had been pulled around the ship every day, making certain that the additional stores, even the movement of powder and shot from one part of the hull to another, would in no way impede her agility under all conditions. He smiled to himself. Even in action again.

He thought of the noisy celebration to welcome Bellairs to the wardroom. He had made the right decision; Bellairs had all the marks of a fine officer. He recalled the rear-admiral's interest. *Has he family? Connections?* But there were many senior officers who thought exactly like Marlow when it came to promotion; he could recall one post-captain who had been quite frank about his reluctance to promote any man from the lower deck to commissioned rank. 'All you do,' he had insisted, 'is lose a good man, and create a bad officer!'

Midshipman Fielding had the tiller, and Adam guessed it had been Galbraith's decision. Homey, the midshipman who had been killed, had been his best friend. A good choice for two reasons.

Fielding said, 'Boats alongside, sir!'

Sir Lewis Bazeley and his party had arrived in his absence. No ceremony, Marlow had said.

Adam said, 'Pull right round the ship, Mr Fielding. I am not yet done.'

Jago was watching Fielding's performance on the tiller, but his thoughts were elsewhere, on the day when the dead Lovatt's son had been sent for. Told to collect his gear and report to the quarterdeck. Just a boy, with a long journey before him, to caring people in Kent. Jago had heard the captain dictating a letter to his clerk. And all paid for out of Adam Bolitho's pocket. There had been a sea fight and men had died. It happened, and would continue to happen as long as ships sailed the seven seas and men were mad enough to serve them. Lovatt had died, but so had the flag lieutenant who had served the captain's uncle. And young Homey, who had not been a bad little nipper for a 'young gentleman'. He thought of the other one, Sandell. San-*dell*. Nobody would have shed a tear for that little ratbag.

He looked over at the captain now. Remembering his face when he had torn open his breeches, the dead midshipman's blood and bone clinging to his fingers. Then the surprise when he had found the smashed watch, pieces of broken glass like bloody thorns. Why surprise? *That I should care?*

He felt the captain touch his arm. 'Bring her round now.' They both looked up as the jib boom swung overhead like a lance, the beautiful figurehead too proud to offer them a glance, her eyes already on another horizon.

He heard him say, 'Fine sight, eh?'

But all Jago could think of was the small figure of Lovatt's son, his father's sword tucked under one arm, pausing only to hold the hand of the cabin servant Napier, who had cared for him.

Jago had felt anger then. Not even a word or a look for the one man who had tried to help his father. And him.

He stared over towards the two prizes. They had done it, together . . .

Adam was watching the Indiaman, already making sail, her yards alive with men, and imagined what Catherine must have felt, leaving Malta for the last time in such a vessel.

Midshipman Fielding cleared his throat noisily. *'Bows!'*

The side party was already in position. *The captain was coming aboard.* Adam tested his leg and felt the pain again. The decks of that same Indiaman were probably lined with rich passengers, observing the little ceremony about to take place aboard just another of His Majesty's ships.

'Toss your oars . . . *up!*'

Jago winced, and saw the bowman thrust out to soften the impact alongside. But he would learn. He saw the captain reach for the first handhold, felt his muscles tighten in sympathy as if sharing his uncertainty.

Then the captain turned and looked down at him, and Jago saw the grin he remembered from that day when they had blown up the battery, before the attack on Washington.

Adam said, 'Equal strain on all parts, eh?'

Jago saw the young midshipman standing in the boat, hat in

hand but grinning up at his captain, all else, for the moment, forgotten.

Jago nodded slowly. 'You'll do me, *sir*!' Then he laughed out loud, because he found that he meant it.

Sir Lewis Bazeley was tall, but gave an immediate impression of strength rather than height. Broad-shouldered, and with a mane of thick grey hair which, although cut in the modern style, still singled him out from anyone else.

Adam strode from the entry port and extended his hand.

'I am sorry that I was not aboard to greet you, Sir Lewis.'

The handshake too was strong: a man not afraid of hard work, or of showing an example to others.

Bazeley smiled and waved vaguely towards the open sea.

'I knew this was not one of John Company's ships, Captain. I'll expect no special favours. A quick passage, and I can see for myself she's a fine sailer, and I'll ask no more of any man.' The smile broadened. 'I am sure that the women will endure it for three days.'

Adam glanced at Galbraith. 'Women? I was not told –' He saw the quick, answering nod; Galbraith had dealt with it.

Bazeley was already thinking of something else. 'I promised to pay a private visit to the lieutenant-governor, Captain. If you can provide a boat for me?'

Adam said, 'Mr Galbraith, call away the gig again,' and lowered his voice as Bazeley moved away to speak with one of his own men. 'What the hell is going on?'

'I took the women aft, sir, as you would have wished. And I've already told Mr Partridge to make sure all working parties are decently dressed, and to mark their language.'

Adam stared aft. 'How many?'

Galbraith turned as Bazeley called out something, and said, 'Only two, sir.' He hesitated. 'I will happily vacate my cabin, sir.'

'No. The chart room will suffice. I doubt I shall get much sleep, fast passage or not.'

He saw Bazeley waiting for him, feet tapping restlessly. He seemed full of energy, as if he could barely contain it. He appeared to be in his late forties, although possibly older; it was difficult to tell. Even his style of dress was unusual, more like a uniform than the clothing of a successful man of business. Or *trade*, as Rear-Admiral Marlow would no doubt describe it.

He recalled the discreet wording of his orders. *To offer every facility*. Bethune would know what to do; he was used to it.

He said, 'Perhaps you would care to sup with me and my officers, Sir Lewis. Once we are clear of the approaches.'

It would be a far cry from the Indiaman's table, he thought, and expected Bazeley to make his excuses. But he said immediately, 'A pleasure. Look forward to it.' He saw the gig being warped alongside and beckoned to one of his party.

He paused in the entry port. 'I shall not miss the ship, Captain.'

Adam touched his hat, and said to Galbraith, 'Is everyone accounted for?'

'The purser's due back on board shortly, sir. The surgeon is at the garrison – there are still two of our people there.'

Adam saw Napier hovering by the quarterdeck ladder. 'Call me when you're ready.' And grimaced as another pain lanced through him. 'I'll not be much of a host tonight!'

He made his way aft, where seamen were stowing away chests and some cases of wine which obviously belonged to Bazeley's group. Something else for Partridge to keep his eye on.

The marine sentry straightened his back as Adam passed, then leaned towards the slatted screen with sudden interest.

Adam thrust open the door, and stared at the litter of bags and boxes which appeared to cover the deck of the main cabin. A woman was sitting on one of the boxes, frowning with apparent pain while another, younger woman was kneeling at her feet, trying to drag off one of her shoes.

Adam said, 'I – I am sorry, I did not realise . . .'

The younger woman twisted round and looked up at him. Woman; she was no more than a girl, with long hair, and a wide-brimmed straw hat which was hanging down over her back. In her efforts to drag off the offending shoe some of the hair had fallen across her eyes, and one shoulder was bare and luminous in the reflected sunlight.

Adam saw all this, and that her eyes were blue, and also that she was angry. He made another attempt. 'We were not forewarned of your arrival, otherwise you would have been offered more assistance.' He gestured wordlessly at the disordered cabin. 'Your father said nothing to me about all this!'

She seemed to relax slightly, and sat on the deck looking up at him.

'Sir Lewis is my husband, Lieutenant. That you *should* have been told.'

Adam could feel the other woman watching him, and, he thought, enjoying his discomfort.

'I am Captain Adam Bolitho, ma'am.'

She stood lightly and pushed the hair from her forehead, all in one movement.

'There now, *Captain*. We all make mistakes, it would seem!' She looked around the cabin. 'Yours, I believe.' It seemed to amuse her. 'We are honoured.'

The other woman had managed to remove her shoe, and was staring glumly at her swollen foot. Lady Bazeley said gravely, 'This is Hilda. She takes care of everything.'

She laughed, and the other woman's face responded as if she had never learned to resist the sound.

The girl moved just as swiftly to the stern windows and looked at the panorama of masts and colourful lateen sails, then she faced him again, her body outlined against the blue water. 'And this is a man-of-war.' She sat on the bench seat, the hair falling across her bare shoulder. 'And you are her captain.'

Adam wondered at his own silence, his inability to answer, to be himself. She was laughing at him, teasing him, and probably very aware of the effect it had on him and anyone else she cared to confront.

She pointed at the adjoining sleeping cabin. 'I see you are not married, Captain.'

He said coolly, 'You have a keen eye, ma'am.'

'And that surprises you? Perhaps you take a dim view of a woman's place in the scheme of things!' She laughed again, and did not wait for a reply. 'You have been in a battle, I understand, and you have been injured?'

'Many were less fortunate.'

She nodded slowly. 'I am sorry for it. I have not experienced

202

war at close quarters, but I have seen what it has done to people. Those close to me.' She tossed her head, the mood passing as quickly. 'Now you really must excuse me, Captain. I must prepare myself.' She walked past him, and he could feel the impact of her presence as if they had touched. She was lovely, and she would know it, and that alone must act as a warning, before he made a complete fool of himself. Bazeley was not the sort of man who would forgive even a casual offence.

'If you will excuse me also, m' lady, *I* must prepare the ship for leaving harbour.'

She regarded him steadily, her eyes much darker in this confined space. Violet.

He glanced at the sleeping cabin, where his cot had already been folded away. Where he had dreamed, and remembered. He turned away from it. Where Lovatt had coughed out his life . . .

'My servant will assist you. He is a good lad. If you require anything else, my officers will do their best to make your stay aboard as comfortable as possible.'

'In the *Cumberland*, the captain said I was to ask *him*. Are the King's ships so different?'

She was playing with him again. Was she so young that she did not understand what she could do, was doing? Or did she not care?

He answered, 'Then ask me, m' lady, and I will try to oblige you.'

She watched him, one hand resting on the empty sword rack, her eyes thoughtful.

'A duty, then?'

He smiled and heard the sentry move away from the door. *To offer every facility.*

'I hope it may also be a pleasure, m' lady.'

He turned to the door and the pain hit him again like a bullet.

A reminder; if so, it was just in time. He walked quickly to the companion ladder, his mind clearing as the pain retreated.

Galbraith was waiting for him, with one of his lists already in his hands.

He said, 'I've spread Sir Lewis's people as evenly as

possible amongst the warrant officers. Two will be in the wardroom.'

Rank and status. Always separated, no matter how small the ship. He heard her voice again, mocking him. *Are the King's ships so different?*

Galbraith said, 'Lady Bazeley is a very striking woman, sir. I shall endeavour to make certain that she is not offended by some careless word or deed.'

He was so serious that Adam wanted to laugh, and did, at the sheer absurdity of it.

'And that includes the captain, I take it?'

Acting Lieutenant Bellairs heard him laugh, and saw the surprise and bewilderment on Galbraith's face.

He thought of the lovely woman in the cabin; she had smiled at him.

And he was a part of it.

Adam Bolitho tried to ease the discomfort in his legs on the makeshift mattress and stared at the spiralling lantern above the chart table. It was an effort to think clearly, to determine each sound and movement. Here, in the chart room, it even felt different. Like another ship.

He rubbed his eyes, and knew he would get no more sleep. He had already been on deck when *Unrivalled* had shortened sail for the night, and had sensed the growing strength of the wind, holding the ship over; the darkness had been filled with flying spray.

It had done something to clear his head. But not much.

He heard the muffled sounds of blocks, the stamp of bare feet somewhere overhead; even that seemed strangely distorted.

It was useless. He swung his legs over the side of the mattress and felt the ship rising, rising, before ploughing down again. He could see it in his mind, as clearly as if he were up there with Massie. He licked his dry lips. The middle watch. How much wine had they had?

The three lieutenants, and O'Beirne the surgeon, sitting around the table in his cabin. Lady Bazeley's servant Hilda had supervised the flow of dishes and wines, assisted by young Napier. Bazeley himself had been in good form, recounting his various trips, visits to other countries, and, in passing, his building of fortifications and harbour facilities under government contract. Most of the wine had been his, and he had insisted that they should try whatever they fancied.

Adam had been very conscious of the young woman opposite him, her eyes giving little away while she listened to each officer in turn. He had been conscious, also, of the lack of personal comforts in the great cabin; no wonder she had guessed he was unmarried. The women had probably laughed about it when they had been left alone together.

He felt for a beaker of water but it was empty. And there would be more incidents like the one which had so unreasonably disturbed him. Bazeley had left the table to select a particular bottle of wine, and had paused by one of the cabin lanterns to show them his own name, engraved on the medallion around its neck.

'A Château Lafite, 1806. Now this will appeal to you, Captain.'

The ship had been close-hauled, the deck rising and shuddering to the pressure of sea and rudder. Adam had seen Bazeley put his other hand on his wife's shoulder as if to steady himself as he had stressed the significance of that particular chateau or vintage, Adam could remember neither. He had been watching the hand gripping her naked shoulder, the strong fingers moving occasionally like a small, private intimacy.

And all the while she had been looking at him across the table; her eyes had never left his. Not once did she glance up at the man by her chair, nor had she responded to his touch. Perhaps it meant nothing, although he had heard that they had been married for only six months.

He had tasted the claret; it meant nothing to him. It might as easily have been cider.

He had seen her hand move only once, to readjust the gown across her shoulder. And even then she had looked at him.

He saw the old sword hanging beside his boat cloak, swaying with the heavy motion. Was he so stupid that he could not recognise the danger? A single wrong move, and he would lose everything. He reached out and touched the damp timbers. The ship *was* everything.

He stood slowly, waiting for the pain, but it did not come. He spread his hands on the chart table and stared at Cristie's scribbled notes and the soft cloth he used to polish the ship's chronometer, something he entrusted to no one but himself. A man who had grown up in the same streets as Collingwood; what would he think of his captain if he knew his weakness? Like a false bearing or sounding on a chart. Not to be trusted.

There was a tap on the door: someone needing to examine the chart, to make some new calculation. *If in doubt, call the Captain.* That, too, seemed to mock him.

But it was the boy Napier, his shirt soaked with spray, carrying his shoes in one hand.

'What is it?' Adam seized his wet arm. 'Where have you been?'

Napier said quietly, 'I – I thought I should call you, sir.' He swallowed, perhaps already regretting that he was here. 'The lady –'

'Lady Bazeley? What's happened?' His mind was suddenly quite clear. 'Easy, now. Tell me – take your time.'

The boy stared at him in the swaying light. 'I heard somethin', sir. I was in the pantry, like you told me.' He stared out into the poop's inner darkness. 'She were out there, sir. I tried to help, but she wouldn't move. She was sick, sir.'

Adam snatched his boat cloak and said, 'Show me.'

Once outside the chart room the sound of sea and banging canvas was almost deafening. The deck was streaming with water, shipped each time *Unrivalled* ploughed into the heavy swell.

'Here, sir!' His voice was full of relief, that he had told his captain, that she was still where he had left her.

She was below the quarterdeck ladder on the leeward side of the upper deck; seamen on watch could have passed without seeing her. She could have fallen against one of the tethered eighteen-pounders, broken a rib or her skull. It happened even to experienced sailors.

Adam crouched under the ladder and gathered her into a sitting position. She felt very light in his arms, her hair hiding her face, her feet pale in the darkness. She was wet to the skin and her body was like ice.

206

'Cloak, *here*!' He held her again, feeling her shivering, with cold or nausea, it could be either.

He dragged the cloak round her shoulders, wrapping it with great care as more spray rattled against the ladder and drenched his shirt. He felt her body contract in another spasm and saw Napier with a sand bucket under the ladder.

'Easy, easy!' He did not realise he had spoken aloud. 'I'll bring some help.'

She seemed to understand then what he had said. Who he was. She tried to turn, to struggle round, one hand pushing the hair from her face. As he restrained her he felt the coldness of her skin. She was naked under the dripping gown.

She gasped, 'No.' But when he pulled away she shook her head and said, 'No! Don't go.'

He said, 'Get someone, fast!' But Napier had already disappeared.

Slowly and carefully, he began to drag the girl from beneath the ladder. At any second now someone would come, perhaps call Massie, who was in charge of the watch. And then Bazeley.

She lolled against him and he felt her grip his hand, pulling it against her, across her. She would remember none of it. The rest did not matter.

He felt someone kneel beside him, caught the rich tang of rum. It was Jago, the boy Napier hovering behind him like a nervous ghost.

Jago said between his teeth, 'Trouble, sir?' He did not wait for or seem to expect a reply. 'All women is trouble!'

They guided and half-carried her into the poop again, the sounds becoming muffled, insignificant.

The wardroom door was closed, and there was no sentry at the cabin screen. Jago muttered, 'Just to be on the safe side, sir.'

They found the woman Hilda in a state of anxiety and disbelief.

Adam said, 'Dry her, and get her body warm again. D' you know what to do?'

She took the girl in her arms and led her to the couch which had been prepared in the sleeping cabin. There was no sign of Bazeley, nor were his clothes anywhere to be seen.

She said, 'Too much wine. I tried to warn her.' She combed the wet hair from the girl's face with her fingers. 'You should go now. I can manage.' She called after them, 'Thank you, Captain!'

Outside, it was as if nothing had happened. The sentry had reappeared at the screen, but stood aside as they passed. A ship's boy was climbing the companion ladder, carrying a tarpaulin coat for one of the watchkeepers.

Adam stared at the deckhead, measuring the sounds of rigging and canvas. They would have to take in a reef if the wind did not cease.

'In for a squall.' He had spoken aloud, unconsciously.

Jago thought of the girl sprawled on the couch, the gown plastered to her body, hiding nothing.

Half to himself, he murmured, 'It'll be a bloody hurricane if this little lot gets out!'

Adam reached the chart room and paused. 'Thank you.' But Jago was already melting into the darkness.

He closed the door and stared at the chart, and then down at his shirt and breeches, dark with spray and probably vomit, still feeling the fingers, cold on his wrist where she had pressed his hand against her. She would not remember. And if she did, her shame and disgust would soon change to affront and worse.

He heard footsteps clattering on a ladder: the midshipman of the watch coming to tell his captain that the wind was rising, or it had veered, or it was lessening. *And I shall deal with it.*

He sat on the mattress and waited. But this time the footsteps scurried past.

He lay back and stared at the lantern. And just as they had left the great cabin he had heard the woman Hilda speaking quietly, firmly.

Lifeline or death wish, it no longer seemed to matter.

Her name was Rozanne.

Tomorrow, today, it would be all through the ship. And yet, he knew it would not.

A dream then, soon over, and best forgotten.

When Galbraith came aft to relieve the middle watch, he found his captain fast asleep.

The echoes of the gun salute rolled across the crowded harbour like dying thunder, the smoke barely moving while *Unrivalled* crept to her allotted anchorage preceded by the guardboat, and let go.

Adam Bolitho tugged at his shirt beneath the heavy dress coat and watched the pale buildings of Malta's shoreline shimmering in haze like a mirage. How different from the brusque and fickle winds on their passage from the Rock, and the exhilaration of changing tack in time to outwit every trick.

And then, almost becalmed, they had crawled the last miles to this anchorage, with courses and topsails all but flat against the rigging.

The guardboat was pulling for the shore now, to warn Bethune of his visitors, he thought. Bethune was welcome to this part of it.

He walked to the opposite side of the quarterdeck and saw a few traders already idling nearby, holding up their wares, probably the very same oddments they had offered *Unrivalled* on her first visit here.

Chests and baggage were already being hauled on deck, and cargo nets were laid out in readiness to lower them into the boats. Partridge and his men were swarming around the boat-tier, doubtless speculating on their chances of getting ashore, being free from routine and discipline, perhaps to lose themselves in some of the island's more dubious attractions.

He saw the cabin skylight open and remain so. Lady Bazeley would soon be leaving. He could see it now as it was, in its true perspective, as he might assess the evidence of some offender brought before him for sentence. He had scarcely seen her since that first night. She had been on deck once or twice, but always with the woman Hilda, and once the surgeon, for company.

She had remained for the most part in the great cabin, and had had all her meals sent there. Napier confided that very little had been eaten.

Their eyes had met only once, when he had been standing by the foremast discussing some final repairs with Blane, the carpenter. She had seemed about to raise her hand to him, but had used it instead to adjust the brim of her hat.

Bazeley had spoken to him hardly at all, and then only on matters relating to their progress, the ship's time of arrival, and aspects of her routine. He had made no mention at all of his wife's behaviour, or her illness. Galbraith had solved one mystery. Bazeley had been drinking with some of his companions in the warrant officers' mess when she had left the cabin in her night attire, apparently the worse for drink.

Whenever Bazeley did mention her it was as though he were speaking of a possession. Like the hand on her shoulder that night at the table, it was deliberate. He could not imagine Bazeley doing anything on a whim.

He moved into a patch of shade, angry at himself. Like some moonstruck midshipman . . . It was unlikely that they would ever meet again, and it was just as well. He had been mad even to think about it. And it was dangerous.

Bellairs called, 'They're about to leave, I think, sir.'

Adam watched her stepping through the companion hatch; she even did that gracefully, in spite of her gown. For a moment she stood alone by the untended wheel, looking around, at the men working on deck and up in the yards, and then towards the land, veiled in its dusty heat. And then, finally, at him.

Adam crossed the deck and removed his hat. 'I hope you are feeling well, m' lady?'

He saw her eyes flash. Then she said, 'Better. Much better. Thank you, Captain.'

He relaxed a little. Either she did not remember, or she wanted only to forget.

She said, 'So this is Malta. A place worth fighting and dying for, I'm told.' There was no contempt or sarcasm; if anything, it was resignation.

'Shall you be here long, m' lady?' A voice seemed to warn him. *Stop now.*

'Who can tell?' She looked at him directly, her eyes changing again. Like the sea, he thought. 'And you, Captain? Some other port, perhaps? Some new adventure?' She tossed her head, impatient with the game. 'Some adoring woman?'

Galbraith called, 'Sir Lewis insists that our boats will not be required, sir.'

Adam stared at the shore, and saw several boats pulling smartly towards them. Bazeley was obviously a man of influence. Even Vice-Admiral Bethune was apparently eager to make his acquaintance.

Galbraith strode away to rearrange his preparations for the passengers' departure, and Adam said, almost to himself, 'I have learned that gratitude in a woman can be harmful. To *her*, m' lady.' He saw the sudden uncertainty on her face. 'I had hoped to escort you ashore.' He smiled. 'Another time, maybe.'

Bazeley was here now, calling over his shoulder to one man, beckoning impatiently to another.

He said, 'We take our leave, Captain. Perhaps one day –' And swung round again. 'Be careful with that, you clumsy oaf!'

It was then that she thrust out her hand, and said softly, 'Thank you, Captain Bolitho. You will know what for. It is something we will share with no one.'

He kissed her hand, feeling her eyes on him, and imagining that her fingers closed very slightly around his own.

A bosun's chair was already rigged, and she allowed herself to be settled in it, her gown protected from grease and tar by a canvas apron.

'Hoist away, *'andsomely*!'

Every unemployed hand turned to watch as she was hoisted and then guyed out with great care to be lowered into a waiting boat. Bethune had even sent his flag lieutenant to assist.

Bazeley glanced around, patting his pockets as if to be sure he had left nothing personal below.

Adam thought of the mattresses and bedding strewn across the sleeping cabin. Where they had lain together. Where Bazeley had taken and used her like a plaything.

Bazeley said, 'Good sailing, Captain.' He glanced briefly at his wife in the boat alongside. 'I was told you were reckless.' He held up one hand. 'You get results, that's all important in my view!' Then he laughed, and Adam saw her look up, shading her eyes. 'But you know caution when you see it, eh? And that's no bad thing, either!'

Adam watched the boat bearing off, and said, 'I shall be going ashore in one hour, Mr Galbraith.' He sensed the unspoken question, and added flatly, 'To see the admiral. Perhaps we may be given something useful to do!'

Galbraith watched him walk to the companion way before picking up the duty midshipman's telescope.

Sunlight on her cream-coloured gown, a scarlet ribbon on

211

her wide-brimmed hat which matched the other one in her hair. All compressed into one small, silent picture. There could be nothing between them. How could there be? But today, she had dressed with obvious care, and he had seen her expression when the captain had pressed his lips to her hand.

Wynter had told him what he knew of Sir Lewis Bazeley. A man who had forced himself to the top, offering and no doubt receiving favours on the way. People less accustomed to deception might describe them as bribes, but one thing was certain: he would be a ruthless man to cross. Galbraith had lost his own command because of another's malignant influence and dislike. *Unrivalled* was his only chance of obtaining another.

He smiled grimly. And yet, all he could feel for Adam Bolitho was envy.

Below in the great cabin, Adam looked around; the place was suddenly spacious and bare again, the quarter gallery open as if to clear away the last vestige of their presence here. The bedding had vanished, his own cot was in its place. No wonder she had played with him, when all the time . . .

He saw his boat cloak hanging from the deckhead, where it was never kept. He took it down and folded the collar. The entire garment had been sponged and cleaned, the stains from that night gone completely. He felt inside the deep pocket, although he did not know why.

It was a small, sealed paper. He carried it to the quarter gallery and opened it.

There was no note. But there was a lock of her hair, tied with a piece of scarlet ribbon.

14

Destiny

Vice-Admiral Sir Graham Bethune pushed some of the unopened despatches to one side and got up from the ornate desk.

'Deal with these, Grimes. My head is too full for much more at present.'

He felt the clerk's eyes following him to the window, which looked across the small, sun-drenched courtyard.

The day had started badly with the guardboat's officer reporting that *Unrivalled*'s arrival meant more than simply the delivery of despatches or letters – there were visitors to accommodate and entertain. Bethune felt the same resentment returning as he heard a woman's voice, and saw the gleam of colour from the opposite balcony. His flag lieutenant had insisted that that particular room was the obvious choice for guests who had come with the full blessing of the government and the lords of the Admiralty. He could hear Bazeley's voice too, loud, demanding, authoritative. Full of himself.

He sighed, and walked back to the desk. There was a letter from his wife as well, asking about the possibility of joining him in Malta, or of his coming back to London. She made it sound like the only civilised place to live.

He glanced at Adam Bolitho's report. Two more prizes. Surely their lordships would offer him extra ships now. There was proof enough that the activities of the Dey of Algiers and his equally unpredictable ally in Tunis required swifter, sharper measures. He almost smiled. It would also make an impressive spearhead for his return to another post in London.

Bethune enjoyed the company of women, and they his, but

he had always been discreet. The prospect of his wife joining him in Malta made him realise just how far they had grown apart since her attempts to humiliate Catherine, perhaps even long before that. Of course, he thought bitterly, there were always the children . . .

He looked at the other window, thinking of Lieutenant Avery standing beside him, sharing it, remembering it. And now he was dead. The Happy Few were only ghosts, only memories.

Bazeley's young wife would turn a few heads here when her presence became known. She had probably married the great man for his fortune, which, allegedly, was considerable, but if any of the young bloods from the local garrison got the wrong ideas, they had better watch out. He wondered how Adam had managed to resist her very obvious charm on the passage here from Gibraltar. He was reckless. But he was not a fool.

The flag lieutenant was back. 'Captain Bouverie is here, Sir Graham.'

Bethune nodded. It was even harder to recall Onslow as he had been on that last night together, lying on his back, snoring and drunk. But almost human.

'Very well.'

Onslow smiled, as always apologetic. 'And Captain Bolitho is due shortly. His boat was reported a few minutes ago.'

Bethune turned away and looked across the courtyard.

'I will see them.' He added abruptly, 'Separately.'

Onslow understood, or thought he did. He would do it by seniority.

Bethune was well aware of the peculiar rivalry between Adam Bolitho and Emlyn Bouverie of the frigate *Matchless*. They scarcely knew one another, and yet it had leaped into being. He thought of the successes his small squadron had achieved, despite, or perhaps even because of this personal conflict. It might even be used to greater advantage if he could enlarge his chain of command here. He smiled again. He could never go back to being a mere captain, and he wondered why he had not noticed the change in himself before.

Adam Bolitho stood aside to allow two heavily laden donkeys to push their way through the narrow street. When he glanced up at the strip of blue sky overhead, it seemed the buildings were almost touching.

He had deliberately taken a longer route from the jetty where he had landed from the gig, perhaps for the exercise, maybe to think; his mind was only vaguely aware of the babble of voices around him. So many tongues, so many different nationalities crammed together in apparent harmony. Plenty of uniforms, too. The Union Flag was obviously here to stay.

There were stairs across this part of the street, and he felt the stabbing pain, when earlier he had all but forgotten it.

He paused to give himself time and heard the gentle tap of a hammer. Here the open-fronted shops were as varied as the passers-by. A man selling grain, another asleep beside a pile of gaudy carpets. He ducked beneath a canopy and saw a man sitting cross-legged at a low table. The sound was that of his hammer against a miniature anvil.

He looked up as Adam's shadow fell across shallow baskets full of metal, probably Spanish silver like the chain on Catherine's locket, and asked in faultless English, 'Something for a lady, Captain? I have much to offer.'

Adam shook his head.

'I may return later . . .' He hesitated, and bent to examine a perfect replica of a sword. 'What is this?'

The silversmith shrugged. 'Not old, Captain. Made for a French officer who was here,' he gave a polite smile, 'before you came. But never collected. The war, you understand.'

Adam picked up the sword, so small, but heavy for its size. A brooch, or a clasp of some kind. He smiled; he was being ridiculous, and he knew it.

The silversmith watched him calmly. 'There is an inscription, very small. It must have been important. It says *Destiny*, Captain.' He paused. 'I have other pieces also.'

Adam turned it over in the palm of his hand. 'You speak very good English.'

Again the shrug. 'I learned in Bristol, many years ago!' He laughed, and several people who had paused to observe the transaction joined in.

Adam heard none of them. '*Destiny*.' Like the horizon which never got any nearer.

Somewhere a bell began to chime, and he clapped his hand

to his empty watch pocket. He was late. Outwardly at least, Bethune was tolerant enough, but he was still a vice-admiral.

He said, 'I would like to have it.'

The silversmith watched him take out his purse, and when he was satisfied held up one hand.

'That is *enough*, Captain.' He smiled as Adam held it to the light. 'If the lady declines it, sir, I will buy it back from you, at a consideration, of course.'

Adam returned to the sunlight a little dazed, amazed at his own foolish innocence.

He touched his hat to a Royal Marine sentry and walked into the courtyard.

An unknown French officer, and a silversmith from Bristol.

Then he saw her on the balcony, in the same gown she had been wearing when she had left *Unrivalled*. She was looking down at him, but she did not smile or wave to him.

He felt it again, like a challenge. Destiny. The horizon.

And he knew it was already too late for caution.

Adam was surprised by the warmth of Bethune's welcome, as if he were genuinely pleased, relieved even, to see him.

'Sit here.' He gestured to a chair far from the reflected glare. 'I saw you come through the gates just now – limping, I thought. I read the full report.' He glanced at the dour-faced clerk at the other table. 'Most of it, in any case. I am glad it was nothing worse.'

'The shot struck my watch. Which is why I was late, sir.'

He saw Bethune look meaningly at his flag lieutenant. So they had noticed.

'You are here and you are safe, that's the main thing. I am so damned short of vessels I am beginning to think that nobody cares in the Admiralty.' He laughed, and Adam saw the young officer again.

Bethune said, 'We shall take wine in a moment. I would ask you to stay for a meal, but I have matters which require prompt action.' The easy smile again. 'But you've heard all that before, eh? We all have!'

Adam realised for the first time that Bethune was adrift here in Malta. Perhaps high command was even lonelier than the life of a captain.

'No matter, sir. I have to return to my ship. But thank you.'

Bethune walked to the window, one hand tapping against the flaking shutter.

'Captain Bouverie of *Matchless* was here.'

'I saw him briefly, sir.'

'Not a happy man, I fear. His ship badly requires an overhaul. She has been the longest out here, as far as I am aware.'

Adam thought of something he had heard Jago say. *Like a man who's found a penny but lost a guinea.* It fitted Bouverie well.

And Adam did not need to be told. If *Matchless* was sent to a dockyard in England she might be paid off, laid up, her company disbanded.

It could happen to me. To us.

He saw Bethune step back from the shutter, and knew he had been watching the balcony. Watching *her*. The revelation surprised him, and he began to see him in quite a different light, recalling that Catherine had spoken of him favourably in her letters. Rank had its privileges, and its drawbacks too, apparently.

Bethune said, 'We have received information from what is judged to be a reliable source.' He waited for Adam to join him at the other table where Onslow had arranged a chart, weighed down with carved ivory figurines. 'These islands to the south-west of Malta. Owned by nobody, claimed by many.' He tapped the chart. 'Almost midway 'twixt here and the coast of Tunis. They are useless for trade or habitation except for a few fishermen, and not many of those, with the corsairs so active in these waters.'

He stood aside as Adam bent over the chart.

'I know them, sir, but at a distance. Dangerous shoals, not even safe for an anchorage. But small craft,' he looked up and saw Bethune nod, '*they* would find the islands useful.' There was a sudden silence, broken only by the scratching of the clerk's pen. Even the sounds of the street did not penetrate to this room.

'Some of the islands have high points of ground.' He touched the chart as if to confirm it. 'When this one was last corrected, it stated that two of them could be three hundred feet or more above sea level.'

Bethune rubbed his chin thoughtfully. 'I believe the corsairs are sheltering their chebecks among these islands. The high ground rules out any kind of normal approach. A blind lookout would see our t'gallants before we got within five leagues of the place!'

'And the information is good, sir?'

Bethune glanced towards the window again, but seemed to change his mind.

'Two traders have been attacked in the past week, another is missing. A Sicilian vessel saw the chebecks – her master has given us some useful information over the years. Us *and* the French, of course!'

Adam said quietly, 'My uncle always had the greatest respect for the chebecks, sir. His flagship *Frobisher* was attacked by some of them. Lieutenant Avery told me about it.'

They both looked at the empty chair, and Bethune said, 'He saw what many of us missed.'

Adam walked a few paces. 'A landing party. At night. Volunteers.'

'Royal Marines?'

'I think not, sir. They are fine fighters, but they are foot soldiers at heart. This would require stealth, men used to working aloft in all weathers, sure-footed, eager.'

A door opened and he heard the clink of glasses. No wonder Bouverie had looked so depressed and so angry. His ship was too slow. By the time *Matchless* was restored to her proper trim it might be too late. For him.

Bethune said, 'I can offer *Halcyon* in support. I cannot spare my flagship, and the rest of the squadron is deployed elsewhere.' He banged the table with his fist. 'God, I could find work for ten more frigates!'

Adam knew the other frigate, half *Unrivalled*'s size, twenty-eight guns, with a youthful and zealous captain named Christie. The family again . . . Christie had been a midshipman under James Tyacke at the Nile. They had both been scarred, in different ways, on that terrible day.

Adam could feel Bethune watching him, perhaps seeing

218

himself already there, confronted by an operation which at the best of times could spell disaster. But if the corsairs were using the islands they could not have chosen a more effective lair. A thorn in the side; no. Far deeper than any thorn.

Hazardous or not, Captain Bouverie would perceive it as an act of favouritism. *As I would.* He felt the piece of silver inside his shirt, and wanted to laugh at the absurdity of it.

He recalled a captain who had once said to him after a bitter hand-to-hand engagement, 'You might have been killed, you young idiot! Did you ever pause to consider that?'

He straightened his back and took a goblet from the hovering servant.

'I think it can be done, sir.'

'I hoped you might say that.' Bethune could scarcely conceal his relief. 'But no unnecessary risks.'

Adam smiled tightly. Bethune had never lost his ship, witnessed her agony, and that of her people who had trusted in him.

Perhaps it made it easier for him.

Onslow ventured, 'The reception, Sir Graham?'

Bethune frowned at him. 'It would be better if you weighed at first light. I will have your orders prepared immediately, Christie's too.' He looked at the pile of documents awaiting his signature, and said abruptly, 'Sir Lewis and Lady Bazeley, were they any trouble?'

'We had a fast enough passage, sir.'

Bethune looked at him and smiled. It was not what he had asked.

'There is a reception for them this evening. Short notice, but they are used to that in Malta. *I* am not.'

He walked with him to the door, while Onslow made a display of folding the charts, probably in readiness for the next visitor.

Bethune said, 'Captain Forbes will give you all the help he can. He has served in these waters for many years.' Then, at a complete tangent, 'I am truly sorry that you cannot join us this evening. Everything must appear normal.' He paused, as if he had gone too far. 'A king once said, if you tell your best friend a secret, it is no longer a secret!'

The mood did not last, and he said almost brusquely, 'I will see you when you sign for your orders. No matter what I am doing, I want to be told.'

Adam descended the marble stairs, his mind already on the details of his mission. Total responsibility. He had heard it from his uncle several times. *If you succeed, others will get the reward; if you fail, yours is the total responsibility.*

He saw the flag captain's stocky figure by the entrance. Ready to play his role.

Unrivalled had arrived that morning; tomorrow she would weigh and proceed to sea once more. And suddenly he knew he was not sorry to leave.

Leigh Galbraith stood by the hammock nettings and studied the boats alongside. One of them was *Halcyon*'s gig, her crew very smart in checkered shirts and tarred hats. He smiled. *A ship shall be judged by her boats.*

The other frigate's captain had been down in the great cabin for more than an hour. Each seeing his own ship's part in what lay ahead, the selection of men, and who would lead them.

A landing party. A raid, to flush out the corsairs so that the frigates could get amongst them before they could make good their escape.

He heard Lieutenant Massie, who had the watch, speaking sharply to a boatswain's mate, a man not known for his quick response to anything beyond routine. Massie had little patience with anyone who could not keep up. He was a good gunnery officer, one of the best Galbraith had known, but he was not a man for whom it was possible to feel any affection.

Massie joined him now, breathing hard. 'A bloody block of wood, that man!' Galbraith glanced at the open skylight. *Soon now.* He heard Bolitho laugh. A small thing, but reassuring.

The captain had said to him while they had been waiting for Christie to arrive from *Halcyon*, 'I want you to take charge of the landing party. I've a few suggestions which we can discuss later, but mostly it will be your initiative, and your decision when you get there.' His dark eyes had been intense. 'Not a battle, Leigh. I need you as my senior lieutenant, not as a dead hero. But you are the obvious choice.' He had smiled. 'The *right* choice.'

Massie said, 'One man to be flogged, so why all the fuss?'

A seaman had been found in his mess, off duty and drunk. It seemed they had only just dropped anchor, and now they were leaving again . . . *There will be danger.* Aboard ship it was different. Faces and voices to sustain you, the strength of the timbers surrounding you.

Galbraith said, 'A flogging helps no one at a time like this.'

'They'd laugh in your face without firm, strong discipline, and you know it!' Massie sounded triumphant when Galbraith did not respond. 'They offer us scum to be made into seamen. Well, so be it!'

Galbraith stared at the other ships, their reflections less sharp now in a freshening breeze.

Massie seemed to read his thoughts, and said angrily, 'I expect half of Malta knows what we are about! When we reach those damned islands the birds will have flown, and good riddance, I say!'

Is that what I was hoping? Galbraith thought suddenly of the gathering in the captain's cabin when they had entertained Sir Lewis Bazeley and his young wife at supper. The wine, like the endless procession of tempting and distracting adventures with which Bazeley had dominated the conversation, disappearing bottle by bottle. Like most sea officers, Galbraith had little experience of fine wines. You took what was available, in a far different world from that described by Sir Lewis. But once or twice he had received the impression that Bazeley had not always known the luxury of good food and wine, or beautiful women. He was a hard man in more ways than Galbraith had yet fathomed.

Massie waved an arm towards the shore. 'And a reception, no less! We should be there, after all we've achieved since we joined this damned squadron!'

Galbraith remembered most of all how the young woman had looked at the captain whenever he had answered one of Bazeley's many questions. As if she were learning something. About him, perhaps . . .

He answered wearily, 'Next time, maybe.'

Midshipman Cousens said, 'The captain's coming up, sir.'

Galbraith nodded, glad that the conversation had been interrupted, and that Massie would be quiet for a while.

'Man the side!'

The two captains stood together by the rail and waited for the gig to grapple alongside.

Christie turned and smiled at Galbraith. 'My second lieutenant will be supporting you on this venture. Tom Colpoys – he's an experienced officer, so you'll have no complaint on that score!'

So easily said. As if neither of these young captains had a care or a doubt in the world.

The muskets slapped to the present, a sword sliced through the dusty air, the calls squealed, and moments later Christie's gig pulled smartly out from *Unrivalled*'s shadow.

Adam Bolitho swung on his heel. 'A man for punishment, I understand?'

Galbraith watched his face as Massie reeled off the offences.

'Willis, you say?' Adam paced to the rail and back again. 'Foretopman, starboard watch, correct?'

Massie seemed surprised. 'Aye, sir.'

'First offence?'

Massie was out of his depth. 'Of this kind, sir.'

Adam pointed towards the shimmering rooftops and battlements.

'Over yonder, a good many will be too drunk to stand tonight, Mr Massie. Officers, no less, so think on that too! They shall not be flogged and neither shall Willis. Give him a warning, this time.' He looked keenly at the lieutenant, as if searching for something. 'And a warning for the one who brought him aft in the first place. Responsibility pulls in two directions. I'll not have it used for working off old scores.'

Massie strode away, and Galbraith said, 'I should have dealt with it, sir.' Massie had probably never been spoken to in that manner in his life. Few captains would have cared, in any case.

Adam said, 'I shall be going ashore directly.' And smiled, at something Galbraith did not understand. 'To sign for my destiny.' He looked along his command, and Galbraith wondered how he saw her. Only a captain could answer, and Bolitho would share that with nobody. Unless . . . 'When I return offshore, you will join me in a glass.' The rare, infectious smile again. '*Not* claret, I think.'

Then the mood was gone, just as quickly, and he said, 'The man Willis. His wife has died.' He paused, the memory stirring. 'In Penzance.'

'I did not know, sir.'

'Why should you? But Massie is his lieutenant. *He* should have known, and cared enough to prevent this unnecessary affront.'

Bellairs was hurrying towards them, but he waited for the captain to leave before he produced a list of items he had been told to muster for the proposed landing party.

Galbraith put his hand on the young man's shoulder. 'Later, but not now, my lad.' He shook the shoulder gently. 'I wish you had been here just now. You'd have learned something which would have had your promotion board agog with admiration.' He thought of the captain's expression, the dignity and the fire in the quiet voice. 'About the true qualities which make a King's officer. I certainly did, believe me!'

He knew Bellairs was still gazing after him when he walked away to call the gig's crew. And he was glad he had shared it with him.

Adam chose the same leisurely approach to Bethune's house without truly knowing why. The narrow street was in deeper shadow now, and most of the stalls had been closed or abandoned for the night. He looked towards the low-canopied shop where he had spoken with the silversmith, but that, too, was deserted. As if he had imagined it.

He had left the gig at the jetty alone and had sensed Jago's disapproval; he had even ventured to suggest that he should keep him company. *The whole place is probably full of cutthroats an' thieves.* But he had remained with the boat's crew when Adam had told him that there would not be a man left, hand-picked or not, when he returned.

Like that handshake; Jago had still come only halfway towards sharing his innermost thoughts.

But the old sword at his hip had been loosened in its scabbard all the same.

There had been a couple of small boys begging, and a savage-looking guard dog, but otherwise his walk was undisturbed.

The air was cooler as evening lengthened the shadows, but not much. He thought without pleasure of the reception at Bethune's headquarters, and imagined the press of sweating bodies, and the wine. *Unrivalled* would put to sea in the morning. He had to keep a clear head, to deal with any remaining problems before the two frigates were committed.

He turned the corner and saw the pale gates looming out of the dusk. Every window seemed to be ablaze with light. He could smell cooking, and felt his stomach contract. He had eaten nothing since breakfast; Jago probably knew about that, too.

He touched his hat to a sentry and strode into the courtyard, aware of vague shapes, murmured instructions, and the continuous clatter of dishes and glassware.

He recalled Bethune's casual question about the passage from Gibraltar. Did he see his unwanted visitor as a burden, or a possible stepping-stone to some new appointment? He was welcome to it. His was a world Adam had never known, and had repeatedly told himself he would never willingly share.

There was music, hesitant at first, violins, seemingly at odds with one another and then suddenly sweeping through the courtyard in a single chord.

He stopped and listened as the music faded away, and somebody called out for attention. *Short notice.* Bethune had not approved of that, either.

'Why, Captain Bolitho, is it not? Standing alone and so thoughtful. You are *very* early!'

He turned and saw her in a curved entrance he had not noticed on his previous visit. In the deepening shadows her gown looked blue, perhaps chosen to match her eyes. Her dark hair was piled above her ears, Hilda's work, he thought, and she was wearing earrings, shining like droplets of fire in the last sunlight.

He removed his hat and bowed.

'My lady, I am a visitor, not a guest. I shall be on my way as soon as I have met with Sir Graham or his aide.'

'Ah, I see. More duty, then?' She laughed and flicked open a small fan which had been dangling on a cord at her wrist. 'I had thought we might see more of you.'

He joined her in the paved entrance and caught her perfume,

224

her warmth. The same woman, and yet so different from the one he had held and restrained in her moment of nausea and despair.

'It seems you are well cared for, m' lady.' He looked past her as the music began again. 'I hope the reception is a great success.'

She took his arm, suddenly and deliberately, turning him towards the music, towards her, until they were only inches apart.

'I do not care a fig for the reception, *Captain*! I have seen so many, too many . . . I am concerned that you choose to blame me because of such . . .' She seemed angry that she could not find the word to express her displeasure.

'Necessities, m' lady?'

'No, never that!' She calmed herself; he could feel her fingers gripping his arm, like the night Napier had brought him to her.

She said, 'Walk with me. There is a view of the harbour on the other side.' Her fingers tightened as if to drive away his resistance. 'Nobody will see us. Nobody will care.'

'I do not think you understand . . .'

She shook his arm again. 'Oh, but I do, Captain! I am well aware of the rules, the *etiquette* of King's officers. No talk of women in the mess. But a knowing nod and a quick wink betrays such chivalry!' She laughed, and the sound echoed in the curved archway. 'Listen! D' you hear that?'

They came out on to a paved parapet, beyond which Adam saw the sea, sunset already bronze on the water, the riding lights and small moving craft making patterns all their own.

The hidden orchestra was playing now, and the other sounds of preparation seemed to pause as if servants and orderlies had stopped to listen.

She said almost in a whisper, 'It's beautiful,' and turned to look at him. 'Don't you agree?'

He put his hand on hers and felt her tense. A woman one moment, a child the next. Or was he deluding himself yet again?

'As you have observed, my lady, I am somewhat aback when it comes to the finer points of etiquette.'

She did not respond, but said a moment later, as if she had

225

not heard him, 'A waltz. D' you know that some people still claim it is too risqué, too bold, for public performance?'

He smiled. She was teasing him.

'I am thankful I am spared such hazards!'

She turned towards him again, and removed his hand from hers as if she was about to walk away. Then she took his hands once more, and stood looking at him, her head slightly on one side, deciding perhaps if she had already gone too far.

'Listen. Hear it now? Let it take charge of you.'

She placed his right hand on her waist, pressing it there, like the night when she had refused to release him.

'Now hold me, guide with your left hand, so.'

Adam tightened his grip and felt her move against him. Even in the uncertain light he could see the bare shoulders, the darker shadow between her breasts. His heart was pounding to match the madness, the pain of his longing. And madness it was. At any moment somebody would discover them; rumour could run faster than any wind. And jealousy could match and overwhelm any sense or caution.

But she was moving, taking him closer, and his feet were following hers as if they had always been waiting for this moment.

She said, 'You lead,' and leaned back on his arm, her eyes wide. 'Then I shall *yield*.'

And laughed again. The music had stopped, like the slamming of a single door.

How long they stood in the same position was impossible to know. She did not move, even when he pressed harder against her thighs, until he could feel the heat of her body, her shocked awareness of what was happening.

Then, carefully, firmly, he held her away, gripping the naked shoulders until she was able to look at him again.

He said, 'Now you know, *my lady*, this is no game for tricksters. Bones mend, but not hearts. You would do well to remember that!'

She dragged her hand away and raised it as if to strike him, but shook her head when he seized her wrist. 'It was not a game or a trick, not to me. I cannot explain . . .' She stared at him, her eyes shining with tears, and he felt her come against him again, without protest or amusement. He wanted to push her away, no matter what it might do to each or both of them.

Think what you are doing, of the consequences. Are you beyond reason because of a loss you could never have prevented, a happiness which was never yours to explore?

But there was no solution. Only the realisation that he wanted this woman, this girl, another man's wife.

He heard himself say, 'I must leave you. Now. I have to see the admiral.'

She nodded very slowly, as if the action was painful.

'I understand.' He felt her face against his chest, her mouth damp through his shirt. 'You may despise me now, Captain Bolitho.'

He kissed her shoulder, felt her body tighten, shock, disbelief, it no longer mattered.

There were voices now, and laughter, someone announcing an arrival. She was fading into the shadows, moving away, but with one arm held out.

He followed her through the same low archway, and she said, 'No, no – it was wrong of me!' She shook herself as if to free her body of something. 'Go now, please go!'

He held her, kissing her shoulder again, lingeringly, and with a deep sensuality. There were more voices, closer. Someone looking for him, or for her.

He pressed the small silver sword into her hand and closed her fingers around it, then he walked through the archway and into the courtyard once more, his mind and body fighting every step, almost daring to hope she might run after him and prevent him from leaving. But all he heard was the sound of metal on stone. She had flung the little clasp away from her.

He saw Lieutenant Onslow peering out from the opposite doorway and felt something like relief.

'Captain Bolitho, sir! Sir Graham sends his compliments, but he is unable to receive you this evening. He is with Sir Lewis Bazeley, and before the guests arrived he thought –'

Adam touched his sleeve. 'No matter. I will sign for my orders and leave.'

Onslow said lamely, 'He wishes you every success, sir.'

Adam did not glance up at the balcony. She was there, and

she would know that he knew it. Anything more would be insanity.

He followed the flag lieutenant into another room. While Onslow was taking out the written orders, Adam held out his hand and examined it. It should be shaking, but it was quite steady. He picked up the pen, and thought of Jago down there with the gig's crew.

There were far more dangerous forces abroad this evening than cutthroats and thieves. Perhaps Jago had realised that also.

I wanted her. And she will know it.

He could hear her voice still. *Then I shall yield.*

Perhaps they would never meet again. She would know the perils of any liaison. Even as a game.

The gig's crew sat to attention when he appeared, and the bowman steadied the gunwale for him to step aboard. Jago took the tiller.

'Cast off!'

Captain Bolitho had said nothing. But he could smell perfume, the same she had been using when they had carried her, almost insensible, below.

'Bear off forrard! Out oars!'

Jago smiled to himself. *Get back to sea. Good thing all round.*

'Give way all!'

Adam saw the riding light of his ship drawing nearer and sighed.

Destiny.

15

Close Action

Lieutenant Leigh Galbraith got down on his knees in the cutter's sternsheets and ducked his head under the canvas canopy to peer at the compass. When he opened the lantern's small shutter it seemed as bright as a rocket, just as the normal sounds around him were deafening.

He closed the shutter and regained his seat beside the helmsman. By contrast it was even darker than ever now, and he could imagine the man enjoying his lieutenant's uncertainty. He was Rist, one of *Unrivalled*'s senior master's mates, and the most experienced. The stars, which paved the sky from horizon to horizon, were already paler, but Rist navigated with the assurance of one who lived by them.

Galbraith watched the regular rise and fall of oars, not too fast, not enough to sap a man's strength when he might need it most. Even they sounded particularly loud. He tried to dismiss it from his thoughts and concentrate. The cutter's rowlocks were clogged with grease, the oar looms muffled with sackcloth; nothing had been left to chance.

He imagined their progress as a sea bird might have seen them, had there been any at this hour. Three cutters, each astern of the other, followed by a smaller boat which had been hoisted aboard *Unrivalled* under cover of darkness. Was it only two nights ago? It felt like a week since they had made that early morning departure from Malta.

It had been a quiet night when they had hoisted the other boat aboard, in spite of a steady breeze through the rigging and furled sails, quiet enough to hear the music carried across

229

the harbour from the big white building used by Vice-Admiral Bethune and his staff.

Galbraith had seen the captain by the quarterdeck rail, his hands resting on it as he watched the boat being manhandled into a position away from the others. His head had been turned towards the music, as if his thoughts were elsewhere.

Rist said quietly, 'Not long now, sir.'

Galbraith failed to find comfort in his confidence. A point off-course and the boats might pass the poorly described and charted islet; and he was in command. When daylight came in a mere two hours' time it would lay them bare, all secrecy would be gone, and the chebecks, if they were there, would make their escape.

There were thirty-five all told in the landing party, not an army, but any larger force would increase the risk and the danger of discovery. Captain Bolitho had decided to include some marines after all, only ten, and each man, as well as their own Sergeant Everett, was an expert shot. When Galbraith had carried out a final inspection of the party before they had disembarked he had noticed that even without their uniforms they managed to look smart and disciplined. The others could have been pirates, but all were trained and experienced hands. Even the foul-mouthed hard man, Campbell, was here in the boat. In a fight he would ask no quarter, nor offer any.

Halcyon's second lieutenant, Tom Colpoys, was in the boat furthest astern. It would be his decision either to fight or to run if his leader encountered trouble.

Colpoys was a tough, surprisingly quiet-spoken man, old for his rank, and indeed the oldest man in the landing party. Galbraith had been immediately aware of the respect he was shown by his own sailors, and of a calm assurance which could not have come easily to him. From the lower deck, he had probably served all kinds of officer before rising to that same rank.

It was good to know that he was second-in-command of what his young captain had called this 'venture'.

Galbraith had taken part in several such raids throughout his varied service, but never in this sea. Here there was no running tide to cover your approach, no boom of surf to warn or guide your final decision to land.

230

He thought of the Algerine chebecks he had seen and had heard described by the old Jacks. They were laughed at by those who had never encountered them, as relics from a dead past, from the pharaohs to the rise of the slave trade. But those who had experience of them treated them with respect. Even their rig had improved over the years, so that they could outsail most of the smaller traders on which they preyed. Their long sweeps gave them a manoeuvrability which compensated for their lack of armament. A man-of-war, with a fully trained and disciplined company, but becalmed, could become a victim in minutes. A chebeck could pull around the ship's stern and fire point-blank with her one heavy cannon through the unprotected poop. And then the Algerines would board their victim, without either fear or mercy. It was said that the dead were the lucky ones, compared with the horrors which inevitably followed.

He saw Williams, one of *Unrivalled*'s gunner's mates, bending over the heavy bag he had brought with him. Another professional, he had been entrusted with fuses, powder, and the combining of both into a floating inferno. Galbraith had seen him clambering over the small boat they had hoisted aboard, supervising the placing and lashing of each deadly parcel. If anything could dislodge the chebecks, this miniature fireship would do it. If they were driven from shelter and forced into deeper water, even they would be no match for *Unrivalled*'s speed and armament.

'*Now*, sir!' Rist eased the tiller-bar without waiting for an order. Galbraith saw the man in the bows waving his arm above his head, and then pointing firmly across the starboard bow. Nothing was said, nobody turned to watch, and so break the steady stroke of oars.

Galbraith wanted to wipe his face with his hand. 'Ease the stroke – allow the others to see what we are about!'

He was surprised at the calmness of his own voice. At any moment a shot might shatter the stillness, another boat forge out from the invisible islet. Only the handful of marines had loaded muskets. Anything else would be madness. He himself had been in the middle of a raid when someone had tripped and fallen, exploding his musket and rousing the enemy.

It was no consolation now. He touched the hanger at his side and wondered if he would have time to load his pistol if the worst happened. And then he saw it. Not a shape, not an outline, but like a presence which must have been visible for a long time, and yet hidden, betrayed only by the missing stars which formed its backcloth.

He gripped Rist's shoulder. 'We'll go in! *Beach her!*' Afterwards he wondered how he had managed to grin. 'If there *is* a poxy beach!'

Then he was scrambling through the boat, steadying himself on a shoulder here, an oarsman's arm there. Men he knew, or thought he did, who would trust him, because there was no other choice.

'Boat your oars. Roundly, there!'

Galbraith heaved himself over and almost fell as the water surged around his thighs and boots, dragging at him, while the cutter plunged on towards the paler patch of land.

More men were over the side now, and one gasped aloud as he stumbled on hard sand or shingle. The boat grated noisily aground, men rocking and guiding the suddenly clumsy hull until it eventually came to rest.

Galbraith wiped spray from his mouth and eyes. Figures were hurrying away, like the spokes of a wheel, and he had to shake himself to recall the next details. But all he could think was that *they* had remembered what to do. Exactly as it had been outlined to them on the frigate's familiar deck. Yesterday . . . it was impossible.

Someone said hoarsely, 'Next boat comin' in, sir!'

Galbraith pointed. 'Tell Mr Rist! Then go and help them to beach!'

And suddenly the small hump of beach was full of figures, men seizing their weapons, others making the boats secure, and the gunner's mate, Williams, floundering almost chest-deep in water while he controlled the last boat in the procession.

Lieutenant Colpoys sounded satisfied. 'They'll lie easy enough here, sir.' He was peering up at the ridge of high ground. 'The buggers would be down on us by now if they'd heard anything!'

'I'm going up to get my bearings, Tom.' Galbraith touched his arm. 'Call me Leigh, if you like. Not *sir*, in this god-forsaken place!'

He began to climb, Rist close on his heels, breathing

heavily, more used to *Unrivalled*'s quarterdeck than this kind of exercise.

Galbraith paused and dropped on one knee. He could see the extent of the ridge now, jutting up from nowhere. *Like a cocked hat*, one survey had described it. Darker now, because the stars had almost gone, and sharper in depth and outline as his eyes became accustomed to their barren surroundings.

Then he stood, as if someone had called to him. And there it was, the crude anchorage, with another, larger island beginning to be visible in the far distance. He swore under his breath. *The one they should have landed on.* Despite everything, he had misjudged it.

He felt Rist beside him, watching, listening, wary.

Then he said, 'Fires down yonder, sir!'

Galbraith stared until his eyes watered. Fires on the shore. For warmth, or for cooking? It did not matter. At a guess, they were exactly where his boats would have grated ashore. The rest did not bear thinking about.

Rist summed it up. 'We was lucky, sir.'

Galbraith asked curtly, 'First light?'

'Half an hour, sir. No cloud about.' He nodded to confirm it. 'No longer.'

Galbraith turned his back on the flickering points of fire. It might be long enough. If it failed . . .

He quickened his pace, hearing Adam Bolitho's voice. *Mostly, it will be up to you.*

And that was now.

He was not even breathless when he reached the beach. He had heard it said often enough that the British seaman could adapt to anything, given a little time, and it was true, he thought. Men stood in small groups, some quietly loading muskets, others checking the deadly array of weapons, cutlasses, dirks or boarding axes, the latter always a favourite in a hand-to-hand fight. Colpoys strode to meet him, and listened intently as Galbraith told him what he had seen, and the only possible location for an anchorage. Chebecks drew little water; they could lie close inshore without risk to their graceful hulls.

Colpoys held up his hand and said flatly, 'Wind's backed, si . . .' And grinned awkwardly. 'It will help our ships.' He glanced at the one boat still afloat. 'But it rules out sailing *that* directly amongst the Algerines. One mast and a scrap of sail – they'll see it coming, cut their cables if necessary. No chance!'

Galbraith saw Rist nod, angry with himself for not noticing the slight change of wind.

He said, 'But they're *there*, Tom, I know it. Fires, too.' He pictured the other island, high ground like this. A lookout would be posted as a matter of course at first light, to warn of the approach of danger or a possible victim. It was so simple that he wanted to damn the eyes of everyone who had considered this plan at the beginning. Bethune perhaps, spurred on by some sharp reminder from the Admiralty? Whatever it was, it was too late now.

Colpoys said, 'Not your fault, Leigh. Wrong time, wrong place, that's all.'

Williams, the gunner's mate, leaned towards them, his Welsh accent very pronounced.

'I've trimmed the fuses, sir. It'll go up like a beacon, see?' If anything, he sounded dismayed that his fireship was not going to be used.

Colpoys said, 'The wind. That's all there is to it.'

Galbraith said, 'Unless . . .' *Stop now. Finish it. Pull out while you can.*

He looked around at their faces, vague shapes in the lingering darkness. They had no choice at all.

'Unless we *pull* all the way. We could still do it. I doubt if they'll have much of a watch on deck, as we would!'

Somebody chuckled. Another said, 'Heathen, th' lot of 'em!'

Galbraith licked his lips. His guts felt clenched, as if anticipating the split second before the fatal impact of ball or blade.

'Three volunteers. I shall go myself.'

Colpoys did not question it or argue; he was already thinking ahead, reaching out to separate and to choose as shadowy figures pushed around him.

Two of *Halcyon*'s seamen, and Campbell, as somehow Galbraith had known it would be.

Williams exclaimed, '*I* must be there, sir!'

Galbraith stared at the sky. Lighter still. And they might be seen before . . . He closed his mind, like slamming a hatch.

'Very well. Into the boat!' He paused and gripped Colpoys' arm. 'Take care of them, Tom. Tell my captain about it.'

He threw his coat into the boat and climbed down beside the carefully packed charges. A few voices pursued him but he could not hear them. Colpoys was wading with the others, pushing the boat away from the beach.

Four oars, and a hard, hard pull. He doubted if any of them could swim; few sailors could. For them, the sea was always the real enemy.

He lay back on the loom, his muscles cracking in protest. Williams took the tiller, a slowmatch by his foot shining like a solitary, evil eye.

Campbell said, 'Nice an' steady, lads! We don't want to tire the officer, do we?'

Galbraith pulled steadily; he could not recall when he had last handled an oar. As a midshipman? Was he ever that?

Tell my captain about it. What had he meant? Because there was no one else who would care?

He thought of the girl he had hoped to marry, but he had been about to take up his first command, so the wedding had been postponed.

He closed his eyes and pressed his feet hard into the stretchers, sweat running down his back like ice water.

But she had not waited, and had married another. Why had he thought of her now?

And all for this. A moment's madness, then oblivion. Like George Avery, matter-of-fact about some things, sensitive, even shy, about others. And the traitor Lovatt who had died in the captain's cabin; perhaps he had had some purpose, even to the end . . .

Williams called softly, 'Half a cable!'

Galbraith gasped, *'Oars!'*

The blades still, dripping into the dark water alongside. When he twisted round on the thwart, he saw what he thought at first was a single large vessel, but when he dashed the sweat from his eyes he realised there were two, chebecks, overlapping one another, masts and furled sails stark against the clear sky, rakish hulls still hidden in shadow.

He said, 'We shall grapple the first one, and light the fuses.'
He saw Williams nod, apparently untroubled now that he was
here to do it. 'Then we'll swim for the land. Together.' He
paused, and Williams said gently, 'Can't swim, sir. Never
thought to learn.'

One of the others murmured, 'Me neither.'

Galbraith repeated, '*Together*. Take the bottom boards, we
shall manage.' He looked at Campbell, and saw the evil,
answering grin.

'I'd walk on water just to 'elp an officer, *sir*!'

The long bowsprit and ramlike beakhead swept over them,
as if the chebeck and not the boat was moving.

It was a miracle nobody had seen or challenged them.

Galbraith lurched to his feet and balanced the grapnel on
his hand. Up and over. *Now.*

Even as the grapnel jagged into the vessel's beakhead the
stillness was broken by a wild shout. More like a fiend than
something human. Galbraith staggered and ducked as a musket
exploded directly above him, the sickening crack of the shot
slamming into flesh and bone so close that it must have passed
within inches.

Someone was gasping, 'Oh, dear God, help me! Oh, dear
God, help me!' Over and over, until Campbell silenced him
with a blow to the chin.

The fuse was alight, sparking along the boat, alive, deadly.

'Over, lads!' The water knocked the breath out of him but
he could still think. No more shots. There was still time before
the chebeck's crew discovered what was happening.

And then he was swimming strongly, Williams and the other
man floundering and kicking between them. The wounded
seaman had vanished.

Two shots echoed across the water, and then Galbraith
heard a chorus of yells and screams. They must have realised that the bobbing boat under their bows was not merely
a visitor.

It was madness, and he wanted to laugh even as he spat
out water, trying to guess how far they had come, and if the
Algerines had managed to stop the fuses. Then he gasped as
his foot grated painfully between two sharp stones, and he
realised that he had lost or kicked off his boots. He staggered

into the shallows, one hand groping for his hanger, the other still clinging to the choking gunner's mate.

Campbell was already on his feet, pulling the other seaman on to firm ground.

Galbraith wanted to tell them something, but saw Campbell's eyes light up like the fires he had seen on the beach.

'Get down!' But it came out as a croak. Then the whole world exploded.

Adam Bolitho rested his hands on the quarterdeck rail and listened to the regular creak of rigging, the clatter of a block. Otherwise it seemed unnaturally quiet, the ship forging into the deeper darkness, as if she was not under control.

He shivered; the rail was like ice. But it was not that and he knew it. He could see *Unrivalled* in his mind's eye, ghosting along under topsails and forecourse; to set more canvas would deny them even a faint chance of surprise. He stared up at the main-topmast and thought he could see the masthead pendant licking out towards the lee bow. It would be plain for everyone to see when daylight finally parted sea from sky. To set the topgallants, the 'skyscrapers', would be a gift to any lookout.

He felt the twinge of doubt again. There might be nothing.

They had cleared for action as soon as they had cast off the boats. There had been no excitement, no cheering. It had been like watching men going to their deaths, pulling away into the darkness. *Not just a captain's decision. But mine.*

He walked to the compass box again, the faces of the helmsmen turning towards him like masks in the binnacle light.

One said, 'Sou'-west-by-south, sir. Full an' bye.'

'Very well.' He saw Cristie with a master's mate. Their charts had been taken below; their part was done. The master was probably thinking of his senior mate, Rist, who had gone with Galbraith and the others. Too valuable a man to lose. To throw away.

Suppose Galbraith had misjudged his approach. It was easy enough. It would give the enemy time to cut and run for it, if they were there . . . The slight shift of wind had been noted. Galbraith might have ignored it.

He saw Lieutenant Massie's dark shadow on the opposite

side of the deck, standing in Galbraith's place, but with his heart most likely with his gun crews. The eighteen-pounders were already loaded, double-shotted and with grape. It was inaccurate but devastating, and there would be little time to reload. *If they were there.*

He wondered briefly if Massie was still brooding over the reprimand he had been given. Resenting it, or taking it personally. What did one man matter in any case?

It was an argument Adam had heard many times. He could recall his uncle's insistence that there had to be an alternative, beginning with the conditions under which men were forced to serve in times of war. Strange that Sir Lewis Bazeley had made the same point during that meal in the cabin. To impress the officers, or had he really cared? He had drawn comparisons with the Honourable East India Company's ships, where men were not ruled by the Articles of War, or subject to the moods and temper of a captain.

Adam had heard himself responding, very aware of the girl's eyes, and her hand lying still on the table. The same hand which had later gripped his wrist like steel, refusing to release him.

'So what is the alternative for the captain of a King's ship, Sir Lewis? Restrict their freedom to come and go, when they have none? Deny them their privileges, when they are afforded none? Cut their pay, when it is so meagre after the purser's deductions that were it gone they would scarcely miss it?'

Bazeley had smiled without warmth. 'So you favour the lash?'

Adam had seen her hand clench suddenly, as if she had been sharing it in some way.

He had answered, 'The lash only brutalises the victim, and the man who administers it. But mostly, I think, the man who orders it to be carried out.'

He came out of his thoughts abruptly and stared at the masthead. Colour. Not much, but it was there, the red and white of the long pendant, and even as he watched he saw the first touch of sunlight run down the topgallant mast like paint.

He took a telescope brusquely from Midshipman Cousens and strode to the shrouds, extending the glass as he moved. He rested it on the tightly packed hammocks and stared across the bow. Land, fragments. As if they had been scattered by the gods.

He said, 'Are the leadsmen ready, Mr Bellairs?'

'Aye, sir.'

Cristie said, 'Closer inshore there's some seven fathoms, sir.' He did not add, *or so the notes state*. He knew his captain needed no reminding. Seven fathoms. *Unrivalled* drew three.

Adam looked up at the gently bulging main topsail. He could see most of it, the head in contrast with the foot, which was still in deep shadow. Not long now.

He steadied the glass once more and trained it slowly across the craggy humps of land. He could see the higher ground also, and that one small islet had a solitary pinnacle at its end, like something man-made.

'Bring her up a point. Steer sou'-west.' There was an edge to his voice but he could not help it. 'Rouse the lookouts, Mr Wynter – they must be asleep up there!'

Suppose Galbraith had been taken by surprise and over-whelmed? Thirty-five men. He had not forgotten what Avery had told him about the barbarity of the Algerines towards their captives.

He rested his forehead against the hammock nettings. So cool. Soon it would be a furnace here.

'Sou'-west, sir! Steady she goes!'

A quick glance at the topsails again. Steady enough. Braced close to the wind, such as it was.

He thought of *Halcyon*, in position by now on the other side of this miserable group of tiny islands. The trap was set. He touched his empty watch pocket and felt the pain again.

Somebody moved past him and he saw that it was Napier, his feet bare, as if to avoid being noticed.

Adam said, 'We are cleared for action, Napier. You know your station. Go to it.'

He swung round and stared up again. Very soon now, and the whole ship would be in broad daylight. Or so it would feel.

He realised that the boy was still there. 'Well?'

'I – I'm not afraid, sir. The others think I'm not to be trusted on deck!'

Adam stared at him, surprised that the simplicity could move him, even distract him at this moment.

239

'I understand. Stand with me, then.' He thought he saw Jago grin. 'Madness is catching, it seems!'

'Deck there! Somethin' flashin' from the middle high ground!'

Adam licked his lips. The voice was Sullivan's. Something flashing: it could only be one thing, early sunshine reflecting from a glass. A lookout. *They were there.*

Then came the explosion, which seemed to linger in a slow climax before rolling across the sea and sighing against the ship. *Unrivalled* seemed to quiver in its path.

'One craft under way, sir. 'Nother on fire!' Sullivan was barely able to contain his excitement, which was rare for him.

On the upper deck the gun crews were staring into the retreating shadows or aft at the quarterdeck, trying to guess what was happening. A great pall of smoke had begun to rise, staining the clear, clean sky like something grotesque, obscene. There were more explosions, puny after the first, and smoke spreading still further as if to confirm the success of Galbraith's attack.

But sails were moving, suddenly very bright and sharp in the new sunlight, and Adam had to force himself to see it as it really was. A vessel destroyed: impossible to guess how many had died to achieve that. But the explosion was on a different bearing, so that the alleged anchorage must also be wrongly charted.

Galbraith would stand no chance of getting away. Another chebeck, perhaps two, were using the change of wind which had delayed his attack. They would escape. He steadied the glass again, ignoring everything but the tall triangles of sails, a flurry of foam as the chebeck used her long sweeps to work around the blazing wreck, which was burned almost to the waterline.

Between and beyond was the gleam of water: the line of escape. And *Halcyon* would not be there to prevent it. He swallowed as a second set of sails moved from the smoke, like the fins of a marauding shark. They still had time for revenge. Galbraith's boats would stand no chance, and even if his men broke and scattered ashore they would hunt them down and slaughter them. Revenge . . . *I should have known that, only too well.*

'We will come about, Mr Cristie! Steer nor'-east!'

They were staring at him, and he heard the reluctance in Cristie's response.

'The channel, sir? We don't even know if . . .' It was the closest he had ever come to open disagreement.

Adam swung on him, his dark eyes blazing. '*Men*, Mr Cristie! Remember? I'll roast in hell before I leave Galbraith to die in their hands!'

He strode to the opposite side, ignoring the sudden bustle of seamen and marines as they ran to braces and halliards, as if they had been shaken from a trance.

The leadsmen were in position in the chains, one on either bow, their lines already loosely coiled, ready to heave.

Adam bit his lip. Like a blind man with his stick. There was not a minute more to measure the danger. There was no alternative.

He said, 'Carry on! Put the helm down!' He saw Massie staring at him over the confusion of men already lying back on the braces, his face wild, that of a stranger.

Cristie stood near his helmsmen, one hand almost touching the spokes as the big double-wheel began to turn, and *Unrivalled*'s figurehead gazed at what appeared to be an unbroken line of sun-scorched rocks.

Adam gripped the old sword and forced it against his hip, to steady himself. To remember.

His voice sounded quite level, as if someone else had spoken.

'Then get the hands aloft and shake out the t'gallants!'

He touched his face as the sun reached down between the flapping canvas, and did not see Bellairs pause to watch him.

Then he held out one hand, like someone quieting a nervous horse.

'Steady now! *Steady!*'

Trust.

Adam remained by the nettings and watched the shadows of *Unrivalled*'s topgallants and topsails glide over a long strip of sand and rock, as if some phantom ship were in close company. Some of the gun crews and unemployed seamen were peering into the water, the more experienced to study the patches of weed, black in the weak sunlight, which seemed to line the side of the channel through the islands. They were bedded in rock, any one of which could turn the ship into a wreck.

As if to drive home their danger, the leadsman's voice echoed aft from the chains. 'By the mark ten!'

Adam watched the man hauling in his lead, his bare arm moving deftly, perhaps too engrossed to consider the peril beneath the keel.

Cristie said, 'Narrows a bit here, sir.' It was the first time he had spoken since they had laid the ship on the new tack, and his way of reminding his captain that after this there would be less room to come about, even if that was still possible.

'Wreckage ahead, sir!' That was Midshipman Cousens, very calm, and aware of his new responsibilities now that Bellairs was promoted. Almost.

Adam leaned over to stare at the charred timbers as they parted across *Unrivalled*'s stem. Galbraith's people must have got right alongside the vessel to cause such complete devastation. Perhaps they had all been killed. Somehow he knew Galbraith had done it himself; he would never delegate, particularly when lives were at risk. *And because I would expect it of him.* It was like a taunt.

He could smell it, too. The boat must have exploded like a giant grenade; the fire had done the rest. There were corpses as well, pieces of men, lolling wearily in the frigate's small wash.

'Deep *six*!'

If he went to the side he knew he would be able to see the ship's great shadow on the seabed. He did not move. Men were watching him, seeing their own fate in him. Lieutenant Wynter was by the foremast, staring at another, larger island which appeared to be reaching out to snare them.

Adam said, 'Let her fall off a point.' He saw Captain Bosanquet with one of his corporals positioned by the boat-tier. If she drove aground they would need every boat, perhaps to try and kedge her free again. But men in fear of their lives would see the boats as their only security, their link with the invisible *Halcyon*.

He looked at the masthead pendant again. *How many times?* Holding steady. If the wind backed again they would not weather the next island, with its headland jutting out like a giant horn. *If, if, if.*

He heard the big forecourse flap noisily, and felt the deck heel very slightly.

Jago muttered, 'Just stow that, matey!' Adam had not realised that he was at his side.

'An' a quarter six!'

Adam released his breath very slowly. Slightly deeper here. He had seen the splash of the lead hitting the water, but his mind had rejected it, as if afraid of what it might reveal.

'Deck there! *Boats ahead!*' From his lofty perch Sullivan could very likely see over, if not beyond, the outthrust headland, and on to the next leg of the channel.

Bosanquet snapped, 'Put your men in position, Corporal!'

His best shots, although his chosen marksmen were with the landing party.

Adam said, 'Over here, boy!' He swung Napier round like a puppet and pointed him towards the bows. Then he laid the telescope on his shoulder. 'Breathe easily.' Surely the boy was not afraid of him? With the ship in real danger of being wrecked, perhaps overrun by Algerines, it was impossible. He steadied the shoulder, and said quietly, 'This will show them, eh?'

He saw the leading cutter spring into focus, the oars rising and falling to a fast, desperate stroke. Another cutter was close astern, and the third appeared to be stopped, its oars in confusion. A man was hanging over the gunwale, others were trying to drag him from the looms. They had been fired on, the sound muffled by *Unrivalled*'s shipboard noises. One officer, *Halcyon*'s second lieutenant, a seaman tying a bandage around his arm.

Even at this distance Adam could see Colpoys' disbelief, when he turned and saw *Unrivalled* filling the channel.

And then he saw the chebeck. She must have used her sweeps to cut past the wreckage and overhaul the three cutters. The great, triangular sails were filling, pushing the chebeck over while her sweeps rose and froze in perfect unison. No wonder unarmed merchantmen were terrified of the Barbary pirates.

Adam gritted his teeth, and felt the boy stiffen as the leadsman's chant came aft to remind them of their own peril.

'By th' mark seven!'

He said sharply, 'Stand to your guns, Mr Massie! Bow-chasers, then the smashers!'

He saw Massie look aloft. A split second only, but it said everything. If *Unrivalled* lost a spar, let alone a mast, they would never see open water again.

Adam rubbed his eye and laid his hand on the boy's shoulder again. It was madness, but it reminded him of the instant she had raised her hand to strike him, and he had gripped her wrist with such force that it must have shocked her.

He said, 'Still, now!' and winced as a bow-chaser banged out from the forecastle, the recoil jerking the planks even here at his feet.

He tried again, and then said, 'Over yonder, boy. *You* look. Tell me.'

He thrust the long signals telescope into his hands, and tensed as another shot cracked out from forward. From a corner of his eye he saw one of the cutters passing abeam, suddenly dark in *Unrivalled*'s shadow, men standing to yell and cheer when moments earlier they had been facing death.

There were more shots now, heavy muskets, and the sharper, answering crack of the marines' weapons.

He felt something thud into the packed hammocks, heard the screech of metal as a ball ricocheted from one of the quarter-deck nine-pounders. Men were crouching, peering through open ports, waiting for the first sight of the chebeck, waiting for the order as they had been taught, had had hammered into them day after day.

But Adam did not move an inch. He could not. He had to know.

Then Napier said in a remarkably steady voice, 'It's them, sir! On the headland! Four of them!' The significance of what he had said seemed to reach him and he twisted round, the telescope forgotten. 'Mr Galbraith is safe, sir!'

Then Massie's whistle shrilled and the first great carronade lurched inboard on its slide, the noise matched only by the crash of its massive ball as it exploded into the chebeck's quarter. Timber, spars, oars and fragments of men flew in all directions, but the chebeck came on.

Massie gauged the range, his whistle to his lips. After one shot from the 'smasher', many men were too deaf to hear a shouted order.

The second carronade belched fire, and the ball must have exploded deep within the slender hull.

Adam called, 'As you bear!' He gripped the boy's shoulder. 'I want them to *know*, to feel what it's like!'

There was more firing in the far distance, like thunder on the hills: *Halcyon* in pursuit of the third chebeck, her captain perhaps believing that his consort had been wrecked.

'By th' mark . . .' The rest was lost in the crash of gunfire as Massie strode aft, pausing only to watch each eighteen-pounder fling itself inboard and pour a murderous charge into the stricken chebeck. There were still a few figures waving weapons and firing across the littered water. Even when the final charge smashed into the capsizing hull Adam imagined he could still hear their demented fury.

'By the mark fifteen!'

Adam saw the lead splash down again, could picture the seabed suddenly sliding away into depths of darkness.

'We will heave to directly, Mr Cristie.' He raised his voice; even that was an effort. 'Mr Wynter, stand by to retrieve those boats. Inform the surgeon. I want him on deck when they come aboard.'

He stared at the headland, misty now with drifting smoke.

'I'll take the gig, sir.' It was Jago. 'Fetch Mr Galbraith.'

Adam said, 'I'd be obliged.' He looked away as men hurried past him. 'And, thank you.'

Jago hesitated by the ladder and looked over his shoulder. The captain was standing quite still as orders were shouted and, with her sails in disorder, his ship came slowly round into the wind.

He had kept his word. Jago could hear the boats pulling towards the ship, their crews exhausted but still able to cheer.

He heard the sailing master say quietly to his mate, 'Not a choice I would have cared to make, Mr Woodthorpe.'

Jago shook his head. *Not yours to make, was it?*

As if to put a seal on it, the leadsman, forgotten in the forechains, yelled, *'No bottom, sir!'*

They were through.

16

In Good Hands

The letter lay on the cabin table, held down by the knife Adam had used to open it, its flap moving slightly in a faint breeze from the stern windows, the broken seal shining in the sunlight like droplets of blood. He tried to think it through rationally, as he had taught himself to do with most things.

Unrivalled had anchored that morning, with *Halcyon* entering harbour close astern. A moment of triumph, a lingering excitement after the short, savage encounter with the chebecks and the sheer pleasure of greeting a filthy but grinning Galbraith, his shirt scorched almost from his back, and his equally dirty but jubilant companions.

Adam had taken his report ashore, only to be told that Bethune was neither at his headquarters nor aboard his flagship *Montrose*. He had boarded one of the squadron's brigs, and with Sir Lewis Bazeley had gone to examine potential sites for new defences in Malta and the offshore islands.

He had already noticed that the courier schooner *Gertrude* was in harbour, and she was preparing to weigh and make sail again by the time he had returned to *Unrivalled*. As was the way of fleet couriers.

He had been expecting a letter from Catherine, hoping for one. It was stupid of him and he knew it. She would be recovering from her loss, and would need time to decide what she must do in the immediate future and with the rest of her life. But he had hoped, all the same.

Instead, there had been this letter. The same neat, round handwriting which had followed him from ship to ship, from despair to hope. Always warm, as she had been ever since that first day when he had arrived exhausted at the Roxby house after walking all the way from Penzance. From his mother's deathbed.

Aunt Nancy, Richard Bolitho's youngest sister, was the last person from whom he had been expecting to hear, and yet in his heart he knew there was none better suited to this task.

He walked to the stern windows and stared across at *Halcyon*, swinging to her cable and surrounded by harbour craft, with scarlet coats on her gangways to deter unwanted visitors. He had sent Captain Christie a copy of his report. *Halcyon* had done well, and between them they had lost only four men.

He looked at the letter again, as if his mind were refusing to lose itself in matters concerning the ship and the squadron. That other world seemed very close: rugged cliffs, treacherous rocks, and in contrast rolling hillside pastures and great, empty moors. A county which had produced many fine sailors, probably more than any other part of England. He could see Falmouth in his thoughts . . . the people, the quality of strength in its seamen and fisherfolk.

Where Belinda, whose hand had once rested on his cuff as he had led her up the aisle to marry Falmouth's most famous son, had been killed. Thrown from a horse. *Killed instantly*, Nancy had written. And yet he could not come to terms with it. Perhaps he had never really known Belinda, or been close enough to understand what had destroyed his uncle's marriage; she had always been beautiful, proud, but distant. She had been at the old house, and Adam could guess why, although the family lawyer had touched only in passing on it. Not wishing to trouble a King's officer, *fighting for his country's rights*.

And there was his cousin, Elizabeth. She would be about twelve or thirteen by now. She would stay with Nancy until things were 'more settled'. Adam could almost hear her saying the words.

Nancy had also written to Catherine. The mare given to her by his uncle was now stabled at the Roxby house. Adam had known instantly that Belinda had been riding Tamara at the time of the accident.

The letter ended, *'You must take good care of yourself,*

dear Adam. Here is your home, nobody can ever deny you that.'

The ink was smudged, and he knew she had been crying as she wrote, doubtless angry with herself for giving into it. A sailor's daughter, and the sister of one of England's finest sea officers, she had had plenty of experience of separation and despair. And now that her husband was dead she was alone once again. Elizabeth would be a blessing to her. He picked up the letter, and smiled. *As you were to me.*

Catherine was in London. He wondered if she was alone, and was surprised by how much it could hurt him. Absurd . . . He glanced at the skylight, hearing voices, Jago's carrying easily as he called out to the gig's crew. Vivid memories: the leadsman's chant, the closeness of danger on all sides, Massie and Wynter, and the boy who would rather risk death than take refuge below when the iron began to fly.

And he thought of Falmouth again. The house. The grave portraits, the sea always out there, waiting for the next Bolitho.

He turned almost guiltily as someone rapped at the door. It was Bellairs, who was assisting Wynter as officer of the watch.

'Yes?'

Bellairs glanced around the cabin. His examination was in orders, here in Malta. The next step, or the humiliation of failure.

'Mr Wynter's respects, sir, and a new midshipman has come aboard to join.' He did not blink, although he must have been recalling his own time as a young gentleman.

'Ask Mr Galbraith . . .' He held up his hand. '*No.* I'll see him now.'

Bellairs hurried away, mystified that his captain, who had just inflicted a crushing defeat on some Algerine pirates, should concern himself with such trivialities.

Adam walked to one of the eighteen-pounders which shared his quarters and touched the black breech. Remembering; how could he forget? Anxious, worried, even defiant because he had imagined that his first captain, his uncle, would find fault or cause to dismiss him on that day which was so important to him.

He heard the marine sentry say, 'Go in, *sir.*' Guarded, yet to be proved. A midshipman was neither fish nor fowl.

He saw the newcomer standing by the screen door, his hat beneath his arm.

'Come over here where I can see you!' Again the assault of memory. They were the very words his uncle had used.

When he looked again, the youth was in the centre of the cabin, directly beneath the open skylight. Older than he had expected, about fifteen. With experience he could be very useful.

He took the envelope and slit it with the knife he had used earlier, feeling the midshipman's eyes watching every move. *As I did.* All those years ago.

He was not new, but had been appointed from another frigate, the *Vanoc*, which had been temporarily paid off for a complete overhaul. His name was Richard Deighton. Adam raised his eyes, and saw the youth look away from him.

'Your captain speaks well of you.' A young, roundish face, dark brown hair. He would be fifteen next month, and was tall for his years. Serious features. Troubled.

The name was familiar. 'Your father was a serving officer?' It was not a question. He could see it all more clearly than the chebecks of only three days ago.

The youth said, 'Captain Henry Deighton.' No pride, no defiance.

That was it.

'Commodore Deighton hoisted his broad pendant above my ship, *Valkyrie*, when I was with the Halifax squadron.' So easily said.

The midshipman clenched one fist against his breeches. 'The rank of commodore was never confirmed, sir.'

'I see.' He walked around the table, hearing Jago's voice again. He had been there too on that day when Commodore Deighton had been shot down, it was thought by a Yankee sharpshooter. Except that after the sea burial the surgeon, rather the worse for drink, had told Adam that the angle of entry and the wound were all wrong, and that Deighton had been killed by someone in *Valkyrie*'s own company.

The matter had ended there. Deighton had already been put over the side, with the boy John Whitmarsh and others.

But the faces always returned; there was no escape. The family, they called it.

'Did you ask for *Unrivalled*?'

The midshipman lifted his eyes again. 'Aye, sir. I always hoped, wanted . . .' His voice trailed away.

Bellairs was back. 'Gig's alongside, sir.' He glanced at the new midshipman, but only briefly.

Adam said, 'Take Mr Deighton into your charge, if you please. The first lieutenant will attend to the formalities.'

Then he smiled. 'Welcome aboard, Mr Deighton. You are in good hands.'

As the door closed he took out the letter once more.

It was like seeing yourself again . . . something you should never forget.

He picked up his hat and went out into the sunshine.

Captain Victor Forbes leaned back in Bethune's fine chair and raised a glass.

'I'm glad you chose to come ashore, Adam. I've been reading through your report, Christie's too, and I've made a few notes for the vice-admiral to read on his return.'

Adam sat opposite him, the cognac and the easy use of his first name driving some of his doubts away. The flag captain was obviously making the most of Bethune's absence, although it was apparent from the occasional pause in mid-sentence to listen that, like most serving captains, he was ill at ease away from his ship.

Forbes added, 'I still believe that raids on known anchorages, though damn useful and good for our people's morale, will never solve the whole problem. Like hornets, destroy the nest. Time enough later to catch the stragglers.'

Adam agreed and tried to recall how many glasses he had drunk as Forbes peered at the bottle and shook it against the fading sunlight. 'I'd have given anything to be there with you.' Then he grinned. 'But with any luck *Montrose* will be a private ship again quite soon!'

'You're leaving the squadron?'

Forbes shook his head. 'No. But we are being reinforced by two third-rates, and about time too. Sir Graham Bethune will likely shift his flag to one of them. A damn nice fellow,' he grinned again, 'for an admiral, that is. But I believe he is eager to leave, to get back to a stone frigate, the Admiralty again, most likely. I'll not be sorry. Like you, I prefer to be free of flag officers, good or bad.'

Adam recalled Bethune's restlessness, his sense of displacement even in a world he had once known so well. And there was a wife to consider.

Forbes changed tack. 'I hear that you've got a new midshipman, a replacement for the one who was killed. Deighton – I knew his father, y' know. We were lieutenants together in the old *Resolution* for a year or so. Didn't know him all that well, of course . . .' He hesitated and peered at Adam as though making a decision. 'But when I read the account of your fight with the Yankee *Defender*, in the *Gazette* I think it was, I was a little surprised. He never really struck me as being in the death-or-glory mould, one who would fall in battle like that. His son must be proud of him.' He sat back and smiled. Like a cat, Adam thought, waiting to see which way the mouse would run.

'He was killed by a single shot. It is common enough.'

Forbes exclaimed, 'Thoughtless of me! Your uncle . . . I should have kept my damn mouth shut.'

Adam shrugged, remembering when Keen had left Halifax to return to England for promotion and high command at Plymouth. And to marry again . . . Deighton was to remain as commodore in charge until otherwise decided. He could remember Keen's words to him, like a warning. Or a threat.

'Be patient with him. He is not like us. Not like *you*.'

He said, 'How is Sir Graham getting along with his visitor?'

Forbes gave him the grin again, obviously glad of the change of subject.

'They both know about wine, anyway!'

Adam smiled. 'Claret, of course.'

A servant appeared with another bottle but Forbes waved him away.

He said, 'I shall be dining with the army tonight. Don't want to let our end down!'

Adam prepared to depart. It had been a friendly, informal discussion, but he had been a flag captain himself, and a flag lieutenant to his uncle. Both roles had taught him to sift fact from gossip, truth from rumour, and in this brief meeting he

252

had learned that a new admiral was about to be appointed, and that Bethune would be leaving. The new flag would decide all future operations, as so ordered by the Admiralty. An aggressive demonstration of sea power might deter the Dey from any further attacks on shipping, or from offering refuge to any pirate or turncoat who offered his services in return for sanctuary.

Forbes had made a point of not mentioning Lady Bolitho's death, although it was no doubt common knowledge in a place like this. Adam himself had said nothing about it; it was private, if not personal. Belinda was dead. *I never knew her.* But was it so simple?

Forbes frowned as a shadow moved restlessly beneath the door.

'Not like a ship, Adam. Too many callers, always wanting things. I'd never make an admiral in a thousand years!'

Adam left, cynically amused. He could see Forbes as precisely that.

Outside he paused to study the copper sky. It was a fine, warm evening, and in England the summer was over. It would be the first Christmas without war. And without his uncle.

Forbes had also avoided mentioning Bazeley's lovely young wife. He wondered if she had fared any better aboard the brig, with its cramped quarters and limited comforts. After an Indiaman and then *Unrivalled*, a brig would seem like a work-boat. Eyes watching her every move, men deprived of a woman's touch, the sound of a woman's voice.

He had told Jago to return to the ship, saying that he would take a duty boat from the jetty. He grinned in the shadows. He had been expecting Forbes to ask him to stay. Instead, he would return to his own, remote cabin.

Something moved in a doorway, and his hand was on the hilt of his sword in a second, unconsciously.

'Who is there?'

The action and strain had cost him more than he would have believed.

It was a woman. Not a beggar or a thief.

'Captain Bolitho. It *is* you!'

He turned in a patch of golden light and recognised Lady Bazeley's companion.

253

'I did not know you were here, ma'am. I thought you would be with Sir Lewis and his lady.'

The woman stood very still, and he felt the intensity of her eyes, although her features remained hidden in shadow.

She said, 'We did not go. Her ladyship was unwell. It seemed the safest thing to do.'

He heard footsteps, measured, precise, and relaxed again. It was the marine sentry at the gates, pacing his post, his mind doubtless far removed from this place.

The woman touched his arm, and then withdrew her hand just as quickly, like an unwilling conspirator.

'My lady would like to see you before you leave, sir. We saw you earlier in the day. And then you came back.' She hesitated. 'It is safe, if you will allow me to lead.'

Adam looked back, but there was only silence. Forbes must have known that the women had stayed behind, but had made a point of not mentioning that either.

Was she really unwell, or was she merely bored, needing to be amused? *At my expense.*

He said, 'Lead on, ma'am.' Perhaps she wanted to remind him of his awkward advances, his clumsiness. He thought of the leadsman's cry. *No bottom!* What it had meant, after the risk he had taken for what Lovatt would have called a gesture, a conceit.

The woman walked swiftly ahead of him, untroubled by the rough paving where he guessed guns had stood in the past when Malta had been in constant fear of attack. Perhaps she was used to running errands for her mistress. He recognised the same parapet as before, but knew it was at the opposite side of the rambling building, in shadow now, the old embrasures touched with colour from the melting light.

And the view was the same. When he had held her, and the invisible orchestra had offered its private gift of music. Ships anchored as before, some already displaying lights, topmasts clinging to the last copper glow, flags limp, barely moving.

And then he saw her, her gown pale against the dull stone, the fan open in her hand.

She said, 'So you came, Captain. You honour us.'

He moved closer and took the hand she offered him.

'I thought you were away, m' lady. Otherwise –'

'Ah, that word again.' She did not flinch as he kissed her hand. 'I heard there was fighting. That *you* were fighting.'

It sounded like an accusation, but he said nothing. Nor did he release her hand.

She said in the same level tone, 'But you are safe. I heard you laugh just now. Recognised it. Enjoying some of Sir Graham's cognac in his absence, yes?'

He smiled. 'Something like that. And you, I hear you were unwell?'

She tossed her head, and he saw her hair fall loose across one shoulder.

'I am well enough, thank you.' She withdrew her hand slowly and deliberately, then turned slightly away, towards the ships and the harbour.

She said, 'I was concerned, about you, *for* you. Is that so strange?'

'When we last met –'

She shook her head again. 'No. Do not speak of it! There were so many things I wanted to say, to share, to explain. I could not even manage that unaided.'

There was a catch in her voice, more from anger than despair.

'I showed you arrogance when I wanted only to thank you for helping me as you did. There has been no word of it, so I knew you had said nothing.' She held up the fan to silence him. 'Others would, and well you know it!'

He said, 'Because I cared. I still do. You are another man's wife, and I know what harm this might cause. To both of us.'

She did not seem to hear him. 'I know that people talk behind my back. Giving myself to a much older man, because of power, because of wealth. I am not so young that I do not understand how they think.'

He said abruptly, 'Walk with me.' He took her hand again, expecting her to resist, to turn on him, but she did neither. 'Like old friends, you see?'

She held his arm and fell into step beside him. Only by the parapet could the sounds of the harbour and a nearby street reach them.

She said, 'I spoke with your Captain Forbes. He told me of

255

you and your family.' He felt her turn to look at him. 'Your uncle. I knew some of it. I guessed some of it, too, when I heard you speak that night with such conviction, and when you were talking with your men and did not know I was there.' He felt the pressure of her hand on his arm. 'And then you helped me.'

'When you were sick.'

She laughed softly. 'I was drunk, like some dockside slut!' She quickened her pace, and he could sense her mind moving, exploring it again. 'He came to me that night, did you know? He is like that. He cannot believe that I need to be myself on occasion, a person – not some *thing* to arouse his passion!'

He said, 'I think you should stop, m' lady. I came here because I wanted to see you. Even if you had spat in my face, I would have come.'

She stopped by the parapet once more and stared at the anchored vessels. Almost to herself, she murmured, 'Your world, Adam. Something I can never share.' She turned. 'I did not marry from choice, or out of greed, for myself.'

Without realising what he was doing, he put his fingers to her lips.

'There is no need to tell me. I am not proud of some of the things I have done, or what I might have done, if my life had been different. So let this be a secret between us.'

Gently, firmly, she pulled his hand away.

'My father was a fine man, but when my mother died of fever he seemed to fall apart. Sir Lewis, as he now is, was his junior partner, a man of ambition. He was quick to come to his assistance.' She touched the buttons on his coat. 'And he taught him how to enjoy himself again.' She laughed, a small, bitter sound on the still air. 'Introduced him to others who would help to expand the business, the only thing he had left to care about. Gambling, drink . . . he would not listen to a word against Lewis. He could not see the ground opening beneath his feet. There were debts, broken contracts with government commissions, with the military as well as the navy. In the end,' she gave a little shrug, and Adam felt it like a blow, 'prison was the only reality. We would have been left like beggars. My two brothers also work for the business. I was given little choice. No choice at all.'

He hardly dared to speak, afraid to break the moment.

'So he asked you to marry him, and then all the debts would be made good, and the business restored.'

'You know my husband,' she said. 'What do *you* believe?'

'I believe I should go. Leave here without delay.' He felt her move as though she too would go, but he did not release her. 'I know I have no right, and others would condemn me . . .'

She said softly, 'But?' Only one word.

'That night, aboard my ship, I wanted you.' He pulled her closer, feeling her warmth, her nearness. Her awareness. 'I still do.'

She leaned against him, her face in his shirt, perhaps giving herself time to recognise the danger, and the folly.

She said, 'You have not been fed by the gallant Captain Forbes. I can at least do something about that.' She tried to laugh. 'I can smell the cognac, so I was right about the pair of you!'

But when he held her again she was shivering.

'We will go inside . . . then you can tell me all about yourself.' She could not continue. 'Come, now. Quickly. Banish all doubts!' She paused only to look at the harbour. 'All that can wait, this once.'

Even though he had never set foot in the place before, he knew it was the same. Here Catherine had spent her last night with her Richard, in these rooms which Avery had found so difficult to describe, and of which Bethune had carefully avoided speaking, as if it was too painful even for him.

He walked to a window and eased the shutter aside very slightly and looked down into the courtyard, dark now but for the reflected glow from a copper dusk.

He heard the sentry at the gates stamp his feet, and the clink of metal as he shifted his musket, yawning at the dragging hours.

There were no lights in the windows opposite. Forbes had gone to dine with the army; the staff had probably been left to do as they pleased until Bethune's return.

He felt his muscles contract. Voices now, very low, the sound of glasses. And when he closed the shutter and turned he saw her facing him from the other side of the room, her

257

eyes very clear in the glow of candles which must have been arranged here earlier.

She said, 'A little wine, Adam. It is as cool as can be expected. Some food can be sent for later.'

She watched him cross the room, and turned slightly so that the piece of silver at her breast shone suddenly like a flame. She wore a plain white gown which covered her from her throat to her feet, now bare on the marble floor.

He put his hands on her arms, and said, 'You kept it. I thought you'd thrown it away.'

He touched the small silver sword and felt her stiffen as she answered, 'I am wearing it for you. How could I not wear it?'

He lowered his mouth to her shoulder and kissed it, feeling the smoothness of her skin beneath the gown.

'The *wine*.' She pressed him away. 'While it's cool.'

He brought the glasses from the table and held one to her lips, and they looked at one another over the rims, all pretence gone, all reason scattered.

She did not resist or speak as he kissed her shoulder again, and each breast in turn until she gasped softly and put her arms around him, holding him there, her head moving from side to side as if she could no longer contain herself.

He stood, and held her at arm's length, seeing the darker patches on the silk, where he had kissed and roused the points of her breasts.

There was a tall mirror on the wall and he turned her towards it, his hands around her waist, seeing the reflection of her eyes in the glass, then deliberately he unclipped the little sword, and opened and removed the gown. He looked over her shoulder, his face in her hair as he watched with her, as if they were onlookers, strangers. Exploring her body, feeling every response like his own, until she twisted round in his grip and said, 'Kiss me. Kiss me.'

He lifted her as he had the night aboard *Unrivalled*, holding her tightly as they kissed again. And again. He laid her on the broad bed and threw off his coat, and the old sword slid unnoticed to a rug by his feet.

She propped herself on one elbow, and said, '*No!* Come to me now!'

He knelt beside her, his mind and reason gone as she struggled to free him from his clothes, pulling him down to kiss her mouth once more until they were breathless.

He gazed at her, hungry for her, the hair disordered across the pillows, the hands, suddenly strong, gripping his shoulders, one moment holding him away and then drawing him down to her body, her skin hot and damp as if with fever.

He felt her nails breaking his skin as he came against her, and she moved still further, arching her body until they were almost joined. Then she opened her eyes, and whispered, '*I yield*!' and gave a small, soft cry as he found and entered her.

It was like falling, or being carried along by an endless, unbroken wave.

Even when they lay exhausted she would not release him. They clung to one another, breathless, drained by the intensity of their congress, their need.

Hours later, after they had explored every intimacy, she sat on the bed, her knees drawn up to her chin as she watched him pulling on his breeches and shirt.

'A King's officer. To everyone else but me.' She reached out impetuously and touched him again, held him, while he bent to kiss her. She had found and touched the old wound and had kissed the jagged scar, her passion roused again. *No secrets, Adam . . .*

When he looked again she was dressed in the thin robe, the silver clasp in place, as if the rest had been a wild dream.

A chapel bell was ringing tunelessly; someone was already awake. She opened the door, and he saw that fresh candles had been brought to light the stairs. Hilda, ensuring that nothing would go amiss.

He held her, feeling the supple limbs through the silk, wanting her again in spite of the risks.

She said, 'No regrets.' She was still looking after him when he reached the courtyard.

Her voice seemed to hang in the warm air. *No regrets . . .*

The guard at the gate was being changed, and a corporal was reading out the standing orders, too tired or too bored to see the naval officer striding past.

He paused in a deserted alley, which he thought was the

one where he had purchased the little silver sword. He could still feel her, enclosing him, guiding him, taking him.

He might never see her again; if he did, she might laugh at his desire. Somehow he knew that she would not.

He thought he heard the creak of oars, the guardboat, and quickened his pace.

But regrets? It was far too late for them now.

17

The Family

Adam Bolitho sat at his table, a pen poised over his personal log, the sun through the stern windows warming his shoulder. Another day at anchor, and the ship around him was quietly alive with normal working sounds, and the occasional shouted order.

He stared at the date at the top of the page. *30th September 1815*. So much had happened, and yet at moments like these it was as if time had been frozen.

He thought of his conversation with Captain Forbes earlier in the evening he had ended in the room above the courtyard. That, too, was like a dream. But Forbes had been right in what he had told him, or rather what he had not told him. It had broken over the squadron just two days ago when Bethune had returned from his inspection of coastal defences with Sir Lewis Bazeley. It was no longer a rumour, but a fact. Bethune was leaving as soon as he was relieved. And that was today.

The two third-rates of which Forbes had also spoken had already been sighted by the lookout post ashore.

Adam laid down the pen and recalled his last meeting with Bethune, who had seemed pleased at the prospect of a new position at the Admiralty as assistant to the Third Sea Lord, with all the promise of advancement it would carry for him. But he had been on edge, evasive, although Adam had not known why. And then, with all the other captains and commanders of the squadron, he had partly understood the reason. The new flagship was *Frobisher*, which had been Richard Bolitho's

261

own, and now it was returning to Malta where so much had begun and ended.

The other arrival would be the eighty-gun *Prince Rupert*, which Adam had seen and boarded at Gibraltar. The big two-decker was no longer Rear-Admiral Marlow's flagship, although Pym was still in command, and he had heard the flurry of speculation as to why the new flag officer, a senior admiral, should hoist his flag over the smaller of the two ships.

He was convinced that Bethune, better than anyone, would know the answers. Lord Rhodes had been Controller at the Admiralty when Bethune had been there, and those who understood or were interested in such matters had been convinced that Rhodes had been put forward for First Lord, supported by no less than the Prince Regent. Then the appointment had been suspended, quashed, and now it was obvious that Rhodes had been given the Mediterranean station as an honourable demotion. Rhodes would not need reminding that Lord Collingwood, Nelson's friend and his second-in-command at Trafalgar, had been given the same command. For some reason Collingwood had neither been promoted to admiral nor allowed to return home, even though illness had forced him to apply many times for relief. He had died at sea, five long years after leading the Lee Division against the combined fleets of France and Spain.

And now *Frobisher* was here again. Different faces perhaps, but the same ship. New compared to most ships of the line, she would be about nine years old now, French-built, and taken as a prize on passage to Brest some five years back. He turned it over in his mind warily, like a hunter looking for traps. James Tyacke had been his uncle's flag captain, and his predecessor had been a Captain Oliphant, a cousin of Lord Rhodes, a favour which perhaps had misfired. In one of her letters Catherine had mentioned meeting Rhodes just prior to the choice of flagship, and it had been obvious that she had disliked him. It could be that Rhodes had chosen *Frobisher* merely because she was the better ship. He considered Bethune's uncharacteristic evasiveness and doubted it.

There was a tap at the door and Galbraith peered in at him.

'The flagship has been sighted, sir.'

Adam nodded. Not *new* flagship; Galbraith would know his captain's thoughts about *Frobisher*, and how he would feel when he was summoned aboard for the first time. The memories, and the ghosts.

Galbraith said, 'I have made certain that all hands will be properly turned out. Yards will be manned, and we will cheer-ship if necessary.' He smiled. 'I understand that Admiral Lord Rhodes will expect it. Two or three of the older hands have served under him.'

Adam closed his log. That said it all. It was a long time since Rhodes had walked the deck of his own flagship; he would be looking for flaws, if only to prove he had forgotten nothing. Galbraith watched him impassively, recognising the signs.

'Our new lieutenant has settled into his rank quite well, sir. Though I fear Mr Bellairs will need a larger hat if he continues in this fashion!'

But there was no malice in the comment, and Adam knew he was as pleased as most of the others when Bellairs had returned from his promotional examination with his *scrap of parchment*, as the old timers called it. An extra lieutenant. That would not be tolerated, beneficial though it might be for running the ship.

Adam leaned back slightly. 'There will be an opening in the squadron, or perhaps within the fleet before long.' He saw Galbraith stiffen. It was the moment he had been hoping for, what every lieutenant dreamed of. 'You held a command before you came to *Unrivalled*. Your experience and example did much to iron out the wrinkles, so to speak, before we were all put to the test. Perhaps we did not always agree about certain matters.' He smiled suddenly, the strain and the tension dropping away like the years. 'But as your commanding officer I, of course, always have the advantage of being right!'

Galbraith said, 'I am well content here, sir . . .'

Adam held up his hand. 'Never say that. Never even think it. My uncle once described a command, especially a first one, as *the most coveted gift*. I have never forgotten it. Nor must you.'

They both looked at the glittering water beyond the anchored vessels astern as the first crash of cannon fire rolled across the harbour. The response, gun by gun, from the battery wall seemed even louder.

Adam said, 'We'll go up, shall we?'

He clipped on the old sword, then he said, 'Mr Bellairs will have no sword as yet.' He gestured to his own curved hanger in its rack. 'He may have that one if he chooses to wait until his parents do him the honour!'

He touched the sword at his hip. So many times. So many hands. And he was reminded of the note Catherine had written for him, and had left with the sword at Falmouth.

The sword outwore its scabbard. Wear it with pride, as he always wanted.

Frobisher was back. And *he* would know.

Vice-Admiral Sir Graham Bethune winced as the Royal Marine guard of honour slammed to attention once more, a cloud of pipeclay floating over their leather hats like smoke while the band struck up a lively march. The ceremony was almost finished. Bethune could not recall how many he had witnessed or participated in since he had entered the navy. Probably thousands. He tried to relax his muscles. Why, then, was he so disturbed, even agitated, when this was opening new doors to his own future?

He glanced at the man for whose benefit this ceremony had been mounted. His successor: to him it might seem the end of everything, rather than a fresh challenge.

Admiral Lord Rhodes was shaking hands with the governor's representative, but it was impossible to tell what he was thinking. Rhodes had been at the Admiralty when Bethune had been appointed there, and for a good many years before that, and they had met occasionally, but Bethune had never really known him. His elevation to First Lord had been taken for granted, until the day Sillitoe had burst unannounced into the office and had demanded to speak with Rhodes. Bethune had learned only then that he had been appointed the Prince Regent's Inspector-General.

It had been Rhodes' cousin, once *Frobisher*'s captain, who had attempted to rape Catherine. *Because I allowed her to go home unescorted.* He thought of Adam's face when he had mentioned Rhodes' particular interest in Sir Richard Bolitho's flagship. He had been ashamed that he could conceal the full truth, but it would have helped no one, least of all Catherine, and he had to consider what old hatreds might do to his own future, as well as Adam's.

But the much-used code of conduct failed to afford him any comfort. It seemed in this instance merely a device which placed expediency before honour and friendship.

He studied his successor once more. Rhodes was tall and heavily built, and had once been handsome. His face was dominated by a strong, beaked nose which made his eyes appear small by comparison, but the eyes, overshadowed though they were, missed nothing. The band was comprised of soldiers borrowed at short notice from the garrison commander, a friend of Captain Forbes; the frigates carried Royal Marine drummers and fifers but they had not yet paraded together. Rhodes had commented on the music, a military quick march, which he thought inappropriate.

The walls had been lined with people watching the ceremony, and Bethune had found himself wondering how long it would take news of Rhodes' appointment to reach the Dey of Algiers.

He walked across the dusty jetty as the guard was dismissed and the onlookers began to disperse. He saw Sir Lewis Bazeley standing in the shade of a clump of sun-dried trees; how would he get along with Rhodes, if he stayed in Malta? An energetic man, eager, Bethune had thought, to impress on younger men what he could do, although Bethune could not imagine him having anything in common with the girl he had married. He had never known if Lady Bazeley had really been in ill health when she had declined to accompany them in the brig. He had thought about Adam's presence here during that time, but Forbes had said nothing to him on the subject, and he was, after all, his flag captain.

And finally, he considered England, the grey skies and chill breezes of October. He smiled. It would be wonderful.

Rhodes strode over to join him. 'Smart turn-out, Sir Graham. Standards – they count more than ever, eh?'

Bethune said, 'I shall show you the temporary headquarters building, m' lord. I have sent for a carriage.'

Rhodes grinned. 'Not a bit of it, we'll walk. I can see the great barn of a place from here!' He gestured to his flag lieutenant. 'Tell the others!'

Bethune sighed. Another Bazeley, or so it seemed.

By the time they had gone halfway Rhodes was breathing heavily, and his face was blotched with sweat, but he had never stopped firing questions. About the six frigates in the squadron, and the expectations of getting more. About the many smaller craft, brigs, schooners and cutters which were the eyes and ears of the man whose flag flew in command.

They paused in deep, refreshing shadow while Rhodes turned to stare at the anchored men-of-war, shimmering in haze above their reflections.

'And *Unrivalled*'s one of them, is she?' He looked at Bethune, his eyes like black olives. 'Bolitho, what's he like?'

'A good captain, m' lord. Successful as well as experienced. What the navy is going to need more than ever now.'

'Ambitious, then?' He looked at the ships again. 'He's done well, I'll give him that. Father a traitor, mother a whore. He's done *very* well, I'd say!' He laughed and strode on.

Bethune contained his fury, at Rhodes and with himself. When he reached the Admiralty perhaps he could discover some way to transfer Adam. But not without *Unrivalled*. She was all he had.

Rhodes had stopped once more, his breathless retinue filling the street.

'And who is *that*, sir?'

Bethune saw a flash of colour on the balcony as Lady Bazeley withdrew into the shadows.

'Sir Lewis Bazeley's wife, m' lord. I explained –'

Rhodes grunted, 'Women in their place, that's one thing.' Again the short, barking laugh Bethune had often heard in London. 'But I'll not have them lifting their skirts to my staff!'

Bethune said nothing. But if it came to drawing a card, his own money would be on Bazeley rather than Rhodes.

And then he knew he was glad to be leaving Malta.

Luke Jago bowed his legs slightly and peered at *Halcyon*'s stout anchor cable to gauge the distance as the gig swept beneath her tapering jib boom, then glanced at the stroke oar and over the heads of the crew, easing the tiller-bar until the flagship appeared to be pinioned on the stemhead. They were a good boat's crew, and he would make certain they stayed that way.

He saw the captain's bright epaulettes catch the sunlight as he leaned over to gaze at the anchored seventy-four.

Professional interest? It was more than that and Jago knew it. Felt it. There were plenty of other boats arriving and leaving *at God's command*.

Vice-Admiral Bethune at least had seemed human enough, and had obviously got on well with the captain. Now he had gone. Jago had seen Captain Bolitho and the first lieutenant watching the courier brig as she had made sail, with the vice-admiral her only passenger. Most senior officers would have expected something grander than a brig, he thought. Bethune must have been that eager to get away.

And now there was Lord Rhodes, a true bastard to all accounts. More trouble.

Jago looked at the midshipman sitting below him. The new one, Deighton. Very quiet, so far, not like his father had been. He wondered if the boy had any idea of the truth. *Killed in action, for King and Country*. His lip almost curled with contempt. Deighton had been scared rotten even before the ball had marked him down.

The flagship was towering over them now, masts and spars black against a clear blue sky. Every piece of canvas in place, paintwork shining like glass.

A ship, any ship, could look very different in the eyes of those who saw her. Jago knew from hard experience how it could be. To the terrified landsman, snatched from his daily life by the hated press gang, the ship was a thing of overwhelming terror and threat, where only the strong and the cunning survived. To a midshipman boarding his first vessel she would appear awesome, forbidding, but the light of excitement was already kindled, ready to be encouraged or snuffed out.

He looked at the captain's shoulders, squared now as if to meet an adversary. To him, she would seem different again.

He saw him shade his eyes and raise his head, knew what he was looking for, and what it meant to him. Today. Now. The Cross of St George lifting and rippling from *Frobisher*'s mainmast truck: the admiral's flag, where his uncle's had been flying when they had shot him down.

He had died bravely, they said. Without complaint. Jago found he could accept it, especially when he looked at his own captain.

'Bows!' He did not even have to raise his voice. Other coxswains were here, watching, and there were several, grander launches with coloured canopies over their sternsheets.

Jago swore silently. He had almost misjudged the final approach to *Frobisher*'s main chains, where white-gloved sideboys were waiting to assist their betters to the entry port.

'*Oars!*' He counted seconds. '*Up!*'

The gig came to rest alongside perfectly. *So you could crack an egg between them*, as old coxswains boasted.

But it had been close. Jago had seen the canopied launches. It usually meant that women would be present, officers' wives maybe, or those of the governor's staff. But there was only one who troubled him, and he could see her now, half-naked, her gown soaked with spray and worse. And the captain holding her. Not scornful, or making a meal of it like some, *most*, would have done.

Adam got to his feet, one hand automatically adjusting his sword. For only an instant their eyes met, then Jago said formally, 'We shall be waitin', sir.'

Adam nodded, and looked at the midshipman. 'Listen and learn, Mr Deighton. *Your* choice, remember?'

The midshipman removed his hat as Adam reached for the hand ropes. They heard the twitter of calls and the bark of commands, then he asked quietly, 'You were there too, weren't you? When my father . . .'

Jago answered sharply, 'Aye, sir. A lot of us was there that day. Now take the tiller an' cast off the gig, can you manage that?'

The youth dropped his lashes. It was as if Jago had told him what he had not dared to ask.

Above their heads, as the gig cast off to make way for another visitor, Adam replaced his hat and shook the hand of *Frobisher*'s captain, a lantern-jawed Scot named Duncan Ogilvie. He was well over six feet tall, and it was hard to imagine him living comfortably in any ship smaller than this.

'You must allow the admiral a few minutes to bid farewell to an early visitor.' He gestured vaguely with his head. 'Commodore from the Dutch frigate yonder.'

Adam had watched her anchor and had felt the old uneasiness at the sight of her flag amongst the squadron's ships. The flag of a once respected enemy, but an enemy for all that. It would take even stronger determination when the French ships began to appear. He turned to say something, but the other captain was already greeting a new arrival, and his eyes were moving swiftly beyond him to yet another boat heading for the chains.

Adam had been a flag captain twice, with his uncle and with Valentine Keen. It was never an easy appointment. To be Rhodes' flag captain would be impossible.

A harassed lieutenant eventually found him and escorted him aft to the great cabin. Even with all the screens removed and furniture kept to a minimum, the whole of the admiral's quarters was packed with uniforms, red and scarlet, and the blue and white of sea officers. And women. Bare shoulders, bold glances from the younger ones, something like disdain from the not so young.

The lieutenant called out Adam's name and ship, and a marine orderly appeared as if by magic with a tray of glasses.

'Better take the red wine, sir. T' other's not much good.' Then, as an afterthought, he murmured, 'Corporal Figg, sir. Me brother's one o' your Royals!' He hurried away, wine slopping unheeded over his sleeve.

Adam smiled. The family again.

'Ah, there you are, Bolitho!' It sounded like *at last*. Rhodes waited for him to push through the crowd, his head bowed between the deck beams. He was almost as tall as his flag captain.

Rhodes said loudly, 'I don't suppose you've had the pleasure of meeting Captain Bolitho? Commands one of my frigates.'

And there she was, smiling a little as she stepped from behind the admiral's considerable bulk. She was all in blue, her hair piled above her ears, the luminous skin of throat and shoulders as he remembered.

She said, 'On the contrary, Lord Rhodes, we know one

another quite well,' and offered her hand deliberately, unaware or indifferent to the eyes upon them.

An officer was speaking urgently to the admiral, and Rhodes had turned away, obviously angered by the interruption.

As Adam raised the hand to his lips, she added softly, 'I should have said, *very well.*'

They stood by the stern windows, watching their reflections in the thickened glass. They did not touch, but Adam could feel her as if she was pressed against him.

She said, 'We shall be leaving Malta very soon.' She turned as if to follow another reflection, but the figure melted away and was lost in the throng.

Then she moved slightly, with one hand raised. 'Look at me.'

Adam saw the little silver sword at her breast. There were so many things he wanted to say, needed to ask, but he could sense the urgency, the hopeless finality. Of a dream.

She said, 'You look wonderful.' Her free hand moved and withdrew. As if she had been about to touch him, had forgotten where they were. 'The bruise? Is it gone?'

Their eyes met, and he felt the irresistible thrill of danger as she murmured, 'My mother said when I was a child and I hurt myself, *I'll kiss it better, Rozanne.*' She looked away. 'It was so beautiful, all of it.' Her lip quivered. 'I shall not spoil it now.'

'You couldn't spoil anything . . .' He lingered over the name. 'Rozanne.'

He heard Rhodes' voice again, and Bazeley's, and their laughter. She raised her chin, and said steadily, 'You see, *Captain*, I love you!'

Bazeley said loudly, 'Here she is!' and, as they turned, 'Captain Bolitho. More adventures, I hear!' He took his wife's arm. 'That's a sailor's life! Not for me, I'm afraid. I like to build things, not knock 'em down.'

Rhodes' eyes were on Bazeley's hand around her bare arm. 'Sometimes we have to do one before we can afford the other, Sir Lewis!'

Bazeley grinned broadly. 'There, what did I tell you?' He made a show of dragging out his watch. 'I must make our excuses, m' lord. I have to see some people.' He looked at

Adam. 'I wish you well.' He did not offer his hand, or remove it from her arm.

A lieutenant was waiting anxiously. 'I have summoned your boat, Sir Lewis.'

Bazeley nodded, dismissing him. 'Given the backing of Parliament, we shall see Malta turned into a fortress. It makes me feel humble to be offered the task, huge though it is!'

They moved away into the crowd, but when Bazeley paused to speak with a senior army officer and clasp him ostentatiously around the shoulders, Rozanne turned and looked directly at Adam.

No words. Just the hand on the little silver sword, pressed against her breast. Nothing more was needed.

Rhodes was saying thickly, 'If *he's* humble, then I'm the bloody Iron Duke!'

Adam realised that Captain Forbes had joined him, and was holding two glasses, one of which he offered.

Forbes said, 'Quite a gathering,' and sighed. 'And ours is a private ship again, for better or worse.' Then he murmured, 'I heard before you joined the squadron that you were not afraid to take a risk, if you considered it justified.' His eyes shifted to the admiral. '*Now*, I understand.'

When Adam looked again, she had gone.

Catherine Somervell turned away from the low stone wall and watched the coachman and groom adjusting the harness, and quieting the two horses which had just been led from the stables. A smart carriage, but it was strange not to see the familiar crest on its door. This one was Roxby's. She smiled sadly, reminiscently. *The King of Cornwall*, as he had been known, affectionately for the most part, although not, perhaps, to those who had appeared before him in his capacity as magistrate.

She saw Roxby's widow, Nancy, giving a parcel to the coachman and emphasising something with a gesture. Food for the journey. Like Grace Ferguson at the old Bolitho house, Nancy always seemed to think she was not getting enough to eat.

She turned her back on the drive and the house and gazed at the nearest hillside. Smooth and green, and yet the sea lay just beyond it. Lying in wait . . .

She had stayed for a single night here with Richard's youngest sister. Now she would return to Plymouth, where Sillitoe was waiting. She had had mixed emotions about meeting Valentine Keen again, but she need not have worried; he and his wife had made her more than welcome, and Sillitoe also. There had been no questions or hints, not even the revival of old memories. Keen would never change, and his second marriage was obviously a success. Gilia was exactly what he needed, and Catherine knew simply by talking to her that Keen was still unaware of Adam's love for Zenoria.

Coming back to the old house below Pendennis Castle had been very hard for her. So many familiar faces, obviously delighted to see her again: Bryan and Grace, Young Matthew, so many of them. And one other. Daniel Yovell, Richard's secretary, had moved back into his little cottage and Bryan Ferguson had signed him on as his deputy, with obvious relief. One of *the little crew*, as Richard used to call them. There had been no time to visit Fallowfield, and she still did not know if she was relieved or saddened by it. Seeing Allday again so soon might have been more than she could bear. With Keen and the others it was difficult enough; she thought Allday would have broken down her last defences.

Nancy joined her by the wall, wrapped in a thick shawl.

'There'll be an early winter, I think.' Catherine felt the eyes on her, full of affection and anxiety. 'If only you could stay a while longer. But if there's anything you need, you have only to write and let me know.' She slipped an arm around her waist, like a young girl again. The girl who had been in love with a midshipman, the young Richard Bolitho's best friend.

'We have many things to do before we sail for Spain, Nancy. I have so enjoyed being here with you.'

They stood in silence for a moment.

'You mustn't worry about Tamara. She'll be well exercised and cared for, until . . .' She broke off. 'You know what I mean.'

Catherine said deliberately, 'I am not living at Chelsea now, Nancy. I am staying at Lord Sillitoe's house in Chiswick.' She had started; she could not stop. 'I have never felt the same about the Chelsea house since that night.' She felt Nancy's grip tighten around her waist. 'Sometimes of late I have seen men watching the house, or imagined I have. Waiting for a chance to see *that woman*.'

Nancy asked softly, 'Shall you marry this Sillitoe? It is obvious to me that he adores you, and rightly so. Remember, I did not marry Roxby for love, but it grew to something even stronger. I still miss him.'

They turned away from the wall and faced the carriage. It was time.

Catherine said, 'He gave up his appointment to the Prince Regent because of me. I shall not destroy his life as well with another scandal.' She inclined her head, as if someone had spoken to her. 'I shall tell you, you of all people.'

There were faces at the upper windows, servants looking out as *that woman* prepared to leave their ordered world. And Elizabeth would be here tomorrow. Another challenge, for both of them. Nancy had sent her to Bodmin with her governess to arrange for some more appropriate clothing and to see something of the town.

Growing up fast, Nancy had said. A withdrawn, demure child who had been too long in the company of older people. She had told Catherine about the day following the girl's arrival. It had been hard to tell how she had been affected by her mother's untimely death, and even now she was still not sure.

But on that day Nancy had taken her down to one of the beaches where Catherine had so often walked with Richard. Some children had been standing in the shallows, hunting for shells, Nancy thought. Elizabeth had remarked on their bare feet. *Had the children no shoes? Were they too poor to own them?*

She had said, 'My word, when I think what *we* used to do at her age!'

Catherine turned and embraced her with great feeling.

'I shall never forget your kindness, and your love. I have always known why Richard cared so much for you.'

The door was open, a gloved hand was held out to support her wrist, Nancy was crying, and suddenly the wheels were moving.

Out on to the road, which ran in the other direction to the old grey house. Where she had waited, and hoped, for the sound of his voice.

When she looked again, the hillside had moved out to hide the house and the small figure who was still waving.

She sat back against the soft leather and stared at the parcel wrapped in its spotless napkin. His old boat cloak was folded beside it, which she had always worn when the wind was blowing coldly off the Bay. There were scissors in the pocket, and she had found one rose still alive and blooming in that familiar garden.

But she had been unable to cut it. And was glad. It was a part of her. It belonged there.

The last rose.

Unis Allday knotted the ties of a fresh apron behind her back and gave herself a critical glance in the parlour glass. The first customers would be arriving soon, most likely buyers and auctioneers on their way to market in Falmouth, and it would be busy at the Old Hyperion inn. She checked each item in her mind, as she did every day. Deliveries of meat and fowl, ale from the brewery.

She walked to the door of the Long Room. Rugs brushed clean of the mud from farm workers' boots, shining mugs and fashionable glasses for the salesmen, and a fire burning in the grate even though it was only October.

A carter had told her that fishermen had reported heavy mist around Rosemullion Head. They were all talking of an early winter.

Little Kate was out walking with Nessa, the new servant at the inn, a tall, dark woman who rarely smiled but had drawn many an admiring glance nevertheless. Not least from Unis's brother, the other John. She was younger than he, but Unis thought she would be good for him; it would be a new beginning for both of them. Nessa had fallen for a soldier from the garrison at Truro; it was a familiar enough tale. She had carried and lost his child, and her lover had been posted with unseemly haste to the West Indies.

Nessa's parents were good chapel people, well known in Falmouth for their strict Christian beliefs. They had turned their daughter out of the house without hesitation.

Unis had taken her into the inn and she had settled down,

perhaps grateful for Unis's trust, and her own sturdy interpretation of Christian charity.

The door from the stable yard swung open and John Allday strode into the parlour.

She knew instantly that something was wrong with him, her man, her love. She also thought she knew what it was.

Allday said heavily, 'I just seen Toby the cooper's mate. He told me Lady Catherine was up at the house. Yesterday, he said.' It sounded like an accusation.

She faced him; she had been right. 'I did hear something about it.' She put a hand on his sleeve; it looked very small and neat on his massive arm.

'You never said?'

She regarded him calmly. 'And well you knows why, John. You're coming to terms with things. So let you think of her, too. Poor lamb, she's got more'n enough to carry.'

Allday smiled fondly. Small, neat and pretty. His Unis. But woe betide anyone who tried to take advantage of her. She was strong. *Stronger than me in many ways.*

They walked to the window together. The place had been in debt when she had bought it. Now it was prospering and looked pleased with itself. One of the ostlers was doing his usual trick with a potato, making it disappear in mid-air and then holding out both tightly clenched fists and letting little Kate choose the one where it was hidden. The child was thinking about it now, her face screwed up with concentration, while Unis's brother stood nearby, watching the dark-haired Nessa.

The child tapped a fist, and it was of course empty, and she screamed with delight and frustration. It never failed.

'We've done well, John.' And they were widening the lane across Greenacre Farm; coaches would be stopping here soon. People had laughed at old Perrow when the plan had been made public, but they would be laughing on the other sides of their faces before long. The wily squire would charge a toll for every coach that crossed his land.

Allday said, '*You've* done well, lass.'

It was there again, the old sense of loss. Like when he had told her about Captain Tyacke calling at Falmouth in his new command.

She heard her brother's wooden leg thudding across the

275

floor, and wondered what Nessa thought about that, or if she had even guessed his feelings for her.

He said, 'Someone asking for you, John.'

Allday came out of his thoughts. 'Me? Who is it?'

He grinned. 'Didn't offer, John.' He added, 'Odd-looking cove. Knows *you* right enough.'

Allday opened the other door and stared past the fire. There were two people in the room already, a black dog snoozing between them.

For a moment he thought he was mistaken. The wrong surroundings. The wrong background.

Then he strode across the room and grasped the newcomer around his narrow shoulders.

'*Tom!* In God's name, Tom Ozzard! Where in *hell* have you been hiding?'

'Oh, here and there. Up home in London, mostly.'

'Well, I'll be double-damned! You skipped off the ship the minute we was paid off. Not a word out of you. What are you doing here?'

Ozzard had not changed in one way. He was as curt and abrupt as ever, the pointed features unsmiling.

He said, 'Thought you'd have a corner where I could pipe down before moving on.'

Moving on. Up home in London. Ozzard had no home.

'*Course* you can stay, you old bugger!'

Unis observed this from the doorway, seeing all things which her beloved John did not see, or want to see. The split shoes, and the threadbare coat with its missing button, the fading hair tied back with a piece of worn ribbon. But this man was part of a world which she could only share at a distance, the life which had taken one husband and had given her another, this big, shambling man who was so glad to see one of its ghosts return. He had spoken often of Ozzard, Sir Richard's personal servant. Like Ferguson, joined now by Yovell up at the house, he was part of the little crew.

She said gently, 'I've some stew on the fire. Maybe you've not eaten yet.'

Ozzard stared at her with eyes which were almost hostile. 'I haven't come because I need anything!'

Allday said quietly, 'Easy, Tom. You're among friends

276

here,' and frowned as voices echoed from the yard. The first of the road labourers were arriving.

Unis was aware of two things. That Ozzard was wary, even distrustful of women, and that her John's pleasure was changing to distress.

She said, 'Come into the parlour. That lot are too noisy for greeting old friends.'

Ozzard sat silently at the table, staring around the room until his eyes came to rest on the model of *Hyperion* in its place of honour.

Allday wanted to talk, if only to reassure him, but was afraid to break something so tentative, so fragile.

Unis was stirring the pot in the kitchen, but her mind was elsewhere.

She said over her shoulder, 'Of course, you being used to Sir Richard an' the likes of other naval gentlemen, you'll know all about wines an' that like.'

Ozzard said suspiciously, 'More than some, yes.'

'I was thinking. With the trade improving on this road, you could be a help to us. To me. There's a room over the tack store. You'd be more'n welcome until you want to move on again.'

She sensed Allday's pleasure and added casually, 'I can't vouch for the money though.'

She had to say something, she thought. Anything. She had noticed the torn cuffs and broken, dirty nails. But he was one of the men who had been with her John and Sir Richard in battles she dared not even begin to imagine.

She came over with the bowl and said, 'Game stew. Get that inside you, an' think about what I said.'

Ozzard bowed his head and blindly picked up the spoon. Then he broke.

'I've got nowhere else,' was all he said.

Much later, when they were alone together, and the inn was quiet until the new day, Allday held her in his arms and murmured, 'How did you know, Unis love?'

She pulled his shaggy head down to her breast. 'Cause I knows *you*, John Allday. An' that's no error!'

She could taste the rum in his kiss, and she was content.

18

Of One Company

'Heave, lads! Heave away!'

With both of *Unrivalled*'s capstans fully manned and every available seaman putting his weight on the bars, the cable was barely moving. Adam Bolitho stood by the quarterdeck rail, his hands clasped beneath his coattails, watching the strange light and the low, scudding clouds. The harbour walls, like the waterfront buildings, seemed to glow with a dull yellow texture, and although it was morning it seemed more like sunset.

The wind had risen slightly, hot against his face, and he tasted grit between his teeth, as if they were already standing off some desert shore. He heard Midshipman Sandell shout impatiently, 'Start that man! Put some weight on the bars there!'

And, instantly, Galbraith's curt, 'Belay that! The cable's moving at last!' He sounded impatient, frustrated, perhaps because of the time wasted here in Malta since Admiral Lord Rhodes had hoisted his flag, which had been followed by this sudden order to get the ships under way.

Clank. The iron pawl of the capstan dropped into position. *Clank*, and then the next one.

Someone said, 'Flagship's cable is shortening, sir!'

Galbraith retorted, 'They have six hundred idle hands to play with!'

Adam looked forward where Massie was peering through the beakhead to watch the bar-taut cable. All of *Unrivalled*'s tonnage and the pressure of wind, set against muscle and sweat.

278

Clank. Clank. As if to a signal he heard the scrape of a violin and then the shantyman's quavery voice. So many times. Leaving harbour. For the sailor the future was always unknown, like the next horizon.

> When first I went to sea as a lad . . .
> *Heave, me bullies, heave!*
> A fine new knife was all I had!
> *Heave, me bullies, heave!*

Adam relaxed slightly. To sea again. But this time under the Flag. The fleet's apron strings, as he had heard other frigate captains describe it.

> And I've sailed for fifty years an' three
> *Heave, lads, heave!*

It was coming in faster now, the capstans turning like human wheels.

> To the coasts of gold and ivory!

Midshipman Sandell hurried past, pointing out something to the new member, Midshipman Deighton.

He had heard Jago remark, 'Look at 'im, will you? Cocking his chest like a half-pay admiral!'

Another memory. What Allday had often said to describe some upstart.

He thought of Admiral Rhodes' hurried conference aboard the flagship. He had received news of another unwarranted attack on some innocent fishermen. A battery had fired on the vessels, and then chebecks had appeared as if from nowhere and had captured or massacred the luckless crews. One of the squadron's armed schooners had been nearby and had attempted to offer assistance, only to be driven off herself. It had been a close thing, to all accounts.

Rhodes had been beside himself with anger. *An example must be made*, before the weather changed yet again. He would delay no longer; all available ships must be ready to sail.

The squadron had been reinforced by a bomb vessel named *Atlas*. She had sailed at first light with *Matchless* as escort.

Adam knew from experience that bomb vessels were difficult at the best of times, being clumsy and unhandy sailers. To use just one such craft without waiting for promised reinforcements would be asking for trouble, no matter how experienced her company might be.

At the captains' conference aboard *Frobisher* he had said as much. Rhodes had turned on him instantly, as if he had been waiting for the chance.

'Of *course*, Captain Bolitho. I almost forgot! A frigate captain of your style and record would condemn the more controlled approach.'

Only Captain Bouverie of *Matchless* had laughed. The others had waited in silence.

Rhodes had continued, 'No daring cutting-out, or some hand-to-hand skirmish with undisciplined renegades, so *you* consider this is not a useful undertaking!'

'I resent that, my lord.' The words had hung in the air, while Rhodes had made a point of studying one of his charts. 'To break the Dey's hold over the Algerine pirates, as he chooses to call them when it suits his purpose, a fleet action will be required.'

Rhodes had shrugged. 'Knowledge is not necessarily wisdom, Captain Bolitho. I trust you will remember it.' He had looked pointedly at the others. 'All of you.'

The shantyman's reedy voice broke into his thoughts again.

And now at the end of a lucky life!

Massie yelled from the forecastle, 'Anchor's hove short, sir!'

Adam nodded, satisfied. 'Loose the heads'ls!' He stared up at the braced yards. 'Hands aloft and loose tops'ls!'

Midshipman Cousens, who had not lowered his telescope and was still watching the flagship, shouted, 'Signal from Flag, sir! *General . . . Make haste!*'

Adam saw the wind feeling its way into the loosely brailed topsails. It was easy to contain your anger when the enemy was so obvious.

The shantyman ended with a flourish, 'Well, still I've got that same old knife!'

'Anchor's aweigh, sir!'

Adam walked to the opposite side to watch the land sliding away, as more men released from the capstan bars hurried to add their weight to the braces, to haul the yards round and capture the wind.

He took a telescope from its rack and trained it on the ancient battlements, and the gaping embrasures where cannon had once dominated the harbour. Where they had held one another. And had loved, impossible though it was to believe.

Galbraith had found him on deck during the morning watch, and had probably imagined he had risen early to see the bomb vessel and the weed-encrusted *Matchless* clearing the harbour.

Or had he guessed that he had been watching the third ship making an early departure, tall and somehow invulnerable with her spreading canvas. A merchantman, the *Aranmore*, bound for Southampton. Had she also been on deck to watch the anchored men-of-war, he wondered? Had she already forgotten, or locked it away, another hidden secret?

He said, 'Take station on the Flag, Mr Galbraith, and lay her on the starboard tack once we are clear.' He tried to smile, to lighten it. 'As ordered, remember?'

He paced to the compass box and back again. And then there was Catherine's letter. Perhaps it would have been better to have sailed earlier, before the latest courier had anchored. *My dear Adam* . . .

What, after all, had he expected? She had nobody to care for her, to protect her from malicious gossip and worse.

He raised the glass again and waited for the image to focus on the first patch of windblown water. *Frobisher*. Much as she had been when she had quit Malta with his uncle's flag at the main. He had felt it when he had walked her deck, sensed it in the watching faces, though few, if any, could have been aboard on that fatal day.

He lowered the glass and looked at his own ship, the seamen flaking down lines and securing halliards. In spite of everything, he had seen the bond grow and strengthen. They were one company.

Perhaps he was wrong about Rhodes, and a show of force was all that it needed. But in his heart he knew it was something else. Unsaid, like that which Bethune had left behind, as dangerous as *Unrivalled*'s shadow on the seabed when they had entered the shallows.

He saw Napier coming aft with something on a covered tray. The boy who had trusted him enough to come and tell him of Lady Bazeley's plight. He laid his palm briefly on the polished wood of the ladder where she had been lying helpless.

He should be able to accept it. Instead, he was behaving like some moonstruck youth.

He heard Cristie give a little cough, waiting to make his report, course to steer, estimated time of arrival. Then the purser would come: provisions and fresh water, and this time, no doubt with Forbes' influence, some welcome casks of beer from the army.

'Signal from Flag, sir!' Midshipman Cousens sounded subdued. '*Make more sail!*'

'Acknowledge.' Adam turned away and saw Midshipman Deighton speaking with the newly minted lieutenant, Bellairs. It gave him time to think, to recall Forbes' words on board *Frobisher. Not afraid to take a risk if you thought it justified.*

He said, 'Be patient, Mr Cousens. I fear you will be much in demand until we sight an enemy!'

Those around him laughed, and others who were out of earshot paused in their work as if to share it.

Adam looked through the great web of spars and rigging. Perhaps Rhodes was watching *Unrivalled* at this very moment.

Aloud he said, 'I'll see you damned, *my lord*!'

Bellairs watched the captain walk to the companion way and then gave his attention to the new midshipman again. It was hard to believe that he had been one himself, and so recently given his commission. It would make his parents in Bristol very proud.

The war was over, but for the navy the fighting was never very far away. Like this new challenge, the Algerine pirates. He found violent death more acceptable than the prospect of life as one of those he had seen left wounded and hopelessly crippled.

He touched the fine, curved hanger at his side. He had been astounded when the first lieutenant had told him of the captain's offer.

He suddenly realised what Midshipman Deighton had been asking him about the ship and her young captain.

He said simply, *'I'd* follow him to the cannon's mouth.'

He touched the hanger again and grinned. A King's officer.

Midshipman Cousens lowered the big signals telescope and dashed spray from his tanned features with his sleeve.

'Boat's casting off from the flagship now, sir!'

Lieutenant Galbraith crossed to the nettings and stared at the lively, broken water, the crests dirty yellow in the strange glare. The weather had worsened almost as soon as they had left Malta, wind whipping the sea into serried ranks of angry waves, spray pouring from sails and rigging alike as if they were fighting through a tropical rainstorm. If the wind did not ease, the ships would be scattered overnight. As they had been last night, and they had struggled to reform to the admiral's satisfaction.

As Cristie had often said, the Mediterranean could never be trusted, especially when you needed perfect conditions.

He saw the cutter staggering clear of *Frobisher*'s glistening side; it was a wonder that it had not capsized in its first crossing. To use the gig had been out of the question. A cutter was heavier and had the extra brawn to carry her through this kind of sea.

He had been both doubtful and anxious when Captain Bolitho had told him he was going across to the flagship to see Rhodes in person, after three signals to the admiral requesting an audience. Each had been denied without explanation, as was any admiral's right. But it was also the right of any captain to see his flag officer, if he was prepared to risk reprimand for wasting the great man's time.

With his own coxswain at the tiller Bolitho had headed away, his boat cloak black with spray before they had covered a few yards. It would not have been the first time a captain had been marooned aboard a flagship because of bad weather. Suppose it had happened now? The captain would have had to endure the sight of his own command hove to under storm canvas, and another man's voice at the quarterdeck rail. *Mine.*

He watched the cutter lifting, porpoising slightly before riding the next trough of dark water, the oars rising and dipping, holding the hull under control. At other times he could scarcely see more than the bowed heads and shoulders of the boat's crew, as if they were already going under.

Galbraith felt only relief. He had heard the rumours about Bolitho's disagreement with the admiral at the last conference, the hostility and the sarcasm, as if Rhodes were trying to goad him into something which would be used against him. It was something personal, and therefore dangerous, even to others who might be tempted to take sides in the matter.

The cutter plunged into a trough and then lifted her stem again like a leaping porpoise. Even without a glass he could see the grin on the captain's face, stronger than any words or code of discipline. He had seen it at first hand in action, when these same men had doubted their own ability to fight and win, had seen how some of them had touched his arm when he had passed amongst them. The victors.

He called sharply, 'Stand by to receive the captain!'

But the boatswain and his party were already there. Like himself, they had been waiting with their blocks and tackles, perhaps without even knowing why.

He saw a small figure in a plain blue coat, drenched through like the rest of them: Ritzen, the purser's clerk. A quiet, thoughtful man, and an unlikely one to spark off a chain of events which might end in a court martial, or worse. But Ritzen was different from the others around him. He was Dutch, and had signed on with the King's navy when he had been rescued by an English sloop after being washed overboard in a storm and left for dead by his own captain.

Ritzen had been ashore in Malta with Tregillis, the purser, buying fruit from local traders rather than spend a small fortune at the authorised suppliers. He had fallen in with some seamen from the Dutch frigate *Triton* which had called briefly at the island. Her captain, a commodore, had paid a visit to Lord Rhodes.

Galbraith could recall the moment exactly, after another long day of sail and gun drill, and a seemingly endless stream of signals, mostly, it appeared, directed at *Unrivalled*.

Everyone knew it was wrong, unfair, but who would dare to say as much? Galbraith had gone to the great cabin, where he had found the captain in his chair, some letters open on his lap, and a goblet of cognac quivering beside him to each thud of the tiller head.

Despair, resignation, anger: it had been all and none of them.

After reporting the state of the ship and the preparations for station-keeping overnight, Galbraith had told him about the purser's clerk. Ritzen had overheard that the Dutch frigate was on passage to Algiers, her sale already approved and encouraged by the Dutch government. It had been like seeing someone coming alive again, a door to freedom opening, when moments earlier there had been only a captive.

'I knew there was something strange when I heard it aboard *Frobisher*!' Adam had gone from the chair to the salt-stained stern windows in two strides, the dark hair falling over his forehead, the weight of command momentarily forgotten. 'A commodore in charge of a single frigate! That alone should have told me, if nobody else was prepared to!'

Perhaps Rhodes had forgotten, or thought it no one else's business. Maybe Bethune's records had not been examined. Galbraith thought it unlikely, and when he had seen the light in the captain's eyes he knew it for certain.

'I shall see the admiral . . .' He must have seen the doubt in Galbraith's face. To risk another confrontation, and all on the word of the purser's clerk, seemed reckless if not downright dangerous. But there had been no such doubt in Bolitho's voice. 'Such intelligence is valuable beyond measure, Leigh! To *any* sea officer, time and distance are the true enemies. This man spoke out, and I intend that his words should be heard!'

He had stared at the leaping spectres of spray breaking across the thick glass, and it had been then that Galbraith had seen the locket on the table beside the goblet. The beautiful face and high cheekbones, the naked shoulders. He had never laid eyes on her, but he had known that it was Catherine Somervell. *That woman*, who had scorned society and won the hearts of the fleet, and of the nation.

Galbraith stood back from the dripping hammock nettings. He was soaked to the skin, but he had felt nothing. He suppressed a shiver, but it was not cold or fear. It was something far stronger.

'After you have secured the cutter, Mr Partridge, pass my compliments to the purser and have a double tot issued to the boat's crew.' He saw the little clerk staring up at him. 'And also for Ritzen.'

And, as suddenly as he had departed, the captain was here on the streaming deck with his gasping, triumphant oarsmen.

He shook his cocked hat and tossed it to his servant.

'All officers and warrant ranks aft in ten minutes, if you please.' The dark eyes were everywhere, even as he pushed the dripping hair from his face. 'But I must speak first with you.'

Galbraith waited, remembering the moment when Bazeley's wife had offered her hand to be kissed. The notion had touched him then: how right they had looked together. He had wanted to laugh at his own stupidity. Now, he was not so sure.

Then Adam spoke quietly, so softly that he could have been talking to himself. Or to the ship, Galbraith thought.

'I pray to God for a fair wind tomorrow.' He touched his lieutenant's arm, and Galbraith knew the gesture was unconscious. 'For then we must fight, and only He can help us.'

Lieutenant Massie looked around the crowded cabin, his swarthy features expressionless.

'All present, sir.'

Adam said, 'Sit where you can, *if* you can.' It gave him more time to think, to assemble what he would say.

The cabin was full; even the junior warrant officers were present, some of them staring around as if they expected to discover something different in this most sacred part of their ship.

Adam could feel the hull moving heavily beneath him, but steadier now, the wind holding her over, all sounds muffled by distance.

He could picture Galbraith moving about the quarterdeck overhead, and recalled his face when he had outlined the possibilities of action, as he had to Lord Rhodes.

Now Galbraith was on watch, the only officer absent from the cabin.

The two Royal Marine officers, a bright patch of colour, the midshipmen in their own whispering group, and young Bellairs standing with Lieutenant Wynter and Cristie, the taciturn sailing master. The surgeon was present also, dwarfing the scrawy figure of Tregillis the purser. Despite the lack of space the other warrant officers, the backbone of any fighting ship, managed to keep apart. Stranace the gunner stood with his friend the carpenter, 'Old Blane' as he was known, although he was not yet forty. Neither of them could work out a course or compass bearing on a chart, and like most professional sailors they were content to leave such matters to those trained for it. But lay them alongside an enemy ship and they would keep the guns firing, and repair the damage from every murderous broadside. And the master's mates: they would keep the ship under command, knowing they were prime targets for any enemy marksman. The flag and the cause were incidental when it came to surviving the first deadly embrace.

He knew without looking that his clerk, Usher, was at the table, ready to record this rare meeting, with a handkerchief balled in one fist to muffle the cough which was slowly killing him.

The only missing face was that of George Avery. Even as Adam had outlined his convictions to Admiral Rhodes he had thought of Avery, as if he had been speaking for him.

So many times they had talked together, about his service with Sir Richard, his friendship with Catherine. Galbraith had touched upon it too, only a few moments ago in this same cabin.

I think he knew he was going to die, sir. I think he had given up the will to live.

He glanced along the cabin's side. The big eighteen-pounders were held firmly behind their sealed ports, but dragging at the stout breeching ropes with the sway of the deck. As if they were restless, eager.

But instead he saw *Frobisher*'s stern cabin, the great ship riding almost disdainfully across the broken water. Where his uncle had sat and dreamed; had believed, perhaps, that a hand was reaching out at last.

The surprising part had been the admiral's frowning silence while he had explained the reason for his visit.

Avery again . . . How he had described their meeting with Mehmet Pasha, the Dey's governor and commander-in-chief in Algiers. Face to face, with no ships to support them but for the smaller twenty-eight gun frigate *Halcyon*. She was out there now, riding out the same weather, with the same young captain who had served under James Tyacke as a midshipman, in this very sea at the Battle of the Nile.

Avery had forgotten nothing, and had filled a notebook with facts of every kind, from the barbarous cruelties he had witnessed, not so far from where they had cut out *La Fortune*, a thousand years ago, or so it felt, even to the names of ships moored there, and the Spanish mercenary, Captain Martinez, who had changed sides too many times for his own good. This command would be his last, one way or the other. Adam seemed to hear Lovatt's despairing voice while he lay dying, here, just beyond the screen of his sleeping quarters. Where he had held the boy Napier circled in his arm, to make himself believe he was the son who had turned away from him.

He licked dry lips, aware of the silence, the intent, watching faces, barely able to accept that he had been talking to these men for several minutes. Even the shipboard noises seemed muted, so that the scrape of Usher's pen seemed loud in the stillness.

He said, 'I believe we shall fight. The main attack will be carried out by the flagship and *Prince Rupert*, and at the right moment by the bomb vessel *Atlas*. Perhaps this is merely a gesture, one worth risking ships and lives. It is not my place to judge.' He held the bitterness at bay, like an enemy. '*Unrivalled*'s place will be up to wind'rd. Ours is the fastest vessel, and apart from the two liners the best armed.' He smiled, as he had done in the cutter to give his oarsmen heart for the return pull. 'I do not need to add, *the best ship*!'

Rhodes would have his way. The bombardment would be carried out without delay after yet another reported attack on helpless fishermen and the murder of their crews. It might make a fitting beginning to the admiral's appointment.

He thought of the Dutch frigate again. Expedience, greed, who could say? The great minds who planned such transactions

288

never had to face the brutal consequences of close action. Maybe the Dutch government had fresh plans for expansion overseas. They already held territories in the West and East Indies, so why not Africa, where rulers like the Dey could obstruct even the strongest moves of empire?

Such deals were left to men like Bazeley . . . his mind faltered for a second . . . and Sillitoe. He saw Lieutenant Wynter watching him fixedly. Or *his* father in the House of Commons and those like him.

'The Dutch frigate *Triton*, or whatever she may now be called, is a powerful vessel . . .'

He heard Rhodes again, his confidence and bluster returning like a strong squall.

'They would not dare! I could blow that ship out of the water!'

He continued, 'I know not what to expect. I merely wanted to share it with you.' He paused, and saw O'Beirne glance around as if he expected to see a newcomer in the cabin. 'For we are of one company.'

He had already seen the doubt on Massie's dark countenance. He knew the chart, the notes in Cristie's log, and now he knew *Unrivalled*'s holding station, well up to windward. Rhodes could not have made it plainer.

'Be content to watch the flank for a change!'

Even the flag captain had warned him openly before he had climbed down to the pitching cutter.

'You've made an enemy there, Bolitho! You sail too close to the wind!'

He would, of course, deny any such remark at a court martial.

They were filing out of the cabin now, and Usher bowed his head in a fit of coughing.

O'Beirne was the last to leave, as Adam had known he would be. They faced one another, like two men meeting unexpectedly in a lane or on some busy street.

O'Beirne said, 'I am glad I wear a sword only for the adornment, sir. I consider myself a fair man and a competent surgeon.' He tried to smile. 'But command? I can only watch at a distance, and be thankful!'

The surgeon walked out into the daylight, and was surprised

to see the planking steaming in the warm wind as if the very ship were burning. There was so much he had wanted to say, to share. And now it was too late. Before sailing from England he had met *Frobisher*'s previous surgeon, Paul Lefroy; they had known one another for years. He smiled sadly. Lefroy was completely bald now, his head like polished mahogany. A good doctor, and a firm friend. He had been with Sir Richard Bolitho when he had died. O'Beirne had pictured it in his friend's words, just as he had seen some of it in his youthful captain's face, and he glanced aft now as if he expected to see him.

Lefroy had said, 'When he died, I felt I had lost a part of myself.'

He shook his head. For a ship's surgeon, even after several glasses of rum, that was indeed something.

But for some reason the levity did not help. The image remained.

Napier, the captain's servant, watched O'Beirne leave, and knew his captain would be alone, perhaps needing a drink, or simply to talk, as he did sometimes. Perhaps the captain did not understand what it meant to him. The boy who had wanted to go to sea, to become someone.

And now he was.

He touched his pocket and felt the broken watch, its guard punched in two by a musket ball, where the little mermaid had been engraved.

The captain had seemed surprised when he had asked if he could keep it, instead of pitching it outboard.

He turned as he heard the sound of a grindstone and the rasp of steel. The gunner was back, too, supervising the sharpening of cutlasses and the deadly boarding axes.

He found that he could face it. Accept it.

He touched the broken watch again and smiled gravely. He was no longer alone.

Joseph Sullivan, the seaman who had taken part in the Battle of Trafalgar and who was *Unrivalled*'s most experienced lookout, paused in his climb to the crosstrees and glanced down at the ship. It took some men years to become used to the height from the deck, the quivering shrouds and treacherous rigging;

some never did. Others were never afforded the chance. Falls were common, and even if the unfortunate lookout fell into the sea it was unlikely that he would recover. If the ship hove to in time.

Sullivan was completely at ease working aloft, and always had been. He looked briefly into the fighting top he had just passed, where some Royal Marines were occupied with a swivel gun and checking their arms and powder. Marines were always busy, he thought.

Sullivan took the weight on his bare soles, so hardened and calloused over the years that he scarcely felt the tarred ratlines, and linked an arm through the shrouds.

The ship had been up and about since before first light, as he had known she would be. He could still taste the rum on his tongue, the pork in his belly. It was a hard life, but he was as content as any true sailor could be.

He peered up at the black shrouds, the big main topsail filling and emptying while the wind tried to make up its mind. No need to hurry. It was too dark to see more than a few yards. He shifted the knife which he carried across his spine like most seamen, where it could not snare anything, but could be drawn in a second.

He smiled. Like the Jack in the shantyman's song when they had weighed anchor, he thought. Sullivan had been in the navy for as long as he could remember. Good ships and foul ones. Fair captains and tyrants. Like the shanty. The old knife was about the only possession he still owned from those first days at sea.

He could smell smoke and grease and heard a splash alongside. The galley fire had been doused; the ship was cleared for action. He sighed. From what he had heard, *Unrivalled* would be well out of it when the guns started to roar. He thought of the captain's face. He was feeling it. He grinned. A real goer, like his uncle to all accounts. But a man. Not afraid to stop and ask one of his men what he was doing, or how he felt. Rare, then.

He began the final climb, pleased that he was not breathless like some half his age. He saw the masthead pendant streaming away to leeward towards the larboard bow. Lifting, then curling again, undecided. He grinned again. Like the bloody admiral.

He reached his position in the crosstrees and hooked his leg around a stay. The wind was steady enough, from the north-east, but the bluster had gone out of it. That would mean that overnight the other ships would have drifted off their stations.

A bombardment, they said. He rubbed his chin doubtfully. It was to be hoped that the admiral knew what he was about. A two-decker made a fine target. It only needed some heated shot to upset the best-laid plans.

He shaded his eyes as the first sunlight played across the sails and braced yards; it was a view which never failed to stir him. People you knew, moving about the deck like ants, and other, isolated scarlet coats like those in the maintop. Marks of discipline, like the blue and white uniforms on the quarterdeck and down by the foremast at the first division of eighteen-pounders. His eyes crinkled as he recalled his captain climbing up to join him. No fuss, no swagger. He had just sat here with him. Not too many could say that.

He could see the coloured bunting scattered over the deck by the flag lockers. Signals to be made and answered, once *Frobisher* was in sight. He could see some of the others now, the bigger *Prince Rupert*, sails apparently limp and useless, and a frigate just off her starboard quarter. That would be *Montrose*, although she was well off station.

He felt the mast shiver, shrouds murmuring as the wind pressed into the topsails again. *Unrivalled* was standing well up to windward, while nearer the coast the whole squadron might become becalmed.

He stared beyond the larboard bow again, but the coast was still little more than a shapeless blur. There could be a mist, too.

He turned his head as a cloud of sea birds took off suddenly from the water and circled angrily over the ship. The spirits of dead Jacks, they said. Surely, he thought, they could find something better to come back as?

He laughed and began to whistle softly to himself. Whistling was forbidden on board a man-of-war, because it could be mistaken for the pipe of a boatswain's call. *They* said. It was more likely because some old admiral in the past had said as much.

That was another part of it. The freedom. Up here, you were your own man. Experience taught you the shades and colours of the sea that governed your life. The depths and the shoals, the sandbars and the deeps. Like when young Captain Bolitho had taken her right through that narrow strait . . . Even Sullivan had felt uneasy about that.

He peered down again and saw one of the midshipmen training his telescope, adjusting it for a new day. And he remembered the captain's surprise, that time when he had proved his skill as a lookout.

He glanced at his arm, the tattoos of ships and places he could scarcely remember. They all swore that they hated it, but what else was there? Perhaps when *Unrivalled* eventually paid off . . . He shook his head, dismissing it. How many times had he said that?

He looked up again and the whistle died on his lips. For only a moment longer he held on to the view, the wheeling gulls, the pale deck far below, the men who were his companions from choice or otherwise.

He held one hand to his mouth, surprised that he had been caught out.

'Deck thar! Sail on th' starboard bow!'

He was too old a hand to consider pride. He was, after all, a good lookout.

293

19

'Trust Me . . .'

Joshua Cristie, the master, watched his captain stride from the chart to the compass box, and said, 'Wind's still holdin' steady from the nor'-east, sir.'

Adam Bolitho stared at the great span of hardening canvas, the masthead pendant reaching out towards the bow like a lance.

He said, 'Make to Flag. *Sail in sight to the west.*' He paused long enough to see Midshipman Cousens and his signals party bending double to fasten the flags into order for hoisting, and caught sight of Bellairs turning from the rail, his eyes anxious, as if he were concerned that someone else was carrying out what had been his duty before his examination for lieutenant.

He forgot them as he raised a telescope and levelled it on the flagship. The other ships were badly scattered, and *Frobisher's* yards seemed to be a mass of signals as Rhodes tried to muster his command.

It was not long before Cousens shouted, 'Acknowledged, sir!' But it felt like an age. Then Cousens called again, '*Disregard, Remain on station.*'

Adam turned away. 'God damn him!'

Galbraith joined him. 'Shall I send Bellairs aloft, sir? Sullivan's a good hand, but . . .'

Adam looked at him. 'There is a ship, right enough, and we both know which one she is!'

He swung round again as a rocket exploded like a small star against the dusty shoreline. The bomb vessel was moving into position between the flagship and the old fortifications.

Rhodes' *show of strength*. Adam knew that anger was blunting his judgment, but he could not help it. If Algiers had any doubts before, they would be gone now.

Even if it was the Dutch frigate, one such ship could do little against Rhodes' array of force.

He thought of the response to his signal. Like a slap in the face, which would soon be known to every man here today. It was cheap. And it was dangerous.

He saw Napier standing by the companion hatch and said, 'Here, take my coat and hat.' He saw Galbraith open his mouth as if to protest, then close it again. Perhaps he was embarrassed to see his own captain making a fool of himself, or maybe he felt it as a slight on his ability that he had not been consulted.

If I am wrong, my friend, it is better for you to know nothing.

Jago was here too, but took his sword and tucked it under his arm without comment.

Adam strode to the shrouds, where he turned and looked back at Galbraith.

'Trust me.' That was all.

Then he was climbing the ratlines, his boots slipping on the taut cordage, his hands and arms grazed by rigging he did not even feel. As he drew level with the maintop the marines stared at him with surprise, then some of them grinned, and one even gave a cheeky wave. Perhaps the man whose brother was a corporal in the flagship.

On and on, higher and higher, until his heart was pounding at his ribs like a fist.

He took Sullivan's hard hand for the last heave up on to the crosstrees, and gasped, 'Where away?'

Sullivan pointed without hesitation, and might even have smiled as Adam dragged out the small telescope which could easily be slung over one shoulder.

The light was still poor, high though he was above the tilting deck, but the other ship was a frigate right enough. Standing away, with all plain sail set and filling to the fresh north-easterly.

He swung the glass to larboard and studied the scattered ships. The two liners were on course again, *Frobisher* in the lead, with *Matchless* and *Montrose* standing well away on either quarter. And, far away, her masts and topsails shimmering in haze, was *Halcyon*, the admiral's 'eyes', leading the squadron.

Then he saw the bomb vessel *Atlas* and found time to pity her commander as he sweated to work his ship into a position from which he could fire. From here it was all a sand-coloured blur, with only the slow-moving ships making sense. Adam had been aboard a bomb vessel during the campaign against the Americans, and *Atlas* seemed little improved. Bluff-bowed, and very heavily constructed for her hundred feet in length; bombs were always hard to handle. Apart from two immensely heavy mortars, they also carried a formidable armament of twenty-four pounder carronades as well as small weapons to fight off boarders. But the mortars were their reason for being. Each was thirteen inches in diameter and fired a massive shot, which, because of its high trajectory, would fall directly on top of its target before exploding. Adam felt his own ship riding over again to the wind. They could keep their bomb vessels . . .

Sullivan said, almost patiently, 'I reckon that when the light clears a bit we'll see the other ship, sir.'

Adam allowed the glass to fall on to its sling and stared at him.

'I saw the frigate. Surely there's no other.'

Sullivan gazed beyond his shoulder. 'She's there, sir. A big 'un.' He looked directly into his eyes. Not the captain, but a visitor to his world. 'But I reckon you already knew that, sir?'

Adam gazed down at the deck. The upturned faces. Waiting . . .

'There could only be one. The merchantman that left Malta when *Atlas* sailed. *Aranmore*.'

Sullivan nodded slowly. 'Might well be, sir.'

Adam reached across and touched his leg. 'A prize indeed.'

He knew Sullivan was leaning over to watch him descend. Even the marines in the fighting top remained quiet and unsmiling as he clambered down past the barricade and its swivel gun, the daisy-cutter, as the sailors called them. Perhaps they saw it in his face, even as he felt it like a tightening grip around his heart.

296

Galbraith hurried to meet him, barely able to drag his eyes away from the tar-stained shirt and the blood soaking through one knee of his breeches.

'I think the frigate is chasing *Aranmore*, Leigh.' He leaned on the chart, his scarred hands taking the weight.

Galbraith said, 'Suppose you're wrong, sir?'

Cristie forced a grin, and said, 'There was only one man who was never wrong, Mr Galbraith, an' they crucified *him*!'

Adam lingered on the warning, and knew what it must have cost Galbraith to say it.

'But if I'm not? If the Algerines capture *Aranmore*,' he hesitated, loathing it, 'it will make Lord Rhodes a laughing-stock. The hostages could be used for bargaining, and so much for "a show of strength".'

Galbraith nodded, understanding. Experience, instinct; he did not know how it came about. And he was ashamed that he was glad the choice was not his. Nor probably ever would be.

He watched the captain's face as he beckoned to Midshipman Cousens. Outwardly calm again, his voice unhurried, thinking aloud while he held out one arm to allow his coxswain to clip the old sword into position.

'Make to Flag, Mr Cousens. *Enemy in sight to the west, steering west-by-south.*' He saw Cristie acknowledge it. '*In pursuit of . . .*' He smiled at the youth's frowing features. 'Spell it out. *Aranmore.*'

It took physical effort to take and raise the spare telescope. The next few hours would be vital. He heard the flags squeaking aloft and in his mind saw them breaking out at the yard and, across that mile or so of lively water, another signals midshipman like Cousens reading the signal, as someone else wrote it down on a slate.

Cousens' brow was furrowed in concentration. 'From Flag, sir. *Acknowledged.*' He sounded rather subdued. 'Flag's calling up *Halcyon*, sir.'

Adam snapped, 'No use! *Halcyon*'s too far downwind – it will take her a whole watch to close with them!'

Cousens confirmed it. '*Chase*, sir.'

Galbraith was beside him again. 'They might run for it when they see *Halcyon*, sir.'

'I think not. The man in command will lose his head if he fails this time. And he will know it!'

He looked back at the signals party.

'Anything, Mr Cousens?'

Sullivan's voice broke the spell, '*Deck thar!* Frigate's opened fire, sir!'

He heard the distant thuds, bow-chasers, he thought, testing the range, hoping for a crippling shot.

Cousens shouted, 'Signal *Chase* is still flying, sir!'

Adam walked to the compass, the helmsmen gazing past him as if he was invisible, the big double-wheel moving slightly this way or that, each sail filled and fighting the rudder.

He said, 'Then acknowledge it, Mr Cousens.' And swung away, as if he might see in the boy's eyes the folly of his own decision. 'Get the hands aloft, Mr Galbraith! T'gallants and royals!' He grinned, the strain and doubt recoiling like beaten enemies. 'The stuns'ls too, when we may!' He strode over to Cristie and his mates. 'How so?'

'West-by-north, sir.' The master gave a wintry smile, as if the madness was infectious. 'It'll give 'er room to run down on the bugger!'

'Stand by, on the quarterdeck! Man the braces there!'

Another squall moaned through the stays and shrouds, and the canvas cracked as if it would tear itself from the yards as the helm went over.

'Flag is repeating our number, sir!' Cousens' words were almost drowned by the distant reverberating crash of mortars. The bombardment had begun.

Galbraith shook his head. 'Hoist another ensign, Mr Cousens,' and attempted to smile, to share what the captain was doing. 'That will be duty enough for you today!'

He watched the seamen running from one task to the next, not one tripping over a gun tackle or snatching up the wrong line or halliard. All the training and the hard knocks had paid off. It was insanity, and he could feel it driving away his reserve and his concern at the captain's deliberate misinterpretation of the admiral's signal. He had even found time to note it and sign the log, so that no one else could be officially blamed.

Galbraith saw Napier handing his captain a clean shirt, laughing at something he said as he pulled it over his unruly hair. The sunlight was stronger now, enough to shine briefly on the locket the captain was wearing, the one he had seen in the cabin with the letters.

He felt a sudden chill as the boy handed Captain Bolitho his coat, not the one he had been wearing when he had first appeared on deck, if he had ever left it, but the gold-laced dress uniform coat with the bright epaulettes. A ready target for any marksman. Madness again, but Galbraith could imagine him wearing no other this day.

'West-by-north, sir! Steady she goes!'

Adam looked along his ship, hearing the intermittent crash of gunfire. *Halcyon* was under fire already, long-range shots, like the ones laid on *Aranmore*.

He thought of Avery, his comments concerning the infamous Captain Martinez, and touched the locket beneath the clean shirt, and said aloud, 'You were right, George, and nobody saw it. The face in the crowd.'

He turned to see the other ensign breaking to the wind, seeming to trail on the dark horizon as the ship heeled over, knowing that his mind must be empty now of everything which might weaken his resolve. But a memory of his uncle came, as he had seen him all those other times.

'So let's be about it, then!'

Luke Jago stood by the mainmast's great trunk and looked along the frigate's maindeck. So many times; different ships and in all weathers, but always the same pattern. The whole larboard battery of eighteen-pounders had been run in, hauled up the tilting deck by their sweating crews, held in position by their taut tackles and ready for loading. Each crew was standing by with the tools of their trade, rammers and sponges, handspikes and charges, while every gun captain had already selected a perfect ball from his shot garland for the first, perhaps vital broadside. Around and at the foot of every mast the boarding pikes had been freed from their lashings, ready to snatch up and spit anyone brave or stupid enough to attempt to board them. The weapons chests were empty, and each man had armed himself with cutlass or axe with no more uncertainty than a farm-hand selecting a pitchfork.

He could sense the new midshipman watching him, breathing hard in his efforts to keep up with the captain's coxswain. Jago had wondered why the captain had given him the task of nursing Commodore Deighton's son. One day he would be an officer like Massie or so many others he had known, quick to forget past favours, and the secret skills which only true seamen knew and could pass on.

He felt the deck jerk to the double crash of the bomb's two mortars. Even at this distance, the ships were barely visible through the haze and dust, and yet the mortars' recoil seemed to rebound from the very seabed.

He had heard some of the men joking about the captain's reading of the flagship's signal. They would be putting bets on it too, if he had made a serious mistake. He loosened the cutlass in his belt, swearing quietly. Captain Bolitho would be a marked man anyway, as far as the admiral was concerned.

He said to the midshipman, 'You'll be needed to pass messages between the forrard guns, under Mr Massie,' he jerked his thumb in the direction of the quarterdeck, 'an' the cap'n. And if *he* falls, to th' next in command aft.'

He saw the boy blink, but he showed no fear. And he listened. He glanced at Midshipman Sandell by the empty boat-tier, even now snapping at some luckless seaman. He'd be no bloody loss to anyone.

He said, 'An' remember, Mr Deighton, always *walk*, never run. That only makes the lads jumpy.' He grinned at Deighton's seriousness. 'Stops you bein' a target too!'

Then, seeing his expression, he touched the midshipman's arm. 'Forget I said that. It just came out.'

He stared at his own scarred hand on the boy's sleeve. *Let him think what he damn well likes. He'll not care a straw for a common seaman.* But it would not hold.

He said, 'Now we'll carry on aft.'

Deighton said, 'It seems so empty without the boats on deck.'

'Never you mind them. We'll pick 'em up afore sunset.'

Deighton said softly, 'Do you believe that, really?'

Jago nodded to Campbell, who was leaning on a handspike near his gun. Like most of the crews he had stripped to the waist, his scarred back a living testimony to his strength.

300

Jago sighed. Or stupidity. It was not long since he had done the same, his defiance of the authority which had wrongly punished him, leaving him scarred until the day he dropped.

The boy was murmuring, 'I've never been in a real sea fight before.'

Jago knew that Deighton had transferred from the old *Vanoc*, a frigate said to be so infested with rot that she was as ripe as a pear, with only her copper holding her together.

He looked up at the towering masts and their bulging pyramids of canvas. From down here, the topgallant masts appeared to be bending like whips to the mounting pressure.

It was there again. Pride. Something he had all but taken an oath against. But she was flying through the water, spray bursting through the beakhead and drenching the figurehead's naked shoulders, a veritable sea nymph. He saw *Halcyon*, so much closer now, heeling over at a steep angle from *Unrivalled*'s bow. A well-handled ship, he conceded. But no match for the big Dutchman.

And the lookouts had reported that the merchantman *Aranmore* was somewhere ahead. Victim or prize, it depended on which side you took.

Jago thought of the girl he had helped to carry below. He stared at the poop, the officers' figures leaning over to the sloping deck as if they were nailed to it to hold them in position. And now she was out there with her bullyboy of a husband and God alone knew how many other important passengers. Jago had seen the captain's face that night, and again when he had gone ashore to see her, even if he had not intended to meet her or it had been a complete accident. Jago thought otherwise. He shaded his eyes and saw the captain standing with one hand on the quarterdeck rail. By that same ladder.

And why not? As smart as paint, she was. He smiled crookedly. And she knew it, what's more.

The sound of cannon fire across the sea's face, and for an instant Jago imagined that the wind had changed direction.

Sullivan's voice cut through the boom of canvas and the groan of straining cordage. 'Deck thar! *Halcyon*'s under fire!'

Jago ran to the side and stood on a gun truck to get a better view. *Halcyon* was as before, cutting through the water, her ensigns very white against the hazy sky, their scarlet crosses

301

like blood. Then there was a sudden groan, and her foretopmast and spars began to topple; the sea and wind muffled the sound, and yet he seemed to hear it clearly, the slithering tangle of masts and rigging, snapping cordage and torn canvas, and then the complete mass plunging over the lee bow, flinging up spectres of spray. There would be men there, too, some killed in the fall, others dragged over the side by broken shrouds and stays, dying even as he watched, while others ran to hack the debris away. There was never time for pity.

Within minutes the fallen foretopmast was dragging *Halcyon* around like a giant sea anchor, and her guns were pointing impotently at open water.

'Stand by to wear ship!' That was the first lieutenant, voice distorted by his speaking trumpet. *'Pipe the hands to the braces!'*

Jago waited, feeling the ship's response to wind and rudder. The afterguard tramping past those same officers, hauling at the mizzen braces while *Unrivalled* altered course to windward, as close as she'd come, some of the sails already whipping and cracking in protest until more hands brought them under control.

Midshipman Deighton called, 'What are we doing?'

Jago watched the tapering bowsprit and jib boom, the enemy frigate clearly visible for the first time, as if sliding downwind to larboard. Captain Bolitho was going to try and overreach the enemy, to claw into the wind and then run down on them, much as he had heard the dour sailing master describe.

But all he said was, 'We're going to fight. So be ready!' Then, together, they climbed the ladder to the quarterdeck.

Adam Bolitho looked only briefly at the scene on the quarterdeck. The marines, their boots skidding on the wet planking while they secured the braces again before snatching up their muskets and running back to their stations. Four men on the wheel now, one of Cristie's mates adding his weight to the fight against wind and rudder.

He glanced up at the masthead pendant, almost hidden by the wildly cracking canvas. The wind was still steady, from the north-east, but from aft he could believe it was almost directly abeam. The ship lay hard over, and his eyes stung as a shaft of sunlight found them for the first time.

And the enemy was still firing at *Halcyon*. There was no smoke to betray the shots, the wind was too strong, but he could see the other frigate's sails pockmarked with holes, and great, raw gashes along her engaged side; the enemy was trying to rid himself of one foe before dealing with the real threat from *Unrivalled*. He fought back the anger. Rhodes was so intent on humiliating him that he had been blind to the true danger. Dutch-built frigates were heavier, and could take a lot of punishment. *Halcyon* could not even close the range and hit back. He saw her main-topmast reel drunkenly now in a tangle of black cordage, like something trapped in a net, before crashing down across her gangway.

He took a telescope from its rack and trained it on the other frigate. Magnified in the powerful glass, he could see terrible damage, could feel her pain, and knew he was thinking of his beloved *Anemone* in her last fight against odds. When he had been badly wounded, and unable to prevent her colours being struck to the American.

He heard Cristie yell, 'As close as she'll come, sir! Nor'-west-by-west!'

He realised that Midshipman Deighton was beside him at the rail, and said, 'Take a good look, Mr Deighton. That is a ship to be proud of.' He lowered the glass, but not before he had seen the tiny threads of scarlet running down *Halcyon*'s tumblehome from the forward scuppers, as if the ship and not her people was bleeding to death. But an ensign was still flying, and from what he had heard of her captain another would be in readiness to bend on if it was shot away.

What sort of men were they about to fight?

He had heard one of the master's mates ask Cristie the same question.

He had answered harshly, 'The scum of a dozen waterfronts, gallows-bait the lot of 'em! But they'll fight right enough. Pirates, deserters, mutineers, they've no choice left any more!'

More shots found their mark in *Halcyon*. Her steering had been carried away, or perhaps there were only dead men at her wheel now. She was drifting, but occasionally a single gun would fire at her attacker, despite the range.

Adam said, 'You may load and run out now.' The gun captains would know. Single shots this time; an overloaded eighteen-pounder would be useless. He watched the sea boiling away from the lee side, the one thing he had dreaded about holding the wind-gage. Maximum elevation for the first broadside. And after that . . .

He found that he was holding the locket through his spray-soaked shirt. At least she was free of the worry and the strain at every separation.

And I have nobody to grieve for me.

'Sir!' It was Galbraith, reaching out as if to drag him from his sudden despair.

'What is it?'

Galbraith could not seem to find the words immediately. '*Halcyon*, sir! They're cheering!' He fell silent, as if shocked at his own emotion. '*Cheering us!*'

Adam stared across the wind-torn water at the battered, defiant ship, and faintly, above the shipboard sounds and the squeal of gun trucks, he heard it. The hand reaching out again. The lifeline.

He shouted, 'As you bear, Mr Massie! On the uproll!'

It was too far, but the other frigate was changing tack. Preparing to fight, and, if possible, to board on their own terms.

'*Fire!*'

Adam gripped young Deighton's arm and felt him jump as if he had been shot.

'Go forrard to the carronades. Remind them *not to fire* until ordered!' He shook him gently. 'Can you do that?'

Surprisingly, the youth smiled, for the first time.

'Aye, ready, sir!'

He hurried down the ladder and walked purposefully forward, not even faltering when, gun by gun, the larboard battery recoiled from their open ports. Adam heard muffled shouts and felt the impact of a heavy ball smashing into the side, and thought of O'Beirne below in his domain, his glittering instruments laid out with the same care as these gun captains took with theirs.

'*Sponge out! Reload!* Move yerself, that man!'

'Take in the courses, Mr Galbraith.' Adam leaned over the rail and saw the spare hands running to obey the call. With the big courses brailed up and loosely furled it was like being stripped naked, with the ship open from forecastle to taffrail.

And there was the enemy. In mid-tack, sails all in disarray, some ports empty, others with their guns already run out for the next encounter.

'*Ready*, sir!'

Every gun captain was staring aft with raised fist, the gun crews barely flinching as another mass of iron slammed into the lower hull. They were on a converging tack, like a great arrowhead painted on the sea. Two ships, all else unimportant, and even *Halcyon*'s brave defiance forgotten. The other ship was beginning to lean to the wind on the opposite tack, but just for a minute she would be bows-on, unable to lay a single gun on *Unrivalled*. A minute, maybe less.

Adam found that his sword was in his hand, and that he was standing away from the rail, and yet he remembered neither.

'As you bear, lads!' How could a minute last so long?

He thought he heard the far-off rumble of heavy guns. Rhodes was still bombarding the fortifications, as timeless as those ancient ramparts in Malta where the invisible orchestra had played for them and they had taken, one from the other. Without question.

The sword sliced down, like glass in the sunlight.

'*Fire!*'

Gun by gun, each hurling itself inboard to be manhandled and reloaded without a second to fumble or consider.

He saw holes appear in the other ship's foresail and jib, and long fragments of gilded woodwork blasted from the ornate beakhead. But she was swinging through the wind; they would be alongside and mad for revenge. The boarding nets would merely delay the inevitable.

He heard Napier shout; it was more like a scream. '*Foremast*, sir!'

Adam had seen some of *Unrivalled*'s shots cutting through the water beyond the target. It was too difficult for them to lay their guns with any hope of accuracy.

It was impossible, but the enemy's whole foremast was going over the side, as if severed by some great, invisible axe.

Shots hammered into the deck and he saw two marines fall

305

from the hammock nettings. He heard the bang of swivels from the tops and knew that Bosanquet's men were following their orders, their marksmen already firing down into the mass of figures scrambling through and over the fallen mast to reach the point of collision. But Bosanquet would never know. He lay with one immaculate leg bent under him, his face destroyed by a splintered ball which had come through one of the gunports.

Luxmore, his second-in-command, was already down there with his own party, bayonets gleaming in the smoky light, all mercy gone as the first boarders leaped wildly across the narrow gap of water only to be hacked down or impaled. Closer and closer, until *Unrivalled*'s long jib boom, its canvas in rags, was pointing directly at the enemy's forecastle.

Adam sliced the air with his sword again. Had the carronade crews understood? Had Deighton managed to reach them or had he, too, been killed? But Deighton was here beside him, and he shook himself, feeling the despair falling away.

It was more a sensation than a sound; the carronades were almost touching the other ship when they belched smoke and lurched inboard on their slides.

Adam yelled, 'To me, *Unrivalled*!' Then he ran along the gangway, hearing the shots, feeling some of them crack into wood and metal and flesh. The nets hung in shreds, and the massed boarding party was blasted into a pile of bloody gruel. Men were running to follow him, and he saw Campbell wielding a boarding axe, hacking down anyone who tried to prevent *Unrivalled*'s people from boarding.

And all the while, through the bang of muskets and the clash of steel in the hand-to-hand fighting, and the screams and pleas which went unheard in any language, he could think only of one fact which stood out above all else. Pirates, corsairs, mercenaries, the names by which the enemy were known meant nothing. Somehow he knew that the man who had offered shelter to the French frigates in the event of Napoleon's escape from Elba was here *in this ship*. It was all that counted. Martinez, indirectly or otherwise, had killed Richard Bolitho, as surely as if he had aimed the weapon.

Someone lunged at him with a sword and he heard Jago

shout, 'Down *you* go, you bastard!' The man fell over some broken timber to be crushed between the two hulls.

His arm felt like lead and throbbed with pain, and there was blood on his hand, his own or another's he neither knew nor cared.

They were halfway along the unfamiliar deck, some of the enemy still putting up a fierce resistance, but many falling as his marines directed a swivel gun from the ship's gangway.

Massie was down, his hands like claws across his stomach as he fell. Adam saw Lieutenant Wynter stoop to help him, and Massie's angry rejection, shaking his head as if to urge him back into the fight. Then the blood came and it did not stop. Massie had had his way, and had remained quite alone to the end.

He heard Galbraith shouting above the din, and saw more men climbing over the fallen rigging to join the first boarders and their own captain. There was cheering too, and he wondered how they could find the strength. He hacked a sword aside and felt the pain tear his muscles as the point grated against the man's ribs before the blade found its mark, choking the scream before it had begun. It seemed to take all his strength to tug it free. Somehow he had dragged himself up a ladder, where smaller groups of figures were locked in what he knew was the final resistance.

Jago gasped, 'I can see smoke, sir! Fire below, by my guess!'

Adam gripped a stanchion and gulped at the air. 'Get our wounded across to the ship! Leave *nobody*!'

Jago peered at him. How did he know it was over? Men were still fighting, or chasing some of the defenders, hacking them down.

Adam wiped his face with his sleeve and almost laughed. It was his best uniform, the one he had been wearing when he had gone to her room. Madness. A wild dream. He gripped his sword even more tightly, knowing that if he allowed himself to laugh he would be unable to stop it.

He heard someone gasp and swung round to see Napier on one knee, a wood splinter protruding from his thigh like a bloody quill.

'Here, my lad, you're coming with me!' Then, as he bent

to give the boy his arm, he saw Martinez, crouching behind a raised hatch, a pistol in one hand. It had to be him; but how could he be so sure? It was only a glimpse, too quick for him to see the dark eyes widen with shocked disbelief as he had stared first at the slim figure in a post-captain's soiled coat, and then, instantly, at the old sword. Something like recognition, something he had never forgotten.

And it was too late. Adam could not reach him with his sword, and if Martinez fired now he would surely kill the boy he had lifted from this stained and fought-over planking.

Martinez said thickly, '*Bo-lye-tho.*' And took careful aim.

But the shot seemed louder, or came from a different bearing. It was the marine corporal Bloxham, Bosanquet's crack shot. He stepped carefully over a corpse and kicked the unfired pistol across the deck.

He said, ''Ere, sir, I'll take the lad from you,' and grinned, the strain slipping from his features. 'But I'll just reload old Bess 'ere first, to be on the safe side!'

Adam touched his arm, and walked across to look at the dead man. He heard the sudden wave of frantic cheering. The fight was over.

My men. And they had won the day, because of a trust which few could explain. Until the next time. Now he must go and face these same men, and share it with them before the pain of loss intruded.

He gazed along the disputed deck, with its bloody scars of battle. Soon only the dead and the poor wretches who had fled below would remain.

He saw his own ship angled away from the bows, suddenly clear in the fresh sunlight, her wounds hidden by drifting smoke, and only then did he know what had held him here. He looked down into the dead face, frozen at the instant of impact. As he had sworn to do.

Perhaps he had expected elation, or a sense of revenge. There was nothing.

He heard voices calling out and knew they would come to find him, interrupting this moment which he could share with only one.

He let his sword arm fall to his side and turned once more

to look at his ship, and smiled a little, as if he had heard someone speak.

'Thank you, Uncle.'

The Most Coveted Gift.